The Power and
THE GLORY

The Power and
THE GLORY

WILLIAM C. HAMMOND

McBooks
Press

Guilford, Connecticut

An imprint of Globe Pequot, the trade division of
The Rowman & Littlefield Publishing Group, Inc.
4501 Forbes Blvd., Ste. 200
Lanham, MD 20706
www.rowman.com

Distributed by NATIONAL BOOK NETWORK

British Library Cataloguing in Publication Information available

Library of Congress Cataloging-in-Publication Data

ISBN 978-1-4930-5815-0 (paper)
ISBN 978-1-4930-5816-7 (electronic)

In loving memory of my parents,
BILL AND TRUDY HAMMOND,
and of my parents-in-law,
LAMBERT AND VLASTA KAREL

Act well your part; there all honor lies.
ALEXANDER POPE

Prologue

THE APRIL 22, 1793, proclamation notifying the world that
the United States would remain
neutral in the gathering storm between Great Britain and France was, at
its core, a meaningless decree. President George Washington had to
deliver it nonetheless. The government over which he presided had few
systems in place and a laughable presence on the world stage. What is
more, it had no credit abroad and scant enforcement capabilities. A
small band of ill-trained, ill-equipped soldiers served, in effect, as a glo-
rified police force, and a few lightly armed cutters of the U.S. Treasury
did their best to guard the coast against smugglers, pirates, and other
maritime miscreants. So puny was America's military presence that
Treasury Secretary Alexander Hamilton was prompted to comment in
disgust: "A nation, despicable in its weakness, forfeits even the privilege
of being neutral."

At sea, European maritime nations preyed on America's carrying
trade under the pretext of blocking shipments of wartime contraband
to enemy ports. On land, the recalcitrant British retained possession of
valuable fur trading posts in the Northwest that under the Treaty of
Paris belonged to the United States. Along the western frontier, British and Spanish agents stirred up the Creeks and Cherokees to hinder
inland migration from the seaboard states and to harass American shipping on the Mississippi. America was a country rich in resources with
a promising future and a mercantile fleet to rival any in the Old World.
But like a stricken beast bobbing on a perilous sea, its wounded corpus

was beset time and again by the savage forays of human sharks feeding in a frenzy of ripe pickings.

Internally, the situation was not much better. From its birth, the United States had been a divided nation. In the North, the Federalists held sway under the auspices of John Adams, Alexander Hamilton, and other proponents of commercial enterprise. Advocating a strong central government with the power to tax its citizens, they called for a standing army and, more important, a strong navy to convoy the lifeblood of the infant republic to Europe and the West Indies. Such commerce involved great risks and skyrocketing insurance rates, but it was also, potentially, the source of enormous profits because the belligerent powers desperately wanted to buy what America had to sell. Decidedly pro-British in their outlook and dress, the Federalists disdained their political opponents, who regarded powdered wigs, silk neck stocks, and other trappings of wealth as symbols of elitism, patronage, and decadence.

The Republicans were concentrated in the South and were led by such heroes of the Revolution as Thomas Jefferson, James Madison, and James Monroe. They trumpeted the frontier spirit on which their country was founded, advocating not the banks and bonds and privileges of the elite, but the principles of limited federal powers; the inherent rights of Man as espoused by Rousseau, Locke, and their own Bill of Rights; and, as economic policy, minimal levels of taxation and national debt. Most detestable to Federalists, the Republicans were decidedly pro-French in their outlook and dress. They continued to idolize the principles of the French Revolution long after King Louis XVI had lost his head to the guillotine and the Great Terror had dragged countless others to their death. Those aristocrats who managed to escape the bloody blade—including such ardent patriots as the marquis de Lafayette—did so by fleeing their homeland for a foreign sanctuary, there to fade into the mists of history.

Such was the pro-French sentiment of the citizens of Charleston, South Carolina, that they allowed French privateers to use their seaport as a base from which to attack British shipping along the Atlantic sealanes. Even after a tax uprising in western Pennsylvania known as the Whiskey Rebellion had spread fears of a Jacobin nightmare appropriating the American dream, Virginians and Carolinians and Georgians continued to wear the tricolor cockade in their hats and to toast the success of Robespierre in Paris—though perhaps with less enthusiasm than in former days.

President Washington was not a man easily intimidated. He stood firm when Citizen Edmund-Charles Genet, the French ambassador in Philadelphia, threatened to appeal directly to the American people to repeal the Neutrality Act if the U.S. government did not suspend its pro-British policies. In 1794 he sent Genet packing and commissioned Chief Justice John Jay as special envoy to the Court of Saint James to repair relations with the former Mother Country and to reopen vital trade routes between America and the British sugar islands of the West Indies—trade that had been crippled by an embargo imposed by Parliament several years earlier and vigorously enforced by the Royal Navy. Jay succeeded in his mission, to the satisfaction of the Federalists if not the Republicans, but the signing of the Treaty of London had immediate consequences. Once its pro-British terms were aired in Paris, the Committee of Public Safety, which now constituted the government of the Republic of France, abrogated the Treaty of 1778, expelled U.S. ambassador Charles T. Pinckney, and declared what amounted to a *guerre de course*—a worldwide commercial war—against its former ally. In the West Indies, French warships based in Guadeloupe and Saint-Domingue seized American vessels and impounded their cargoes of southern cotton and tobacco. Too often the Frenchmen slew the innocent crew and heaved their bodies overboard, thereby blurring the lines between privateers operating under official letters of marque and outright piracy. Throughout the South, toasts to revolutionary France became less frequent and less fervent in tone. And French privateers were no longer welcomed in Charleston.

All was not doom and gloom, however. By September 1796 a few threads of encouragement had managed to weave their way into the complex fabric of international diplomacy. The Mediterranean Sea had by now become a relatively safe haven for American enterprise, with fewer American merchantmen falling into the clutches of Barbary corsairs. True, the Barbary States of Algiers, Tunis, and Tripoli continued to hold American sailors in their dank prisons, as they had for more than a decade, but the seeds of American mediation in North Africa were finally beginning to bear fruit. Interrupted by the French Revolution and stalled by the untimely death of John Paul Jones, America's chief envoy to the Barbary States, negotiations with the dey of Algiers were under way and fast approaching a satisfactory conclusion. For the price of one million U.S. dollars, an amount approximating 13 percent of the nation's annual expenditures in 1795, plus the promise of a newly built warship in the future, Algiers and its Arab neighbors promised to release the hostage American seamen.

In response to the rape of the nation's carrying trade in the Mediterranean and Caribbean, and sick to death of America being the plaything of Europe, Congress in 1794 voted 50 to 39 to build six frigates under the auspices of a new cabinet-level Navy Department, itself a subset of the newly created War Department. President Washington chose the names of the warships while his successor, John Adams, a strong proponent and organizer of the Continental navy during the war with England, took a more active role, to the point of personally selecting certain of the ships' commissioned officers.

These six men-of-war bore little resemblance to the ships of the Continental navy, or to the warships of the European powers. Designed by Joshua Humphreys, a Quaker shipwright from Philadelphia, they were longer, heavier, and narrower than other men-of-war in their class— hybrids, really, between a traditional 36-gun frigate and a third rate of 74 guns, the standard line-of-battle ship deployed by the Royal Navy.

The officers who commanded the U.S. Navy's new frigates would soon discover that they possessed a secret weapon that had nothing to do with ordnance. It was, rather, the wood used for key pieces of the ship's frame. Called *Quercus virens* by botanists, this wood came from a live oak with olive-green leaves that grew along a narrow swath of the Coastal Plain extending from Virginia to Georgia and across northern Florida. It could be found only in the American South, and its texture was far stronger than New Hampshire white oak, stronger even than English oak, which for centuries had been the mainstay of British hegemony at sea. Enemy shot directed at the hull of one of these newly built frigates bounced off as though it had struck not wood but iron.

One

Mary Beth, off Matanzas, Cuba
June 1797

THE MASTER of the schooner *Mary Beth*, out of New York, was suspicious the instant he noticed the full press of sail sweeping toward him from the north coast of Cuba. That the two-masted brig was flying Spanish colors mattered not at all. Cuba was Spain's principal colony in the West Indies, and the only beef Spain had with the United States these days involved shipping rights on the Mississippi River. Nonetheless, Tobias Taylor knew that for the past year Spain had again been an ally of France, the residue of what two decades earlier had been a powerful military alliance between the two Bourbon kings. And France, he also knew, was no longer a friend of the United States. That brig, Taylor was convinced, was flying the red and gold of Spain as a *ruse de guerre*.

The likelihood of encountering such a vessel was why he had shaped a course to Jamaica around the western tip of Cuba. Pirates and privateers were known to prowl the Windward Passage, a fifty-mile stretch of water separating the eastern shore of Cuba from the western shore of Saint-Domingue. These cutthroats and marauders operated with the tacit approval—if not the outright support—of the colonial governor of the French West Indies. And the colonial governor of the French West Indies took his orders from the National Directory in Paris.

The brig was closing too quickly for Taylor to consider flight. Besides, where in these waters would he go? He glanced up at the ensign fluttering abaft the schooner's mainmast. She was flying the Stars and Stripes, and why not? She could hardly be mistaken for anything other than an American merchantman. The unique design of a Baltimore-built schooner was familiar to anyone engaged in international commerce.

Taylor scoured the horizons with a long glass, hoping against hope to find a Royal Navy vessel out on patrol from the British base at Fort Montego. But the sea was empty save for the brig, now closing fast and less than two miles away.

"Mr. Pate!" he shouted to his mate. "Heave to and run out the guns!"

Billy Pate hesitated before giving the order. *Mary Beth* was a merchant vessel, and like many American merchant vessels she was armed: three guns on her starboard side, another three to larboard. But these were 3-pounders, popguns compared with the long 9s the brig likely carried, six per side. Fighting off a small pirate barque was one thing; challenging what amounted to a brig of war was another. Not only was *Mary Beth* seriously outclassed in weight of broadside, but her crew of fourteen, master and mate included, would be no match for the much larger crew on the brig should they grapple and board the schooner.

"Mr. Pate!" Taylor cried again, his voice laced with frustration and anger. The redoubtable privateer captain he had been during the war with England would not permit him to give up the ship without a fight. "Obey my order, damn your eyes!"

Reluctantly, Pate complied. With her sails set to counteract each other, *Mary Beth* drifted to a standstill as her crew, freed from their sailing duties, loaded and ran out her guns. Presenting her puny broadside to the oncoming brig, she bobbed up and down on the dazzling blue sea like a tiny cork of defiance.

The brig's captain dispensed with the formality of demanding surrender. Veering off the wind, he brought his larboard guns to bear and opened fire in rapid sequence. *Mary Beth* answered, the high-pitched bark of her guns drowned out by the ominous roar of her tormentor's. Iron balls and grapeshot shrieked into the schooner, smashing through bulwarks, chewing up rigging, butchering anyone caught in their path. A sailor stationed by the foremast was struck full in the chest by a round shot. In a fraction of a second his tanned and sinewy torso was pulverized into splinters of bone and flecks of gore.

"Sweet Jesus, Captain!" Pate implored as the brig swept on by, wore ship, then made ready her starboard guns to deliver another glimpse of hell. "We must strike!"

Realizing the hopelessness of further resistance, Taylor nodded his agreement. He ordered the American ensign hauled down and watched helplessly as the brig backed her topsail and maneuvered into position alongside his schooner. Bare-chested sailors heaved over ropes, the iron claws at their ends banging onto the schooner's deck. The claws gripped the bulwarks and the two vessels were pulled close together. As the brig's captain stepped on board *Mary Beth,* Taylor prayed silently that these pirates would somehow be different from others of his experience.

His prayer went unanswered. Furious at being shot at by these upstart Americans, the pirate captain ordered Taylor sent below under guard. Taylor sat in the dank hold, his back against the hull, teeth clenched and eyes closed, but unable to escape the horror of the screams erupting from up on the weather deck. The screams were followed by the sound of bodies splashing into the sea just a few feet away from where he was sitting, to be followed by more screams and then horrible gurgles as the waiting sharks circled in and struck, drawn by their keen sense of smell to waters made bloody, Taylor suffered no doubts, by jugular veins slashed open with a knife.

When all was quiet and Taylor had fought back the urge to shriek like a madman at the inhumanity of it all, he began to contemplate his own fate. He was to learn that fate some time later when he was seized by guards and strong-armed topside. At the larboard entry port he was dispatched below into a boat in which four pigtailed sailors sat waiting with oars raised before a heavily armed coxswain at the tiller. Once Taylor was secure on the after thwart, his hands were tied loosely behind him.

As he was rowed ashore to what appeared to be a small, deserted island, he tried to determine, based on approximate time elapsed and probable speed, where he was. His best guess was somewhere within one of the southern archipelagos of the Bahamas—the Exumas, perhaps. Wherever he was, he could bet it was far removed from the Old Bahama Channel and other well-traversed sea-lanes.

When the bow of the boat hissed onto the sand, he was summarily dumped overboard. He splashed onto the wet sand and shallow water, then battled himself to his knees and upright to face his captors, to stare them in the eye.

"*Au revoir, Capitaine,*" the coxswain sneered. "*Appréciez votre séjour sur cette belle île.*" That remark set the four oarsmen to laughing. The American captain was very unlikely indeed to enjoy his sojourn.

Before shoving off, the coxswain gently lobbed a dirty canvas bag up onto dry sand.

Taylor's gaze never left the boat as he slowly twisted his hands free of their binding. Only after the boat had been hauled on board the brig and the brig was making sail in company with *Mary Beth* did he turn to look about him. What he saw was not encouraging. The island was indeed small, a mere speck of land surrounded by a vast expanse of glittering blue sea. At first blush it appeared bereft of anything to sustain life.

He picked up the canvas bag and pulled apart the opening. Inside he found a half bottle of dark rum wrapped in rags. A further search revealed a small pistol, together with powder and ball to fire one shot.

Two

Boston, Massachusetts
September 1797

Young Will Cutler saw them first: two glints of white on the distant horizon beyond Outer Brewster Island, the massive outcropping of bedrock at the entrance to Boston Harbor. He turned the lens of his long glass to bring the glints into sharper focus. She was a double-topsail schooner—that much he could determine from the two massive fore-and-aft sails now beginning to take shape beneath the furled topsails—but he could not yet see her hull despite his elevation on the roof of his family's counting house on Long Wharf. He could see that her course was north-north-westerly and that she was making for the Graves, as though intending to bypass Boston. But the sailor in Will knew that counted for naught. Although the fifteen-knot southwesterly breeze hit squarely abaft her beam, the schooner had taken in her topsails, which she would not have done had she intended to carry on to some farther destination. Boston was her destination. Will was convinced of that. Once she sailed past the Graves up toward Nahant, she would swing her bow through the wind on a new course that would take her southward between Deer Island and Long Island Head.

As the schooner rose higher on the horizon, Will waited in agonizing suspense. He had a strong hunch, but it was only a hunch. He would not know for certain until he saw her hull, more specifically the color of her hull. When the mainsail took full form just above her deck, he held his breath and stood on tiptoes, as though those extra few inches might make all the difference. Almost there . . . almost there . . . *yes!* A brilliant flash of yellow reflected the sun, and Will whooped for joy. He knew of only one yellow-hulled, double-topsail schooner sailing in these waters, and that beautiful and graceful vessel sailed in the employ of his family.

"Jamie!" he shouted down to his younger brother lolling about on the wharf below, inspecting the merchant vessels nested tight against each other, their yards a-cockbill to avoid entanglement. The boy glanced up. "Get Father! I see her! She's coming!"

Jamie Cutler looked up, shading his eyes. "You see her, Will? Are you sure?"

"Of course I'm sure, you twit. Now hurry! Father's at McMurray's, with Mr. Hunt."

"I know that!" Jamie took off at a full sprint. At the age of thirteen he was, like his brother, a fine physical specimen, consistently finishing first or second in footraces against his classmates at Derby Academy in Hingham. Within minutes he was across from Faneuil Hall and inside McMurray's, an establishment renowned for the quantity and quality of its shepherd's pie. He found his father in the dimly lit oaken room sitting by a window and having dinner with George Hunt, the diminutive, soft-spoken, and yet highly competent administrator of Cutler & Sons.

"Father!" Jamie cried out, bursting into their conversation. Patrons chatting at nearby tables stopped in mid-sentence to take note of the excited lad dressed in ordinary brown trousers and open-necked white shirt. "It's *Falcon,* Father! Will's seen her. She's coming! She's almost here, Father!"

A blond-haired man in his mid-thirties placed a large hand on Jamie's shoulder, the sky blue of his eyes boring into the rich hazel of his son's. They were expecting *Falcon.* All of Boston, all of New England, all of America was expecting *Falcon.* Her imminent arrival was the reason he had allowed his sons to abandon school and sail with him to Boston from Hingham every day this week, and would continue to do so until the day *Falcon* arrived. But could today really be that day? She was a fast ship. No one understood *Falcon*'s sailing qualities better than Richard Cutler. But could Agreen truly have sailed from Algiers to Boston in just five weeks?

Answers to those questions were obvious in the eager expression on Jamie's face and the way he kept shifting his weight from one foot to the other, edging toward the door. Richard stood up. "Will you settle this, Mr. Hunt?" he asked, meaning the bill.

"That will not be necessary, Mr. Cutler," a voice cut in. "Today your meal is on the house." In a loud voice of authority the headwaiter proclaimed to the tavern at large, "On this glorious day, all food and drink are on the house, compliments of Mr. Charles Wheeler, proprietor of McMurray's Tavern!"

That announcement was met with a round of applause reinforced by whistling and shouting and stamping of feet. Some patrons bolted for the door.

"You go on, Mr. Cutler," George Hunt said amid the din. "I'll be right along. At my age I'm not as fleet of foot as you and your son." He smiled warmly at Jamie.

Richard bowed in appreciation to both Hunt and the waiter and followed his son out the door. The dazzling hues of early autumn struck his eyes, and a refreshing breeze ruffled his hair. Bells began to toll, first from one church, then from another, then from another and another and another until it seemed to those gathering on and near Long Wharf that the joyous peals must go far beyond the confines of Boston and Cambridge, all the way to the western frontiers of the young republic.

A large crowd was gathering on the waterfront. Wives, parents, siblings, and sweethearts had waited ten years for this day, and they would not be denied. When word had arrived almost a year ago that a treaty had been signed in Algiers, hope soared that every American sailor held captive in Barbary would soon be home. As always, however, the devil was in the details. Another ten months would pass before the disorganized U.S. government could raise the agreed-upon ransom and hammer out those details to the satisfaction of the Arab rulers of North Africa and the advisers and magistrates and self-seeking connivers lurking in their courts. It was not until early June, three months after the Treaty of Tripoli had been ratified by Congress and signed by President Adams, that American vessels were allowed safe passage along the Barbary Coast. Even then, bureaucratic inexperience and ineptitude caused one delay after another, adding to the national sense of anger and despair.

Finally, in mid-July, a special communiqué was relayed to the European ministers and American negotiators in North Africa. After holding Americans captive for more than a decade and forcing them to labor on barely sustainable rations, the dey of Algiers, along with the bey of Tunis and the bashaw of Tripoli, grandly announced that on August 10, 1797, all prisoners held in the Barbary States would be released. On August 7 Agreen Crabtree, the most trusted ship's master in the Cutler merchant fleet, set sail on board *Falcon* to Algiers from Gibraltar, where he had been biding his time for three weeks in the cordial company of Richard's brother-in-law, Jeremy Hardcastle, a senior post captain attached to the Royal Navy's Mediterranean Squadron.

RICHARD AND JAMIE wove their way along Long Wharf through the throngs of citizens straining to reach the spot where dockhands were clearing a space for the schooner to tie up. Some in the crowd recognized the elder Cutler and made room for him and his son to pass through. More than one reached out to touch him in gratitude, for the men returning home on board this particular schooner were in the employ of Cutler & Sons. Muslim pirates had seized the company's brig *Eagle* in the Mediterranean in August 1787. Since then, Cutler & Sons had done what it could to secure the release of its sailors, sending Richard Cutler and Agreen Crabtree to Algiers with $60,000 in ransom money raised from family members on both sides of the Atlantic. Although that ransom attempt had failed to achieve its primary purpose, the imprisoned Americans at least knew that their country had not forgotten them and that their employer had not forgotten their families. Speaking on behalf of the Cutler family, Richard had promised *Eagle*'s crew prior to leaving Algiers that Cutler & Sons would look after their families for as long as necessary. Although the cash squeeze on the shipping company had been extreme at the time, the Cutler family had kept its promise.

Will Cutler dipped and bobbed his way over to his father and brother when he saw them wending their way to the Long Wharf counting house. "See, Jamie, I told you!" he crowed.

"Mr. Cutler! Mr. Cutler, sir!"

Richard turned to see a small-boned, thirty-ish woman in a faded blue cotton dress and plain white mobcap coming toward him. Her face was familiar, but her name escaped him. "I'm Jane Reed," she said, sensing his uncertainty when she was close to him, "wife to Jim Reed."

"Yes, of course, Jane. I'm sorry. It's been a few years, and in all this confusion . . ."

"Mr. Cutler," she interrupted him, "I've something to say to you." Taking a deep breath and fighting back tears, she leaned in so that he could hear her amid the clanging of bells and the bustle at dockside. "Thank you," she said, her voice breaking. "Thank you and your dear family for all you have done for me and my Jim. You, sir, are a saint." She swiped away tears and then reached up to kiss him on the cheek.

Richard had to fight the lump in his throat to reply. "I'm hardly that, Jane. It's God's blessing that *Eagle*'s crew has come home to us today."

"His, yes," she agreed, "and yours, Mr. Cutler." She touched his arm before moving off into a crowd that was growing ever more jubilant as *Falcon,* lying a short way off the quay with her bowsprit facing toward the east whence she had come, made ready to be warped in. Sailors at her bow and stern heaved coiled ropes to dockers stationed fore and aft on the merchant vessels bracketing the space cleared for *Falcon* along the half-mile stretch of Boston's longest commercial wharf. The dockers caught the ropes and, aided by deckhands, ran the bitter ends through hawser holes and onto cylindrical capstans bolted amidships on each of the two vessels. Once the end of each rope was secured to a capstan and a signal given, men stationed in a circle around the giant winches pushed hard on the metal bars at the top, taking in first the slack of rope and then the full weight of the schooner herself, coaxing her slowly inward toward the wharf.

Members of the schooner's crew working in the rigging had by now assumed distinct form, as had the passengers lining her larboard railing. The former hostages stood listening to the bells and watching the goings-on ashore as if in a trance, as though unable to accept the blessed gift of homecoming after enduring so much for so long in a wretched Arab prison. Many let tears stream unabashedly down their cheeks.

As dockers cranked *Falcon* in the last few feet, the crowd stepped back in deference to the Cutler brothers—Richard on the dock and Caleb, his younger brother, standing amidships near *Falcon*'s entry port. The two brothers locked eyes as onlookers cheered, waved their hats in the air, and beckoned joyously to loved ones now just a few feet away and drawing closer. As *Falcon* bumped against the massive stone-and-wood structure, Caleb formed a fist with his right hand and brought it over his heart, in the same gesture of the Roman general Fabius Maximus with which he had said good-bye to Richard in the dey's prison those many years ago. Richard returned the gesture and then allowed his gaze to wander over the cluster of men around Caleb, who were becoming more animated as they recognized family and friends on the dock. He looked aft to the helm, to the tall, muscular, tawny-haired ship's master standing by the tiller. When their eyes met, Agreen Crabtree snapped a salute, a gesture familiar from their days as midshipmen in the Continental warship *Ranger* and then as acting lieutenants in *Bonhomme Richard*, both ships under the command of John Paul Jones.

Dockers on board the merchantmen eased the strain on the giant winches as sailors on the schooner cast mooring lines to dockers on the quay, who secured them to bollards with a series of clove hitches. *Falcon* was home.

The larboard entry port opened and a gangway was pushed down to the dock. First off, by protocol, was James Dickerson, *Eagle*'s master. During his mission to North Africa in 1787, Richard had met with Dickerson and Caleb in a prison chamber and had learned from his brother just how crucial Captain Dickerson's role had been in keeping his men alive and safe while catering to the whims of his captors. So impressed was the dey of Algiers with Dickerson that he had allowed extra provisions and medical attention to be brought into the prison when Dickerson requested them. Most noteworthy, not a single member of *Eagle*'s crew had been sold into the flesh markets of Tunis and Tripoli, a fate suffered by the one hundred other American prisoners in Barbary and countless others enslaved while sailing under a flag of Christendom.

Dickerson's reply to Richard Cutler's emotional expression of gratitude as he met him by the gangway was the same this day as it had been back then. "My duty, Mr. Cutler," he said. He grasped Richard's hand in both of his and bowed before taking his leave. As he made his way through the throng, citizens of Boston clapped him on the back, albeit gently, for all could see that he was raw-boned and weary.

Then Caleb limped down the gangway and a great cheer went up as the two brothers embraced, the grip of one hard upon that of the other.

"You look well," Richard managed after he had eased his grip sufficiently to give his brother a quick once-over. He could feel Caleb's ribs through his shirt and jacket. "Far better than I expected."

Caleb was equally beset by emotions. "You sent enough food to feed an army," he said. "And Agreen brought fresh provisions from Gibraltar. My shipmates and I had naught to do on the entire voyage home but eat and sleep."

"Well, Edna's in charge of you now," Richard grinned, referring to the tried-and-true Cutler housekeeper of many years. "So you'd best get used to that lifestyle. Here, let's move back a ways, shall we, and let others through." With Will and Jamie in tow, they edged against the flow of a closely packed crowd surging forward to greet those disembarking one by one from *Falcon*. Conditions were less frenetic at the entrance of Cutler & Sons.

"A swift passage, eh, Caleb?" Richard asked to make conversation. He could not take his eyes off the brother he had been forced to abandon.

"Fair winds all the way. Agreen told us he had never seen the like on an Atlantic crossing."

"I imagine *any* wind would have seemed fair to you on this voyage."

"There is that," Caleb confessed.

Richard motioned to his sons. "Will, Jamie, you remember your uncle, don't you?"

"I remember him," Will chimed in. "But Jamie doesn't. He was just a baby when you sailed for Algiers, Uncle Caleb."

"I do so remember him!" Jamie's defiant look swung from his brother to his uncle. "And I was not a baby. I was three years old," he said, as though therein lay the proof of the pudding.

"Well, we have a lot of catching up to do in any case," Caleb said. "Captain Crabtree tells me your father is planning a short cruise just for us four so that we can get to know one other again. Are you willing?"

Both boys nodded eagerly.

"Good. It's a pity Diana won't be joining us."

Will shrugged. "She wouldn't want to come. She's too little, and besides, she'd rather go riding with mother every day."

"Well, if your sister looks anything like I remember your mother, she must be one lovely young lady."

Will shrugged again. "She looks fine, I guess."

As former hostages mingled happily with family and friends, Boston Harbor came alive with small craft commissioned by the Cutler family to transport them to their homes on the South Shore. The Cutlers had their own coastal packet awaiting them at the far end of the wharf, but they would not depart for Hingham until Richard had personally welcomed home every member of *Eagle*'s crew. That took some doing, because each crewman had much to say to him. Last up was Addison Percy, a Harvard-educated physician from Cohasset who had served as ship's surgeon on *Falcon*'s cruise to Algiers and home.

"Truth be told, Mr. Cutler," he reported, "I am pleased with what I've seen. I had expected much worse." Not a seasoned sailor, he was having trouble finding his balance ashore after weeks on a rolling deck. "Several cases require further scrutiny, and I am concerned about Captain Dickerson. But no lives appear to be in danger. I am finishing up a report that I will give to you and your father tomorrow morning, if that is convenient for you."

"It is, Doctor. Shall we say ten o'clock?"

Agreen Crabtree remained on board while George Hunt paid off *Falcon*'s crew. Only when he was certain that everything above and belowdecks was stowed in Bristol fashion did he excuse the last of the crew and step ashore to join the Cutlers.

"Welcome home, Agee," Richard said. He offered his hand to Agreen's tough, leathery grip. "Thank you for bringing the men home safely."

"That's what you pay me for," Agreen said dismissively. Feeling awkward in the face of the powerful emotions of the day, he made a funny face at the two boys that made them giggle. "How long you reckon they'll keep up these bells? Damn, they're beautiful. It means a lot t' the men. Many of 'em broke down like babies as we came in."

A brief silence ensued, as if to honor that simple observation. Then Richard motioned up the quay. "Shall we? Anne and Lavinia are waiting for you at home, Caleb. Frederick and Stephen will join us as soon as we send word to them. Two weeks from now we have a grand reception planned for you and your shipmates. In the meantime, we'll take that cruise I promised you, and you can eat and sleep to your heart's content." His gaze swung over to Agreen. "Speaking of things beautiful, Agee, your wife has some news for you."

"Is she all right?" Agreen demanded, his tone turning instantly serious.

"She's fine, just fine. Katherine's with her every day, and Dr. Prescott looks in on her regularly. The baby's kicking up a fuss, is what I meant."

"God be praised," Agreen muttered reverently. He set off with the others toward the single-masted packet bobbing at her mooring at the far end of the wharf.

ONCE *Falcon* had made her sweep through the wind toward Boston Harbor and her identity was confirmed, a swift vessel had set sail for Hingham to alert the village and the Cutler family. Such a courtesy, it turned out, was hardly necessary. Bells chiming in unison from North Church and South Church and every church in between were picked up and echoed by churches in Dorchester and Milton and Weymouth. Their joyful peals were clearly audible on board the Cutler packet as she skimmed across the sheltered waters of Hingham Bay. By the time the packet had nosed her way through the flotilla of small craft swarming around her and had Otis Hill in sight, the bells of First Parish Church, Second Parish Church, and the Old Meetinghouse were in full swing.

Richard knew that Katherine would not be on the wharf to greet them. By prearrangement, she was waiting up on Otis Hill in the company of Elizabeth Cutler Crabtree, Richard's first cousin and Katherine's closest friend since their childhood in England. Up there, removed from the high-spirited crowd jostling and jockeying below on Broad Cove Lane and in the broad stretch of land adjacent to the Hingham docks, they were out of harm's way. Lizzy was seven months pregnant, and if safely delivered, this baby would be her first. At age thirty-six, she was almost a year younger than Katherine, who nine years ago had borne her third child. In consideration of Lizzy's age, the Cutler family doctor had warned her not to do anything that might physically upset her—or worse, upend her. Given the miscarriage she had suffered two years earlier, Dr. Prescott had reminded her, it was a miracle that she had conceived at all.

Thomas Cutler was on the quay, however. He stood as far out on the main wharf as he could get, at the location where the incoming packet was to be moored. The patriarch of the Cutler family in America, he had sailed with his bride to Boston a half-century earlier, seeking new opportunities in the new land. His older brother, William, had remained behind in England to manage the British end of their shipping business, which had grown sufficiently over the years to embrace the high risks and high rewards of West Indian sugar and rum production.

As he stood on the Hingham quay and watched the packet's bow inch in toward dockside, it was all he could do to keep his emotions in check. Before the packet was secured to the dock, Caleb swung a leg over her side and jumped down onto the wharf, dropping to a knee from the pain in his left leg. His father gently drew him up and embraced him as those standing nearby looked on in respectful silence.

"How I wish your mother were here today to see this," Thomas said, choking on the words. Elizabeth Cutler had succumbed two years earlier to the crippling effects of ill health suffered over many years. Caleb had read about his mother's death in a letter his father had sent him through the British consul in Algiers. "Her last wish was to see you safely home."

"She knows, Father," Caleb said, his own voice unsteady. "I'm sure she knows I'm home with you today."

Richard and Agreen remained on the packet until father and son had turned to walk down the quay together. Then they jumped off, followed by Will and Jamie.

"I'll get Katherine, Father," Richard called out when they were on dry land. He squeezed Caleb's arm in passing and smiled at Anne and Lavinia, his sisters, who had rushed to dockside with the first peal of church bells. Lavinia, the youngest Cutler sibling at age thirty, wept openly as she took Caleb in her arms.

"Stay here with your uncle," Richard shouted to his sons. It was difficult to make himself heard over the chime of bells in the distance and the excited jabber of people close by.

On their way up Otis Hill, Richard had to hoof it to keep pace with Agreen. Katherine and Lizzy had spotted them and were waving. Standing beside her mother was Diana Cutler, a lass who had inherited so many of her mother's physical attributes that even at the tender age of nine she was showing all the signs of someday becoming a very comely woman. Behind them, puffing contentedly on a long-stemmed white clay pipe, stood Benjamin Lincoln, the owner of the blue-shuttered gray clapboard house where the women were waiting. As General Washington's second in command at Yorktown and the senior officer who had accepted Lord Cornwallis' sword of surrender, Lincoln was Hingham's most distinguished war hero.

When the men reached the crest of the hill, Katherine stepped close to her husband. "How is Caleb?" she asked anxiously. "And the rest of the crew?"

"Better than we expected," Richard assured her. "You'll be amazed at how well Caleb looks."

Diana tugged on her mother's sleeve. "Can we go down to the docks, Mommy? Can we, please?" She looked beseechingly up at her father, her white cotton dress billowing in the soft autumn breeze. "Oh *please* can we?"

Richard smiled at his wife. Diana Cutler was clearly Katherine's daughter, and not just in physical appearance. Like her mother—like most attractive females of his acquaintance—Diana had seemed to grasp from an early age just how beguiling and irresistible the feminine mystique can be. He stooped down and placed his right hand on the side of her face, pushing back the silky chestnut curls tumbling down across her shoulders.

"So you're anxious to meet your Uncle Caleb, are you, Poppet?"
She nodded.

"Well, I have it on good authority that he's just as anxious to meet you." He stood up. "Your mother will take you to the docks. I'll be along after a word with the general." He brushed his lips against Katherine's cheek in a token show of affection, their custom when in public or in the company of their children.

"Come, Diana," Katherine said, taking her daughter's hand. With a farewell wave to Lizzy and Agreen they set off down Broad Cove Lane. Richard turned in the opposite direction, walking toward the older man who was striking flint on steel to relight his pipe.

"You're right," Agreen exulted as Richard passed by. He had his hand on Lizzy's stomach. "It *is* kickin' up a fuss."

"Takes after its father," Richard replied with a grin. "You're in for it now, Liz. I tried to warn you. But you wouldn't listen. Now you're going to have *two* fusspots living with you."

Lizzy returned his smile, the glow of pending motherhood lighting her gentle features, but said only, "We'll see you at your father's."

A few yards farther on, before the porch of the two-story house with a white widow's walk on the tiled roof, stood a man dressed as casually as Richard in homespun white trousers and a loose-fitting blue cotton shirt tied with strings at the chest and neck. Except that the general's ensemble required a good deal more fabric in the fitting, the inevitable consequence of advancing age and a wife with a deserved reputation for lavish entertainment.

"A glorious day, eh, Richard?" he beamed. He pointed his pipe toward the bay and the flotilla of small craft tacking this way and that. Beyond, in the far distance, they could discern the beacon pole perched atop Boston's highest hill. "Now *there's* a sight to warm the heart of an old soldier."

"I suspect it is, General," Richard said. "When I told Caleb what you have in store for him and his shipmates, he was deeply moved. I want you to know that. All of Hingham is indebted to you."

Lincoln waved that away. "Nonsense, my boy. I am honored to do what I can and happy to offer my farm for the occasion." He sucked in a mouthful of smoke and blew it out contemplatively. "It's going to be quite the event. Most of Hingham will be there," he said, adding, with a flash of mischief, "and perhaps others from farther away. Perhaps even as far away as Belknap Street in Boston." He paused, waiting for Richard to rise to the bait. When he didn't, Lincoln looked up at the sky, the farmer in him weighing the odds of continuing fair weather during the fickle early weeks of autumn. "Let's hope this weather holds and we're able to stockpile enough food and spirits to keep everybody happy. The date is set for two weeks from today, but I suggest we move it up a few days now that we have our lads safely home. We still must allow time to send word to everyone and allow them to make arrangements, of course."

"Whatever you say, General. Just please let us help wherever we can."

"It's always a pleasure to call on the Cutler family. Especially your beautiful women."

With that, Lincoln's jocular tone turned more serious. "Have you responded to the president? He's home, you know, and has sent word that he and Mrs. Adams are planning to attend our celebration. In his letter, he asked me to press you about your proposed commission on board . . . *Constellation*, isn't it?"

"Yes, sir."

"She's the one being fitted out in Baltimore."

"Yes, sir. At Fell's Point."

"Well, the shipwrights of Baltimore are famous for building quality schooners. Let's see how they do with a Navy frigate." Lincoln shook his head. "I must say, I was surprised and not a little disappointed that you were not awarded a commission in *Constitution*." Lincoln said this as though it had been a foregone conclusion that Richard Cutler would be selected from among a sea of worthy officer candidates to serve in the ship of his choice in the new U.S. Navy. "Though I do understand the logic of having officers from different parts of the country serving on board each ship. And I understand that *Constellation* is now off her cradle and at dockside."

"That's my understanding as well, sir."

"And? How have you left things with Mr. Adams?"

"By now he should have my response. I wrote to thank him for his patronage and to say that I would be honored to meet with Captain Truxtun."

"Excellent. Well done, my boy. When do you think this meeting with Truxtun will take place?"

"I don't know, sir. That depends on Captain Truxtun."

"Yes, of course, of course. Everything in its own good time. I should tell you that sources of mine who are acquainted with Thomas Truxtun assure me that he is an excellent sea officer. You may be aware that he was impressed into the Royal Navy before the war and was offered a midshipman's warrant—which he declined. During the war he earned quite the reputation as a privateer captain." He slowly exhaled a lingering wisp of tobacco smoke. "Is Katherine accepting of all this?"

"I believe she is, General," Richard replied, although his tone suggested that he was not entirely convinced. "She is the daughter of a Royal Navy captain, you know, so she's used to this sort of thing. And Lord knows she has uncanny instincts. I'd wager that she has been expecting this to happen for some time."

Lincoln smiled. "Knowing your wife as I do, Richard, I won't take that wager. What about the rest of your family?"

"The same. I haven't told Caleb yet."

Lincoln clapped a hand on Richard's shoulder and looked him square in the eye. "I'm proud of you, my boy. We all are. No man has a greater calling than to serve his country in her time of need. And despite what many of our countrymen seem unable or unwilling to accept, this *is* a time of need. America can make peace only if she is prepared to make war. And I fear it's going to take a war to convince the world that the United States is willing to stand up for its principles. If we're not willing to stand up, if we don't put an end to these despicable attacks on our merchant fleet, then Mr. Hamilton is right. We are a bankrupt nation, morally and financially. We will have fought the Revolution for nothing. We'd have been better off remaining a British colony."

"I agree, General," Richard said, leaving aside for the moment the grim reality that for the Cutler family, this affair was an intensely personal one. Cutler vessels bound to and from the West Indies were among those being targeted by French pirates and privateers.

Richard bowed to Lincoln and took his leave, anxious to join his family at the docks, a reunion that on this splendid day included his brother Caleb.

Three

Hingham, Massachusetts
October 1797

THE PEALING of church bells diminished gradually as the afternoon wore on, and then ceased altogether as lamplighters armed with flasks of spermaceti oil went about their business on the village streets. Inside the home of Thomas Cutler, a short way up from the village proper on Main Street near the Old Meetinghouse, the glow of celebration continued well into the night, until Jamie and Diana fell asleep on a sofa in the parlor and Caleb, drugged with fatigue and wine and no longer able to resist the allure of goose-down bedding, shuffled upstairs to his room on the second floor.

At 10:40 the next morning he appeared in the kitchen down the back stairway, unshaven and unkempt. He noted the time with astonishment and slid onto a chair at the long kitchen table just as Edna Stowe, the Cutler family's housekeeper since 1783, plopped down a plate of six fried eggs, rashers of bacon, and a healthy wedge of cheese; a basket of freshly baked biscuits; tins of strawberry jam and freshly made butter; and a mug of steaming coffee.

Caleb's jaw went slack. "Sweet Jesus in heaven, Edna!" he exclaimed as he gazed down at the bounty. "Is this all for me? It's a week's ration in Algiers, and this is *real food*."

"Good morning to you, too," Edna replied in a mock scolding voice. "And I'll hear no more blasphemy from you, young man, thank you very much. I put the eggs on when I heard you rumbling about upstairs.

Now sit there and eat. More eggs and bacon are on the way. I aim to put some meat on those pathetic-looking bones of yours, whether you like it or not. You heard me! Eat!"

"Yes, ma'am." Caleb picked up a fork, smiling at the thought of Edna's reaction had she witnessed his skeletal frame at its worst. Smiling, too, because he was home in his kitchen in Hingham, with Edna fussing over him the way she used to do, as though he had never left. Ten years suddenly seemed not such a vast span of time.

"Where is everybody?" he asked after he had made short shrift of the first helping of eggs and bacon and was happily into the second.

"Anne and Lavinia are with Katherine," Edna answered as she refilled his cup from a fresh pot of coffee. "They're going riding with Diana. Your father and Richard are with Dr. Percy down at Barker Yard," she added, referring to the area of Hingham Harbor where the Cutler family maintained a modest office, as much for nostalgic as for business reasons. It was where Cutler & Sons had first taken root in colonial America.

"I should be with them," Caleb said, pushing away his coffee.

"No, you should not. You were exactly where you should have been: upstairs asleep. And now you're doing exactly what you should be doing: eating in my kitchen like a horse. Besides, they said they wouldn't be gone long. I expect them home at any moment."

True to her prediction, a few minutes later they heard the front door open and footsteps approach through the parlor.

"Up at last, I see," Richard teased Caleb as he and the elder Cutler entered the kitchen. He doffed his jacket, hooked it on a peg on the wall, and walked over to the table. "Hungry, are we?" He nodded at Caleb's plate smeared with egg yolk and freckled with breadcrumbs and bits of bacon.

"Famished. What's for dinner?"

"Sheep stomach and fish guts cooked in olive oil, parsley, and sesame and served over rice," Richard responded grandly. "Edna's been preparing for your homecoming, and she's become quite the Arabian cook in the process. Isn't that so, Edna?" Richard grinned at her scowl. "By the way, Father and I just met with Dr. Percy. You'll be glad to hear that your shipmates are coming along smartly, even Captain Dickerson. They'll need time to fully recover, but recover they will." He went over to the open hearth and dropped a fresh birch log on the low-burning fire. Dry white bark flamed up, crackling and popping agreeably. "You slept well?"

"Like old times."

"Good for you, son." Thomas Cutler sat down next to Caleb as Richard took a seat across from him. Edna served a mug of coffee to each.

Richard scooped a spoonful of sugar into his mug and stirred it in.

Caleb, watching him, asked, "Is that our sugar?"

His father answered. "Direct from Barbados. Richard was there recently to visit with Robin and John," referring to Caleb's first cousins, the two sons of William Cutler in England and brothers of Elizabeth Cutler Crabtree. "You have some catching up to do, but here's the gist. Two years ago, John and Cynthia and their young son Joseph returned to the Indies from England to help Robin and Julia manage the family business there, particularly on the sales end. John, it seems, has a natural talent for sales, and we sorely need that talent in these difficult times. I tried to keep you informed in the letters I wrote, but I don't know how many of them got through.

"I don't know, for example, if you are aware of how serious the threat is these days to our carrying trade. French pirates and privateers are attacking our merchantmen—in the Indies and even off our coast. They seize our vessels, do what they will to our crews, and sell off our cargoes on Guadeloupe, Saint-Domingue, or some other French island. These attacks have forced insurance rates to unheard-of levels. Some shipping families have had to suspend business because they can't afford to pay them. The Swifts and the Guilds are two examples.

"We're more fortunate than most other shipping families. Hugh Hardcastle—you remember him, Katherine's brother—remains on station with the Windward Squadron in Bridgetown. Whenever possible, he arranges for a British warship to escort our vessels through the danger zones to open water. And you may recall that Julia is a daughter of a Mount Gay rum family. That connection helps as well. Understand: there's a reason for such cooperation from the British. Their colonies in the Indies rely heavily on our trade, so it's in their interest to protect that trade. But with trouble brewing in Europe, and with so many ships being recalled to Spithead, the Royal Navy is limited in its abilities. What ships they still have on station in the Caribbean can't be everywhere at once. So the attacks continue."

Caleb nodded. "I read about all that in the letters that did get through," he said. "But we're responding to the threat, aren't we? Hasn't Congress approved a new navy? That's what Agee told us on the cruise home."

Thomas Cutler deferred to Richard.

"It's true, in part," Richard said. "Three years ago, Congress authorized the construction of six frigates. But the Republicans in the southern states managed to add a provision to the bill stipulating that since the purpose of these new frigates was to protect American commerce in the Mediterranean, construction on three of the frigates must cease if the United States should sign a peace treaty with the Barbary States. Which of course is what we did. What these Republicans don't understand is that the Barbary States are by no means the only threat to our carrying trade. Today they're not much of a threat at all. France is the threat, and France is not acting alone. Pirates in every sea are capitalizing on our inability to fight back. It galls me no end, I can tell you. Mr. Jefferson told me, face to face in the consulate in Paris back in '89, that he strongly supported the construction of a navy. But apparently he has had a change of heart. President Adams is pushing Congress hard to approve all six frigates *and* to approve the construction and acquisition of additional warships. Please God he succeeds. We'll need every ship we can lay our hands on if we're to challenge the French navy."

"The French *navy*? I didn't think the French had a navy anymore."

"They do, though certainly it's not what it used to be. Nearly all its commissioned officers were aristocrats, and most of them were carted off to the guillotine or murdered by mutinous crews. Former merchant captains command most French naval vessels today, and few of them have experience in battle. British intelligence reports a handful of French frigates in the Indies, though the main fleets remain bottled up in Toulon and Brest. French privateers and pirates do most of their country's dirty work in the Indies."

"I don't understand, Richard." Caleb shook his head in confusion. "Why are the French so bent on war with us? Don't they have enough troubles in Europe dealing with the British? And anyway, don't we have a treaty with France?"

"That treaty has gone by the boards. France claims that we violated it, first, by our proclamation of neutrality and, second, by signing the Treaty of London, the one Mr. Jay negotiated with the British. So the French declared the Treaty of Alliance null and void at the same time they declared a *guerre de course* against us. That declaration gives them the right to seize and search any American vessel bound for a British port. Or so they claim in theory. In practice, they claim it gives them the right to seize any American vessel bound for *any* port."

"Don't they have cause? I mean, France is at war with England, right? So if the Royal Navy is openly protecting American merchant vessels . . ."

Richard shrugged. "That depends on your perspective. We are English by descent and we have family in England with whom we are in business. When it comes to war, naturally we favor England over France. But when it comes to commerce, we don't play favorites. We support free trade—with every country. We'll treat with the French or the British. Or with the Dutch or the Russians or the Malays. But it's not the Dutch or the Russians or the Malays who last year seized more than three hundred of our merchantmen. It was French cutthroats perpetrating the worst kinds of atrocities. You want an example? Here's one. A few months ago a schooner out of New York bound for Jamaica was attacked somewhere off the north coast of Cuba. She was armed and her captain may have put up a fight. If so, he was likely outgunned and forced to strike his colors. No one knows what happened next. No one on board the schooner lived to tell about it. A few corpses washed up on the shore, or what was left after the sharks finished with them. Pickering, our secretary of state, protested to the Spanish ambassador. But what was Spain, a puppet of France, going to do? The answer is they did nothing beyond confirming that a schooner had been sighted sailing westward off Havana shortly before she disappeared.

"I agree with Father that the British can only do so much. It's up to us, not the British, to protect our merchantmen and answer these atrocities. And the only answer the French seem to understand these days is one delivered by powder and shot." He uttered those last three words with bitter precision.

"President Adams sent a peace delegation to Paris in July," Thomas Cutler said in a calmer voice. "John Marshall, the leader of the delegation, is an honorable man. So is his colleague Charles Pinckney of South Carolina. The third delegate, Elbridge Gerry, is a Massachusetts man from Marblehead. While I commend the president for this initiative and his choice of envoys, I seriously question their chances for success. The French don't want peace. They want funds to finance their war in Europe, and privateering is a lucrative source for those funds. They won't give it up easily."

Caleb took a moment to absorb that. Then a notion struck him. "What's your role in all this, Richard?" he asked. "It certainly sounds as though you have one."

Richard nodded. "I have been approached, Caleb."

"By whom?"

"By our president," his father answered for him. "Mr. Adams has commended Richard to Thomas Truxtun, captain of *Constellation*. Richard's name was also put forth by our dear friend Alexander Hamilton."

Caleb's eyes never left Richard's. "When do you report to Captain Truxtun?"

"Fairly soon, I suspect."

"The decision is final, then?"

"No naval officer's commission is final until it is proposed by a ship's captain and approved by the Senate."

"But if offered, you will accept it?"

"I will, barring the unforeseen."

"How do I enlist?"

Richard's eyebrows shot up. "*Enlist?* Jesus Christ, Caleb, you just got home."

Caleb shook his head. "That doesn't matter, Richard. I sat in an Arab prison for ten years, and I have no intention of sitting any longer. I want my life back. I want to get back to sea, and I want to serve my country. I can do both in the Navy."

Richard met his brother's hard stare until their father intervened.

"That is very noble of you, Caleb, given the hell you've had to endure these past ten years. You make me proud. But the fact is, I can't afford to have both you and Richard taking leave of Cutler & Sons. Agreen is likely to be called up, and if he is . . ." Thomas held up his hands. "I need you here with me. I need you to help manage the family business."

"In what capacity, Father?"

"In any capacity you choose. You want to go to sea? I can guarantee you that. You want to serve your country? You can, in a most meaningful way. Our carrying trade is our country's lifeblood, Caleb. Without it our economy would collapse, along with our family's fortunes. I am hoping that you will sail to Barbados within the year to learn the family business from that end. John and Robin would welcome your company and your assistance. Please, son, give this matter some serious thought before making your decision."

It took Caleb only a moment to respond. "I don't need to give it serious thought, Father. Of course I will comply with your wishes. If I learned anything while in prison in Algiers, it's that nothing matters more than family and country. And I can't deny that I have much to learn about our business." He scraped back his chair.

"Where are you going, son?"

"To visit Mother."

Richard stood up across from him. "I'll go with you, Caleb."

THE NEXT SEVERAL DAYS saw lively debate as to where Richard would take his sons and Caleb on the short cruise he had promised them. Will and Jamie fancied the Isles of Shoals, two low, treeless islands off the coast of Portsmouth, New Hampshire. Their father, however, thought those islands too far away and peopled by fisher-folk too long cut off from the mores and morals of the mainland. He suggested the Misery Islands in Salem Sound off the North Shore of Boston. These two islands—one big, one small—were an easy day's sail from Hingham and afforded both sheltered coves for anchorage and sweeping vistas of Cape Ann, so named by King Charles I of England to honor his mother, Anne of Denmark.

As it turned out, the cruise had to be scrapped. The following Thursday, a day before the Cutlers were to set sail, the wind strengthened to a full gale, whipping up white foam even within the protected waters of Hingham Bay. Moisture-laden clouds gloomed in from the southwest and stalled over Boston, pummeling its shores and streets with a cold, drenching rain. As the days elapsed and the storm lagged on, concern mounted that the homecoming celebration to honor *Eagle*'s crew would also have to be scrapped.

Providence proved kind, however. Three days before the planned event, the storm blew itself out. Hingham awoke to a soothing, warm October sun, a gentle westerly breeze, and a bright blue sky accentuating the red-gold, brilliant yellow, and tarnished bronze of autumn foliage. Such conditions boded well for what had to be done, and quickly. Scores of men and women converged on the Lincoln farm south of Hingham to prepare for the many hundreds, perhaps thousands, of people who would attend, for it was a well-publicized event open to everyone. Tent tops were erected, tables were brought in, and a makeshift dais was set up for speeches, with chairs set to accommodate the elderly and infirm. Numerous pits were filled with combustibles to slow-cook the beef, venison, and pork that would accompany rounds of beer, wine, and ale. By Saturday morning the broad green pastures surrounding the Lincoln farmstead had been transformed from a serene, pastoral setting into a veritable fairground.

No one appeared more pleased with the results than the host of the event, Benjamin Lincoln. Dressed in a blue uniform coat with buff facings and gold buttons—three silver stars on the twin epaulettes signifying the rank of brigadier general—he strode about the grounds arm-in-arm with his wife, a tall, pewter-haired woman of grace and gentility. Together they greeted those who arrived on foot from nearby farms or by horse and carriage from locations farther away. Adults and children alike came dressed in their Sunday best.

The Cutlers arrived early, before noon, to help out where they could and to be on hand to greet the members of *Eagle*'s crew. Their wagon had hardly ground to a halt before Will and Jamie jumped off and darted ahead to where meats lanced on iron spits sizzled over blazing fires. Richard and Katherine, meanwhile, took Stephen Starbuck, Lavinia's husband, a shopkeeper from Duxbury, and Frederick Seymour, husband to Anne Cutler and a physician from Cambridge, to greet the general and his wife.

"Welcome," General Lincoln said, shaking each man's hand in turn. "Mrs. Lincoln and I are honored that you are able to join us today."

"You must travel to Hingham more often," Mrs. Lincoln admonished. "We miss your wives and we miss seeing you. I remember your sons, Doctor. They are a handsome brood, though from the look of them they must be quite the handful."

"That they are," Anne confirmed.

As morning melded into afternoon, Richard and Katherine strolled about among the guests, talking to as many people as possible. At one point they saw Caleb in the company of four of his shipmates walking toward the dais where Benjamin Lincoln was preparing to speak. What he had to say was indistinct—Richard and Katherine were too far away—though his intent was clear enough. One by one, each member of *Eagle*'s crew was invited up to the platform to stand between the general and his wife and receive the cheers and applause of those gathered around. This day, there would be no talk of war or piracy or an agrarian economy going to seed.

"Darling," Katherine said, after the crew had received their due, "I see Joan Keating over there. I fancy a word with her. Please excuse me for a moment."

Richard smiled to himself. Experience had taught him that a "word" between Katherine Cutler and Joan Keating would likely last a great deal longer than a "moment." He contented himself by watching the proceedings on the dais until he noticed Agreen Crabtree trying to make his way toward him. It was slow going, for there were many partygoers in between, and Agreen cut a popular swath in Hingham.

"Ahoy, Agee," Richard said when they were together. "How's Lizzy?"

"Doin' fine," Agreen said. "Disappointed not t' be here. Dr. Prescott's given her strict orders t' stay put. I don't plan t' stay long myself. Just wanted t' pay my respects t' the men." His eyes narrowed. "Anne told Lizzy you've heard from Captain Truxtun."

"That's right, I have. A post arrived yesterday."

"And?"

"I'm to meet with him in three weeks' time. He'll size me up and figure out what to do with me—if anything. While I'm down there I plan to stroll around a bit, maybe talk to a few people. Father thinks we should consider opening a second office in Baltimore. It's our westernmost seaport, and it has easy access to Pennsylvania and the Ohio Valley. From there we can ship our goods inland. Plus, it's well protected from storms and invasion. And, it's a lot closer to the Indies than Boston."

"That's true; all of it. Baltimore's quite the place, I'm here t' tell you. I dropped anchor there twice while in Sloane's employ. I'd give a sow's ear t' join you on *this* cruise 'cause I'd enjoy takin' you around t' some of the choice spots. 'Course, seein' as how you're so prim and proper and all, I'd have t' limit my tour t' the respectable establishments. But no matter, you haven't invited me; and besides, I wouldn't want t' leave Lizzy in her state."

Richard nodded his agreement. "You're on the beach until the baby's delivered, no question. Maybe after that . . . What is it, Agee?" he asked when he noticed Agreen's attention focusing on something over his shoulder. "Why the silly grin?"

"Ah, Richard? Friendly fire's comin' up aft. I suggest you wear ship."

Richard turned around to find Anne-Marie Endicott standing demurely before him. She was dressed simply, as was her custom since casting off the trappings of a marquise and fleeing France back in '89. But the simple rose-colored cotton dress and the off-white shawl draped across her slender shoulders neither concealed nor diminished a physical presence so alluring that, in pre-revolutionary France, *la crème de la crème* of Parisian society had characterized the Swiss-born beauty as *une belle femme du monde,* an expression denoting either high praise or deep envy, depending on who was offering the comment. A flourish of thick, flowing curls framed delicate facial features, the black locks a sharp contrast to Richard's yellow hair. Yet the eyes settling affectionately upon him were as bright a sky blue as his own.

"Hello, Richard," she greeted him. "You seem surprised to see me."

He kept his expression noncommittal. "Not surprised, Anne-Marie. Happy. I'm always happy to see you."

"Well, I'm grateful for that."

His gaze took her in with the same pulse of warmth he had felt when he first met her in Paris back in '78 while in the company of Captain Jones and Benjamin Franklin. And when, weeks later following a performance of *The Barber of Seville* at the Tuilleries, they had first nestled naked on her bed and she had initiated him into the glorious rites of manhood. He had felt that same pulse when, years later, he met her again in Paris, this time under far less romantic circumstances, for he was married and the father of three children, and she was newly widowed. Her husband, Bernard-René de Launay, had several weeks earlier been seized by the mob and dragged off to the place de Grève. There they had held down this royal commander of the Bastille and cut off his head with a dull knife, then jabbed it onto a long pike and paraded it through the streets of the city.

Ruthlessly, relentlessly, the wolves of revolution had stalked his widow and their two daughters, as they did every Parisian of noble blood, and Richard had risked his life to spirit them out of Paris to the French seaport of Lorient, and from there to America on board *Falcon*. During the three-week voyage home, Agreen had served as sailing master and—so chortled the local gossipmongers in Hingham—as chaperone, in alliance with Gertrud, the brawny German woman who had been Anne-Marie's childhood nurse and who now guarded her interests and those of her daughters with fierce maternal tenacity.

"Is Jack here?" he asked, referring to the Boston widower and wealthy merchant who had finally won her hand in marriage after many months of ardent pursuit.

"Yes, somewhere. He's hoping to find time to chat with you. About business, of course. Jack's a dear, but Lord knows, he is *always* about business." She leaned in close enough to brush off a shred of lint from Richard's white linen neck stock. "Truth be known, Richard, Adele was equally keen to travel here today. She's over there . . . with Will."

Richard followed her gaze to see his son standing before a girl of his own age and height dressed as simply as her mother and with nearly identical physical attributes. Adele had been born Adélaide de Launay, but when the family reached America her mother had changed her name to sever as cleanly as possible her family ties to France. Beside her was her younger sister, Frances, née Françoise, equally fetching though somewhat shorter and with straight ginger-colored hair that was shiny as a foal's. Will had his hands in his pockets and was staring down at the ground, looking up occasionally when spoken to or, more rarely, when he was doing the speaking. Jamie was nowhere in sight.

As he watched them Richard recalled his own youth. He had been as awkward and tongue-tied in the company of a pretty girl as Will seemed to be now.

"Diana is around here somewhere," he said to Anne-Marie, "and will be delighted to see Frances. Tell her to look for a gaggle of prattling girls. Will you be staying over? Katherine and I would be pleased if you would visit us."

"We'd love to, but Jack wants to return to Boston before it gets dark. For reasons of business, you understand." She gave him a rueful look.

Richard nodded. "Some other time, then."

"Absolutely. Adele will insist on it."

They both smiled at that. Their eyes locked during a brief moment of silence that was broken only by background laughter and chatter. Richard's mind whirled with questions he longed to ask. Was Anne-Marie happy? Were her daughters adjusting to life in America? And how was Gertrud? He had heard that she was not well. But he never seemed to have either the courage or the occasion to ask them. Why, he had often wondered, was it so difficult for him to talk to Anne-Marie now? Was it because he somehow felt responsible for her fortunes in America? It was he who had convinced her to flee her adopted country and sail away with him to Boston. Was the state of her marriage to Jack Endicott, good or bad, somehow a reflection on him? Or was his reluctance something darker, the underside of jealousy, perhaps, envy of a man who now possessed what had once been so blissfully his? Whatever the reason, words failed him, and he felt a mixture of relief and frustration when her eyes shifted away from him.

"Please excuse my bad manners, Agee," Anne-Marie said. "How are you? And how is your dear wife? I understand that you two are expecting a child."

Agreen doffed his tricorne hat. "Yes, ma'am, we are. In just a few weeks' time."

"That's wonderful. I am so happy for you, Agee. May God watch over you and your family." She gave him an amused look. "And may God grant me my most ardent wish, that someday you will call me Anne-Marie, rather than 'ma'am.'"

"Yes, ma'am," Agreen replied, grinning.

Just then a great roar of applause rose up from around the platform. They turned to see a rather short, stubby man of advancing years approaching the much taller and more robust Benjamin Lincoln. The shorter man was dressed in a plain suit of light brown cloth, a bottle-green waistcoat, and a white shirt and neck stock. His round head was bald on top, though sprouting out from its sides were thick mounds of gray hair and sideburns flecked with white. Nothing about him, however, suggested either frailty or aloofness as he waved out at a crowd pushing in from all sides.

"Who is that, Richard?" Anne-Marie asked. "Why all the ado?"

"That's our president," Katherine Cutler answered. She had walked up alongside her husband and slipped her arm proprietarily through his. "Hello, Anne-Marie," she said just a shade too sweetly. "How nice to see you. Richard didn't tell me that you were coming today."

"Hello, Katherine. It's nice to see you too. You look lovely, as always. And don't blame Richard for anything. I didn't tell him we would be here. It was Jack's idea. He so enjoys talking commerce and always appreciates an opportunity to pester Richard about it."

"I see. Will you be staying long?"

"Alas, no. We must take our leave shortly. Jack needs to return to Boston."

"What a pity," Katherine said, smiling graciously.

The applause eased as Benjamin Lincoln offered an introduction that was hardly necessary. John Adams was a Braintree man, a South Shore man.

"We should move in closer," Katherine said. "To hear what Mr. Adams has to say and to pay our respects to Mrs. Adams. Caleb and Pappy are there already," she added, using the family nickname for Thomas Cutler.

"I agree. Will you join us, Anne-Marie? Agee?"

"You three go ahead," Anne-Marie said. "I'll find Jack and then we'll join you." She bowed slightly to Katherine and sent Richard a mischievous twinkle before parting.

"RICHARD, YOU SHOULD HAVE WARNED me about Anne-Marie. You know how much I hate being caught unaware."

They were in their bedroom on the second floor of their home on South Street. Richard had taken off his waistcoat and neck stock and had cracked open the window to admit the cool autumn air. From outside they could hear a dog bark, but other than that only the small nighttime sounds of the village broke the silence.

"How could I have told you when I didn't know, Katherine? I haven't seen Anne-Marie in weeks. She doesn't inform me of her every intention."

"Surely you suspected she might be here."

"As no doubt you did. Besides, you heard her. Coming here was Jack's idea . . . and Adele's."

"Adele? What does she have to do with this?"

"Apparently she has eyes for Will."

Katherine threw up her arms. "Oh, wonderful. That's just perfect. That's exactly what we need!"

Richard lit a second candle from the one he had carried into the room and came over to where Katherine stood with her arms crossed firmly over her chest. He set the candle on the table next to the bed and gripped his wife gently by the shoulders.

"Come now, Katherine. Why do you always get unhinged when Anne-Marie's name is mentioned? She means you no harm. She has told me many times that she wants to be your friend."

"Oh posh, Richard! Those are just words. They mean nothing. Even a dullard can see that she still has feelings for you. I heard people tittering and twittering behind my back all afternoon—the same sort of blather I hear every time Anne-Marie appears. Which is far too often for my taste."

"You're making a haystack from a blade of grass, Katherine. It's just good-natured fun. Our friends and neighbors mean no harm or insult to you."

"It may be just good-natured fun to you and Agreen and General Lincoln. But I assure you it's not good-natured fun to me. Too many people around here are having too much *fun* at my expense."

"Busybodies like that live in every town. They have nothing to crow about in their own lives and so they inquire into the lives of others, hoping to find the excitement that they lack. Pay them no mind." He leaned in to kiss her. She let him, though she placed her palms flat against his chest, denying him full access. "Besides," he soothed, "have you quite forgotten your own past affairs? What about the legions of handsome young men who paid court to you in Fareham? One of them, a Royal Navy captain—remind me, what was his name? Ah, yes, Horatio Nelson, that's it—was so entranced by your charms that he asked you to marry him. And I seem to recall that you accepted his entreaty." He kissed her again.

"That is *not* a fair comparison," she protested hotly. "Horatio and I may have been betrothed, but we never allowed our relationship to . . . *progress* the way yours apparently did with Anne-Marie."

"That was years ago, Katherine. I was young and impressionable, and her country and mine were not at war with each other. If anything, you should thank Anne-Marie. She made me realize once and for all where my heart truly lies. Remind me: was it not *you* I begged to marry me?"

She blinked once, sighed, and blinked again. Slowly she slid her hands from his chest to his hips.

"You have a glib tongue, Mr. Cutler, I'll give you that. But don't you go getting smug on me. I still . . ." She looked down. "Here, what are you doing?"

"I am undressing you, Mrs. Cutler, as you can plainly see." He was loosening button under button on the front of her dress. When he had them all undone, he eased the bodice from her shoulders and let it fall to the floor. "Since my kisses aren't having the desired effect, I find I must resort to stiffer measures."

She suppressed a smile. "The children . . ."

"Are in bed. If they're not asleep, their doors are closed." He scooped her up in his arms and carried her over to their four-poster bed. "So if just this once you could temper those rock-shivering moans of yours, no one will be the wiser."

As he stretched her out on top of the red-and-yellow-checkered bedspread and began removing the remainder of her clothing, she reached in as best she could to undo the buttons of his trousers. "Richard Cutler," she murmured, "you are a wicked man. Satan will strike you down."

"No doubt he will, my lady," Richard murmured in reply. He slid her last line of defense down her long, slender legs and tossed the cotton undergarment aside. Quickly he peeled off his own clothing. "And when he does, I shall rejoice in the certainty that I will be spending eternity with you." He gave her an arch look before delving into the garden of delight planted there before him.

Four

Baltimore, Maryland
November 1797

"TILGHMAN ISLAND, SIR, closing to larboard. Shall I tack her around?"

Caught daydreaming, Richard Cutler cursed under his breath. It was the last thing he should be doing while sailing in these ever-narrowing waters. But as *Elizabeth* approached Maryland's Eastern Shore on a close haul, Richard's mind had been swamped by memories of a man with whom he had served on board *Bonhomme Richard* during the war. A Londoner by birth, a naval gunner by trade, Henry Sawyer had come over from the British side vowing that when the war was over he would leave behind everything bad in his life in Southwark and swallow the anchor somewhere among the eelgrass and cattails of the Choptank River. Sadly, it was not to be. Early on during the battle with HMS *Serapis* in the North Sea, Henry Sawyer's dream of living out his days as a Marylander died the instant an 18-pounder on the lower deck misfired and exploded into shards of scalding iron.

Richard glanced down at the chart cradled in his lap. "Give it another half-cable, Mr. Wadsworth," he called back from the mainmast chains. "The water is deep close in, eight fathoms at a minimum."

"Another half-cable, aye, Captain."

Richard rose and walked slowly forward past duck-trousered sailors making ready to ease off the jib sheets and lay the sloop on a northwesterly course toward the old colonial capital of Annapolis, a town made rich by the slave trade.

It was a bracing November day. A brisk northwesterly breeze persisted, but it carried little of the blustery cold it had when Richard had departed Hingham in the single-masted topsail sloop a few days earlier. *Elizabeth* was one of the smaller vessels in the Cutler merchant fleet, yet built seaworthy enough to withstand foul weather. He gripped the forestay and gazed out upon the thick woodland splendor of Tilghman Island and beyond, across the wide mouth of the Choptank River past Cook Point. He had been in the Chesapeake Bay before, back in '81 during the siege of Yorktown, but the demands of war had kept him along its southern perimeter from Cape Charles to the Potomac. Never had he ventured this far north, and what he had seen thus far confirmed the lore of a place that bordered on legend for both mariners and lubbers: a coastline laced with peninsulas, coves, and inlets where fresh and salt water converged to provide excellent anchorage and hauls of bounty for the fleets of oystermen, crabbers, and other watermen who worked these tidal estuaries. Geese, gulls, ducks, osprey, and terns abounded, swooping low over the water or soaring high above in flawless V formations, their calls at once piercing and pleasing to the ear.

"All hands, ready about! Stations for stays!" Wadsworth shouted the orders to eight crewmen on deck who were standing by to tack. High above, on footropes beneath the single yardarm, four other sailors had clawed in the topsail and lashed it to its spar.

"Ready! . . . Ready! . . . Helm's a-lee!" Wadsworth shouted the signal to let fly the head sheets. Smoothly, deliberately, *Elizabeth*'s bow swung into the wind.

"Haul taut! Mind the boom!"

With the sloop momentarily in stays, and with her three foresails and mainsail jouncing about in the lighter breeze close to a lee shore, sailors in the bow secured the foresail sheets to larboard as others amidships heaved on the mainsheets and boom to force the gaff-topsail up into the wind, using that wide spread of canvas like a giant weathervane to help coax the sloop's bow off the wind to leeward. In an admirable span of time *Elizabeth* lay on a comfortable starboard tack, her stout cutwater knifing through the bay's light chop.

"I'm going below, Mr. Wadsworth," Richard said to his mate. "Please inform me when you have Baltimore in sight."

"Aye, Captain," Wadsworth replied. "It won't be long now."

FROM A DISTANCE Baltimore appeared not unlike Boston, although its population of 20,000 was smaller. Structures of various sizes—made mostly of wood with deeply canted, shingled rooftops, but a few, those of the wealthy, of imported red brick—held sway along a complex of narrow, intersecting cobblestone streets rising up from the waterfront atop small hills under the dominion of a much larger hill to the south. As in Boston, water dominated the visual senses of those arriving by boat: the sparkling blue of the great bay, an inner harbor affording excellent anchorage, the many rivers and streams. The broad and deep Patapsco provided a waterway through the heart of Baltimore much as the Charles did in Boston, while myriad other waterways meandered among the wheat fields and pastures and orchards to the north and south. These swift-flowing streams drained the Tidewater and powered the local millstones that in earlier years had provided the wherewithal to feed General Washington's army. Also as in Boston, white church steeples dominated within the city limits and long stone warehouses lined the quays. The latter stored the local produce of farmers and millers and fishermen that would either be sold outright at nearby Lexington Market, an area of retail commerce not unlike Faneuil Hall in Boston, or shipped off to some other port.

The city formed an imposing panorama, but that was not what commanded Richard's attention as *Elizabeth* coasted inward from the outer reaches of Baltimore Harbor under mainsail and jib. He focused his glass instead on an area he estimated to be a mile downriver and to the east of Baltimore proper, down to where the Patapsco joined forces with a smaller river—Harris Creek, he recalled from Truxtun's correspondence. There, across a narrow span of water from what the chart identified as Whetstone Point, secured broadside to him alongside a sturdy wooden structure providing dockage for the David Stodder Shipyard visible in the immediate background, lay USS *Constellation*.

"Bring her fifty feet off her beam, Mr. Wadsworth," he said, the calm in his voice belying his inner excitement. "See that schooner there under sail? We'll drop anchor where she is now."

"Aye, Captain."

Richard again lifted the glass to his eye. He saw no activity on board the frigate, though he could hear the distant rasp of saws, the ringing of hammers and caulking mallets, the pounding of iron on anvils—sounds emanating either from on board the ship or beyond in the shipyard, he couldn't tell which. He placed the glass back in its becket by the binnacle and walked forward, his senses stirred by the very sight of her.

She was far from sea-ready. Only two of her three masts had been stepped, and those just the lower ones on her mizzen and mainmast: two black spars rising up aft and amidships, bereft of yards or rigging or topmasts or shrouds. Forward of the mainmast was blank space: nothing to see there beyond a rounded iron smokestack jutting up over the bulwarks like a crooked black finger pointing forward. Nor had the jib boom been adjoined to the bowsprit. One day the stubby thumb jutting out from the ship's stem would be a long, thin, graceful arm pointing skyward at a forty-five-degree angle. The fact that the bowsprit shrouds and bobstays were in place suggested that day might come soon.

As *Elizabeth* came abeam of *Constellation*, Richard's gaze swept down the frigate's entire length. She was painted black except for a broad white stripe running along her gun-port strake. Her rounded bow boasted a fine sweep, her stern a jaunty undercut. But what impressed Richard most was her sheer size. She was a fifth rate, a frigate, but really she was a hybrid between a traditionally built Royal Navy frigate and a ship of the line. Except that this ship, just as he had observed on *Constitution* in Boston, had a flush deck: no raised quarterdeck, no forecastle, no substantial deck structure of any kind marred the perfection of her lines.

His view was temporarily lost as *Elizabeth* swung into the wind. His own ship's single quadrilateral sail began to dance about as she came to a virtual stop in the face of the gentle breeze.

"Away anchor!" Wadsworth shouted. In short order, both jib and mainsail were doused and furled to their booms and the sloop was bobbing at her ease upon the sun-jeweled water of the Chesapeake.

"Shall I lower away your gig, sir?"

"Yes, do, Mr. Wadsworth. I'm going below. You may arrange shore leave for the men in two shifts. Later today I plan to have my first look around town. You're welcome to join me if you're so inclined."

"I'd be delighted, Mr. Cutler. Thank you."

When Richard reemerged on deck, he looked every bit the prosperous merchant in buff-colored knee-length trousers, stockings, and waistcoat, and a pure white cotton shirt and linen neck stock. The pale green sea coat he wore over this ensemble added an extra layer of warmth against the morning chill, and a black ribbon kept his shoulder-length blond hair tidy under a beaver-felt tricorne hat. Without fanfare he climbed down a boarding ladder into the waiting gig and took position on the after thwart. Two oarsmen on the starboard side eased off from the sloop's hull as the two on the larboard side backed oars to turn the gig about.

"Good luck, Mr. Cutler," a crewman named Avery called out from the sloop. His hail was taken up by others.

Richard shifted in the stern sheets to turn his head aft. "Thank you, lads," he called back. He raised his hat high in salute, then brought his gaze back to the ship lying directly ahead, made even more majestic by his perspective at sea level. She now seemed the mightiest of sea creatures contemplating with disinterest the tiniest of water bugs.

The gig coasted in aft of *Constellation*, toward a ladder leading up from the waterline to the wooden platform. As Richard clambered up the ladder, he glanced over at the plain glass windows on the frigate's stern. He saw no ornately carved balconies or large tortoiseshell glass windows as he had seen on many European men-of-war and on *Bonhomme Richard*. This frigate, he mused, was not built to coddle her officers.

When he reached the top rung of the ladder, he cupped a hand at his mouth. "Shove off, lads," he shouted down to the gig. "I'll find my way back or signal to be picked up."

No one was there to greet Richard. Nor did anyone pay him much attention as he slowly strolled along the quay beside the frigate. He could hear activity on board her and saw plenty of it in the vast shipyard beyond, with its clusters of mast and boat sheds, joiner's and blacksmith's shops, lofts housing sawyers, sail-makers, coopers, rope-makers, woodcarvers, and glaziers. Closer to him, not far from where he was at the moment, he noted several of the ship's spars submerged in a shallow, man-made pond, being properly seasoned before they were hoisted on board ship and stepped into place. He noted, too, the line of square gun ports cut out of her hull, the ports themselves raised up on their tricing tackle to allow free flow of air across the gun deck. That the square holes were void of black muzzles came as no surprise to him. He knew of only two foundries capable of manufacturing naval cannon within the sixteen states that now constituted the United States.

Unchallenged at the entry port, Richard walked up *Constellation*'s long gangway and stepped onto her weather deck. There he found a tall, stocky man dressed casually in olive-colored breeches, silver-buckled shoes, and a heavy knitted jersey. His back to Richard, he was talking in animated tones to two others, shipyard workers, presumably, and judging by the way he kept jabbing his finger at them, he was none too pleased with whatever it was they were discussing. Richard held back until the two men had been summarily dismissed and the older man wheeled around with a look of disgust.

"Excuse me, sir," Richard said, approaching him. "Can you tell me if Captain Truxtun is on board? And if so, where I might find him?"

The man stopped short and regarded Richard with a wary eye. "Who inquires?"

"My name is Richard Cutler, sir. I have come to Baltimore from Boston at Captain Truxtun's request."

The man's stern facial features relaxed into a smile. "By Jove! Is that your sloop out there?" He pointed at *Elizabeth* riding at anchor fifty feet away."

"She is, sir."

"Well damme, Mr. Cutler," the man exclaimed, "that was handsomely done, the way you brought her in. I have always maintained that seamanship is best demonstrated by the way a vessel is brought to or from her anchorage. You, sir, measured up." He stressed those last four words as if they bestowed the highest possible praise for a sea captain.

"Thank you, sir. I am fortunate to have a good crew."

The smile disappeared. "Fortunate? I think not, sir. Fortune has little to do with shaping a ship's crew. I maintain that a ship should be judged not by her crew but by her officers, who make her crew what it is—or is not—and whose first duty is to inspire confidence of leadership among the crew. Do you not agree?"

"I cannot disagree," Richard said, puzzled by this turn of conversation. Then, with a flash of awareness, he said, "May I presume, sir, that *you* are Captain Truxtun?"

The man offered Richard his hand. "You may, Mr. Cutler, you may. Welcome on board."

Richard felt the firm grip. "I apologize for being so casual, Captain. I did not recognize your rank."

"I did not find you casual, Mr. Cutler; nor could you have possibly recognized my rank in this garb. I assure you I *do* have a proper uniform, which is about all I have as captain of this ship. Why it takes so damnably long to get anything done around here is utterly beyond me. Here I am, appointed master and building superintendent of *Constellation*, and I can do nothing, absolutely nothing, to hurry things along. I got more done a damned sight more quickly when I was a privateer captain, I can assure you of that. McHenry wants this ship ready for sea come March. March? Ha! What a lark! Our secretary of war has a keen sense of humor, wouldn't you say, Mr. Cutler, from what you have observed here on deck?" Truxtun's sweeping gesture encompassed the ship from bow to stern. "And among the things you *won't* find anywhere on board is her crew. That's because we don't yet have a crew. Though it shouldn't take long to man and employ this ship once we set about recruiting."

"I understand your frustration, Captain," Richard said. "If it's any consolation, what you just described applies equally to *Constitution.* It took the Hartt Shipyard I don't recall how many months just to get southern oak for her planking and frame. And her masts have yet to be floated down from Maine."

"So I've heard," Truxtun said, the anger in his voice easing. He shook his head as he added, "That southern oak had damned well better prove its worth. We've spent a king's ransom in time lost harvesting it. Not to mention lives lost to malaria in those stinking Georgia swamps. Horrible way to die, shivering and sweating and lying there helpless in your own vomit and shit."

"Yes sir," Richard said, because there was nothing else to say. Several awkward moments ticked by.

"Well, Mr. Cutler," Truxtun said, "enough of that depressing talk. What say you and I tour this ship? It won't be a long tour, I assure you. There's not much to see yet." He beckoned over a carpenter's mate plying his trade by the capstan abaft the mainmast. "Be a good lad," he said to the disheveled young fellow freckled in sawdust and smelling of it, "and send word to Mr. Sterrett. I believe you know him. I noticed you two talking together yesterday."

The lad nodded eagerly. "It's as ye say, Cap'm. I do know Mr. Sterrett. He lives up yonder off Philpot Street. He goes to worship service at the Methodist Meetin' House, same as me."

"Well that's fine, just fine. I'd be much obliged if you'd tell him that his captain requests his presence on board ship. You may advise him that Mr. Cutler has arrived from Boston. This is for your trouble." He pressed a silver coin into the young man's palm.

The lad brightened at the sight of the coin. "Thank ye kindly, Cap'm. I'll be back with Mr. Sterrett quick as kiss me hand, or my name ain't Thad Joe Wilkins."

"Who is Mr. Sterrett?" Richard inquired as the lad raced away. He and Truxtun began walking forward toward the main hatchway, a large rectangular hole amidships. That hatchway by itself defined a major difference between British and American naval architecture. On board every Royal Navy frigate of Richard's acquaintance, the weather deck remained open to the gun deck below, save for a narrow gangway running along each side of the ship that connected the forecastle to the quarterdeck. On *Constellation*, the deck was flush from stem to stern, the only open access belowdecks afforded by the rectangular hatchway. The rest of the spar deck was heavily planked, save for a much smaller hatchway forward and another one aft, before what appeared to be a skylight cut in abaft the mizzenmast to provide light and ventilation for the captain's cabin.

Truxtun paused at the broad, sturdy ladder. "Andrew Sterrett is my third lieutenant. He comes from a good family here in Baltimore, and he has impressive bluewater experience for someone his age. Which, by the bye, is twenty-two. John Rodgers is my first. At the moment he is with his family in Havre de Grace, a town north of here on the Chesapeake. It also happens to be the home of the Cecil Iron Works, where I plan to purchase the guns for this ship. And to our further good fortune, John's father is a lifelong friend of the foundry's owner.

"The cost?" Truxtun asked, picking the question from Richard's mind. "The cost is $225 per 24-pound gun. That adds up to a bit more than $5,000 just to arm the gun deck. Add another $1,500 or so for the smaller guns on the weather deck, and another $500 for swivel guns, and you have the grand total. Wouldn't want to be responsible for *that* bill, eh, Mr. Cutler?"

"No indeed, sir," Richard agreed. He made a mental note of what Truxtun had just said and stored it away for future use.

Truxtun clambered down the pinewood steps and turned aft. Richard followed behind, taking note of the gun deck, empty save for neatly stacked piles of heavy canvas panels that someday would define the captain's quarters, now open to view. As he walked past a wasp-waisted drum—the bottom half of the capstan he had seen on the deck above—he ran his fingers along the smoothly polished oak base and the twelve iron pigeonholes set higher up. Someday soon, sailors would insert metal bars into those holes and push together to hoist the ship's anchor from the river bottom.

"Mind your head," Truxtun cautioned, as he made ready to descend to the next deck. "We're heading for the orlop. There's something down there I want to show you."

They did not linger on the berthing deck. There was not much to see beyond additional stacks of canvas panels and jalousie doors that would define the officers' cabins located on either side of the wardroom, which was directly beneath the captain's cabin. Slicing down through a circular opening cut out of the deckhead above was the mizzenmast, stepped below on the lowest deck, the orlop. Forward, toward the bow of the ship, the crew would someday sling their hammocks. In the open space between the crew's quarters and the wardroom, as on most naval vessels, would be quarters for the ship's complement of Marines, a human barricade that protected the officers aft from the crew forward should any thoughts of mutiny arise.

Richard followed Truxtun down to where, normally, the most fetid odors of man and ship festered. Today, Richard's nose was filled with the more appealing scent of freshly hewn Carolina pine and red cedar. Truxtun struck steel on flint from a tinderbox and lit two whale oil lanterns hooked on the base of the ladder. He handed one to Richard and kept the other for himself. Together they moved forward on the orlop as though into some dark cavern. Except that in here, Richard had to remove his hat and stoop low, his six-foot frame a full foot taller than the distance between deck and deckhead. They crept forward, Truxtun in the lead, away from the ship's magazine, already sheathed in copper sheeting, past the midshipmen's mess and the cockpit where the ship's surgeon would ply his trade, to an area just forward of the stepped mainmast. Here, in the light admitted by two deadlights of thick Williamsburg glass, their vision improved slightly. A short way farther on, approximately amidships, Truxtun raised his lantern.

"This is what I want to show you, Mr. Cutler. Do you recognize them?"

Richard raised his own lantern. In the dim light he observed what appeared to be wooden supports about a foot thick and two feet wide cut into the deckhead that followed the curve of the ship's hull all the way down to the keelson. He counted twelve such supports, six per side—three running forward and three running aft.

"I've never seen their like before," he allowed, "and I don't remember what they're called. But I suspect their purpose is to prevent hogging." He was referring to a potentially disastrous flaw in ship construction that under certain weight and buoyancy conditions forced the ship's bow and stern to droop and her keel and bottom to arch upward.

Truxtun lowered his lantern. "You are correct, Mr. Cutler. They are called diagonal riders, and they are there for the purpose you specified. Without them, a ship of *Constellation*'s length and beam would likely founder in a storm. The shipwrights in this yard might take their merry time with things and frustrate me no end, but I do credit them for knowing their business. Speaking of which, did you know that David

Stodder, the owner of this shipyard, learned his trade in your hometown of Hingham? It's true," he said to Richard's startled expression. "At the yard of a fellow named Jeremiah Stodder, a relative of sorts. Ah, I see you recognize the name though apparently you've never made the connection. In any event, I had my doubts about Humphrey's so-called innovations in ship design, but I am willing to put those reservations to rest, at least until her sea trials. Those trials will tell us the true story."

"She *is* a fine ship, sir."

IN SHEER SIZE, Captain Truxtun's cabin emulated the after cabin of a large British warship, running athwartship the entire thirty-foot width of the frigate, from the larboard to the starboard quarter. Today, size was about the only comparison one could make. Whereas a British warship housed its commander luxuriously, precious little graced the captain's day cabin on board *Constellation* beyond a rectangular table placed directly beneath the skylight, a small cedar cabinet off to the side, and four straight-back wooden chairs. Directly behind the day cabin, at the very stern of the ship, were the captain's personal quarters. On the starboard side, against the bulkhead, Richard noted an empty alcove that would serve as the captain's dining area. Across on the larboard side was a second alcove containing a free-swinging bunk attached to the deckhead by four sturdy ropes, a simple bureau, and a sea chest. Neither alcove had a door, though hard canvas partitions erected along the outer sides clearly defined the two spaces. No partitions, as yet, separated the day cabin from the captain's personal quarters aft or the gun deck forward. Compared with his little cuddy on *Elizabeth,* however, the space *Constellation* reserved for her captain was a veritable ballroom.

At Truxtun's invitation, Richard sat down in one of the chairs. Truxtun sat down across from him and rested his clasped hands on the table. Into the silence that ensued Richard interjected, "On the cruise south, Captain, I had occasion to read your book on naval strategy and tactics. I bought it from a Boston bookseller."

"Just so? How did you find it?"

"Very much like the treatises written by Rodney and Hood," Richard enthused, referring to two of England's greatest naval heroes. "And, of course, those by Admiral Nelson." He caught himself when Truxtun gave him what Richard interpreted as a sardonic smile, adding somewhat sheepishly, "I wasn't trying to be self-serving in saying that, Captain."

"I didn't think you were, Mr. Cutler. I am flattered by the comparisons and impressed by the quality of your reading. But what truly delights me no end is the knowledge that I have now sold at least one copy of my latest book. That makes one copy more than of my first book, on wind currents."

They chuckled comfortably together before Truxtun rose. "Excuse me a moment, Mr. Cutler, while I see to our refreshment."

Truxtun walked over to the cedar cabinet and poured out two glasses of claret from a cut-glass decanter. He handed one to Richard and resumed his seat across the table from him.

"To book sales," he said, raising his glass. "And confusion to our enemies." He downed a swig, sighed contentedly, and leaned back, crossing his right leg over his left. Moments ticked by as each man silently took the measure of the other. Richard absorbed the pewter-gray eyes that served as focal points of a broad, clean-shaven, middle-aged face; the broad nose, thin lips, and short neck. Truxtun's thinning, tawny hair was pulled straight back in a tightly bound queue. Richard found himself wondering if this seemingly hard-bitten sea officer ever indulged himself with a sniff of powdered tobacco or donned a perfumed wig. Only when forced to by social convention, he conjectured.

Truxtun broke the silence. "As you can see, Mr. Cutler," he said offhandedly, "I am a simple man with simple tastes. Although I must say that the simplicity of *these* surroundings puts even me on edge. Circumstances will change once my personal stores arrive from Perth Amboy. Though I doubt these accommodations will ever equal those of your brother-in-law . . . Captain Jeremy Hardcastle, isn't it? Attached to the Mediterranean Squadron?"

"Yes, sir. Captain Hardcastle is my wife's oldest brother. I am pleased to report that her other brother, Hugh, was recently promoted to the rank of post captain. He remains attached to the Windward Squadron in Barbados."

"So I understand. Your wife had a third brother, did she not? One serving as midshipman in *Serapis* at the same time you were serving as acting third lieutenant in *Bonhomme Richard*?"

Richard lowered his eyes to his glass. "That is correct, sir. His name was James—his friends called him Jamie. I was honored to be counted among those friends." He said nothing more, surprised by Truxtun's knowledge of his wife's family and wondering what other details of that bitter North Sea naval engagement he might know. The respectful silence that ensued suggested that Truxtun knew, at least, that Midshipman James Makepeace Hardcastle had died in Richard's arms on *Serapis'* weather deck as the battle reached its bloody conclusion.

"Well," the captain said at length, "I am honored to be in the presence of such naval accomplishments."

Richard raised his eyes. "What accomplishments are you referring to, Captain?"

Truxtun smiled. "Come now, Mr. Cutler. You're being a tad modest, aren't you? Your conduct in that battle was well documented in the British and American presses. Not to mention your tête-à-tête with those two Arab xebecs in the Mediterranean."

The sea battle waged nine years ago, after Richard had left Algiers having failed to secure the release of *Eagle's* crew, had been covered rather extensively in the presses. The dey of Algiers had refused the proffered ransom, all of it Cutler family money backed by a government promissory note executed by Alexander Hamilton to someday repay all funds expended, Congress at the time having insufficient resources of its own. In the royal court of Algiers, Richard had found himself enmeshed in a web of intrigue and duplicity. The morning after he departed, two well-armed xebecs attacked his schooner, hoping to take both *Falcon* and the $60,000 of unpaid ransom money stored in her hold. *Falcon*, though, was armed and expecting the attack. Her 6-pounder guns and an odd type of ordnance that had served the roving buccaneer Edward Teach with lethal efficiency in an earlier age of high-seas piracy were more than enough to fight off the two attackers. The battle ended with the obliteration of both xebecs and with *Falcon* limping north toward the French naval hospital in Toulon.

"That must have been one hell of a fight," Truxtun commented.

Richard shrugged and then allowed himself a smile. "We would not have prevailed were it not for those fire-arrows, sir. They caught the Arabs completely by surprise."

"Yes, I daresay. Whose idea was it to employ that particular type of ordnance?"

"Richard Dale's, sir. He and I were prisoners in England during the war. We later served together in *Bonhomme Richard* and have remained friends ever since. I have no idea where he found those fire-arrows, but I owe my life and the lives of many of my crew to the fact that he did."

"I know Mr. Dale. He's a fine naval officer. Are you aware that he was recently awarded command of *Ganges*?" He was referring to a former merchant vessel refitted as a man-of-war carrying twenty-six 9-pounder guns. "She is the first vessel of the United States Navy to put to sea. Captain Dale's orders are to chase down French privateers operating off our coast. Our quarry, when finally we sail, will be French frigates and privateers operating in the Caribbean."

Richard noted the word "our." "I read about Mr. Dale's appointment. It is well earned." He took a sip of claret, investing a moment to enjoy its smooth texture while mulling over Truxtun's last statement. "Might I assume from what you just said, Captain, that you believe war with France is inevitable? That the envoys dispatched by President Adams will fail in their mission? You seem quite certain that *Constellation* will be deployed in the Indies."

Truxtun's reply was quick and emphatic. "I do believe they will fail, Mr. Cutler, though it gives me no pleasure to say it. What's more, I'd wager good money that President Adams was convinced they would fail even before he sent them. His political foes clamor for peace, so Mr. Adams agreed to give peace one final try. Oh, I think his intent is sincere enough. He has no more desire for war or any sort of foreign entanglement than did President Washington. But to avoid *this* entanglement, the French must also desire peace. And that they do not. If they did, why would they increase their attacks on our ships on the very eve of this mission?"

"To gain an upper hand in negotiations?" Richard volunteered. He was thinking to himself that Truxtun's opinions on the odds of war with France coincided with those of his father and General Lincoln.

Truxtun grunted. "What negotiations are you referring to? What terms? We're either at war with France or we're not. *Those* are the terms. *That's* the issue. There's no territory to claim or divide up, no advantage to negotiate. No, France does not want peace. Not with us or with England. The British have captured most of France's islands in the Caribbean—Tobago, Martinique, and Saint Lucia among them. They even took Guadeloupe, and had they been able to hold *that* island, the French would have been finished in the Indies. But the French threw everything they had at Guadeloupe to get it back. You may recall that in '94 the National Directory freed all slaves in French colonies. A French commissioner in Guadeloupe named Sonthonax carried out the order, and now he and a petty tyrant named Hugues are stirring up slave rebellions on British-held islands. You were recently on Barbados. Didn't your brother-in-law tell you any of this?"

"Captain Hardcastle was out on patrol at the time, sir," Richard said. "But I was assured by my cousins on Barbados that the British army is taking every precaution. John and Robin treat their slaves better than most planters do, though I realize that won't count for much if the slaves do rise up."

"I agree," the captain said. "However well you might treat a slave during the day, come nightfall he remains a slave."

Just then they heard steps on the main hatchway ladder. Richard turned to see someone stepping onto the gun deck. He could not distinguish much about the man from that distance, except to note that he was handsomely attired and had curly brown hair and thin sideburns that reached nearly to his chin.

Truxtun held up the flat of his palm. "If you will give us a moment, Mr. Sterrett," he called out.

"Of course, Captain," the man answered, his voice echoing in the vast empty space. He ambled over to an empty gunport and stared discreetly out at the harbor.

Truxtun turned back to Richard and motioned him closer. "My lieutenant's arrival is fortuitous, Mr. Cutler. It forces me to cut to the quick. I am fully aware that you sit here before me qualified to serve as first lieutenant in this or any other of our new frigates. You're not a great deal younger than I am, and yet you have at least as much experience at sea. And you have sailed under Captain Jones, a man the entire world admires and a man whom I know from personal experience greatly admired you. Hell, sir, you could serve as captain of this ship, today! But the reality in this man's Navy is that we have far more officer candidates than we have officer berths. Many highly qualified candidates will never step foot on board an American ship of war. Then, of course, there are the family connections—'interest,' as the British call it—of which you, too, are a beneficiary. None of this is entirely fair, but it *is* the reality. Do you understand what I'm saying?"

"I believe I do, sir."

"*Constellation* is going into battle," Truxtun went on. "Do not doubt it. She won't be ready for sea by March as Mr. McHenry would have it, but by summer, yes. When she is ready, I intend to steer her into harm's way, as Captain Jones so aptly put it. But before I do, I have serious need of a commissioned officer skilled in naval gunnery. I have reviewed your documents and the letters of your sponsors, including that of Mr. Adams. I am convinced that you are that officer. As my second lieutenant you will have absolute command of the gun deck. While you are on the gun deck you shall outrank everyone, including Mr. Rodgers, including even *me*. The gun deck will be your sole responsibility on board ship, aside from watch duty. You will train the men on the guns and you will get them into fighting shape to rival any British crew. It's a tall order, I admit, and one that few men would choose to accept. Will *you*, Mr. Cutler? Will you accept an officer's commission and do me the honor of fighting alongside me against our nation's enemies?"

Richard had not expected an offer to be extended so quickly and in such a fashion. His answer, nonetheless, was never in doubt.

"I accept the commission, Captain Truxtun. And I humbly thank you for it."

Truxtun gave him a warm, broad smile. "Excellent, Mr. Cutler. Let us shake hands on it."

Afterward, Richard asked, "How long do you think the Senate will take to confirm my appointment, Captain? Assuming it does, of course."

Truxtun's smile did not falter. "I wouldn't trouble myself with that formality if I were you, Mr. Cutler. I am given considerable latitude in selecting my officers. And since the members of Congress realize that my self-interest and quite possibly my life depend on the men I choose, they will approve my selections, especially one whose name has been put forth by our president. When can you report?"

"When do you need me?"

"There's no pell-mell rush, as you can plainly see. We're not going anywhere anytime soon. Christmas is coming, and I suggest we celebrate the season with our families. It may be our last visit home for a while. We have Mr. Sterrett to make certain work on board continues in our absence. And we have Mr. Rodgers to see to recruitment and the guns. So shall we say, back here by April 1? If I need you sooner, I'll send word.

"And Mr. Cutler," he added as if as an afterthought, "this I promise you. If by some stroke of fortune our envoys in Paris *do* manage to avert war, I shall not bind you to a long term of service. While I understand one's duty to one's country, I also understand one's duty to his family and his family business."

"Thank you, Captain. By the first of April, then."

Five

Nantucket Sound
December 1797

RICHARD TAPPED HIS finger against the bulb at the base of the weatherglass, as if that might encourage the liquid inside the glass tube to stop its ominous fall of the past two hours. A storm was brewing, and the sailor in him sensed a bad one. The sea was becoming mottled, confused, and the wind had shifted counter-clockwise from the southwest to the northeast. He divined no immediate danger, though, and thus delayed the order to double-reef the mainsail. *Elizabeth* was already sailing under reduced canvas, and they needed to make all the headway they could while they could.

Again he studied the chart spread out before him on the table in the cramped after cabin. By his dead reckoning they were somewhere within Nantucket Sound. He could not determine exactly where—a thickening overcast had prevented a noon sun sighting—but he calculated their position as being a few miles off the southwestern shore of Nantucket Island. If that position was accurate, they should have time to make safe harbor before the storm unleashed its full fury.

There came a knock on the cabin door.

"Enter."

A seaman opened the door and poked his head inside. His blond hair and blue eyes matched Richard's own, though his ancestry was Swedish, not English.

"What is it, Anders?"

"Mr. Wadsworth bids ye topside, Captain. We've sighted a vessel."

"What sort of vessel?"

"Can't tell for certain, sir. That's why Mr. Wadsworth bids ye topside."

"Very well. I'm coming up."

Richard rolled up the chart, slipped on a thick woolen sea jacket, and followed Anders up the ladder to the weather deck. His mate was standing by the starboard shrouds, a long glass to his eye.

Richard walked over, rubbing his hands for warmth. "What do we have, Mr. Wadsworth?"

"Sorry to bother you, sir," the mate replied. "It's probably nothing. Collins spotted that ship yonder, heading straight down for us. Says he can't determine her registry. Nor can I. She's barely hull up."

Richard glanced aloft. Joel Collins was a reliable lookout, one of the best in the employ of Cutler & Sons. He possessed keen eyesight, he was an agile topman, and as the scion of a renowned Boston shipwright family, he recognized American and British ship design as well as anyone. Why, then, was he baffled by what he had observed?

"Shall I go up, sir?"

"No, Mr. Wadsworth, I will. Hand me your glass."

Richard slung the glass by its lanyard over his shoulder and worked his way up the weather ratlines, using the schooner's heel to larboard to facilitate the climb. Halfway up to the crosstrees, he laced his right arm in and around the thick hemp cords of the shrouds and trained the glass northward. Yes, there she was, coming right at them, her bow in full view. She was a two-masted brig; that much was certain. White-water coursed out from the stem of a vessel powered by a full set of square sails on her masts and a fore-and-aft sail, with gaff and boom, abaft her mainmast. He could not see her ensign—a pyramid of white canvas blocked his view; more than likely she wasn't flying one. What demanded his attention and his concern were her sharply curved cut-water and her short yards and narrow top-hamper; neither was typical of a British or American vessel. Of equal concern were her foresails, cut much shorter on the luff than English jibs. And then there was the finely chiseled figurehead at the bow, a cherubic angel serenely leading the ship's complement in crusades that, Richard was now convinced, had nothing to do with service to God.

He re-slung the glass and cupped a hand to his mouth. "You may come down, Collins," he shouted up. He retraced his steps on the shrouds as Collins, above him, crossed a leg over a backstay and slid down hand under hand to the deck.

"She's French," Richard said matter-of-factly to those gathered amidships. He collapsed the glass and handed it to his mate.

"A Frenchie? In these waters? Damn me to hell," Wadsworth cursed out loud. "Where's her base, d'ye think, Captain?"

"Guadeloupe. Or Saint-Domingue. Or Charleston, if the good citizens there have decided to reopen their port to French privateers."

"Damn me to hell," Wadsworth cursed again. Then, in a more disciplined tone: "Shall we come about, sir? Or make for the Vineyard?"

Richard glanced ahead. Little more than a mile separated the two vessels.

"No, Mr. Wadsworth. There's no point. We can't outrun her and we can't fight her. So we'll sail right at her. We're small pickings and we're high on the water, so the Frenchies can see that we carry no cargo. Let's hope that with this storm brewing they'll choose to ignore us, especially if we don't appear threatened by them."

His optimism was dampened minutes later by the report of a ship's cannon to windward, the internationally recognized signal of hostile intent. Acrid smoke swept across the brig's bow to leeward. Ahead, a small plume of water shot into the air.

"So much for hope," Richard said disgustedly. "Heave to, Mr. Wadsworth. Let's see what La Belle France has in store for us." Within minutes his crew had the sloop's jib and mainsail set to counteract each other and *Elizabeth* was drifting uneasily upon the rolling sea.

The brig swept on past, then wore ship, feathering in and off the wind until she was abreast of the schooner. When her foretopsail was laid against the mast, she, too, lost all headway. The Americans watched warily as a launch was swung out. Seven men clambered down into it. In short order five Frenchmen were on board *Elizabeth*, two of them wielding muskets. Two others remained in the launch, fending off. None of the men wore any sort of uniform.

Hands on his hips, the apparent leader of the group strode across the deck. He glanced this way and that, making no effort to hide his contempt for the assembled knot of Americans. He was red-bearded and powerfully built, and he wore no visible insignia of command, save for a small tricolor rosette pinned to the front of his red woolen stocking cap. As he returned to the entry port, he unbuttoned his coat and drew back its flaps to reveal a brace of pistols tucked crossways under his belt at the front of his wide-bottomed, red-striped trousers.

"*Eh bien*," he said to the sloop's crew. "*Je m'appelle Paul-Louis du Bourg. Je suis le capitaine de ce visseau là.*" He pointed at the brig drifting slightly ahead of the sloop. "*Qui est votre capitaine?*"

Richard Cutler stepped forward. "*Je suis le capitaine*," he said. "*Que faites-vous à bord mon vaisseau?*" His tone made clear his conviction that the Frenchmen had no right to be on his vessel.

The Frenchman, seemingly caught off guard by Richard's command of the language, regarded him with hostile eyes. He answered the demand with a demand of his own.

"*Votre rôle d'équipage, s'il vous plaît.*" He was referring to the roster of crew and cargo that the French government required every American vessel at sea to carry. Without it, the National Directory had decreed, an American vessel was subject to search and seizure if found to be carrying goods to or from a British port. At least, Richard consoled himself, these men were privateers. Pirates rarely bothered with such formalities.

"I do not have such a document," Richard replied angrily in French. "Nor do I need one, even under your state-sanctioned rules of piracy. We are sailing in home waters. You are the ones here illegally, and I demand you depart at once. *Immédiatement! Comprenez-vous, monsieur?*" He spat out that last word.

The Frenchman's thin, condescending smile did nothing to temper Richard's outrage. He motioned to his men. "*Fouillez ce vaisseau!*"

Jake Wadsworth did not speak French, but he understood the order to search the vessel when two of the privateers advanced toward the hatchway leading belowdecks. Wadsworth stepped in front of the hatchway and crossed his arms over his chest, blocking their path.

"*Vos fusils, mes hommes!*" the officer shouted.

Two of the Frenchmen drew pistols. Two others lowered their muskets to waist level, aiming the barrels directly at Wadsworth's stomach.

"Ease off, Jake," Richard said. "Let them go below. They won't find anything of value down there."

Grudgingly, Wadsworth stepped aside. Two privateers pushed past him and disappeared down the ladder. The others remained on guard on deck. The wind, meanwhile, had strengthened and was carrying needle-sharp pellets of freezing rain that stung exposed flesh.

"*Vite!*" the French captain yelled down the hatchway.

The two privateers emerged topside to report that the American schooner carried no cargo, only stores for her crew. Their captain ordered them back belowdecks to appropriate those stores and then strode aft toward Richard.

"Why no cargo?" he demanded in broken English.

"None of your fucking business," Richard replied, his voice low and dangerous.

The Frenchman narrowed his eyes. The ruddy color on his face darkened and his upper lip curled, exposing yellow teeth. Suddenly his right fist lashed out, catching Richard square on the jaw. "*Cochon insolent!*" he sneered. "*Je suggère que vous apprenez quelques manières, monsieur!*"

The blow sent Richard reeling backward. He grabbed hold of the mast, steadied himself, then felt with his index finger the cut on his lower lip. Blood trickled down his chin.

Wadsworth advanced two steps. Several of the crew followed him.

"As you were, Wadsworth!" Richard shouted.

"We can take them, Captain," Wadsworth snarled. His hands were balled into fists and his eyes were glued on a youthful privateer brandishing a musket at waist level, its aim wavering now in the face of the challenge. "We outnumber the bastards."

"That's sheer folly, Jake. They'll kill you certain. Even if we did manage to overcome them, that brig over there would blow us out of the water. Stand down, all of you. *Stand down! Now! By my order!*"

Wadsworth muttered something incomprehensible. Nonetheless, he motioned to the crew to back off. Richard faced the privateer captain.

"Monsieur," he said in French with as much deference as he could muster, "what you are doing makes no sense for either of us. Take what stores you require and leave us. A bad storm is coming. You can see that. You can also see that you are putting your brig in grave danger by staying so close to land. You need sea-room, and plenty of it."

He spoke not as an enemy to an enemy, nor as a victim to his tormentor, but rather as one sea captain to another. As the privateers finished offloading barrels of provisions into the launch, their captain considered his choices.

"*Très bien,*" he said, his mind made up. "*Vous avez raison, monsieur. Merci pour votre provisions.*" With that, he strode to the entry port and ordered his men back into the launch. As he turned around to descend the short ladder, Richard noticed his right hand gripping a pistol by the barrel. He was about to shout out a warning, but the Frenchman was too quick. Whipping out his arm, he slammed the butt of the pistol hard against Wadsworth's face. Wadsworth's knees buckled and he collapsed on the deck, blood pulsing from an ugly wound between his nose and upper lip. Cursing, he sat up and spat out fragments of a front tooth.

"Son of a *bitch*!" Richard seethed in angst and anger and an appalling sense of helplessness. "Back off!" he managed to shout to his crew.

"*Quelque chose pour se souvenir,*" the French captain jeered. "*Au revoir, mes amis.*" He stepped down into the launch.

As the oarsmen struggled against cresting waves to get back to their brig, Richard focused a glass on the ship's stern where the name *Le Léopard* was displayed in bold gilt lettering. Fitting, he thought, for a ship like that to bear such a name. He vowed never to forget this ship, or this captain. Someday, somehow, he would again cross tacks with this particular leopard, under far different circumstances.

RICHARD'S WARNING about the storm proved all too accurate. Within an hour after parting ways with the French brig he was forced to reduce canvas to a small triangular storm jib and a double-reefed mainsail. Two hours later, *Elizabeth* battled her way northward past the islands of Muskeget and Tuckernut, barely visible to starboard in the gathering mist and uniform gloom. The hum of the wind in the rigging had intensified from a low, sinister moan to a wild, agonized shriek. Gray seas whipped with foam crashed against her hull, battering her timbers, washing her weather deck with icy seawater, and sending shudders of agony through the fabric of the sloop.

Immediately on shortening sail, Richard had ordered six of his crew below and the hatch cover battened down tight with tarpaulins. He and Wadsworth remained at the helm, his mate having convinced Richard that his nose was not broken. The bleeding had stopped, and it would take a damned sight more than a tooth knocked out by a turd-sucking, frog-faced Frenchman to keep him from his duty. Collins was posted at the bow as lookout, and able seaman George Avery stood by the mainsail sheets. All four men were tethered to a rope linked to a jack-line running amidships from stem to stern, the loop at the bowline knot attached to the jack-line, allowing them free movement about the deck. No one could see much. Freezing rain had yielded to sleet and then to swirling snow, and the darkening cloud cover had now combined forces with fog so thick that sea could no longer be distinguished from sky.

When Richard judged that *Elizabeth* had fought her way sufficiently northward, and that her furled sails were in peril of being ripped from their gaskets by the sheer weight of the wind, he cupped his hands directly over Wadsworth's ear. "Bring her about, Jake," he shouted. "And brace yourself. This won't be easy."

Wadsworth nodded in reply. He waited for the right moment and then, with Richard's help, pushed the tiller hard to larboard, forcing the sloop's bow to starboard. Richard signaled Avery to release the mainsheet. As her bow tore through the wind, *Elizabeth* took the full brunt of the near-hurricane-force winds on her larboard side. She yawed sharply over to starboard, close to her beam ends. Avery slipped and fell onto his back and slid helter-skelter across the deck until the rope securing him to the jack-line jerked him to a halt just shy of the bulwarks. He struggled to his feet, groping wildly for the flailing mainsheet. He managed to seize hold of it, wrestling it as though a bucking stallion were at its other end. As *Elizabeth* slowly came to rights, Richard eased her bow back to eastward, forcing the wind from the mainsail, which thundered in protest. Wadsworth, again judging the moment right, surrendered the tiller to Richard and stumbled forward to where Avery was battling the mainsheet. Together they hauled in the unruly beast and secured it to a belaying pin. At the tiller, Richard eased *Elizabeth* off the wind until her double-reefed mainsail came taut, her rudder found traction, and she plunged ahead into the frothing, mounting swells.

Wadsworth fought his way back to the helm, and Richard yielded the tiller. The oilskins both men wore to protect them from the storm were weighted with snow and ice. "Steer by the binnacle, Jake," he shouted in encouragement. "Keep her as steady as you can on a course south by east."

"South by east, aye, Captain," Wadsworth shouted back into the screaming wind.

That course, Richard calculated, would take them inside the great sandy wings of Nantucket Island, a landfall that he pictured as a gargantuan manta ray swimming upon the ocean's surface in a southeasterly direction. Her outer shores might feel the shock and surge of the stormy Atlantic, but once inside those protective wings, the eastern one capped by a towering wooden lighthouse on Sandy Point, a vessel found safety as long as the wind did not rage from due north, which it rarely did. The harbor of Nantucket Town was *Elizabeth*'s destination, and they would get there none too soon, unless one of the two hundred whaling ships that called Nantucket home suddenly appeared before them in the murk. A collision would likely mean the swift end of everyone on board the sloop. At this time of year, the life expectancy of a man immersed in these waters could be measured in minutes.

Gradually the seas subsided, although a stark wilderness of wind and snow continued to engulf them. Forward, Joel Collins grabbed hold of the jack-line and trudged aft, hand over hand, toward the helm.

"The fog lifted long enough for me to catch the shore, Captain," he shouted when he reached the binnacle. He pointed in the general direction. "Brant Point lies two points to larboard. Land's coming up fast, sir," he warned.

"Understood, Joel," Richard yelled back. "Alert the men. We'll need their help. It may be safer now on deck, but I want everyone on deck tied on until we've passed the point."

Their ordeal wasn't over yet. Land was closing too rapidly to steer into the northeaster on a close haul to the harbor entrance. They had to swing *Elizabeth* around to northward, back into the fierce onslaught of wind and waves, to the outer reaches of the protective wings, before she could make one last final lunge to safety on a broad reach.

In due course *Elizabeth* glided past Brant Point and into the harbor's sheltered waters. One final swerve to the northeast and her crew dropped anchor and doused her small strips of sail. Around them, vessels of various sizes and descriptions bobbed at anchor, their top-hampers white with snow and ice, an armada of ghost ships facing into the wind.

Richard ordered everyone below and the hatchway secured. In his cabin he peeled off his oilskins and seaboots and leaned against a bulkhead, closing his eyes as he uttered a short, silent prayer of thanksgiving. Wearily, his energy spent, he went to his sea chest and pulled out a thick woolen sweater, adding it to the two layers he already wore. Gathering up the remainder of his dry clothing, he carried it forward to where his crew had slumped down onto the damp deck. Most had their heads down with their arms dangling across their knees.

Richard tossed his spare clothing onto the deck. "For anyone who needs these," he said. He looked around at his spent crew. "Let's see where we are, lads. For starters, has anyone taken inventory of our stores?"

"I have, Captain," replied Timothy Cates, a young topman who did double duty as ship's cook. "They didn't leave much. We have a few biscuits and some bits of meat. That's about it. We do have wood for the stove. And," a grin lit his face, "they didn't take the rum, sir. I reckon they didn't find it, stored up forward. We have all four casks."

"Well, at least there's that," Richard acknowledged, adding, in a more hopeful tone: "All right, lads, here's the drill. We'll get the galley stove going and we'll keep it going. Everyone sleeps here tonight, by the stove. We'll maintain five watches of two hours each, two men each. Collins and I will take the first watch. Each watch has two responsibilities: to make certain the fire doesn't go out and to go up there," indicating the hatchway ladder, "every hour to clear away the snow and ice from the hatch cover. Unless, of course, you enjoy it down here so much you'd prefer to stay the winter." He attempted a smile. No one seemed able to summon much of a reaction. The eyes fixed upon him were those of the half-dead.

"Right. I suggest we indulge ourselves with a tot of rum and what biscuit we can spare. Mind you, no one gets drunk tonight. We must keep our wits about us. We won't feast, but we won't starve either. Tomorrow, when this storm blows over, we'll find provisions ashore to see us home."

Two days passed before *Elizabeth*'s crew was able to climb up on deck and begin the arduous task of dumping snow overboard and chipping away at the inch-thick ice on the standing rigging. The morning was brilliant and bitterly cold, with a cloudless sky and a moderate northwesterly breeze. Snow, perhaps two feet of it, with drifts considerably higher, cast an almost blinding white pallor over Nantucket Village, a cluster of shops and homes nestled close together by the harbor's edge. Wisps of smoke curled up from many of those homes, some of them, those belonging to whaling captains and ship owners rising up in the background, as elegant in federalist design and red brick construction as anything Richard had seen in Louisburg Square in Boston.

His first order of business: find food for his crew. The meager rations they had managed to unearth had run out the previous afternoon. Seeing no activity ashore, Richard scanned the decks of vessels anchored nearby, most of them whalers of one design or another. He saw no activity there, either, except on board one ship-rigged vessel anchored not far away. On her deck, men were chipping away at ice-coated rigging with iron mallets, just as his own crew was doing.

"Call out the gig," he ordered. "Cates, go below and bring up a cask. Put it in the bow of the gig."

"A cask, sir?" Cates questioned.

"Yes, Cates, you heard me. A cask. A *full* cask."

"Aye, Captain."

Swinging out the boat was a relatively easy task, secured as it was to the weather deck bottom-up. The men had just to flip it over, loosen the binds holding the oars, insert tholepins into the gunwale on both sides, and hoist it out and down with tackle rigged on stays and the yardarm with a midshipman's hitch. Richard was soon on board, seated on the center thwart and rowing toward the whaler.

"Ahoy!" he cried up to a deckhand breaking ice on lower shrouds at the fore chain-wale. The man was so heavily clothed that Richard could distinguish nothing about him except that his beard was long, curly, and coal black. "Is your master aboard?"

"No," the man yelled down. "He be ashore."

"Are his mates aboard?"

"One is. What can I do fer ye?"

Richard shipped an oar and brought his free hand to his mouth.

"I am the master of the sloop you see over there. We were caught in the storm on our way home to Boston. I need provisions for my crew."

"Sorry," the mate declared unsympathetically. "We've no provisions to spare. Try ashore in town."

"I cannot," Richard persisted. "You can see for yourself that everything is closed up tight and will be for some time. Please, sir, my men are hungry. They have not eaten since yesterday. There are ten of us, and we need only a two-day supply."

"Sorry, mate," the man shouted again, irritation entering his voice. "I can't help you." He went back to chipping at the ice-laden shrouds.

"I am prepared to pay!" Richard shouted up at him.

"Do tell. With what? Spanish gold?" The man guffawed at his own wit and whacked a shroud with his mallet. Shards of ice clinked onto the deck and splashed into the water.

"No. With something better than Spanish gold."

"And what would that be, pray?"

Richard pointed his thumb back at the large wooden cask. "West Indian rum."

The man paused in his work. For several moments he stared down at Richard and the cask set behind him.

"Rum, you say?"

"Aye. Barbados dark rum, the best you've ever tasted. As you and your mates will agree once you sample it."

Early the next morning *Elizabeth* set sail for home, her crew content with full stomachs.

NORTHWARD BOUND, they could see evidence ashore that the blizzard had struck the mainland of Cape Cod with the same devastating force as it had the islands. Each picturesque coastal village they passed—Chatham, Wellfleet, Truro, Provincetown—lay entombed in white, and hardly a glimpse of human activity was to be seen anywhere. The fishermen and tradesmen of these seaside communities sat huddled inside their homes before the hearth, taking what comfort and solace they could from human fellowship and a crackling fire, in the same way their Saxon and Celtic ancestors had done when confronted with such a calamity. Aboard *Elizabeth*, as she sailed past wintry scenes that were at once spectacular and horrifying to the eye, every man prayed that his own family was safe and warm and somehow managing to cope.

As it turned out, the storm had only grazed the South Shore of Boston before it howled eastward into the Atlantic. Because every member of his crew lived in or near Hingham, Richard decided to bypass Long Wharf and steer directly for Crow Point. It would be late in the evening by the time they arrived there, too late for those who lived farther away to get home that night. But at least those who lived near the docks could be with their families.

"Goodnight, lads," Richard said later that evening to the four sailors remaining on board. It was 9:30, and *Elizabeth* lay snug against a Hingham quay. "I'll be back in the morning with horse and carriage to take you home."

"Thank ye kindly," one of the four replied. "An' Cap'm, seeing as how we're off duty, do ye mind a-tall if me and the boys nip into that last cask of rum?"

"Nip to your heart's content, Pulley," Richard urged. "Lord knows you've earned the right. Tomorrow I'll bring along some extra hands in case we should need to carry you and your mates aboard the carriage."

The full moon cast an amber glow as Richard trudged through several inches of freshly fallen snow to his home on South Street. He hoped his family would still be up, although he realized that was not likely. The black shroud of winter closed in early over New England in December, and the one sure way to keep warm during those long, bitter hours was to wrap up inside thick woolen blankets and sleep through the night.

At the entry to his home he paused, listening. No sound. He creaked open the door and stepped inside. Still hearing nothing, he closed the door gently behind him. He removed his seaboots and struck a spark on a tinderbox to light a candle kept on a shelf near the door. A quick survey of the downstairs confirmed that his family had indeed gone upstairs to bed, although not long ago, judging by the low fires still burning in the parlor and kitchen. He tossed several fresh logs onto each hearth. Flames crackled up, adding warmth to the rooms downstairs and, to a lesser degree, those above.

He unbuttoned his sea coat and shrugged it off, placing it on a wooden peg in the foyer above his boots. Candle in hand, he climbed the stairs in stocking feet. On the second floor he paused outside the first room in the hallway to the right, cracked open the door, and peeked in. Will was curled up asleep on one bed, Jamie on the other. He was tempted to wake them but decided against it, imagining their surprise the next morning when they came downstairs for breakfast and found him at the kitchen table. He closed that door and clicked open the next one down the hall.

"Is that you, Mommy?" a sleepy voice called from the shadows.

Richard placed the candle in a sconce on a side table and sat down on the edge of the bed. "No, Poppet. It's me."

"Father!" Diana mumbled with sleepy delight. She sat up, now fully awake. "When did you get home?"

"Just now."

"Does Mommy know?"

"Not yet."

"Well you must go and tell her, Father. Right away."

"Why, Poppet?" Richard asked with concern.

"She's very upset, Father. I saw her crying this afternoon. I asked her what was wrong, but she wouldn't tell me. I told Will, and he said to mind my own business. But she's worried, Father. She's worried sick, I just know she is."

"Worried sick about what?"

"Why, I should think about *you*, Father."

A lump formed in Richard's throat. He swallowed hard. "Well," he managed, "Mommy's a very lucky mommy to have a daughter like you who cares about her so much. I'll go see her right away, all right?"

"All right." When she had settled back, Richard pulled the comforter up to her chin and kissed her forehead. As he did so, she reached up and wrapped her arms around his neck. "Father?"

"Yes, Poppet?"

"I'm so happy you're home. I've missed you. We all have."

Another lump. Another hard swallow. "I've missed you too. Go to sleep now. Promise?"

"I promise. Good night, Father."

"Goodnight, Diana. I love you."

At his own bedroom at the far end of the hall to the left, he opened the door and crept inside. Katherine was asleep on the far side of the bed, her back to him, her chestnut curls flowing across the checkerboard coverlet. He set down the candle and watched her sleep as he stripped off his clothing, a hundred thoughts, memories, desires infusing a mind beset by what his daughter had told him. It was one thing for a man to face the dangers of the sea, but quite another for his family to suffer because of it.

He lifted the blankets and slipped in naked beside her, nestling close, savoring her body heat and feminine scent, allowing his body to warm before touching her. She stirred when she felt him nuzzling her ear and cheek.

"Mmm, Richard?" she murmured dreamily.

"Yes, my love. Were you expecting someone else?"

Her eyes flew open. "*Richard!*"

She turned about and was upon him in an instant, kissing him, running her hands over him, clawing at him with frantic intensity. "I thought you weren't coming back," she wailed. "I thought you were gone!" Weeping openly, she clutched him to her, squeezed him, touched him everywhere, her wild ministrations inspiring more pain than pleasure.

"Gone where? Don't you know that I'll always come home to you?"

She stopped short, as if slapped. Then, as though emerging from a hypnotic trance, she brought her hand to his cheek and gazed deep into his eyes, convincing herself that, yes, she was awake; yes, he was home; no, this was not a dream; yes, the nightmare was over. "I heard tell," she half-whispered, "of a terrible storm south of here. I heard tell of many ships lost at sea."

"Who told you that?"

"Captain Bennett," she said in that same faraway tone. "I heard him talking to people in a village shop on Monday. He said it was the worst storm he had ever seen, by half. He said that his was the last ship to escape hell. And he said that no ship could survive such a storm, that any ship caught in it must be presumed lost. I hurried home, but I didn't say anything to anyone except Agee and Lizzy. I *had* to tell them, Richard. I know I shouldn't have. Lizzy is so close to her time and mustn't be made to worry. But I had to tell *someone*."

He tucked a loose strand of chestnut hair behind her ear. "Well, Frank's a good man, not one to spread panic. And he was right; there *was* a fierce storm off the Cape. But we were in no danger. We rode it out in Nantucket, which is why it took us so long to get home. We'll set Agee and Lizzy straight in the morning, after I see to my crew."

She let out a long, heartfelt sigh that sounded more like a lament. "Oh, dear God, Richard, you must forgive me. I don't know what possessed me. I've never reacted this way with you away at sea. I—"

He brought a finger to her lips. "Ssh, Katherine. It's all right. It's all right, my love. We're together now. We shall always be together, you and I."

"Oh yes, my dearest, my darling! Oh yes!"

She closed her eyes and brought her lips softly to his as her hand slid down to fondle him with a gentle, willful touch born of carnal knowledge and a thousand nights as his lover. They held each other, pleasured each other, loved each other until long after the candle had guttered into darkness, and the warmth that sustained them through the cold of that long December night was theirs and theirs alone.

Six

Hingham, Massachusetts
Winter 1798

T HE CUTLERS celebrated the Yuletide of 1797 in customary fashion. Thomas Cutler invited friends and neighbors to come to his home on Main Street early on Christmas Eve to enjoy a round of spiced punch and seasonal tunes orchestrated by Anne and Lavinia, who were holding forth at the piano. Later that night, their guests gone, the Cutler family settled in to listen to the family patriarch read Scripture by the light of red Christmas candles. At ten o'clock they gathered close by the fire and went around the room, each adult in turn relating his or her best memory, first, of Elizabeth Cutler, then of Will Cutler, the eldest son who had been brutally flogged and hanged on board a Royal Navy frigate in 1775 for striking a king's officer. It was an emotional ordeal for those who spoke, the passage of years notwithstanding. But it was a meaningful way to hold the family matriarch and her eldest son in the sacred light of Christmas, and for the budding branches of young Cutler cousins to learn more about their family tree.

The next morning, after attending the service at First Parish Church, the Cutlers attacked platters of roast venison, candied fruits, squash, and potatoes. This feast was followed, to the children's delight, by a smorgasbord of pumpkin, raisin, grape, and apple pies baked by the indefatigable Edna Stowe. As the Christmas meal drew to its gratifying conclusion, Jeffrey Seymour commented that his aunt must *really* have gorged herself on pies; just look at the size of her belly—a comment that ignited a round of giggles from his cousins and a look of censure from his mother. Before Anne Cutler Seymour could reprimand her son for his crude remark, Lizzy Crabtree spoke up.

"It was those last two pies that did me in, Jeffrey," she said solemnly, patting her swollen stomach. "I should have quit after the third one." Her comment set the adults to laughing and brought puzzled expressions to the faces of the other children. Agreen drew her close with one arm and planted a fond kiss on her cheek.

There were gifts to exchange, by tradition one gift per family member to each other family member. But the gift that had meant the most to Richard and Katherine had been given to their son Will eleven days earlier, on the occasion of his sixteenth birthday.

"What is it, Father?" he had asked as he took the small package wrapped in simple brown paper.

"Open it and see, Will."

The boy opened the package to find a small, leatherbound book. Will flipped through the thin white pages. On each right-hand page was a date in the month of September 1781. Notes and observations had been written beneath each date in his father's bold handwriting.

"But what is it?" Will asked again.

"A journal I kept," his father informed him, "before the Battle of Yorktown. I was serving at the time in an 80-gun French man-of-war. I wrote in that journal every night in my cabin until the sea battle off the Chesapeake. After that, I was stationed ashore with General Lafayette's division. My commanding officer was Colonel Hamilton."

"Your father wants you to have this journal," Katherine explained further. "You are our firstborn, so the honor falls to you. But it's really for all three of you. We ask that you keep it safe, Will, and share it with Jamie and Diana when they are old enough to appreciate what a truly precious gift this is."

"Thank you, Father," Will said with feeling, grateful nonetheless for the new bamboo fishing pole he had also received as a birthday gift.

JANUARY WAS UNUSUALLY MILD for southern New England. What snow there was either quickly melted or changed over to rain along the immediate coast, making it possible for the Cutlers to sail to and from Long Wharf whenever it suited their purpose. George Hunt rarely had good news to report, however. Increased raids on American commerce had by mid-January sent marine insurance rates rocketing as high as 27 percent of the estimated value of a ship's cargo. Each new report strengthened Richard's resolve to find privateer captain Paul-Louis du Bourg and exact revenge.

"These rates are crippling us," Hunt said, stating the painfully obvious to Richard, Caleb, and Thomas Cutler inside the Cutler & Sons counting house. Outside, a cold, dreary rain drummed against the window glass. "If they go any higher, well . . ." He threw up his hands.

"Father," Caleb volunteered, "why pay for insurance at all? Since the Royal Navy protects many of our vessels in the Indies, what if we inform Mr. Church that we no longer intend to purchase insurance? Even if we lost a cargo or two, wouldn't we still come out ahead?"

Thomas Cutler shook his head. "No, Caleb. I understand what you're saying, and I know that other shippers are doing just that. But I will not. The risk is too great. If just one of our vessels is seized, that's the equivalent of a 100 percent insurance rate on her cargo. And bear in mind that we're not talking just about cargoes here. Men's lives are at stake. Men who work for us and whose families depend on us."

"I realize that, Father. But once a vessel is boarded, men's lives are at stake regardless of whether or not her cargo is insured. And a vessel escorted by a warship isn't likely to be attacked in the first place."

"I concede the point, Caleb. But you're forgetting that these days, the Royal Navy has fewer ships in the Indies than before. You're also forgetting what Richard found out for himself—that French privateers are operating right here off our coast, where the Royal Navy cannot protect them. No, we *must* carry insurance unless we're willing to court financial disaster with every ship that sails. And *that* I am not prepared to do."

That statement settled the matter. After a pause, George Hunt said to Richard, "Mr. Endicott was here inquiring after you the other day, Mr. Cutler. He asked me to tell you that he is hoping to see you as soon as that may be convenient."

"Did he say why he wants to see me?"

"He didn't, though I suspect it has something to do with trade to the Orient. I hear he has been saying quite a lot about that recently."

"What do you think, Father?" Richard asked. "We as a family have discussed it before, of course, but never in conjunction with Jack Endicott."

Thomas Cutler shrugged. "Jack Endicott can be a pompous ass at times, and he's a bit too presumptuous for my taste. But we'd be fools not to listen to him. He's a shrewd businessman and we would do well to cultivate him. I particularly admire his willingness to allow his personnel to invest along with him in his business ventures. It's something we should consider doing. And he has excellent relations with the Crowninshields and Derbys," referring to two of Salem's most powerful shipping families. "Having said that, we are in no position to start a new venture of any kind, especially now that Agreen has been commissioned to serve in *Constitution*. In a few months you'll both be on leave from Cutler & Sons. That's a big sacrifice for an enterprise like ours to make."

"I understand, Father. With any luck, our stint in the Navy will be brief. No doubt Captain Nicholson will grant Agee the same consideration that Captain Truxtun gave me, to cut short my service if war is averted." He turned to George and added, "Will you set up this meeting with Endicott?"

"Of course, Mr. Cutler."

THE FOLLOWING MONDAY, in the bedroom of her modest home on Pleasant Street, Lizzy Cutler Crabtree gave birth to a baby boy. It was not an easy delivery. Katherine and Edna Stowe, hastily summoned by Agreen at the first throbs of contractions, did what they could to help under the supervision of James Prescott, the Cutler family physician. Even with the windows cracked open and cool wintry air seeping in, Lizzy stewed in sweat, her thick yellow hair plastered against skin drained of color, her eyes closed tight in anguish, her teeth clenched hard on the soft leather bit Dr. Prescott had tucked into her mouth. Hours slogged by, with Lizzy suffering one form of hell upstairs and Agreen suffering another downstairs. Finally, with one "give-it-all-you've-got-left" push, the baby slid out, and the high-pitched wail emanating from the Crabtree bedroom was no longer that of a woman in the throes of labor but of her newborn child come into the world at last.

Katherine summoned Agreen upstairs.

"You have a son, Agee," Lizzy smiled weakly as her husband rushed to her side. Supine, her head propped up on two pillows, she was too bone-tired to take her son from Edna Stowe, who had cleaned the infant and wrapped him in a light woolen blanket.

"Yes, and I have a wife," Agreen choked. He smoothed back the damp golden locks and kissed her forehead. "Dear God, Lizzy, I thought I was losin' you."

"I'm fine, dearest, honestly I am," she murmured. "Here, see to your son."

Agreen rose to his feet. With painstaking care fortified by stiff apprehension he took the baby from Edna. For long moments he stood in silence, gazing down in wonder at the babe in his arms as his son stared blankly back. "Sweet Jesus Christ God Almighty damn!" was all he could muster. Katherine turned away to hide a smile as Edna sniffed disapprovingly.

The next morning, Richard, Katherine, and Diana dropped by for a visit. Agreen met them in the downstairs hallway looking every bit the picture of a proud father, despite his bloodshot eyes. Beyond him, they could hear Edna puttering about in the kitchen.

"Congratulations, Agee," Richard said. "The whole town's talking about baby Zeke. Once Lizzy is up and about, you'll have more visitors than you can manage. People always want to help at a time like this."

"People *are* helpin'," Agreen said. "You could feed a frigate's crew on the food that's been left on the front stoop so far."

"Can we see the baby now?" Diana urged.

"In a moment," Katherine said. "If it's all right with you, Agee, Richard would like a minute or two with Lizzy first. They have been so very close for so many years."

Agreen glanced inquiringly at Richard, who nodded in silent reply.

"Hell's bells, Richard, I'm not denyin' you *anything*. Not with the wages you're payin' me to sit around and do nothin'."

Upstairs, Richard knocked gently on the door to Lizzy's room and announced himself. The door was slightly ajar. When bidden in, he pushed it open. At the threshold he hesitated. Lizzy was sitting up in bed, her flushed face reflecting the warmth and radiance of the sun-filled room. She was nursing her son, and even with the sheets and blankets thrust up about her middle, her swollen breasts were largely exposed to view.

"I'm not embarrassed if you're not," Lizzy happily welcomed him.

Richard smiled. "I'm the father of three children, Lizzy," he said, walking over to her. "I doubt there's much about the ways of a woman's body that can embarrass me." He sat down on the edge of the bed and kissed her cheek. "After what Katherine told me, I'm relieved to find you looking so well."

"It wasn't so bad, really. And I'm feeling much better now. Dr. Prescott wants me to remain a-bed until the weekend, but I'll be up in a day or two. Don't worry. I shan't do anything I shouldn't." She gazed down upon her son sucking hungrily. "Isn't he just the handsomest little tyke?"

"He is. That's because he takes after his mother. And I see he slobbers over his food just like his father. How did you two come up with the name 'Zeke'?"

"It was Agee's wish. I rather like it as a nickname. For his real name I wanted something a bit more distinguished, so on the parish rolls he is Alexander Cutler Crabtree. But we'll call him Zeke."

"Sounds like a good compromise to me. When will you write your family?"

"Soon. Oh, Richard, I *do* so hope Zeke and I can visit my parents. Father writes that Mother is not well. He says that another Atlantic crossing is not possible for her. So we must go to England if they are to see their grandson."

"We'll make that happen, Lizzy. I promise you we'll make that happen. Katherine wants to see her family too, for the same reason. It's been too many years since we were all together for your wedding. And Diana was just a wee babe back then. So let's plan a family reunion in Fareham for next summer. I don't know if Agee and I can join you, but even if we can't, you and Katherine should go with the children."

"That's sweet of you, Richard. Truly it is. I do so hope that you and Agee will be able to come. I pray every day that you both will receive an early discharge. I can't bear the thought of either of you being in any sort of battle at sea."

"You needn't worry, Liz. That's what I've been wanting to tell you. One visit to *Constitution* in Boston and you'll worry far more about our enemies than us. *Constellation* is the same sort of ship. The French have nothing to match her, should it come to that."

"Please God it does not come to that, Richard."

THE MEETING WITH JOHN ENDICOTT, set for six o'clock on Friday evening of the following week, did not take place in the offices of Cutler & Sons as George Hunt had assumed it would. Rather, it was held at the Endicott residence at Fourteen Belknap Street on Beacon Hill in Boston. Knowing that the meeting would last late into the evening, Richard made arrangements to stay the night on board a Cutler vessel moored at Long Wharf.

He had been to the Endicott residence before and knew what to expect: a freestanding red-brick edifice of federalist construction facing east toward the harbor. Inside, at ground level, were four rooms in addition to the kitchen, each stylishly appointed. A butler took Richard's hat and helped him off with his coat, then escorted him to the elegant parlor. The wingback chairs that graced the room were covered in exquisitely embroidered fabrics, the end of each armrest curling in intricate patterns. So, too, the ornate camelback sofa, the oak parquet floor covered with Persian carpets that glowed in jewel-like colors, the neatly stocked bookcases, the murals of merchant ships and horses and bowls of daffodils, the gold-lacquer Louis XIV escritoire, the Georgian chest-on-chest highboy with polished brass handles, the white marble hearth in which a fire crackled. All, in sum, defined for Richard the difference between the comfortable lifestyle he was accustomed to and true financial wealth.

"Good evening, Richard. What joy it is to see you."

Richard looked up from the book he was perusing and smiled at Anne-Marie. She was dressed tastefully in a dark blue velvet dress with a belt to match and a delicate cotton fichu that covered her shoulders and neck. Her hair had been meticulously coiffed and tumbled down in rich ebony curls that contrasted sharply with the pure white of her shawl. About her were the faint, alluring scents of rosewater and jasmine.

"May I offer you a glass of Madeira?" she inquired when he failed to respond right away. "It's what Jack and I are having. He'll be down in a moment. He's so looking forward to this evening."

"Madeira is fine, thank you," Richard said. He added, with sincerity, "You look lovely, Anne-Marie. As lovely as the day we met in Paris. And not one day older."

She laughed easily. "What a shameless flatterer you have become, Richard Cutler. But who am I to gainsay flattery? Gallantry counts in my book, and deserves its reward."

She drew close and kissed him on the cheek, her lips lingering a moment or two longer than propriety might dictate. When she drew back, their eyes met in a silent communication. In the ensuing quiet Richard thought to say something lighthearted, more to put himself at ease than her, but his intent was truncated by a cultured young female voice.

"Good evening, Mr. Cutler. I hope we're not intruding."

"Not at all, Adele," her mother said, quickly composing herself. "Please join us. Mr. Cutler is delighted to see you and Frances."

"I am indeed," Richard said. He bowed in response to the girls' quick knee-bend, a far cry from the grand sweeping curtsy of French aristocrats that they had performed for him when they were first introduced in the de Launay residence in Paris. Both girls were filling out beguilingly into womanhood, especially Adele, who already, Richard noted with a stab of fond remembrance, bore a striking resemblance to her mother at age eighteen.

"My family sends their greetings," Richard told them. "Will sends you a special greeting, Adele."

Adele blushed prettily. "Thank you, Mr. Cutler. I am so pleased to hear that. Please send Will my warmest regards in return. I look forward to seeing him again soon, as I look forward to seeing every member of your family."

The quick tapping of footsteps on the stairway was followed moments later by John Endicott's grand entrance into the room. A servant followed close behind bearing a tray with three glasses, each filled halfway with robust Portuguese wine.

"Ah, Richard," Endicott greeted, crossing the room with his right arm outstretched. "You do us great honor by coming here this evening. There is no one my family would rather host."

"The honor is mine, Jack," Richard said, bowing slightly to the stout, ruddy-faced, slightly balding man who was several inches shorter than he. Endicott was dressed similarly to Richard, though the cut of his cloth was finer, the fabric richer, and the fit precise to a fault. He took a glass of Madeira from the tray and raised it.

"To our health, our country, our friendship." He drank deeply, nearly draining his glass. "Right," he said, after a brief round of pleasantries had been exchanged, "not to move things along too quickly, I suggest we proceed to the dining room. We can continue our conversation there. Adele, Frances, you may return later this evening to bid Mr. Cutler goodnight."

"Yes, Papa," Frances replied, dutifully bending her right knee.

"Well-mannered young ladies, aren't they," Endicott said with the full pride of ownership as he watched the two girls disappear upstairs.

"Their mother raised them well," Richard commented dryly. A sideways glance at Anne-Marie confirmed that she, at least, had caught his meaning.

"Yes, quite. Well, shall we?" Endicott encouraged.

The dining area was next to the kitchen and, as anyone who had surveyed the rest of the downstairs would have anticipated, superbly furnished. Dominating the space, set upon a thick Turkish carpet, was a rectangular mahogany table with graceful cabriole legs and claw-and-ball feet. Eight matching armchairs surrounded it, each with identical leaf-green upholstery on the seats. Two silver candelabras provided light and a sense of conviviality, reinforced by a fire ablaze in a sizable red marble hearth. Oil paintings graced the walls. In the far corner, near the twin oriel windows, a Chippendale china cabinet displayed fragile blue-on-white dishes and tea sets.

"How is Gertrud?" Richard asked Anne-Marie after they were seated, both to make conversation and because he was genuinely concerned.

"Not well, I'm afraid," Anne-Marie replied. She was at the end of the table with Richard to her left, her husband to her right. "The doctors think she may have an ailment of the kidney. She's upstairs in bed but asked me to send you her regards."

"Please send mine to her. I'm sorry she's not well."

"We all are. Tell us," she went on in a brighter tone, as a liveried servant began ladling out an orange seafood-based bisque from a silver tureen, "what is the news from Hingham?"

"Lizzy had a baby boy," Richard told her. "His name is Zeke."

"How wonderful! I am so pleased. Mother and son are doing well, I hope?"

"Very."

"And Agee?"

"Even better," Richard grinned.

"I can't tell you how delighted I am. Do remind me to send a bottle of our best port back with you as a gift."

John Endicott cleared his throat. "Yes, do that, my dear; a capital notion. Our congratulations all around. Now then, Richard," he continued, his measured tone wiping the slate clean of other topics of conversation, "before the evening wears on and we get too relaxed, I want to discuss a matter of some importance to me—a business proposition that I believe may be of some importance to you and your family as well. Will you hear me out?"

"Of course, Jack. Isn't that the reason I was invited here tonight?"

"Not the *only* reason," Anne-Marie interjected softly.

Endicott again cleared his throat. "Yes, quite. Well, you see, I have been thinking and corresponding and what have you, and I have come to the conclusion that the interests of our two families can and should be combined to our mutual advantage. This is my proposition."

For the next twenty minutes, while finishing off his soup and then dabbing at a plate of creamed codfish, fricassee of turnips, and sautéed potatoes, John Endicott laid out what he saw as a unique business opportunity in opening new trade routes to the Far East. Specifically, he meant Java, going so far as to broach the possibility of opening a shipping office in Batavia under dual ownership. He had been in contact,

he said, with Dutch officials who seemed intrigued with the notion—
assuming, of course, that they received a reasonable percentage of the
profits.

Richard winced at that, the guile and avarice of Dutch bankers
and merchants being well established in world commerce. But it was a
known fact that recent military setbacks against France had weakened
Holland's monopoly in the East Indies and had opened the islands to
outside interests. Dutch traders had by now come to rely on those interests to replenish their coffers.

"Think on it, Richard," Endicott urged. "A bale of cotton selling for
ten dollars in Savannah now fetches twenty-three dollars in Brest and
forty dollars in Saint Petersburg. Imagine what that same bale would
fetch in Java and China! And imagine what Java's coffee, calicoes, nutmeg, and cinnamon would fetch in Boston on the return voyage. Less
than 2 percent of American trade now goes to the Orient. That's all,
Richard; 2 percent. And in that 2 percent you'll find your soon-to-be
naval commander. Ah, I see that statement struck home. Yes, it's true.
Reliable sources inform me that Tom Truxtun has invested a good
portion of his privateering earnings in the China trade. Apparently he
knows a good thing when he sees it. The question before us this evening, Richard," he added encouragingly, as if the answer were a foregone conclusion, "is whether you and your family see it."

"We see the opportunity," Richard said guardedly. In truth, he was
intrigued by Endicott's reference to Captain Truxtun. "My family has
been considering something like this for many years. But I'm curious,
Jack. Surely you have the means to do this on your own. Why do you
need Cutler & Sons as a partner? And why now?"

Endicott refilled Richard's wineglass, then his own. "I'll answer your
last question first. As you are aware, timing is critical in a venture such
as this. If you're not among the first to get in, you're likely to be among
the first to be forced out. As regards our return on investment, this is
the ideal time to do what I propose, what with the Dutch losing their
grip on the islands. We have perhaps two to three years to act before
the window opens too far and lets everybody come rushing in. Other
shipping families are not as well . . . *endowed*, shall we say. And with
our own economy on the brink of disaster, they are loath to try anything new. They are paralyzed with fear and uncertainty. If we act now,
we can exploit that fear and use it to our advantage. How? Simple.
Fear and uncertainty minimize competition: from our fellow Americans, who have limited resources and who have become averse to risk,

and from Europeans, who are distracted by Bonaparte. We can make handsome profits, your family and mine, if we act fast, strike hard, and stay the course.

"As to my having the means," he went on in answer to Richard's initial question, "that does not necessarily mean having the will. To do this properly we shall require larger vessels than either of us has at present. I need not tell you that large ships require large investments. To your point, yes, I can afford to make such investments. But I'd prefer to do it in equal partnership with someone who is prepared to share the risks and rewards of such an enterprise."

"*Equal* partnership, Jack?" Richard looked incredulous. "Surely you don't believe that my family has your financial resources."

Endicott gave him a smile that Richard took to be condescending. "No, I don't believe that, Richard. But financial resources are only part of the equation. For a business partnership to succeed, each party to the agreement must contribute a unique asset—an advantage, if you will—something that complements other assets and gives the business a better overall chance to succeed. Money is one such asset—a critical one, no doubt. But it is not the only one."

"I'm confused, Jack. In your vision, who is contributing what assets to this proposed enterprise?"

Endicott's smile broadened. "My family will contribute the bulk of the financial investment. Exactly how much is open to discussion. For starters I propose 75 percent of the projected costs."

"And my family? What do we contribute aside from the other 25 percent?"

"Seasoned captains and crews, which you already have. And guns."

"*Guns?*"

"Yes, Richard, guns. Ships' cannon. As you know from your own experience, pirates are the biggest threat to this venture. Muslim pirates, the same sort you encountered in Barbary. We cannot allow our ships to sail into Eastern waters unarmed. Every ship of the Dutch East India Company, for example, is armed to the teeth. Ours must be too."

Richard understood what Endicott was saying. Every Boston mercantile family was aware that Muslim pirates were the major threat to shipping in Far Eastern waters. They were a particularly vicious lot, especially those lurking in and around the Malacca Strait. No European power, including Holland, had significant naval forces in the South China Sea. Which is why every maritime nation armed every merchant ship bound for the Orient.

"That's all well and good, Jack. But how do you propose that we procure these guns?"

"That's where you come in, Richard. That's your asset—your advantage, if you will. You are a naval officer. You have contacts with our military. You can secure the guns we need even as you serve our country."

Richard chuckled. "You jest, Jack. I can't do that. Frigate captains are having enough trouble securing guns for warships. What clout would I have, as a mere lieutenant, seeking guns for commercial use?"

Endicott beamed. "The same sort of clout you used as the mere master of a merchant schooner to arm your vessel and defeat the Barbary pirates. You got the job done then, Richard, and I have every confidence you can get the job done now."

Richard had no immediate reply. He looked hard at Endicott, who regarded him just as keenly over the rim of his wineglass. "This is all quite fascinating, Jack," he said at length. "But I'm really not the one you should be talking to. My father and Caleb are managing Cutler & Sons now. In a few weeks I'll be on sea duty for an indefinite period. There's not much I can do along those lines while I'm away."

"Ah, we have arrived at the crux of the matter," Endicott said, somewhat mysteriously. He had a calculating glint in his eye as he continued. "In fact, there is a great deal you can do, Richard, starting as early as tomorrow. You are the only member of your family who can secure the guns we need for our enterprise. In addition, you are the only one who can convince your father to undertake the business opportunities we are discussing. That's what we must do, isn't it? Convince him?" Endicott held Richard's gaze as he casually twirled the stem of his wineglass between his fingers. "In doing that, you will be serving us both." Richard mistook the meaning of "us both" until Endicott flicked his gaze over to Anne-Marie. "I admire your father," he went on, his gaze resting once again on Richard. "Truly I do. Why else would I seek him as a partner in what could be the most promising business venture of my life? But when it comes to matters of commerce, I have observed him to be, perhaps, overly cautious and unable to see the opportunity staring him in the face. To put it bluntly, Richard— and I mean no offense in saying this—I am hoping that your . . . prior relationship with my wife and the affection you still hold for each other might persuade you to make a rather convincing argument."

"I see," said Richard softly. He glanced over at Anne-Marie, who looked steadfastly down at her plate, a muscle twitching in her jaw the only sign of her distress.

The evening wore on for another thirty minutes, much of the conversation forced, as though what had to be said had been said and the three of them were compelled for decorum's sake to carry on for an interval of small talk. When the Gütlin clock on the mantel chimed ten times, Richard excused himself and bade his hosts goodnight.

"I hope you're not angry with Jack," Anne-Marie said with concern after she alone had walked him to the front door. She handed him the bottle of aged port her husband had summoned from the basement as a gift for Agreen and Lizzy. "He was a bit forward this evening. That's just his way, I'm afraid. He did speak the truth when he said how much he admires your father. You must believe that, if nothing else. It's just that he wants so very much for his vision to succeed."

"Is it what you want, Anne-Marie?"

She lowered her eyes. "Yes, Richard, it is."

"Why?" he half-whispered.

When she lifted her eyes to his, he had his answer. Feeling himself coming undone, he buttoned up his overcoat and took his tricorne hat off the rack. "I promised Jack that my family will give his proposal a fair hearing," he said in a business-like tone. "I intend to keep my promise. Give us time to consider what's involved, and we'll see where we go from there." He turned to open the door.

"Richard?"

He turned back.

She took his hat from him and placed it just so on his head. Her voice was low, her tone earnest. About her was a heart-touching look of profound concern. "I won't see you again before you sail for Baltimore. So I must say this now: be careful, Richard. I beg you. Be careful. Come home safely. To Katherine. To your children and your family. To all those who dearly love you." She brought her lips to his and kissed him, her mouth opening briefly, suggestively, before she pulled herself away. She stepped aside and opened the door for him.

"Go with God, Richard," he heard her call out softly as he made his way through the feeble yellow glow of whale oil lamplight on Mount Vernon Street. He had an urge to look back but forced himself to keep walking down Belknap Street toward Beacon Street, and on to the harbor beyond.

THE NEXT MORNING found Richard at Long Wharf in consultation with George Hunt. A northeasterly wind pelted the city of Boston with a wintry mixture of sleet and rain that swept in gray veils across the harbor and made dockside loading and unloading a miserable affair. Such inclemency was more a nuisance than a hazard, however, and Richard remained determined to sail to Hingham that afternoon after he had reviewed the monthly accounts with Hunt and arranged to have *Elizabeth* made ready to convey him, his father, and brother to Baltimore two weeks hence.

Hunt arched his eyebrows.

"Your father and Caleb are sailing with you?"

"Yes. They want to visit Baltimore, and I'm betting they'll like what they see. I certainly did."

"I take it that Caleb will be involved in the decision to open a shipping office there."

"Yes. He must be. My father is relying on him to learn the ropes and assume responsibility wherever he can. Later this year, Caleb will sail to Barbados to visit with John and Robin."

"I'm glad to hear it. I'm impressed with your brother, Mr. Cutler. He's a fine young man, eager to learn. And he seems to have your father's business instincts. Though I must say, I shall sorely miss *your* counsel whilst you're away."

"Thank you, George. The feeling is mutual. And don't worry. I doubt I'll be gone long. For the life of me, I can't understand why the French are courting war with us. I have to believe that, ultimately, common sense will prevail in Paris. When it does, I'll be back here pestering you as if I'd never been away. I'll make you wish I had never come back."

"Oh no, Mr. Cutler," Hunt said emphatically, as though Richard had meant what he had said. "That could never happen."

Hunt understood that it was not his place to inquire about the meeting with John Endicott unless Richard first broached the subject. Which he did not do. Only the next morning in his father's house on Main Street did he repeat Endicott's words. The previous evening, over a late supper with Katherine, he had recounted the gist of what Endicott had proposed. She had expressed little interest in the subject and had little to offer in return. Richard did not pursue the matter. He sensed Katherine's indifference; and besides, the memory of Anne-Marie's kiss pressed guiltily on his mind.

The next morning, Thomas Cutler had more to say. "I'm opposed," he said bluntly, after he had repeated out loud the main points of what

John Endicott had proposed, "and not because I don't recognize the opportunity."

"Why, then, Father?"

"This is simply not the time for us to invest in an enterprise of this magnitude."

"Why?" Richard asked again. He was neither resentful nor surprised. He simply needed to understand.

"What we're discussing here is a Cutler family investment of $100,000, give or take, even if we were to put up only the 25 percent Endicott proposes. We can't invest that much money until we're able to replenish our accounts. And we can't replenish our accounts until financial conditions improve. And financial conditions won't improve until the threat of war is over. You reviewed the accounts yesterday, Richard. You saw where we stand. I cannot in good conscience risk much of what we have at present for a promise of more in the future. As to your finding guns, do that if you can. If nothing else, we can use them on our own vessels. Mind you, I don't resent Endicott for wanting to use our money and connections for his own purposes. In principle, as equal partners, we'd be coming *out* of the bargain as well as he. But going *in,* we'd be placing a great deal more at risk. For now, my decision is no. Circumstances may change in the future. We'll have to wait and see."

After a pause in the conversation Caleb asked, "Would Uncle William be willing to share our side of the risk?"

"I'd ask him," his father replied, "if I didn't already know his answer. You would do well to remember, Caleb, that *our* side is *his* side. Your uncle is our one true business partner, and he and I tend to think alike. We are willing to take a calculated risk if and when circumstances warrant it. But with war with France now appearing inevitable, circumstances most definitely do not warrant taking such a risk."

Richard blinked. "Inevitable? What do you mean, Father? Is there word from Paris?"

Thomas Cutler nodded grimly. "Had I mentioned this first, we would not have given Endicott the fair hearing he deserves."

"Mentioned what first?"

"An express rider delivered two dispatches late yesterday. One was from Mr. Hamilton. Our State Department has finally heard from our envoys in Paris, and the result, I'm afraid, is not encouraging. The second dispatch is from Captain Truxtun. I didn't open it. It's addressed to you. But I have a strong hunch that I know what's inside."

As did Richard. There could be only one reason why Captain Truxtun was contacting him. "Did Mr. Hamilton provide details?"

"Not many. The details have yet to be made public. What I understand is that after all these months of waiting and waffling, Talleyrand has announced that he will not receive our envoys unless and until Congress pays him a handsome tribute. And paying such a tribute only ensures that negotiations will begin. It does not guarantee their outcome. If it is true, President Adams has no choice. Our national honor has been impugned. It will mean war."

Seven

USS *Constellation,* at Sea
July–August 1798

THE DETAILS, when published, confirmed a reality far worse than Thomas Cutler or anyone in the State Department had first imagined. After being kept waiting for months, the American envoys were finally informed by three French agents that Charles Maurice de Talleyrand-Périgord, the French foreign minister, would receive them as soon as the American government agreed to pay what was delicately referred to in European diplomatic circles as *un douceur*, essentially a bribe. In this case, a bribe of $220,000 was to be paid simply for the privilege of opening negotiations. Adding insult to injury, the French agents insisted that two additional conditions be met before negotiations could begin. First, the U.S. government must guarantee a loan of $2 million—which amount the French openly admitted would be invested in their war against England—and, second, the United States must extend a formal apology to France for the allegations of tyranny and radicalism perpetrated by President Adams, Treasury Secretary Hamilton, and other Federalist statesmen during and after the French Revolution.

After sending high-priority dispatches to Secretary of State Timothy Pickering in Philadelphia, envoys John Marshall and Charles Pinckney departed France in a huff, convinced that the National Directory sought to delay resolution of its conflict with America in order to continue plundering her merchantmen and to line the pockets of the individual members of the Directory. Elbridge Gerry remained in the French capital, hoping against hope to talk sense into these people. The American press, meanwhile, was having a field day with this turn of events.

"No, no, not a sixpence!" was the reported response of an apoplectic Pickering upon reading the delegation's report. "Millions for defense, I say, but not one penny for tribute!"

"Damn the villains!" screamed the *Boston Traveler* and other Federalist newspapers.

Cries of high dudgeon resounded through the halls of Congress in Philadelphia, though not in every office. Some southern Republicans, convinced that Adams and Hamilton had somehow concocted the whole affair to provoke war with France, demanded that details of the delegation's report be made public. President Adams was only too happy to oblige. He ordered ten thousand copies of the report to be printed and distributed throughout the states, changing only the names of the three French agents in the eye of the storm to the code letters X, Y, and Z. The result was a volcanic eruption of anti-French sentiment flowing hot within the psyche of the young republic, and with it a national drumbeat for war.

The American public responded to a call to arms that bordered on hysteria after former secretary of war Henry Knox warned that France was preparing to attack the American South with West Indian garrisons reinforced by legions of former African slaves bent on revenge. In reply, President Adams ordered an army of 14,000 men to be raised and commanded by George Washington—coaxed out of retirement by his sense of duty and his love of country—with the ambitious Alexander Hamilton as his second in command and his chief secretary, Tobias Lear, as his aide-de-camp.

In the front ranks of the military buildup was the newly minted U.S. Navy. Work on the second three frigates picked up in cadence with the war drums, while American agents in Europe and the Caribbean hurriedly shopped for other vessels of war, primarily in the dockyards and arsenals of Great Britain—America's preferred source for military hardware. In negotiating such transactions, many Britons regarded America's interests as their own. Every American gun aimed at a French warship, Rear Adm. Horatio Lord Nelson thundered in Parliament and Whitehall, meant one less British gun that would have to be aimed at the French. American naval personnel away on leave were hastily summoned back to duty.

"WHEN WILL CONGRESS declare war, do you think?"

That popular question was posed by Andrew Sterrett during a supper of thick mutton stew laden with potatoes, peas, and turnips brought aft by wardroom stewards from the camboose stove located forward in the galley. Three bottles of red Bordeaux contributed by the third lieutenant from his personal stores supplemented the meal and promoted lively conversation. During *Constellation*'s second morning at sea, Captain Truxtun had been invited to dine with his commissioned and senior warrant officers in the wardroom, which was located aft on the berthing deck directly beneath the captain's cabin. All three lieutenants were present, as was Lt. James Carter of the newly formed Marine Corps, and the ship's surgeon, George Balfour. To each side of the large oval dining table, to larboard and starboard, were the officer's cabins—cubicles, really—set off from each other by thick canvas walls and with a rectangular piece of canvas on hinges serving as a door. Beyond the table, abaft the mizzenmast, was the tiller room housing the rudder. Clusters of candles set about the area provided light, their flames barely flickering in the still air. *Constellation* was rigged for night sailing and was making sluggish headway in a diminishing breeze on a calm sea.

Sterrett had put the question to the table, although he glanced in Truxtun's direction as though expecting the captain to answer.

John Rodgers spoke instead. "It's been more than two months since we received word from Paris," the first lieutenant observed. "Thus far, Congress has done the one thing it does well, which is, of course, nothing. I'm beginning to doubt it *will* declare war."

Richard was not surprised by the conviction behind that remark. He had come to esteem this tall, dark-haired, sea officer despite his relative youth and lack of naval experience. Rodgers, he had learned, had commanded his first merchant vessel at the age of eighteen, a credential that demanded respect, and he understood the workings of a square-rigger better than most sea captains of Richard's acquaintance. As first lieutenant, that was Rodgers' primary responsibility: management of the ship's business on a day-to-day basis, with sole oversight of the station bill—a list of who did what, when, and where on board ship while under way—and the watch bill, which rotated two watches of equal size throughout the day and night for the routine sailing of the ship. He also assumed command of the ship should the captain step ashore or become incapacitated, and when the ship was coming to or weighing anchor.

Even more important, this educated, self-confident Marylander with bushy sideburns had in spades what Captain Truxtun appeared to value most in his chain of command. A month ago, during the memorable evening when the ship's officers had gathered together in the captain's cabin for the first time, Truxtun had defined for them his vision of a naval officer. "A man of good education, good character, good connections, and manly deportment," he had stated, "who is thoroughly grounded in the minutiae of naval affairs and who exhibits zeal, dignity, enterprise, and prudence—and who, above all, is well-mannered, self-disciplined, courageous, and has a passion for honor and glory." The difficulty, he had confessed at the time, was finding officers who possessed such qualities. Which was why, he concluded, it pleased him to have so many of them serving in his ship. That remark had caused the elders of the eight midshipmen to steal glances at each other, and the younger ones to blush.

"Why ever not, sir?" a thin-boned, sandy-haired boy of fourteen inquired of Rodgers, his voice edged with disappointment. He was one of two midshipmen invited up from the orlop deck to the wardroom, the two senior midshipmen now serving as officers of the deck under the critical eye of Nate Waverly, the ship's master. "When the envoys' report was published and the riots broke out, I assumed war was inevitable. My father has been a Republican since before I can remember, and even he now wears the black cockade," referring to a Federalist adornment worn in the hat to signify opposition to France.

"Quite so, Mr. Dent. But I believe you misunderstand me. What I am referring to is a *declared* war."

John Dent continued to stare at him, his face full of questions. "My apologies, sir, but I'm afraid I don't take your meaning."

"Perhaps I can explain, Mr. Dent."

All eyes swung to Captain Truxtun, who leaned forward on his chair at the far end of the table. Soon after entering the wardroom he had removed his blue dress coat with buff lapels and twin gold epaulets and had draped it over the back of his chair, an invitation for everyone present to do likewise. He had taken a seat and crossed one leg casually over the other, listening to the conversation in buff breeches and a buff vest with a gold button on each of the four pockets, each emblazoned with the same fouled anchor and American eagle design evident on the buttons of his discarded dress coat.

"I believe the point Mr. Rodgers is making is that many of our fellow citizens, particularly those living in the South and West, continue to believe, whatever evidence may exist to the contrary, that President

Adams and the Federalist Party are to blame for our current impasse with France." He held out his arms expansively. "I trust no one in this cabin shares the folly of their thinking. But once a man grabs hold of such a position, it is often difficult to get him to let go, your father's admirable example notwithstanding, Mr. Dent.

"Thus, the reasoning goes in Congress, if the United States declares war on France, Republican extremists in the South and West may demand secession from the Union. And there just may be enough of them to cause damage to our young republic. Am I stating your position fairly enough, Mr. Rodgers?"

"To a T, sir. Thank you."

"Do you understand now, Mr. Dent?"

"I understand better, sir. But with respect, I remain confused about our role. Are we simply to patrol the seas and convey merchantmen back and forth to the Indies, as we are now doing? So far we've seen naught of interest beyond two jackass brigs," referring to the popular term for a schooner-rigged vessel of the Revenue Cutter Service, a subset of the Treasury Department whose mission was to guard the coast against maritime misfits.

"That is what I have told you, have I not?"

"Yes, sir, you have."

"Yet despite what I have told you, you remain unconvinced. Is it because you signed on for something other than convoy duty, which in fact you find rather dull? You would prefer something a bit more exciting, perhaps, an engagement with the enemy, yardarm to yardarm?"

Dent dropped his eyes. "No sir, I—"

"Be not timid, Mr. Dent!" Truxtun pronounced. "Stand up for what you believe! I respect that in a man, whatever his views, whatever his age. And I commend any man who seeks battle with his country's enemies. Too many do-gooders in Congress speak boldly from under their desks. I applaud a man who puts himself out there front and center, with feet squared."

Dent nodded appreciatively.

"Captain, if I may," the captain of Marines joined in. Lt. James Carter was of average height with whitish-blond hair and a nononsense look about him. The cerulean-blue dress coat draped over the back of his chair sported red lapels and cuffs, and red lining on the stand-up collar. On its right shoulder the tassels of a single gold epaulet gleamed in the shimmering light of a wide-bottomed candle ensconced on the dining table. "As you indicated when explaining our orders, sir, if fired upon, we are permitted to return fire. But are we permitted such liberty only if and when we ourselves or a vessel in our charge is fired upon first?" It was a question for which every one of the 343 sailors serving in the ship desired an answer, for it underscored why many of them had signed on with *Constellation*: for hearth and home, yes; for honor and glory, of course; but primarily for prize money, to supplement an otherwise modest salary of fifteen dollars per month.

"Those are our orders, Mr. Carter," Truxtun replied stiffly, adding in a more conciliatory tone, "although I am quick to point out that those orders are subject to change. They may already have changed. Three weeks ago I was at the Navy Department on Walnut Street, where I met with Mr. Stoddert." He was referring to Benjamin Stoddert, the newly appointed secretary of the Navy, the first to hold that position within the newly created Navy Department, itself a subset of the War Department. "Among other items, Mr. Stoddert advised me that if the United States or one of its ships is attacked by a country that has declared war on us, our Constitution permits the president to act on his own authority to protect American interests. Under these circumstances, the United States may go to war without war actually being declared by Congress. Whether our current *guerre de course* with France qualifies as such an emergency will no doubt be debated for years to come. But for the moment, if the president believes it does, that view prevails."

Silence ensued as each man pondered that statement. Then, ending the evening on a business note, Truxtun announced, "Gentlemen, since it appears certain that *Constellation* is sailing into war, we shall start preparing for battle tomorrow at four bells in the forenoon watch. Mr. Cutler will conduct gun drills in the morning and again in the afternoon. We shall drill twice every day, and we shall improve every day over the previous day's performance. If we do not, we shall drill again in the evening before supper and spirit rations—if I choose to issue spirit rations. We will drill, and we will drill, and we will drill until the gun crews are too exhausted to go on, and then we shall drill some more. We will drill until I am convinced that our crews are as skilled with the guns and small arms as any British crew afloat. I need not remind you gentlemen that British crews routinely fire three rounds every five minutes. That is a round every minute and a half, a rate almost twice that of the average French crew. It's a measure of excellence I expect our own crews to achieve. I will settle for nothing less."

Richard Cutler smiled to himself, recalling the day years ago, during the war with England, when he had heard John Paul Jones exhort his officers using almost those exact words.

Truxtun scraped back his chair and stood up. His officers immediately followed suit. "Good evening to you, gentlemen. It has been a pleasure. Thank you for a delicious supper, and thank *you*, Mr. Sterrett, for that Bordeaux. It was exceptional. Let us credit the French for *something*, at least."

THE NEXT MORNING at precisely ten o'clock, a young Marine drummer stationed amidships on the weather deck launched into a staccato tattoo. His frenzied beat was immediately taken up by a second drummer on the gun deck below. Crews sprang to battle stations, twelve men serving each of the fourteen 24-pounder guns bowsed up tight against the starboard and larboard sides of the frigate, twenty-eight long guns total, each packing enough firepower to break a hole through two feet of solid oak at a range of one thousand yards. On the weather deck, crews of six Marines manned the smaller 12-pounder guns.

Richard stood on the gun deck by the bilge pump afore the mainmast in his long blue dress coat with buff lining, half-lapels, and two vertical rows of brass buttons. In his right hand he held the quarter bill that listed the names of each gun crew and each man's assignment. With the captain's approval he had divided the gun deck batteries into three divisions—ten, ten, and eight. The guns in the first division were numbered one through five, larboard and starboard; the second division six through ten, larboard and starboard; and the third division eleven through fourteen, larboard and starboard. Each gun crew thus served two guns of the same number. It was an innovation recently decreed in *Marine Rules and Regulations*, a uniquely American document that nonetheless took its cue from the venerable *British Regulations and Instructions Relating to His Majesty's Service at Sea*.

With a practiced eye, Richard watched as the gunner's mate in charge of each crew assembled his men in position with the spongers, rammers, and wormers to do the job. Earlier, during the frigate's weeklong shakedown cruise, he had exercised the men in the evolutions of gun drill, which had changed little since the days of the Continental navy. Except that, by 1798, the linstock formerly used to fire a gun had yielded to the more efficient British-engineered bronze flintlock, which functioned much like the mechanism on a muzzle-loading musket.

The high-pitched squeals of boatswain's whistles reinforced the drumbeat, directing the sailors to clear the decks for action. Galley fires were extinguished, pumps were made ready, and sand was strewn around the deck. Topmen, the elite of any square-rigger, scampered aloft to reduce canvas to fighting sail—foresails, topsails, topgallants, and driver. Waisters on the weather deck worked in tandem with sailors stationed on the fighting tops and on footropes to lower the royal yardarms and clew up the fore and main courses until they hung loosely in their gear like curtains draped above a window. Belowdecks, men unhinged the canvas partitions that defined the officers' and captain's cabins and stowed them aft in steerage, along with artwork, chairs, desks, chests, and anything else portable that could splinter into deadly wooden shrapnel when struck by enemy shot. As a final measure, and for the same reason, the ships' boats were lowered over the side and towed behind.

With everyone and everything in its proper place, more or less, Captain Truxtun sent Midn. David Porter forward amidships to the large rectangular main hatch, its ornate latticework cover now removed and stowed.

Porter cupped his hands at his mouth. "Captain's compliments, Mr. Cutler, and you may begin the exercise!"

Richard returned the midshipman's salute. Facing forward, he brought a speaking trumpet to his mouth. "Cast loose the larboard guns!" As he pivoted aft to repeat the order, sailors on the fourteen larboard guns cast off the lashings that secured the guns to the ship's side and ran the guns inboard on their side tackle until checked by their breeching ropes. With the ten-foot length of the gun inside the ship, sailors removed the wooden tampion plugging the muzzle and made ready to ram a flannel bag of powder down the bore. This would be followed by a round shot taken from a shot rack amidships, followed by a wad made of rope yarn to secure the ball within.

"Run out the guns!"

Some men in quick time, others less so, heaved on train tackle and hauled the six-thousand-pound guns forward on their red-painted trucks until the front end of the carriages banged against the bulwarks and the gun muzzles protruded their maximum distance through the square ports. When all was ready, gun captains lined up a notch filed on the top of the base ring with another notch on the swell of the muzzle and took aim at an imaginary target at sea.

Richard gave the order. *"Fire!"*

Gun captains yanked hard on lanyards attached to flintlocks. One metallic *click!* after another resounded around the gun deck.

"Run in your guns!"

The process was repeated, again and again and again, with the added step of swabbing out the bore with a wet piece of sheepskin affixed to the end of a long wooden staff to extinguish lingering sparks or a smoldering piece of flannel that might later drift out and upward to ignite dry canvas—or worse, prematurely set off a newly inserted bag of powder. Then another cartridge was rammed home, the gun was run out above a protest of squeaking wheels, and the lanyard yanked hard again.

Together with Edward Oates, a former Royal Navy chief gunnery officer, Richard paced the deck back and forth, back and forth, from the camboose stove forward to the captain's quarters aft, now open to view. He held a watch in one hand as he encouraged one crew, instructed another, reprimanding a gun captain only when he chose to make an example of an error or when he noticed one of his crew slacking off.

As the sun approached its zenith and commissioned officers and midshipmen were summoned to the ship's helm for a noon sighting, Richard called an end to the exercise. Men stopped in their tracks and bent over with hands on knees, some panting hard.

"Well done, lads!" Richard shouted out. "You've earned your gill of grog this noon—after ship inspection." That rally cry inspired a weak round of cheers.

That was as far as the evolutions went that morning, although they were repeated several more times that afternoon while under full sail, this time to allow the convoy of fourteen brigs, schooners, and ship-rigged merchant vessels to make decent headway toward their destination. And they continued to fire imaginary shot, as they had done since the shakedown cruise. *Constellation* carried a limited supply of ammunition in her magazine, and Truxtun wanted to conserve it.

"Overall I am quite content with what I observed today," he allowed in his after cabin during his nightly seven o'clock meeting with his officers. The western sky offered a brilliant display of red, yellow, and pink, and the evening muster of divisions at the start of the second dogwatch had passed without incident. Outside the closed door, a Marine sentry in blue uniform and white cross-belts stood at stiff attention.

The officers had covered several routine issues and were now broaching meatier matters. "Your thoughts, Mr. Cutler? Are you satisfied with today's performance?"

"Quite satisfied, sir. The men continue to go above and beyond what is demanded of them, and much is being demanded. We still have far to go, but after observing the men today, I have every confidence we'll get there."

"Which is why you felt justified in declaring 'up spirits' this noon?"

Richard gave Truxtun a puzzled look. "Justified, sir? I don't understand."

Truxtun grimaced. "Mr. Cutler, I shall not argue the merits of what you did; nor did I wish to gainsay my lieutenant in front of the ship's company, especially over a subject as sensitive as rum rations. I, too, prefer to reward men for hard work. You have heard me say many times that sailors are better led by force of character and example than by threat of the lash. But the fact remains that *Constellation* is not one of your family's merchant vessels on which you may dispense rum at your pleasure. She is a ship of war and therefore subject to strict regulations. Do I make myself clear?"

Richard met his captain's hard glare. "You do, sir. But with respect, the regulations state—"

"The regulations *state*, Mr. Cutler, that the issuance of rum shall be the custom of our American Navy. A *custom*, I need not remind you, is subject to the captain's approval. Did you not hear me say, just yesterday in this cabin, that I may withhold spirit rations when and if I so choose?"

That was not what Richard recalled hearing the captain say. Nonetheless, there was only one possible response. "Yes, sir. I apologize, sir."

"Very well. Your apology is accepted, Mr. Cutler. And may this serve as a lesson to all you officers. In the future, you must seek my approval on all matters of protocol. Am I understood?"

He was.

"Now then, Mr. Cutler, on a far more positive note, I quite agree that the men are showing admirable improvement. I therefore believe it is time for us to exercise the guns with live shot. We need the practice, and one day of live exercise will do our supply no harm. I have every confidence we can resupply from the British once we reach Port Royal."

"I understand, sir."

"We never know," Truxtun went on, "when we might find a French dog sniffing about on the horizon. Mr. Waverly," he said, changing course and settling his gaze upon the sailing master seated at the other end of the table. "For a man not known for reticence, you have been surprisingly quiet this evening. You have now had several days to observe the ways of our ship. What insights might you have for us?"

The sailing master, Nate Waverly, was the oldest and most seasoned sailor on board the ship. His sailing credentials dated back to before the war with England, when he had signed on as cabin boy on HMS *Rose,* based in Newport, Rhode Island. From there, he had climbed his way up the petty officer ladder to quartermaster's mate. When war threatened, he jumped ship and joined the Continental navy, serving as quartermaster of the frigate *Providence*, twenty-eight guns, until she was captured by the Royal Navy. When the war ended, he returned to the maritime trade and mastered the intricacies of navigation, log-keeping, and maintaining a ship in proper trim whatever the conditions at sea.

"Sorry to be so quiet, sir," he said, as though Truxtun had been serious in his reprimand. As he spoke, he drummed his fingers on his right thigh, by his own admission a nervous habit he had acquired as a youth when faced with a socially awkward situation. "Like you, I had my doubts about this ship. *Constellation* seemed too long in proportion to her beam. She'll buckle for sure, I convinced myself, no matter how many riders she has down there on her keelson." When he noted his fellow officers hanging on his every word, his voice gained in confidence. "What's more, I found her wales too low, her bow and stern too sharp, and her yards too long, the way they stick out beyond the railing. But stap me if that renegade Quaker"—referring to Philadelphia shipwright Joshua Humphreys, the designer of the *Constitution* class of super frigates—"hasn't proven me wrong, sir. This ship is not only sturdy, she's reliable, too. And she's fast. Were it not for the drills, and did we not have to constantly reduce sail to let the convoy to catch up to us, we'd be in Jamaica in record time."

Truxtun allowed a faint smile. "Thank you for your observations, Mr. Waverly. We can all take heart from them. That's all I have for you this evening, gentlemen, except to note that tomorrow evening I shall be meeting in private with Mr. Carter and Mr. Cutler. On Wednesday we shall resume our normal schedule. Which is our *custom*, eh, Mr. Cutler?"

TOPSIDE A FEW MINUTES LATER, John Rodgers approached Richard amidships. The cloud-spotted summer evening sky had become less brilliantly streaked as the ball of yellow sun dipped toward the western horizon. *Constellation* remained under full sail, a spread of canvas approximating an acre in dimension, although at the end of the second dogwatch, at eight o'clock, sailors aloft would take in the two courses and all three topgallants and hoist a lantern up to the main, foremast, and mizzen crosstrees, the night recognition signal that each vessel in the convoy would replicate in order to keep track of one another during the night hours. They had made their turn eastward, away from the Carolina coast, on a course they would maintain until they swung to the southwest, running free before the prevailing northeasterly trades on a straight line through the Windward Passage to the eastern tip of Jamaica.

"Richard. A word if you please," Rodgers said when he had caught up.

Richard turned around. "Yes, sir?"

Rodgers nodded to starboard, away from the main hatchway, where they could speak with a degree of privacy. They returned the salutes of two pigtailed sailors who were polishing the ship's brightwork with brick dust, and of two others who were mopping a spot on the deck, then walked on ahead to stand beside the foremast. They faced seaward, feeling the warm caress of a setting summer sun and a gentle southerly breeze—a topgallant breeze, the sort of breeze that could lull a man into a state of blissful complacency.

"We're off duty," Rodgers said as he leaned forward against the bulwark. He rested his forearms on the smooth, glossy rail and clasped his hands together. "Please call me John."

"Very well, John. What's on your mind?"

"I just want to say," Rodgers said, careful to keep his voice low, "that I found the captain's behavior rather odd this evening, the way he singled you out. What he said was unjustified, in my opinion. Issuing rum is more than just a bloody custom, and he jolly well knows it!"

When Richard did not reply, Rodgers continued. "Every sea captain has his quirks, and I suspect we have just witnessed one of Captain Truxtun's. He wasn't really questioning your knowledge of the rules. He was making a point, and he was using you to make that point. About his authority, you understand. Then again, I am hardly in a position to lecture you on the eccentricities of sea captains. You've seen more of them in your lifetime than I am ever likely to see in mine. Truth be told, Richard, I am honored to be serving with you. I may outrank you except on the gun deck, but I admire what you have accomplished down there. I could not have done as well. And I suffer no illusions that I will continue to outrank you once our Navy is better organized. Which is why I feel somewhat embarrassed whenever you call me 'sir.'"

Richard was shocked by such an admission from a superior officer. It would be unthinkable in the Royal Navy. "Thank you," he said. "Though I fear you overrate me at the same time you underrate yourself. Look around you, John," he said with a sweeping gesture. "Any officer able to get a ship like this in such fine shape in so short a time deserves the highest praise. *My* truth be told, I stand in awe of *you*. And the quality of the guns, which I understand we also owe to you, is second to none."

Rodgers shrugged. "We have my father to thank for the guns, Richard. More specifically, we have Mr. Howard Cecil to thank. He gave *Constellation* top priority. As to putting this ship to rights, I had help from many people—Andrew in particular. He shows remarkable perseverance and attention to detail for someone of his age and experience."

As Rodgers spoke, the image of Jack Endicott flashed through Richard's mind. He made a mental note of Howard Cecil, proprietor of Cecil Iron Works, as a name worth remembering.

In a lighter, more affable tone, Rodgers said, "Tell me a little more about yourself, Richard. We really haven't had much of an opportunity to get to know each other. You told me you are married. How many children do you have?"

"I have three. My oldest son will be seventeen in December. My daughter, my youngest, turned ten in April. Jamie is fifteen. You?"

"I have four boys and three girls, aged two to sixteen. They keep their mother on her toes! Martha's her name, and I miss her more with each cruise. Incredible, isn't it, after so many years of marriage and so many children, to miss a woman that much."

"It's the same for me, John. And I believe we are very fortunate to have it so. Perhaps being separated in the short run makes for a happier marriage in the long run. The days Katherine and I have together become that much more meaningful."

"Not to mention the nights."

Richard returned Rodgers' smile. "Yes, well, there is that. Every homecoming certainly has its rewards."

"Indeed. It's *why* we have seven children."

They laughed comfortably until Rodgers said, in a more somber tone, "It's harder when it comes to the children, though, isn't it."

That statement triggered complex emotions within Richard. He stood with his hands resting on the rail, contemplating the great blue expanse of ocean as the wind fluttered his white cotton shirt and tousled unruly strands of blond hair about his face. Behind them they heard the slap of bare feet on the wooden deck, but the man passed on forward, returning them to quiet.

"Yes," he replied at length, as if to his inner self, his voice barely audible, "it *is* harder when it comes to the children."

"How do you reconcile it, if you don't mind my asking. I mean, your duty to your country with your duty to your family?"

Richard looked askance at him. "I've asked myself that question many times, John. The only answer I can accept is that my duty to my country *is* my duty to my family."

After a pause, Rodgers nodded. "Thank you, Richard. That's an answer I can take home with me."

Side by side, the two men stared out to sea. The sun, half-hidden on the western horizon, cast a golden glow upon the white canvas of the merchant vessels lazily keeping pace to starboard and larboard. By rote, Richard made the count. Fourteen vessels, all within easy sight of the frigate's weather deck. He scanned the horizon and sky. Noting nothing there of consequence, he allowed his thoughts to drift northward, to Hingham and the memories of warm summer evenings of yore. An image lingered of a flaxen-haired beauty who had taken a fancy to his brother Will, and then, after Will had died, to Richard. Twenty-two years ago almost to the night, two weeks after the signing of the Great Proclamation in Philadelphia, he and Sarah Fearing were strolling hand in hand along a moon-washed Hingham beach when suddenly she stopped and faced him. Wrapping her arms around his waist, she drew him to her and said, in an urgent whisper, that they dare not waste the hot summer night, the blood-warm seawater, the privacy of the cove in which they found themselves, so wouldn't it be just the thing to—

John Rodgers shattered the alluring mental image. "Why do you think Captain Truxtun wants to meet alone with you and Lieutenant Carter tomorrow evening?"

Richard shook his head, casting out the angels of remembrance. "I have no idea. I was hoping you could tell me."

"Sorry, mate. I can't."

Eight bells sounded. Boatswain's whistles piped the starboard watch below to hammocks and the larboard watch aloft to its duty on the weather deck and in the rigging.

"I must take my leave, John. I'm officer of the deck. I enjoyed our talk."

"So did I, Richard. Good luck tomorrow with the guns."

GUN DRILLS RESUMED at ten the next morning, this time using live ammunition. Because *Constellation* was positioned to leeward of her convoy, she exercised only her larboard guns. As always, rate of fire trumped accuracy in hitting a target, which was just as well because there weren't any targets to shoot at. One by one, the guns on the two upper decks roared, vomiting tongues of orange and white sparks before they were run in, sponged out, wormed, and reloaded with round shot delivered by powder monkeys. The sole responsibility of these young boys during battle drill was to lug shot and powder as Edward Oates parceled it out in the copper-sheathed magazine, carrying it through the berthing deck to the gun decks and into the hands of a gun captain or onto shot racks. For two hours, gun captains yanked the firing mechanism, estimated the distance of the plume of seawater towering skyward when the ball struck, then adjusted the quoin on its bed to measure the effects of maximum elevation, point-blank, and extreme depression. All this was done, to the extent possible, with every crew and every man working together until shot and crew were spent, the deck was consumed with blinding, acrid smoke, and the exposed skin on a gunner's arms and face was the glistening black of a native-born African. As the echoes of the final salvo dissolved into peals of distant thunder, Truxtun ordered an end to the morning exercise and a double ration of grog for each member of each gun crew.

"How did they fare that last round?" he inquired of Richard Cutler at seven o'clock that evening.

They were in Truxtun's after cabin. An hour earlier, during small arms and sword drill on deck, the canvas partitions in the captain's cabin and wardroom had been replaced. A breeze wafted through the open gun ports, mitigating the lingering stench of spent powder. Four 24-pounder guns lay bowsed up tight in the cabin, two to a side, the barrels on the larboard sides still warm from the afternoon drill. Below them, on the berthing deck, the off-duty watch was finishing supper, each mess sitting around its own spread of canvas laid out on the deck as if at a picnic. Down on the orlop, midshipmen dined in a cramped and dank mess void of light, save for candles stuck into wax. Cutler and Carter had not yet eaten, nor did Captain Truxtun offer them anything beyond a single glass of claret poured out by a cabin boy.

Richard consulted his notes. "One minute forty-eight seconds, sir," he reported. "An improvement of three seconds from the previous drill."

"Good. But not good enough," Truxtun groused. "Before I'm satisfied, Mr. Cutler, you'll need to shave off another ten seconds. Shave off twenty and you'll find me very pleased indeed."

"In that case, sir, I shall order the men to find you ecstatic by the time we reach Jamaica."

"Excellent." Truxtun allowed a faint smile before shifting his gaze to the lieutenant of Marines. "And you, Mr. Carter? How did you fare?"

"Not quite as well, sir," Carter confessed.

"So I noticed. Tomorrow I shall ask Mr. Oates to turn his attention to the weather deck. I shall ask the same of you, Mr. Cutler, should circumstances warrant it. The guns up there may be smaller than those down here, but their role in battle is just as critical."

"Aye, aye, sir," both lieutenants acknowledged.

"Now, let us turn our attention to another matter. What I am about to tell you is, for the time being, for your ears only. I will bring Mr. Rodgers and Mr. Sterrett into my confidence shortly, but for now, mum's the word. Only a handful of men are privy to the information I am about to give you. These men are, to my knowledge, Mr. Adams, Mr. Pickering, Mr. Hamilton, Mr. McHenry, Mr. Stoddert, and Mr. Washington. And myself, of course. And you, in a few moments."

The caliber of those names brought both lieutenants slightly forward in their chairs, as if by drawing nearer to Captain Truxtun they might convince him of their discretion.

"What do you know about Saint-Domingue and the political situation there?" he asked them.

The lieutenants glanced at each other.

"I know a little, sir," Richard offered.

Truxtun nodded slowly. "I am all ears, Mr. Cutler."

"Saint-Domingue is a French colony on the western half of the island of Hispaniola, which itself is a hodgepodge of British, French, and Spanish interests. Columbus was the first to plant a flag there, and he claimed the entire island for Spain. His claim notwithstanding, French buccaneers soon settled on the western third of the island. The Spanish did nothing about it because they preferred the eastern parts where the soil is richer. Over the years the French built up quite a presence on Saint-Domingue. The British were latecomers, motivated, I suspect, by the quality and quantity of the island's coffee and cane fields. Until a few years ago they had no legal standing on Hispaniola. That changed when local slaves rose up and began slaughtering their white masters, French and Spanish alike. The Spanish invited the British in to help restore order on the island and at the same time drive out the French. I have heard rumors that there was an agreement between Britain and Spain to divide the colony between them once the French were ousted."

"Who told you that?"

"My cousins, John and Robin Cutler. They make it their business to know what's happening on other islands in the Indies."

"I see. Carry on."

"There's not much more I can tell you, sir. I understand that British forces have captured several fortresses near Port-au-Prince—or Port Républicain as it's now called. But they have failed in their objective to drive out the French. A peace treaty was signed some years back, not long after the National Directory abolished slavery on Saint-Domingue and other French islands. That decree ended the slave rebellion—for a while, at least."

"Is that it?"

"I believe so, sir. As I said, I don't know a lot."

"You know a great deal more than most people, Mr. Cutler, including just about everybody in our State Department. What of the current situation? Anything to add there?"

"No, sir, except to say that I believe the slave rebellion continues in the form of a civil war on Saint-Domingue, pitting former slaves against their former owners."

"Not quite accurate, but close enough. Does the name Rigaud mean anything to either of you? André Rigaud?"

It did not.

"What about Toussaint L'Ouverture?"

"That name's familiar, sir," Carter cut in, relieved to have something to contribute to the conversation. "I read a little about him in a newspaper. He's a leader in the civil war, I believe."

"Quite so, Mr. Carter. On whose side?"

Carter gave him a blank look. "On the side of the former slaves, I should think, sir."

"That would seem a safe assumption, wouldn't it, since Toussaint is as pure-blooded a Negro as there is. But his role is more complicated than that. Toussaint is hardly your everyday slave. He started out that way, as a servant to a benevolent master who, among other privileges, allowed Toussaint to educate himself and learn English. Which he did to the point where he now speaks English better than most Englishmen. Plus, he has taught himself several other languages. Care to guess the title of his favorite book?"

Neither lieutenant did.

"*Caesar's Gallic Wars,*" Truxtun informed them. "In Latin. So what we have here is a man who is both brilliant and a natural-born leader. And he's a man of strict loyalties. When informed of the slave uprising, the first thing he did was to see his master and his master's family safely off the island. He then joined the Spanish against the French, some claim because he preferred allegiance to a king over a republic. By the end of '93, he and his followers controlled much of the island's interior.

"Early in '94 he switched sides and declared himself for France. Exactly why, I cannot say for certain. But since France abolished slavery in the Indies, it's a fair guess Toussaint believed he owed allegiance to France. The Spanish had also promised freedom to their slaves but were slow to act on that promise. Great Britain—Spain's ally at the time, as Mr. Cutler correctly informed us—has in fact reinstated slavery in the areas of Hispaniola it controls. The British fear, legitimately, in my view, that emancipation on one island will encourage slave rebellions on the other islands."

He allowed a moment for that information to sink in. "What you said a moment ago, Mr. Cutler, is accurate. Hispaniola is a hodgepodge of foreign interests, and those interests have little regard for the local citizenry. On Saint-Domingue there are—I should say, *were*—approximately 30,000 whites, the majority of them government administrators, artisans, and shopkeepers. Most supported the French Republic. Others, the wealthier ones—the planters, the so-called *grand blancs*—remained loyal to the Bourbon king, the exiled Louis XVII. When rebellion broke out, these royalists sided with the Spanish and British, hoping, I suppose, to somehow come out of the turmoil with the status quo intact. When that effort failed and the slaughter began anew, the *grand blancs* fled the colony right behind the *petit blancs*. Many of them went to Cuba, taking with them what slaves they could, as well as their knowledge of sugar production.

"Also living on Saint-Domingue are another 30,000 so-called *gens de couleur*, a rather elegant term for citizens of mixed European and African descent. These people are the offspring of white planters and their Negro mistresses who lived together in an odd form of common-law marriage that allows their offspring to inherit property. These people—mulattoes, you and I would call them—are recognized by France as citizens of France. They form an elite group on the island. So elite, in fact, that they consider themselves superior to *both* blacks and whites.

"The third group on the island—by far the most numerous at 400,000 strong—consists of former black slaves. Most of these Negroes came to Saint-Domingue in chains from the west coast of Africa. I need not describe for you the misery of their lives. So it should be easy to understand why they call Toussaint 'Father Toussaint' and look upon him as a saint or savior—which to them, of course, he is. Thousands have flocked to his banner."

"Against whom? The French?"

"Not at all, Mr. Carter. Have you not been listening?" His tone conveyed more humor than reprimand. "As I told you, most of the whites have fled the island. Those who remain are connected in some way to the government or military. No, Toussaint is fighting the *gens de couleur*, the mulatto army led by André Rigaud, the militant extremist whose name I mentioned earlier. Rigaud also knows a thing or two about military affairs—enough to conquer and control what amounts to a semi-autonomous state in the southern regions of Saint-Domingue. His objectives go far beyond that, however. He seeks what Toussaint seeks: to conquer the entire island of Hispaniola. Toussaint seems to have a better chance of succeeding because his army is considerably larger than Rigaud's. That's the point to remember. Two years ago Toussaint thwarted Rigaud's attempt to assassinate the French governor of the colony, a general named Laveaux. As a reward for saving his life, Laveaux appointed Toussaint lieutenant governor of Saint-Domingue and commander in chief of French forces on the island. Have I confused you yet?"

Richard scratched the nape of his neck. "You've done a good job confusing *me*, sir. This is all quite intriguing, but if I may, what does all this have to do with Lieutenant Carter and me?"

"A great deal, Mr. Cutler, which I am about to tell you. Before I do, however, you should know that Toussaint L'Ouverture has been in secret contact with President Adams."

That piece of information caused both lieutenants to blink. Then Truxtun delivered his thunderbolt. "He has formally requested that our government lift our embargo on shipments to Saint-Domingue. He has also requested military supplies and food for his army. In exchange, he has pledged to Mr. Adams that he will deny France the use of Saint-Domingue as a naval base in the West Indies."

Richard and Carter exchanged looks, both men struggling to make sense of a labyrinth of double-dealing that seemed to expand in size and complexity with each sentence Truxtun uttered.

"Captain," Richard managed, "how can that be? Did you not say a moment ago that Toussaint L'Ouverture now commands French forces on Saint Domingue?"

"I said exactly that."

"Forgive me, sir, but how can the commander of French forces deny France the use of a naval base he is pledged to maintain and defend?"

Truxtun's mouth twisted. "I appreciate the difficulty you are having with this, Mr. Cutler. If it's any consolation, I asked my superiors the same questions that you and Mr. Carter are asking me. What you need to understand is that Toussaint's true loyalty lies not with France but with the former slaves. He trusts no foreigner or mulatto. But he will treat with you and me and anyone else he believes can help him realize his ultimate objective."

"Which is?"

"An independent nation ruled by freed black slaves."

Richard shook his head in disbelief. "And the United States is open to this? We're willing to help him realize this objective?"

"I can't answer that. What I *can* tell you is that Mr. Pickering is on board with this initiative, as is Mr. Hamilton. Mr. Stoddert, less so. So you see, gentlemen, we have a government that is split on this issue. But it's a disagreement based more in ignorance than fact. We require more facts, more information, to clarify the situation. We need to understand more about Toussaint's motives and exactly how he intends to use our support, should we decide to lend him that support. Above all, we need to be assured that whatever we decide to do is in the best interests of our country. That requires a fact-finding mission, led in part by an American naval attaché, to meet with Toussaint L'Ouverture on Saint-Domingue and have it out with him, so to speak."

"I see. And that naval attaché is . . ."

Truxtun's smile was benign. "You, Mr. Cutler, as no doubt a man of your intelligence has already concluded. You, escorted by Lieutenant

Carter and a squad of his Marines. Mind you, I am not ordering you to do this. Mr. Stoddert made it quite clear that this mission is to be strictly voluntary, both because of its confidential nature and because there may be danger involved. Having stated that, I am compelled to point out that your name was put forth by both Mr. Adams and Mr. Hamilton. I must therefore ask if you harbor any doubts concerning the wisdom of their choice?"

"No, sir," Richard said, feeling like a pawn in a game of chess.

"Splendid. Apparently my superiors view your past exploits in the Caribbean and Mediterranean as critical factors in this mission. There are further details that I am not at liberty to divulge this evening. Nor, I confess, am I aware of them all. You shall hear more of this when we meet with Vice Admiral Parker in Port Royal."

"Admiral Parker?" Richard probed. "Admiral Hyde Parker? I believe I once met his father. They have the same name."

"You did, Mr. Cutler." Truxtun's tone turned more sober. "Near the end of the war, when Admiral Hyde Parker Senior—'Vinegar Hyde' to some, 'Old Piss and Vinegar' to others—commanded the Windward Squadron in Barbados. Your acquaintance with him is yet another reason why you were recommended for this mission. It's perhaps the most important reason of all. You see, this is to be a joint British-American expedition, and your family's English connections may well decide its outcome."

Eight

Port Royal, Jamaica
August 1798

RICHARD CUTLER knew something of the history of Port Royal—as did most people familiar with the West Indies. Situated at the western tip of a long, thin spit of land shaped like an ostrich leg with an Italy-shaped boot at its western end, the port was in its heyday in the late 1600s the largest, richest, and most debauched British municipality in the Western Hemisphere. Its dubious distinction as the "Sodom of the West Indies" was well deserved. With an economy driven by gold bullion plundered by English privateers off Spanish treasure fleets, Port Royal served as a safe haven for pirates, buccaneers, cutthroats, and other lowlifes keen to pick a farthing or a florin from an unsuspecting tar passed out cold on an alehouse floor or in a dark alley rife with the stench of human waste. In 1680 Port Royal was said to host a tavern for every ten residents. Inside those taverns and on the streets outside, prostitutes brazenly plied their wares, their oft-used bodies tantalizing pie-eyed sailors too long away at sea.

Tottering at the tip of the societal pyramid, the town's few respectable citizens—merchants, mainland planters, and an Anglican priest or two—tried to buy safety from the thieves and other opportunists who scourged the port. They pooled their resources and appointed Henry Morgan, the renowned buccaneer and sworn enemy of propriety and Puritanism, as lieutenant governor. The seemingly insane gamble paid off. Elevated from the base to the apex of society, Morgan found religion and set about to clean up the unholy mess, publicly hanging many of those with whom just a few weeks before he had been in cahoots. His efforts, however, proved too little, too late. At 11:42 on the morning of June 7, 1692, in what was widely perceived as divine punishment for its manifold sins and wickedness, Port Royal was rocked to its core by a violent earthquake that sent much of the city, Atlantis-like, into the sea. The few people who managed to survive the holocaust fled across the bay to the mainland, where, in collaboration with the sugar planters and wealthier merchants already living there, they established a new commercial center. With the devastation of Port Royal fresh in their minds, these citizens of Kingston, as the new community came to be called, lived and worked and prayed as paragons of sobriety and Christian morals—until memories faded.

What remained of Port Royal, meanwhile, was appropriated by the Royal Navy and rebuilt as Britain's flagship base in the West Indies.

"ON DECK, THERE! Land ho! Dead to loo'ard!"

The cry from the foremast crosstrees compelled everyone on *Constellation*'s weather deck to squint ahead beyond the bowsprit and its three cloud-white foresails taut in a stiff northeasterly breeze. Theirs was an instinctive reaction only. Another hour would pass before those on deck could see what the lookouts on high had seen. Not until the sun rose above the yardarms and the crew had been issued its noon ration of rum did a form begin to take shape on the horizon, a dark smudge in between the cerulean sea and the turquoise sky.

"Jamaica, sir," James Jarvis said to Richard, stating the obvious as he handed back the spyglass. The voice of the young midshipman from New York seemed to have suddenly dropped several octaves, as if the mere sight of this fabled island and the possibilities for debauchery it held had instantly transported him beyond puberty.

"Aye, Mr. Jarvis. Jamaica. What you're looking at are the Blue Mountains. Port Royal lies on the other side."

Activity on the weather deck brought John Rodgers up from the wardroom dressed simply in buff breeches and a white cotton shirt that billowed about him in the breeze. As custom dictated, Richard offered him the speaking trumpet, the symbol of authority. As custom suggested, Rodgers declined the honor.

"Carry on, Mr. Cutler," he said.

"A change of course, Mr. Waverly," Richard said to the sailing master. "Bring her southeast by east, a half east. Once we've cleared

Morant Point, go large on a course due west. Mr. Jarvis, signal the convoy to follow."

Waverly repeated the order to the two quartermaster's mates at the helm. Boatswain's whistles twittered along the weather deck as Jarvis proceeded aft to the signal locker near the taffrail. Sailors in the waist adjusted sheets, tacks, and yards, and for the first time in three days *Constellation* tightened sail from a broad to a beam reach. Four hours later, at Waverly's command, her stern swung through the wind until it rested on her starboard quarter. The weather clew of her mainsail was hauled up, and she ran free due west to Kingston, the convoy trailing in her wake.

At eight o'clock that evening, with the sand spit running east to west across the entrance to Kingston Harbor in clear view, all hands prepared the ship to drop anchor. Sailors aloft clewed up the courses, reducing canvas to jib, topsails, and driver. Those on anchor duty removed the hawse-buckles on her best-bower, leaving the great wooden-stocked, fluked anchor cradled to the bows by a single ring-stopper. Astern, at the double wheel, quartermaster's mates made ready to put the helm down and round the frigate into the wind.

As the crew went about its business, Richard brought a glass to his eye. He noticed first an immense bastion at the entrance to the harbor at the western edge of the spit. Built in the 1650s, it had originally been named Fort Cromwell in honor of Oliver Cromwell and his anti-royalist Roundheads. In 1660 the name was changed to Fort Charles after word was received from London that Charles II had restored the Stuart line to the British throne and had ordered the corpse of the erstwhile Lord Protector of England to be dug up, hanged in chains, and beheaded. Whatever its name, Richard thought as he swept the glass along the thick stone parapets, admiring the long black muzzles of cannon protruding out between them, this bastion would give pause to any enemy bent on assault.

Beyond the fortress, within the town of Port Royal proper, he could make out little of note amid the clusters of low buildings. Past them, by the northeast shore of the town, he brought into focus a white stucco building of greater significance, and beyond that a copse of masts: the frigates, brigs, three-masted sloops of war, and other warships that maintained British hegemony throughout the Greater Antilles. Among them, one ship stood out: a first rate with a broad red pennant fluttering from her mainmast truck. HMS *Queen* was the flagship of Vice Admiral Sir Hyde Parker, commander in chief of His Britannic Majesty's naval squadrons in West Indian waters. The ninety-six-gun vessel was a floating fortress so vast that it could house and feed the entire population of a fair-sized English town.

Constellation coasted alone in the lee of Port Royal, her convoy having parted company to follow a more northwesterly tack before swinging southeastward into Kingston Harbor. When she rounded to and lost way, Fort Charles erupted in a thirteen-gun salute. *Constellation* responded with a thirteen-gun salute of her own.

"Let go!" First Lieutenant Rodgers shouted through the trumpet. A whistle shrieked, the ring-stopper was released, the anchor cable rumbled through the hawse-hole, and the frigate's five-thousand-pound wrought iron anchor plunged into the salty depths, bringing an end to this leg of the cruise.

EARLY THE NEXT MORNING, with the sun barely up above a naval base already stirring to life, a clinker-built ship's boat approached *Constellation* where she lay at anchor off the white stucco building, downwind of the British naval squadron. Eight men worked the oars, four to a side. Each was dressed in blue-and-white-striped jersey, flawlessly white trousers, and a wide-brimmed straw hat adorned with a blue ribbon. In the stern sheets, beside the coxswain, sat a British sea officer, the brilliant gold lining on his uniform coat reflecting the early morning sun.

"Boat ahoy!" a junior midshipman chirped from the weather deck of *Constellation*.

"Flag," the coxswain in the gig called out. Instinctively he held up four fingers, four being the number of side boys required by ceremony to pipe a flag officer on board ship.

When the gig bumped gently against the larboard hull of the American frigate, the British officer seized hold of two ropes leading upward between steps built into the frigate's side. At the entry port he was met by Lt. Andrew Sterrett, standing at attention.

"Welcome aboard, Captain," he said, having recognized the British officer's rank by the gold-tasseled epaulet on each shoulder. "Please accept my apologies for not having a side party prepared in your honor. We were not expecting a visitor this early in the day."

The officer returned the salute. "Be at your ease, Lieutenant," he insisted. "I am not here in any sort of official capacity. I have come to visit a fellow officer of yours whom I believe to be on board."

"Oh?" Sterrett remarked, hiding his relief. "Which officer, Captain?"

"Richard Cutler. He is your second, is he not?"

"He is, sir. Are you an acquaintance of Lieutenant Cutler?"

"I daresay I am. Otherwise I would not be here at this moment, would I?"

Sterrett flushed red, although the British captain's smile removed the sting. "Well then, Captain, I am doubly honored to meet you." He bowed slightly. "I am Lt. Andrew Sterrett, sir, at your service. I am *Constellation*'s third. I shall have Lieutenant Cutler summoned on deck right away."

"That is considerate of you, Lieutenant, but might I request permission to go below? I realize my request is somewhat irregular, but I would ever so much enjoy a look about your ship. She is the envy of every sailor in my squadron."

"I am pleased to hear it, Captain," Sterrett said, puffing up a bit in pride. He glanced at John Dent. "Please see the captain below to the wardroom."

"Aye, aye, sir," said Dent, saluting. "If you will follow me, Captain," he added with a note of self-importance.

Down below in the wardroom, American commissioned and senior warrant officers were lounging about the dining table or in front of their cubicles. When the British officer entered, everyone snapped to. Except for one, who came slowly to his feet, his mouth slack-jawed.

"Hugh? Is that you? Is it possible?"

"Good morning, Richard," the officer said cheerfully. He doffed his hat, slid it under his left armpit, and said, with a bow to the wardroom at large, "And a good morning to you gentlemen. Pray forgive me for intruding upon your breakfast. I'm afraid I could not restrain myself. On behalf of His Britannic Majesty King George III, I welcome you to Port Royal. Now please carry on with whatever you were doing. Pay me no mind."

Such a command was impossible to obey. Wardroom officers continued to stand at attention, their eyes shifting from the British captain to the American lieutenant. After an awkward pause, Richard found his bearings.

"Gentlemen," he said, "I introduce you to Capt. Hugh Hardcastle of His Majesty's Ship *Redoubtable*. Captain, may we offer you some coffee or tea? Some breakfast, perhaps?"

"Thank you, no, Lieutenant. Nor, alas, can I remain aboard for any length of time. Might I thus trouble you to arrange a brief word with your Captain Truxtun? And, if possible, a quick tour of the ship? As I indicated topside to Lieutenant Sterrett, this frigate has every British sailor in port gawking. When I departed my own ship a short while ago, every member of my crew on duty was at the rail—and not to see me off, I assure you."

Richard grinned. "Yes, of course. Mr. Dent, please inform the captain that Captain Hardcastle will pay him a visit in . . . shall we say, half an hour?"

Hardcastle nodded his acquiescence.

"Damn, Hugh, it's good to see you," Richard enthused a few minutes later when he and Hugh Hardcastle were alone in the cockpit on the orlop deck. They were seated on two apothecary chests, the deckhead above being too low to accommodate their six-foot frames. Directly forward they could hear muffled chatter coming from the midshipmen's mess, an occasional giggle or two, then a loud belch. A raucous fart brought a more enthusiastic round of high-pitched giggles, followed by a very distinct and harshly plaintive, "Good *Christ*, Harry!" Within the hour the dank, unventilated cockpit would become man-eating hot. For the moment, though, it was bearable, and one of the few places on the ship affording privacy.

"I had no idea you were here in Jamaica," Richard said. "I thought you were still attached to the Windward Squadron."

"I am. Admiral Hyde summoned me here two months ago on special orders. For reasons you will better understand when we meet with him this afternoon." He withdrew a linen handkerchief from a coat pocket and dabbed at beads of sweat popping up in his thick, blondish-brown hair. He still wore it clipped short around the edges, exactly as he had when he and Richard had first met back in '80 when Richard and Katherine had taken up residence in the Cutler compound on Barbados. Although eighteen years had since passed, Hugh Hardcastle remained every bit the handsome man of grace, wit, and charm whom Richard had so admired back then.

"No doubt you have a host of questions for me," Hugh said as he returned the handkerchief to its pocket. "As I have for you, and we have no time now to ask them. This evening we will, I hope. Please dine with me in Kingston. I will arrange for a table at a favorite spot of mine, as well as a carriage to get us there and back. What do you say to that?"

"Of course, Hugh. I can't imagine anything I'd rather do. Subject, of course, to my captain's approval."

"I have no doubt that you shall have your captain's approval. Now, time is getting on and we should set about our tour. I suggest we start off by stirring things up in the midshipmen's mess."

THE ROYAL MARINE SENTRY stationed before the admiral's quarters banged the bronze-plated butt of his musket smartly on the deck and fired a crisp salute as Captain Hardcastle and his party approached the captain's suite from the entry port located directly ahead amidships.

Hugh Hardcastle returned the salute. "Captain Truxtun and Lieutenant Cutler of the American frigate *Constellation* to see Admiral Hyde," he said.

"Aye, aye, sir."

The Marine pivoted sharply, opened the door ajar, and repeated Hugh Hardcastle's words verbatim. A voice on the inside acknowledged. Footsteps faded aft, then returned. "Please show Captain Truxtun and Lieutenant Cutler in," the voice stated.

The sentry swung the door open to reveal a liveried servant resplendent in the impeccable fashion of the English aristocracy, from his ruffled linen neck stock to his brocade coat and vest, down past a pair of spotless white breeches and stockings to his silver-buckled shoes. He bowed low before them. As he did so, Richard caught the pungent scent of a perfumed wig, its color as pure white as the servant's breeches.

"If you will follow me, please," the servant directed.

Following last in line behind his captain, Richard tried to keep himself from gawking at an opulence he had never before witnessed on board a ship. In other English warships of his acquaintance, one entered the captain's day cabin first and his private quarters second, and then only at the captain's invitation. Here, the design was different in a space three to four times the equivalent space on board *Constellation*. By the mizzenmast, which according to Richard's visual calculation from the cutter on the way over was near the break of the quarterdeck and poop deck above, was the admiral's sleeping cabin, followed by a pantry and dining cabin—in area roughly equivalent to Captain Truxtun's entire day cabin—and finally the admiral's day cabin in the very stern of the ship, a sizable space well lighted by rows of stern windows and two layers of quarter-gallery glass that wrapped around from the stern to the quarter on each side. The entire deck within the admiral's suite was spread with a thick white-on-black diamond-patterned rug, and the elegant furnishings seemed more in keeping with a stylish English country manor than a vessel of war. Directly above under the poop deck, Richard assumed, one would find a similar if slightly less spacious configuration to accommodate the ship's captain.

At the jalousie doorway leading into the day cabin, the liveried servant announced the names of the visitors. As the man stepped aside to allow them to enter, Sir Hyde Parker, Vice Admiral of the Red and Commander in Chief of the West India Station, rose to his feet beside a long writing desk set off to the larboard side between two gleaming black 24-pounder guns. He had been dictating correspondence to his clerk, a scrawny, mouselike man who appeared almost embarrassingly diminutive beside the elegant gentleman in the perfect-fitting gold embroidery of a full-dress British admiral's uniform.

"That will be all, Seaver, thank you," the admiral said. The clerk gathered up his papers and slipped unobtrusively from the cabin.

"Welcome, gentlemen," Hyde greeted his guests cordially. He motioned to an area on the starboard side where a cluster of blue-on-white wingback chairs and a sofa had been arranged in a circle, each piece of furniture with a long-legged, delicate side table placed within easy reach. Before the sofa a middle-aged sea officer stood waiting. The gilt linings on his full-dress coat were only a shade less resplendent than the admiral's. The U.S. Navy might resemble the Royal Navy in many ways, Richard thought to himself as he watched the pleasantries unfold, but certainly not in the majesty of its uniforms.

"Gentlemen," Hyde said, addressing the two Americans, "I have the honor of introducing you to Sir Archibald Mason, captain of this ship." The men bowed low to one another. "Before we set about our business," Hyde continued, "might I offer you something to sip?"

"Coffee would be most welcome, Admiral," Truxtun said.

"Coffee for me as well, sir," Richard said, taking his cue from his commanding officer.

"I'm sorry, gentlemen, but coffee will simply not do for this occasion. May I recommend a glass of sherry? It's from Jerez de la Frontera and I can vouch for its quality. You accept? Excellent. Julian, make it so," he instructed a second liveried servant who immediately set about pouring out portions of sherry from a square-sided cut-glass decanter. "Please, gentlemen, sit down. Make yourselves comfortable.

"Well, Captain Truxtun," he went on in grand fashion when everyone was settled. "I believe congratulations are in order."

"Congratulations? Why so, Admiral?"

"You will be pleased to learn that your Navy has taken its first prize: a French privateer by the name of *Croyable*, twelve guns. She has entered your service and has been renamed *Retaliation*. A rather fitting name, what?"

"Who took her?" Truxtun inquired immediately. "And where?" Although his interest had clearly been piqued, he kept his tone subdued.

Hyde consulted the documents he had brought from his writing desk. "Captain Stephen Decatur, off the coast of New Jersey. Near Egg Harbor, it says here."

What Hyde was consulting, Richard had no doubt, was a British intelligence report.

"I know Captain Decatur," Truxtun said. "He commands the sloop of war *Delaware* and has a son of the same name serving as a midshipman aboard *United States*. Admiral, if I may, it's critical for me to understand the circumstances of this engagement. Can you tell me if there was provocation? Did the French fire first?"

Hyde waited until the steward had finished placing a glass of sherry and a small pink napkin upon each of the mahogany side tables.

"That I don't know, Captain," he said before adding, to ease Truxtun's look of disappointment, "but it matters naught in any event." Truxtun's eyes narrowed as Hyde's toothy smile broadened. "I bring you good tidings, Captain," he went on. "In early July, just as you were making ready to sail from Baltimore, your Congress declared your former treaty with France null and void. And that's not all. It also declared that the American Navy"—he glanced down to read verbatim from his notes—"is hereby authorized to engage any armed French vessel found within the jurisdictional limits of the United States —please listen carefully, Captain, here's the critical ruling—*or elsewhere on the high seas.* Elsewhere on the high seas, gentlemen," he repeated with a triumphant smile. "You understand the implication of those words, do you not? They are tantamount to a declaration of war." Hyde raised his glass. "So, gentlemen, here's to victory against our common enemy. Welcome to the good fight."

"Here, here," Captain Mason chimed in.

After the officers had consummated the toast, Truxtun glanced to his left. "Well, Mr. Cutler," he said, "it seems we have received the orders we've been hoping for."

"It would seem so, sir."

"I assume you have confirmation of that authorization?" Truxtun inquired of Hyde.

"Right here on my lap, Captain. Right here on my lap. Along with several personal messages sent to you from your Mr. Stoddert. By reputation he is a man of few words, though it would seem he is somewhat more prolific with the pen. These are rather thick documents. The seals are not broken, as you can see for yourself. I have not read them." He handed over the smooth leather dispatch packet. "By all means, take whatever time you require to verify whatever you wish. I shall not take offense."

"That will not be necessary, Admiral." Truxtun set the packet down against a leg of his chair. "Is there anything else you can tell me about the affairs of my country?" His tone carried more than a hint of irony.

Hyde deferred that question to *Queen*'s captain, who nodded and began to speak. Sir Archibald Mason's voice, to Richard's ear, seemed even more aristocratic than that of Admiral Hyde, if such a thing were possible.

"Are you aware, Captain Truxtun, of the Sedition Act passed by your Congress last month?"

"Sedition Act? No, I am not. I am aware of the Alien Act," referring to an act of Congress passed during the height of anti-French hysteria. At its core, that legislation granted the president the right to deport anyone deemed dangerous to the United States.

"Oh, yes, *that* one," Mason sniffed. "I say, I wish our Parliament had the decency to pass a law along those lines. We could sweep the land clean, eh? Send the frogs and the dagos back to where they belong, to make do in their own bloody ponds—those who manage to keep their wits about them. Not to mention their heads." Admiral Hyde and Hugh Hardcastle echoed his cultured titter, as, after a pause, did the Americans. "Well, it seems," he went on once the jollity had run its course, "that the party of John Adams seeks to deny citizens the right to criticize their government, no matter what the devil that government may decide to do. My God, what a concept! I must say, you chaps in the dominions *are* rather ingenious once you have your own ship. Our Whigs have much to learn from your Federalists." He stated that last sentence emphatically, without a trace of humor.

"We have much to learn from each other," Truxtun declared diplomatically. "Please accept my government's gratitude for the support Great Britain has given the United States in this matter, particularly as it regards our mercantile trade. French raids against our shipping are beginning to fall off, and we have you to thank for that. We also thank you for the use of your naval base on Saint Kitts, where we are bound next."

"Which we can legally do," Mason interjected, "only because the United States and France are not *officially* at war, and because the United States and Great Britain are not *officially* allied against France." He said this straight-faced, although the twinkle in his eye conveyed his opinion that the legal underpinnings of all this mattered naught.

"Yes, quite right, Captain," Truxtun said, playing along. "Thank you for clarifying that point. In Saint Kitts we will be joining with American naval vessels soon to depart from Portsmouth. Five of our merchant-men shall accompany us there. The others, I presume, may remain in Kingston until safe passage can be arranged to other British ports?"

Admiral Hyde made a small gesture, a signal to the servant to dis-pense another round of spirits. "They are most welcome to remain here for as long as they wish, Captain. They are, after all, providing a most critical service to His Majesty's colonies in the West Indies." Hyde shifted his not-inconsiderable weight. "Now then, if I may, I'd like to move on to the main topic we are here to discuss." For the first time that afternoon, Hyde looked directly at Richard Cutler. "I am assum-ing, Lieutenant, that your captain has informed you of circumstances on Saint-Domingue?"

"He has, Admiral."

"Might I trouble you for a summary of your understanding?"

Richard did so as best he could.

"Well done, Lieutenant," Hyde said at its conclusion. "You cer-tainly seem to have a grasp of the situation. Anything more to add, Captain?"

Truxtun shook his head. "Mr. Cutler has correctly summarized what I told him. My understanding is, however, that *you* have something more to add."

"Yes, quite." Hyde coughed delicately into a fist. "For starters, and what may come as a surprise to you, Mr. Cutler—I trust a pleasant one—you will not be alone in meeting with Toussaint L'Ouverture on Saint-Domingue. Captain Hardcastle will be accompanying you to rep-resent British interests."

Richard cast a sideways glance at his brother-in-law, who nodded slightly in reply.

"I am most pleased to hear it, Admiral. I hold Captain Hardcastle in the highest personal and professional esteem."

"As indeed he holds you, Lieutenant. It was he who recommended you for this mission. He was quite adamant about it, I must say. His endorsement carried considerable weight, given his own experience with these islands. Plus, my father holds him in high regard," Hyde concluded, as though that fact alone should be enough to decide the issue.

"Your mission is a critical one. Success means denying France the one naval base it retains in the Greater Antilles: Cap de Môle. Do you know of it? Ah, since you do, you can appreciate why denying France that base is the number-one concern of their lordships of the Admiralty. Their number-one concern thereby becomes *my* number-one concern. And success will bring us additional advantages." He held up a finger. "Coming to terms with Toussaint means reopening trade with Saint-Domingue, trade that will benefit both our countries." He held up a second finger. "Success also mitigates, if not eliminates, the threat of Negro uprisings on British-held islands and in the United States. I doubt Mr. Jefferson and his fellow slave owners suffer any delusions about the gravity of that threat.

"Success, however, depends on two critical assumptions. The first is that Toussaint L'Ouverture is a man we can trust. I must tell you that I am not yet satisfied on that score. I am, however, a man ever willing to consider new and superior information. The second assumption is that with our support Toussaint can defeat André Rigaud and his army of half-breeds. Understand: Rigaud holds Great Britain and the United States in equal contempt. He has made it quite clear that he will not treat with either of our governments under any circumstances. If he manages to defeat Toussaint, Saint-Domingue will remain our enemy for many years to come. By 'our' I mean yours and mine, Mr. Cutler. And be aware that his primary source of arms is France."

"*France*, sir?" Richard looked more confused than ever. "With respect, Admiral, is Toussaint not the lieutenant governor of Saint-Domingue?"

"He is indeed, as you rightly informed us a few moments ago."

"And is he not also commander in chief of the French forces there?"

"He is."

"Then, Admiral, why in heaven's name would France arm the enemy of the officer they have entrusted to defend their colony?"

Hyde nodded sympathetically. "I am pleased you asked that question, Mr. Cutler. It shows you are trying to wrestle with a situation that is difficult to bring to the mat and nigh impossible to hold down. The answer is, as you might suspect, rather elusive. You will not be surprised to learn that, *encore un fois*, France is playing on both sides of the wicket. Toussaint holds the upper hand at the moment, so the French act as though he's their man. But truth be told, André Rigaud is their man. It is on Rigaud that the French hang their hopes for maintaining Saint-Domingue as a French colony. Why? Because Toussaint seeks independence from France while Rigaud does not. Toussaint and Rigaud are engaged in a civil war, and it is a war in which England and America would logically support Toussaint L'Ouverture. Assuming, of course, that all else is equal. But *is* all else equal? That is what you and Captain Hardcastle must determine. Your mission is to gather sufficient facts to allow our governments to decide the proper course."

As Richard reflected on that, Hugh Hardcastle said, "And bear in mind, Lieutenant, that Toussaint is himself no novice in the art of subterfuge. He professes loyalty to France at the same time he secretly communicates with your president and with British agents on Hispaniola. Why? Because he needs American supplies and because he can no longer abide British forces opposing him. What forces he has he must concentrate on what is being called the War of Knives. That name comes from Rigaud's nasty habit of putting captured Negroes to the knife, whether or not they are in uniform, and whether they be man, woman, or child. Toussaint's most trusted general, a man named Dessalines, is accused of retaliating in the same sort of way against captured mulattoes. Higher-ranking Negroes are dealt with differently, if not with more clemency. They are likely to be strapped over the mouth of a cannon and blown to bloody shreds."

"This entire affair is really quite the ugly mess," Mason volunteered. "It seems that no one on that blasted island trusts anyone, and who can blame them? The history of that wretched place is appalling. Everybody is using everybody else for his personal gain and advantage, ethics and honor be damned."

Much like everywhere else, Richard thought. Aloud he said, "Admiral, are the French aware that Toussaint has requested assistance from the United States?"

Hyde gave him a rueful look. "That is a fair question, Lieutenant, but I am unable to give you a definitive answer." He seemed disheartened by a perceived chink in the armor of British intelligence. "As it goes to the crux of the matter, I would be most grateful if you and Captain Hardcastle could provide the answer to that question after meeting with General Toussaint."

Truxtun asked, "What information can you give us on logistics, Admiral? When and where will this parley take place?"

"I can answer the 'where.' It will take place on Île de la Gonâve, a rather large island west of Port-au-Prince, as I prefer to still call the colonial capital. We chose it for reasons of security. Toussaint has agreed to the location. We still have the 'when' to determine. It should take another couple of months to hammer out the details. As soon as I have that information, I shall send word to Saint Kitts. Then, gentlemen, it will be good luck and Godspeed to our two emissaries."

"SO, RICHARD. What do you think of our Admiral Hyde?" Hugh Hardcastle posed that question as the coach-and-two he had hired jounced eastward along the Palisadoes Spit, a seven-mile stretch of limestone running from the naval base on the spit's western tip to the town of Kingston on the mainland. They had met as planned at five o'clock at the white stucco Royal Navy headquarters building at Port Royal and boarded the well-appointed coach summoned from a local livery stable. Being off duty, they were casually dressed. With a rare summer evening breeze kicking up and the coach windows open, the sultry air was almost pleasant.

"A bit different from his father," Richard hedged.

Hugh chuckled, shook his head. "Come now, Richard, you can do better than that. Tell me what you *really* think. I distinctly recall Katherine describing him as an obscenely fat, pompous old windbag. I'd say she nailed her colors to the mast with that one! And don't forget that I served as his flag lieutenant for years before I was finally promoted."

"Which proves that discretion and patience have their rewards."

"That—and kissing an admiral's arse every time he bends over."

Their laughter was cut short when the coach lurched into a sinkhole, the harsh motion nearly flinging them out of their seats. The driver managed to restore stability and urged the horses on with a crack of a whip.

"Reminds a man of his worst days at sea," Hugh remarked as he straightened his coat. "You get used to such inconveniences whilst traveling along this godforsaken tombolo." He glanced out the left window at Kingston Bay and a flotilla of merchant vessels anchored in the far distance. To their right curled the gentle waves of the Caribbean. "Although I will always prefer Barbados, Jamaica has become the choice assignment in our navy. I wish *Constellation* was not pushing off so soon. I was hoping we might investigate some of the charms of this island together."

"I had hoped for that, too, Hugh. Perhaps on another occasion." Richard was looking ahead to clusters of red brick buildings along a cobblestone street alive with the hustle and bustle of empire. "Kingston is a lot bigger than I expected," he commented.

"It's becoming quite the place, "Hugh agreed. "Word has it that the colonial capital will soon be moved from Spanish Town. That would make sense. Kingston is the primary seaport of Jamaica, and naval headquarters is located here. And it has some of the best taverns in the Indies, as you are about to discover."

The coach swung a hard left onto Harbour Street and shivered to a halt in front of Number Sixty-Nine, a combination red-brick and black-wood-timbered tavern displaying a grand slice of yellow cheese on a sign above its door. Richard opened the door and stepped down onto the street. As he stood stretching his legs, two well-endowed and richly appointed young women walked slowly by, each giving him an appreciative once-over and a friendly smile. Richard smiled at them in return and doffed his hat in greeting.

Hugh quickly emerged from around the other side of the coach. "Good evening, ladies. Please do excuse us. I'm afraid we are frightfully late for an appointment." He bowed, gripped Richard by the elbow, and whisked him through the door of the tavern into a dim, cavernous space alive with the rumble of muted conversations and a ballet of waiters weaving among closely spaced circular tables. The room was pleasantly cool compared with the ninety-degree heat outside, and the air was heavy with tantalizing aromas.

"Please don't tell me those women are whores," Richard implored after Hugh had closed the door behind them.

Hugh laughed out loud but kept his voice low. "I hardly think so, Richard, and I doubt the royal governor would appreciate having his beloved niece referred to in that way. She was the taller of the two. Her companion is a daughter of a wealthy planter. No, I was simply protecting my sister's interests out there. Those two kitties looked like they were about to pounce and drag you away."

Richard grinned in disbelief. "That sort of beauty and status would not be allowed out in Boston in the evening without proper escort."

"So it would be in London as well. Here, though, it's considered perfectly respectable."

"Captain Hardcastle! A pleasure as always, sir!" A dark-tanned, middle-aged man whom Richard took to be the proprietor strode up briskly. "Welcome to the Cheshire Cheese. If you will come this way, I have reserved our best table for you and your guest."

That table was situated in a private alcove near the back of the room. Service for two had been set out before two candles flickering cozily upon tin sconces thick with wax. As Richard slid onto a bench on one side, Hugh slipped the host a gold florin and took the bench on the other side. The man bowed low, then snapped his fingers at a nearby waiter, demanding attention to what clearly had become a very high priority table.

"Come here often, do we?" Richard ribbed.

"As often as I can," Hugh replied honestly. "Everything on the menu is delicious. If you like fish, I recommend the grouper. The way they prepare it here is beyond description." He gave the menu a cursory scan, his mind apparently already made up. "Tonight I fancy the flying fish. It's a local delicacy I've never tried."

"Grouper for me," Richard decided.

"We'll have some wine, of course, the best the house has to offer. And don't forget our rule: no talk of business or war this evening, just family matters."

"I won't forget. And thank you again for footing the bill. An officer's wage in the American Navy is hardly what you Royal Navy types are hauling in. Rumor has it that a British frigate captain like yourself can retire in luxury after only ten years of service."

"He can retire in luxury in one year," Hugh affirmed, "if he's lucky enough to come upon the entire French fleet and skilled enough to take it as a prize."

Richard laughed. Then, in a more serious tone, "Hugh, do you ever have occasion to visit my family on Barbados?"

"I do, and I always look forward to it. I was ever so pleased when John returned from England. He's a favorite of mine, despite his rather stuffy behavior. And Cynthia is such a dear. You've never met their son, have you?"

"Actually, I have; years ago. He was quite young then. On my last visit to Barbados he and his mother were in England."

"Yes, they went there to visit a medical specialist in London. As you may be aware, there's something wrong with poor Joseph. It's such a bloody shame. He's a fine-looking, strapping lad, and quite intelligent. But he seems completely disinterested in anything other than mathematics. His parents have tried everything to engage his attention and are at their wits' end. Sadly, no doctor seems able to diagnose the problem or advance any sort of cure."

"I am very sorry to hear that. When I saw John during my last visit, he told me that Joseph had some sort of ailment. But that was about all he told me. You know John: always trying to paint the bright picture. This must be terribly hard on him and Cynthia."

"I can't imagine. At least Joseph is in no physical danger. And he may well grow out of it. On a lighter note, Robin and Julia are expecting their fourth child very soon."

"Are they! Good for them! They're doing well?"

"Very much so. They are one family whom I believe have settled in for good on the Indies. I can't imagine them leaving Barbados. And why would they? The life they enjoy should make anyone envious. It does me."

"That's my impression, too. My younger brother Caleb is planning to visit there in a few months. Father wants him to become more involved in the family business now that I'm in the Navy. I think John and Robin will enjoy having him. They'll make excellent mentors."

"Yes, they will. Now, tell me about your family. I am most interested to hear about Katherine and the children, of course, but do try to include everyone."

As the first bottle of claret yielded to a second, complemented by platters of grilled fish and fresh vegetables and fruits, Richard recounted the news of his life and family. He concluded with the birth of Zeke Crabtree, whose mother, Lizzy Cutler Crabtree, had once been engaged to Hugh's late brother, Jamie.

"I'm so happy for Lizzy," Hugh said, with feeling. "She spent far too many years of her youth mourning Jamie. By the bye, are you aware that my brother Jeremy once carried a flame for her? Oh, yes, and a rather hot one at that. He did nothing about it, of course, whilst Jamie was alive. Later, duty prevented him from going home to England to visit her. By the time he was given leave to return to Fareham, Lizzy had left for America with her father, and your friend Agreen was soon to sail in and board her, so to speak. I suspect Jeremy will always harbor a grudge against him for that."

"If he does, he doesn't show it. Agee visited Jeremy in Gibraltar before sailing on to Algiers. Jeremy showed him every courtesy and ordered *Falcon*'s hold filled to the brim with fresh provisions. I am forever in his debt for the generosity he showed *Eagle*'s crew. He did far more than mere courtesy or family loyalty required."

"Well, that's Jeremy for you—ever the consummate gentleman. I hope to see him when I sail home in a couple of months. It has been too many years since the last time."

Richard's fork stopped halfway to his mouth. "You're going home, Hugh? On leave?"

"On what one day will be permanent leave, Richard. I have decided to swallow the anchor and seek an honorable profession ashore. Ah, I can see you are surprised by that announcement. It surprises me even as I say it. But it is a promise I have given my fiancée, and it's a promise I intend to keep."

Richard placed the fork down on his plate. "Your *fiancée?* Hold on a second, Hugh. One step at a time, if you don't mind. I didn't even know you were engaged. Is she a local woman?"

"Today is full of surprises, isn't it? By the bye, how's your grouper?"

"Delicious. Now please stay on subject."

Hugh grinned. "No. She's from Portsea. You may recall it. It's a town near Fareham. Her name is Phoebe. Phoebe Clausen. She's nine years younger than I and, Lord knows, a great deal better looking. I met her two years ago whilst home in England during the hurricane season. We've been corresponding ever since and seeing each other whenever possible. She visited me on Barbados not long ago, and before sailing to Jamaica I asked for her hand. Displaying shockingly poor judgment, she accepted."

Richard shook his head in delighted disbelief. "My God, Hugh, that's wonderful! Absolutely wonderful! Congratulations to you both. It's high time you struck your colors. Have you written to Katherine?"

"No. You're the first in the family to know. And there's more. Phoebe and I plan to sail to America someday. Her two siblings are already there—one, a sister, lives in Rhode Island, and a brother lives in Connecticut. Her father died unexpectedly several years ago, and her mother, I fear, is not long for this world. As to my side of the family, both my parents are in poor health. And I have been away at sea for so long that I have few meaningful relationships left in England. So starting a new life in America seems just right for us. However, I have told

Phoebe that I cannot leave the service until after my father has passed on. It would break his heart to see me do it. He and I may not always see eye to eye, but he is my father and I owe him that. You understand. You're his son-in-law."

"I do understand," Richard said, thinking of his own past efforts to measure up to his father-in-law's expectations. Then his face lit up. "Hugh, I have a thought: Katherine and Lizzy are planning to sail to England with the children next summer to visit their parents. Might you possibly tie their visit to your wedding? I can't imagine anything that would bring them more joy."

Hugh clapped his hands hard. "By Jove, Richard! What a capital notion! We *must* do that. I shall write to Phoebe first thing in the morning. I shall also write to Katherine, though I suspect you will beat me to the punch. How thrilled Phoebe will be to meet her and Lizzy and the children! Is there any chance, any chance at all, that you might scare up some shore leave and join us?"

"That depends on the French, doesn't it?"

"I daresay it does." Hugh poured out two final glasses of wine with a surprisingly steady hand. He clinked his glass against Richard's.

"To good hunting, brother. And to swift victory."

Nine

Saint Kitts
October 1798

"**Y**OUR REPORT PLEASE, Mr. Porter."

Midn. David Porter, junior officer of the deck and a towering hulk of a youth, cast Lieutenant Sterrett a nervous look. His eyes flicked to westward, where the remnants of a ferocious squall lingered, then back to the third lieutenant. A quarter-hour earlier that squall had lashed the convoy with torrents of heavy rain and windswept seas. So sudden had been its surge that *Constellation*'s crew barely had time to shorten sail, hook relieving tackle to the tiller, remove the hammocks from their nettings and toss them belowdecks, and secure hatches and guns for heavy weather. So violent was the storm's energy that visual contact with other vessels in the convoy had been temporarily lost in the murk and swirling sea froth, along with the strict sailing formation Lt. John Rodgers insisted they follow.

"Four merchantmen are returning to station, sir," Porter responded, his voice fraught with worry, as though what he was about to say was somehow his fault. "But, sir, *Louisa Spaulding* is unaccounted for. She's nowhere to be found." He added hopefully, "I'm sure we'll spot her soon enough."

"Thank you, Mr. Porter," Sterrett said. "You may return to station. And may I remind you once again that when reporting to a superior officer, you must refrain from offering a personal opinion unless that opinion is specifically requested."

"Aye, aye, sir. I do apologize, sir. It won't happen again."

"It had best not, Mr. Porter."

Sterrett answered the midshipman's salute, saw him off, then glanced up at the foremast and mainmast crosstrees. Lookouts had resumed their positions there, searching to westward for the missing two-masted merchant brig. He hesitated a moment, anticipating a cry of discovery from aloft. When none came, he turned aft to where Thomas Truxtun and the other officers had gathered.

Sterrett snapped a salute. "*Louisa Spaulding* is unaccounted for, Captain," he reported.

"I am aware of that, Mr. Sterrett, thank you," Truxtun replied. "We were about to discuss the possibilities. Mr. Rodgers, you were on deck when the storm struck. Did you notice her experiencing difficulties?"

"None, sir, except for the obvious. Being the most eastward, she was the first vessel hit. When the squall struck us, I was more concerned with *Constellation*."

"Quite understandable. Mr. Carter? Mr. Waverly? Anything to add?"

"What I remember, sir," the ship's master replied, the furrows of his brow wrinkled in thought, "is that she was carrying too much canvas when she was hit. She had hell to pay trying to take it in. When the storm hit us, though, I couldn't see much beyond our foredeck." He gazed out westward, as they all did, to where stray beams of sunlight were beginning to break through the thick, grayish gloom. "If you were to ask me what I think, Captain, I'd say she tore her sails or otherwise lost control and was unable to lie to." All of the merchant ships had orders to lie to under reefed main topsail and upper staysails in the event of violent weather and to remain that way until the storm had passed.

"Are you suggesting, Mr. Waverly, that you think *Louisa* was broached-to or pooped?"

"Either is a possibility, Captain. But had she broached-to or pooped, we'd likely have spotted her by now. She could not have drifted far, laid over like that. More likely she was simply carried away. Out there." Again his gaze slid to westward.

Truxtun took a moment to estimate drift, current, wind conditions, and the lapse of time since the squall's onslaught. Before he could speak, a distant rumbling sounded to the west. A positioning signal? A plea for help? Or merely a final peal of thunder?

"Very well, Mr. Waverly," he said, his mind made up. "We shall wear ship. Set her on a course west by south, a half south." The captain then addressed Midn. Harry Ayres on duty nearby. "Mr. Ayres, signal the convoy to assume search formation. Mr. Sterrett, please summon the boatswain. Mr. Dent, my compliments to Lieutenant Cutler and will he please join me on deck."

Sterrett stepped forward, speaking trumpet in hand. "Pass word for the boatswain!"

Boatswain Frederick Bowles quick-stepped aft. As a senior petty officer he wore the standard Navy-issue loose-fitting shirt and trousers and buff vest. His single badge of authority, a polished silver boatswain's whistle, hung at his chest, suspended from a thin leather lanyard draped around his neck.

He saluted smartly. "You sent for me, Captain?"

"Yes, Mr. Bowles. Call all hands. We are about to wear ship in search of *Louisa*. After we've worn, I want the courses clewed up and up buntlines on the tops'ls. Be prepared to drop them at my command. And return hammocks to the nettings. Clear for action and make preparations for beating to quarters. Lieutenant Carter's Marines will assist you."

"Aye, aye, sir." Bowles whirled around and passed by Richard Cutler striding aft.

"Damage to the gun deck, Mr. Cutler?"

Richard saluted. "No, Captain," he said. "Some loose shot rolling about is all. We secured the guns before the storm hit."

"Good. Now let loose the guns, both sides, and open the ports. Double-shot the guns and stand by for further orders."

"Aye, aye, sir."

"Mr. Carter."

"Sir!"

"Once we have gear and furnishings stowed, deploy your Marines behind the hammocks with muskets at the ready. Summon the drummers and stand by to send men to the tops. You have my permission to unlock the magazine. Mr. Dent?"

"Captain!"

"Stand by to convey my orders to the gun deck."

"Aye, aye, sir!" the young midshipman fairly shouted. He squared his shoulders and puffed out his chest, clasping his hands behind him in the age-old stance of a sea officer on his quarterdeck.

"All hands! Stations for wearing ship! Up mainsail and spanker! Brace in the yardarms! Up helm!" At Waverly's commands, the American frigate began the evolutions that brought her from a close haul on a larboard tack, around twenty points on the compass stern-first through the wind, until the strengthening northeasterly breeze fell on her starboard quarter and she had her yards squared and jib sheets drawn and spanker hauled out. With less efficiency, the four merchantmen followed suit. Now on a westerly course, the five vessels in the convoy fanned out along a half-mile stretch of ocean, two merchantmen on each side of the frigate. *Constellation* sailed with her mainsails clewed up and her topsails brailed up as she went in search of the sixth vessel.

Within a quarter-hour the gloom had dissipated to where they could see a half-mile or so ahead. Regardless, *Constellation*'s officers continued to rely more on sound than sight. Yes, there it was again. Closer this time. Much closer. Suddenly, flashes of light flared within the murk, followed seconds later by a sequence of angry rumbles and then one—no, two—flashes to the right of the first flashes, along with milder rumbles.

"Mr. Rodgers," Truxtun commanded, "let go the topsails. Mr. Waverly, please take the helm. Keep her steady as she goes. Gentlemen, we shall beat to quarters."

Rodgers relayed the sailing order to Boatswain Bowles. Amid a twitter of whistle calls, he stepped forward and raised a speaking trumpet to his lips.

"*Beat to quarters!*"

On the weather and gun decks, Marine drummers struck up a staccato tattoo that echoed through the ship, sending men hurtling to battle stations.

Below on the gun deck, Richard Cutler knelt near the stem of the frigate and peered through gun port number one, starboard side. He could not see much from that perspective, just enough to distinguish a pulse of pale yellow within the uniform gray ahead. He counted the seconds. One. Two. Three. Then he heard it: the heavy thud of a gun's discharge.

He rose to his feet and walked along a deck strewn with sand and damp with water sucked out from the pumps. He sensed the eyes of every man upon him. Even without a verbal explanation, everyone on that gun deck understood that this was no drill. The drumbeat had ceased. The space became deathly quiet, save for the sound of seawater gurgling along the frigate's hull and the footfalls of powder monkeys delivering round shot and six-pound flannel bags of powder from the magazine.

"Is your gun ready?" Richard asked each gun captain, forcing his voice to sound nonchalant, as if he were inquiring after the man's health or the welfare of his children. Each captain acknowledged. "Double shot, level aim. Understood?" Again each captain acknowledged.

Richard waited amidships until the head and spindly torso of John Dent appeared in the open hatchway above.

"Stand by to fire number fourteen gun, Mr. Cutler," the midshipman shouted down.

"How much time, Mr. Dent?"

The midshipman glanced forward. "Ten minutes, sir."

"Very well. I'm coming up."

Richard climbed up to the weather deck. He faced aft and saluted Captain Truxtun, acknowledging his order. At the starboard mainmast chain-wale he clung to a weather shroud and searched the waters ahead. With the extra spread of canvas laid on, *Constellation* had gathered speed and was now closing the gap on the drama being acted out dead ahead.

A French brig was perhaps a quarter-mile away, her stern to the American frigate, her starboard guns—eight to a side, 12-pounders most likely—making small play of the two 6-pounder larboard guns being fired boldly but ineffectively by *Louisa Spaulding*. The two ships were half a cable length apart on more or less parallel courses. *Louisa* was in dire straits. Her sails had been ripped and holed by both storm and langrage, and her top-hamper was cut up and sliced through. She was effectively dead in the water, and her tormentor was acutely aware of her handicap. The French captain seemed to be biding his time and enjoying his victim's plight, like a jungle beast stalking a wounded prey, playing with it, taunting it, savoring the conquest that was, by all indications, his.

Richard strained to read the name on the stern of the French brig but could not. If this brig were not *Le Léopard*, as he hoped she was, she had to be a sister ship. His fists clenched. There was a debt to be settled here.

Returning below to the gun deck, he again peered out through gun port number one. *Constellation* was rapidly gaining on the brig. *Louisa* had ceased firing, either because she had lost her will to fight or she could no longer bring her guns to bear. Or perhaps she had seen what the French ship apparently had not yet noticed: an American frigate bearing down on them under three white pyramids of taut canvas, whitewater flying out from her bow, her length considerably longer than the Frenchman's, her firepower considerably greater.

The directive came shortly from Midshipman Dent. "Captain's compliments, Mr. Cutler, and you may fire number fourteen gun."

Number fourteen was the sternmost gun on the starboard side—one of those braced within the captain's quarters—the last gun to bear on the approaching enemy. It carried authority nonetheless, and a firm warning to the brig to strike her colors. When the gun roared its challenge to windward, Richard, in company with everyone else on the frigate, expected the brig to haul down her ensign and surrender.

Incredibly, she did not, although her crew had clearly spotted the frigate bearing down on them and had heard the warning shot. Her deck and standing rigging had come alive with activity. Whether owing to some misplaced Gallic bravado, anger at losing a plump victim, or a conviction that an American warship would not fire upon a French vessel, her captain let fall the courses and made a run for it.

It was a fool's gamble. Not only was *Constellation* bigger and more powerful, she was also faster, even with her courses clewed up. Quickly she closed the distance between them, her forward guns coming to bear on the brig's stern, fifty yards to leeward. Still the brig refused to strike. Suddenly, two forward ports flashed fire. Ahead, off *Constellation*'s starboard bow, two tall spouts of water ranged up.

"*Eh bien,*" Richard muttered to himself. "*Si c'est la façon que vous le voulez . . .*" In a louder voice, he said, "Gun captains, at my command. Battery number one . . . as your guns bear . . . *fire!*"

Five gun captains yanked lanyards, sparking priming powder that raced to the barrels, ignited the main charge, and sent trucks squealing backward and round shot hurtling forward.

Richard strode down the deck, glanced out through gun port number six. He checked the quoins. They were halfway in as ordered, leveling the guns point-blank at the full length of the brig.

"Battery number two . . . on the uproll . . . *fire!*"

Five explosions sent five more trucks lurching backward. Orange flames and white sparks exploded out of the barrels, and acrid smoke curled back across the gun deck and out the larboard ports.

Richard peered out through gun port number eleven, fanning away the thick smoke to improve his vision. What he saw out there—a severely crippled vessel bobbing up and down on the waves like a wounded bird—convinced him to forgo a third salvo. However great his thirst for revenge, he had no stomach for senseless slaughter; 480 pounds of double shot from ten guns had done the job. Lieutenant Carter, in command of the smaller guns up on the weather deck, had apparently drawn the same conclusion. His guns went quiet as well. High above in the fighting tops, the *thump!* and *pop!* of daisy-cutters and musketry became sporadic, then ceased altogether.

Silence enveloped the gun deck, save for the background clatter of men coughing, wheezing, and spitting. Richard walked amidships to the ladder leading up.

"Well done, lads," he congratulated each gun crew as he passed by. "Be at your ease, but remain on station."

On deck, Richard walked slowly aft, his gaze never leaving the brig now sagging off the wind astern. Her larboard railing and deckwork had been ravaged, splintered; and her main chain-wale had been shot away, jeopardizing the stability of her mainmast. At the base of the foremast an ugly white gash showed like teeth; below the chain-wale, not far above the water line, a round shot had smashed a jagged hole through a strake. Even her bowsprit had been shot through, cut in half, denying her jib and flying jib a base of support. Richard searched the after rigging for the ensign. He saw only its severed halyard being dragged behind in the sea. Off in the distance he heard the cheers and huzzahs of *Louisa*'s crew.

At the helm, Captain Truxtun returned his salute. "Well, Lieutenant," he said with an approving nod, "you made short work of them, didn't you? Which is why, I assume, you did not engage the third battery?"

"Yes, sir," Richard said. "The brig was finished. We had her as a prize and I saw no reason to damage her further."

"Very sensible. Please send my compliments to the men."

"I shall do that, Captain. Thank you."

"Quite the day for us, eh, Mr. Cutler? " Truxtun was clearly enjoying the moment. "Our first action, and our first prize."

"Yes, sir. Congratulations, sir." Richard touched his hat. He turned to go, and then turned around to ask, "What is the name of that brig, Captain?"

Truxtun glanced at John Rodgers, who said with a broad smile, "*L'Albatros*, Mr. Cutler. Quite fitting, isn't it. Our first prize, a big sea bird clipped of its wings?"

FOR A SQUARE-RIGGED SHIP, sailing eastward across the Caribbean Sea required a great deal more time than the other way around. Given the prevailing easterlies and a square-rigger's inability to lie closer to the wind than sixty-six degrees off it, a ship sailing upwind from the

Greater to the Lesser Antilles did well to shape a course for Curaçao, off the coast of Venezuela, before tacking due north. As she approached the Puerto Rican archipelago, she could then tack over a final time on a close haul to her destination. Such a zigzag sail plan could add as many as three weeks to the one week a square-rigger usually required to sail downwind from Saint Kitts to Jamaica.

By the time *Constellation* had Saint Kitts somewhere below the distant horizon, *L'Albatros* and *Louisa Spalding* had been sufficiently refitted to have towing lines cast off. The convoy had been joined the day before by the American naval brig *Baltimore*, fortuitously sighted as she emerged through the Leeward Passage east of San Juan. That evening, Thomas Truxtun invited his commissioned officers to dine with him and the brig's captain in his dining alcove.

It seemed at first as though the evening would provide more entertainment than information. Lt. Josiah Speake, *Baltimore*'s captain, had little to report beyond what Admiral Hyde had related on board *Queen* in Port Royal, except for the electrifying news—music to any naval officer's ear—that two months earlier, in August, Horatio Nelson had orchestrated a momentous victory over the French at Aboukir Bay, near Alexandria at the mouth of the Nile. Nelson's force captured or destroyed the bulk of the French Mediterranean fleet—including its one-hundred-gun flagship, *L'Orient*—and stranded Napoleon and his grande armée among the pyramids. Details of the victory had spread rapidly. Speake had learned of them two days before weighing anchor. By now, he predicted, those details should have reached British naval bases throughout the Western Hemisphere.

"It would appear that Boney and his plan for world conquest have just been given a swift kick in the ass, if you'll pardon my French," Speake gleefully concluded his account. Everyone at the table chuckled at his use of words.

"What of Admiral Nelson?" Richard asked in a serious tone after the mirth had quieted. However much he might admire Nelson's well-publicized resolve to position himself on his quarterdeck in full admiral's regalia during battle—to share the same risks as his officers and to serve as an inspiration to his crew—he could not approve of a commander making himself an easy target for enemy sharpshooters. Often in the privacy of his thoughts Richard had placed Horatio Nelson in Thomas Truxtun's position. If ever a sea officer embodied the principles of leadership and naval command espoused by Truxtun, that man was Rear Admiral Sir Horatio Nelson. "How did he fare in the battle?"

"That's a story unto itself," Speake replied, pleasantly aware that the entire company was hanging on his every word. "During the battle Nelson was grazed on the forehead by a round of grapeshot. His surgeon examined him and told him not to worry because the wound was superficial. But, for whatever reason, Nelson did not believe him. Perhaps he had lost a lot of blood. In any event, he was convinced the end was nigh. At the battle's conclusion he requested final rites from the ship's chaplain. Which, glory be, were not necessary. The surgeon was right after all. The wound *was* superficial, and England's hero lives to fight another day!"

"God be praised!" the entire company exclaimed.

Baltimore's captain had another piece of news to cheer the captain's table. Two additional naval vessels, he reported, were scheduled to depart Portsmouth for Saint Kitts. The sloops of war *Virginia* and *Richmond* would bolster what Navy Secretary Benjamin Stoddert now referred to grandly as the Guadeloupe Station because Saint Kitts was ideally positioned to keep close tabs on the last significant French naval base in the West Indies.

"And, sir?" Speake said, smiling, "I am informed that *Constitution* is scheduled to sail from Boston within the fortnight. Her destination is also the Indies."

"Is that a fact?" Truxtun said, his voice laced with sarcasm. "I must say, Lieutenant, you do possess a flair for the dramatic. Exactly *where* in the Indies, might I inquire?"

Speake reached into his left inside coat pocket. "I believe you'll find the answer in here, sir. I've saved the best for last." He passed down the table a small sachet with the name "Captain Thomas Truxtun, USS *Constellation*" written in bold script upon it. "Secretary Stoddert told me to hand this to you personally—and perhaps gave me a clue of what's inside." He said those last few words rather mysteriously, and his eyes twinkled with delight as he met the inquiring gaze of the assembled officers.

"Thank you, Lieutenant," Truxtun said dryly. He broke the official wax seal and unfolded the flaps. "Gentlemen, if you will excuse me for a moment."

His officers watched in silence as Truxtun began reading. He nodded now and again as his eyes followed the script down the page. At its conclusion he arched his eyebrows.

"Well, gentlemen," he said, keeping his eyes transfixed on the letter, "it appears that *Constitution* is bound for the Royal Navy base at

Prince Rupert Bay in Dominica. And she is to be joined there by *United States*."

Each officer at the table recognized the significance of that news. Dominica was as close to Guadeloupe to the south as Saint Kitts was to the north. With the American frigates *Constitution* and *United States* stationed off the island of Dominica, the United States and Great Britain would have the French navy in a vise. Stoddert's widely publicized theory—that the best way to protect American shipping on the eastern seaboard was to take the war to the Indies—was about to be put into practice.

Truxtun waited until the excited chatter subsided and he again commanded his officers' attention. "And," he said, as though what he had to say was nothing out of the ordinary, "it appears that the Navy Department has seen fit to promote me to the rank of commodore." With that, he folded the letter, tucked it into a coat pocket, picked up his knife and fork, and resumed eating.

John Rodgers jumped up. "Congratulations, sir! Congratulations indeed!" He raised his glass. "Gentlemen, I give you Thomas Truxtun, the first commodore of our United States Navy."

The other officers scraped back chairs and rose to their feet.

"Hear! Hear!" they shouted. And for one of the few times in anyone's recollection, Thomas Truxtun did not deflect praise directed at him.

THE TWO LOOKOUTS had been told to search for, and had apparently spotted across twenty miles of open sea, a four-thousand-foot-tall dormant volcano. That was the landmark that charts and sea lore and Mother Nature identified as the island of Saint Kitts. After their initial cries of tentative discovery had drawn all eyes aloft, both lookouts remained mute, as though not yet convinced that the image in the circular lens of their long glasses was not a mirage. Convinced at last, able-rated seaman Toby Higgins cupped his hands to his mouth.

"Deck, there! Land ho! Two points to loo'ard."

"Saint Kitts?" shouted up Robert Simms, a boatswain's mate stationed directly below him at the base of the foremast.

"Aye, sir. Saint Kitts."

"Very good, Higgins. I shall inform the captain."

As *Constellation* and her convoy approached the sixty-eight-square-mile island, its contours began to assume discernible forms. Closer in, it was not Mount Liamuiga that commanded everyone's attention, the volcano's impressive height notwithstanding. Rather, it was the fortress erected upon Brimstone Hill on the island's western shore. Fort George emerged from the distance as a colossal structure of black volcanic rock towering eight hundred feet above sea level. At the bastion's peak, atop its highest tower, fluttered the red cross of Saint George. In 1782, as British forces took leave of America and fought on in the West Indies against France, Britain's ancient enemy, Admiral de Grasse had achieved what many had considered impossible: he had blown open a breach in the seven-foot-thick walls after a long and savage naval bombardment, and he had ordered French Marines inside to overpower the small British army garrison. A year later, with Saint Kitts restored to British hegemony by the Treaty of Paris, British military engineers went to work to ensure that Fort George would never again suffer the humiliation of surrender. By 1798 its massive embrasures and parapets and blockhouses had earned Fort George the nickname "Gibraltar of the West Indies." Like its counterpart on the southern tip of Spain, Fort George stood as proof positive that henceforth it would take an act of God, not man, to wrest Saint Kitts and its sister island of Nevis from the grip of the British Empire.

The American convoy sailed past Fort George, southeastward toward Basseterre Roads on the southwestern tip of the island. As they approached the colonial capital, it occurred to Richard that while Saint Kitts had much to offer Great Britain's army, it had less to offer the Royal Navy. Set within a slight indentation of coastline on an otherwise featureless shore, Basse-Terre's principal claim to safe harbor was its location on the leeward side of the island. Dockage there was rudimentary, unlike anything Richard had experienced at other British naval bases. The few wooden quays were designed to oblige not British warships, but rather the small, single-masted island packets that hauled cargo back and forth between Nevis, Montserrat, Saba, Saint Martin's, and Anguilla. For sailors serving in larger vessels such as *Constellation*, a ship's boat provided the best means of getting ashore.

Clustered within an array of small fishing and transport vessels in the tiny harbor were four Royal Navy vessels: a light frigate, a brig, and two sloops of war. Not much of a squadron, Richard mused, although one perfectly suited to give chase to the brigands and pirates who lurked in the secluded coves and shallow waters of the Lesser Antilles. One also suited to extend military honors. As *Constellation* coasted to her anchorage, the starboard side of the British frigate *Concorde* erupted in salute, an honor immediately answered by the larboard side of the American frigate.

"Anchor's secure, Captain," John Rodgers reported after the anchor line had been paid out ten fathoms and the anchor watch had confirmed that the great iron hook held firm in the sandy bottom. At his captain's insistence, Rodgers used the lower-rank address. Truxtun might be commodore of the squadron, he had told his officers, but he remained captain of this vessel.

"Very well, Mr. Rodgers. Once you have seen to the disposition of *L'Albatros* and her prisoners, you may inform the boatswain that the men are granted shore leave in rotation. However, my word of warning stands that every man be reminded before going ashore that I will not tolerate misconduct or impropriety of any kind. We are guests of the British. We are representatives of our country. And we must act accordingly. I loathe using the lash, but if I hear so much as a rumor of public drunkenness or debauchery, I shall not hesitate to use it. Is that understood?"

"Perfectly, sir," Rodgers said. Nothing in his voice indicated that he had already passed on that warning, in no uncertain terms, to the entire ship's complement. "I quite agree that use of the cat is sometimes necessary to enforce discipline."

"Indeed, Mr. Rodgers," Truxtun said. "But only in extreme circumstances."

Within the hour *Constellation* piped on board Sir Robert Thomson, the regally clad governor of the island, and David Clarkson, a white-goateed, deeply tanned man from Philadelphia who several years ago had settled on the island with his family. Today, Clarkson served as provisioner of British warships, a profession he had learned during the war as purser in the Continental frigate *Trumbull*. Joining them under an eight-foot-tall white canvas awning stretched across the aft half of the frigate was the captain of the British frigate *Concorde*, in full-dress uniform.

"I am honored, Captain Sweeney," Truxtun greeted him once the side party had piped him on board. However gracious and reassuring Thomson and Clarkson had been in welcoming the Americans to Saint Kitts, Edward Sweeney was the man to whom Truxtun most wanted to talk. At the first appropriate pause in the conversation he turned his full attention to the British frigate commander. "Captain, if I may, do you have intelligence from Guadeloupe?"

Edward Sweeney bowed slightly, his diminutive, almost sickly form reminding Richard of Horatio Nelson when they had met years ago in

Antigua. His olive-green eyes shone bright nevertheless, and his face held the hard stamp of a commander in war.

"First, Captain Truxtun, may I say how delighted I am to make your acquaintance. Your reputation precedes you, sir. To answer your question, yes, I do have intelligence from Guadeloupe; though I fear it is not the sort of intelligence you had hoped to hear. Your naval schooner *Retaliation* has been captured by the French."

"*Retaliation*? Isn't that the French privateer that Captain Decatur captured off the coast of New Jersey?"

"The same, Captain."

"How did that happen? And when?"

"On the twentieth of last month, off Guadeloupe. Exactly *how* it happened remains a bit of a mystery. Apparently her captain, a lieutenant named Bainbridge, became separated from his two consorts when they took off in pursuit of a privateer. Sailing on his own, Bainbridge came upon two large vessels he took to be British. He raised the British signal, with no response. Nor was there a response when he raised the American signal. For a reason no one seems able to explain, least of all Bainbridge himself, he decided to take a closer look. What he found were two large French frigates. When they opened fire on him, he surrendered."

"He did not return fire? For the sake of honor?"

"No, Captain, he did not."

Truxtun grimaced. "Go on."

"Captain Bainbridge believed himself hopelessly outgunned. And his consorts were too far away to render assistance. Bainbridge still had a card, however, and he played it well. After his schooner was taken, he managed to convince the French commander that his consorts—the sloops *Montezuma* and *Norfolk*—were too heavily armed for the French to engage. So the French abandoned the chase, allowing the sloops to make good their escape."

"These two French frigates, what were their names?"

"One was *L'Insurgente,* the other *Le Volontaire.*"

"I know of *L'Insurgente*. She's a *Sémillante*-class forty-gun frigate, reputed to be the fastest ship in the French navy. What of *Retaliation*'s officers and crew?"

"Captain Bainbridge and his commissioned officers were released on their parole and have returned to America. The crew were taken to Basse-Terre in Guadeloupe as prisoners."

Standard procedure, Richard mused as he listened to the exchange. The rules of naval engagement were quite specific on the disposition of a captured vessel and her crew, and most maritime powers honored those rules. Would revolutionary France? He had his doubts. "Sir, with your permission?"

"Yes, Mr. Cutler?"

Richard's eyes swung to Sweeney. "Captain, to your knowledge, is Victor Hugues still *commissair civil* on Guadeloupe?" He was referring to the French official known as "the Colonial Robespierre," a fervent revolutionary who had been placed in authority after French forces recaptured Guadeloupe in 1794. Detesting royalist sympathizers in equal measure with the British, Hugues had established a regime in Basse-Terre that mirrored the horrors of revolutionary Paris. He ordered a guillotine erected in the public square of the colonial capital and the head of every accused royalist sympathizer on the island chopped off, along with that of anyone possessing a drop of British blood. So deep ran his hatred for anything British that he had ordered the body of the erstwhile British governor exhumed and his remains tossed into a sewer.

Nor did America escape his wrath. Viewing Americans as British in both body and politics, Hugues granted a privateer's commission to any vessel that applied for one and set loose a fleet to plunder American shipping, claiming a handsome commission on monies raised from the sale of seized goods before sending the balance on to Paris. The view was widely held in European capitals as well as in Philadelphia that if one were to name those French officials most responsible for the current *guerre de course* between the United States and France, Victor Hugues would be high on anyone's short list.

"He is, Lieutenant," Sweeney replied, "although we have reason to believe he won't hold power much longer. Our spies in Basse-Terre report that Hugues has lost favor with the Directory. Apparently he has overstepped his bounds. He has, in fact, become a major obstacle to peace initiatives."

Richard cast him a quizzical look. "Peace initiatives? What peace initiatives, Captain?"

"Why, those involving your country, Lieutenant."

Richard glanced at Truxtun.

"Are you telling us, Captain Sweeney," Truxtun said, "that the French government is pursuing peace initiatives with the United States?"

"I am, Captain Truxtun. France desires peace with your country, and for a very good reason. French islands in the Indies, including Guadeloupe, cannot survive on their own resources. Until recently, privateers brought in the food and supplies they required, but privateering had been on the wane ever since your navy entered these waters. Today, many innocent people on Guadeloupe are suffering, and they blame Victor Hugues for their pain. His support has eroded, which is why we believe he will soon be replaced."

"How soon, do you think?"

"Please God, not *too* soon, Captain. The Royal Navy needs your ships here, since most of ours have been recalled over there." He pointed in the general direction of Europe. "And of course, we are still feeling the effects of the recent mutinies." He was referring to two widely publicized strikes by British sailors—one at Spithead, the other at the Nore—demanding better pay and living conditions on board ship. Shockingly, to those familiar with the unyielding dictates of Whitehall, the British Admiralty agreed to make certain concessions. "As you can imagine, such incidents make us particularly vulnerable in a time of war," Sweeney noted, "and we need the few friends we have to stay with us."

"Thank you for being so forthcoming, Captain. Whatever peace initiatives may be under way, I can assure you that America will do her part for as long as possible."

During the ensuing weeks the crews of the American squadron settled into a lifestyle that, when off duty and not out on patrol, allowed them to revel in the sun-drenched tropical paradise amid a local citizenry eager to accommodate a young topman or waister, or a somewhat older lieutenant of Marines, too long away from the scent of a woman. For the officers and crew of *Constellation*, it was back to strict naval discipline when, in mid-December, signals were received from Fort George announcing that a British mail packet had been sighted closing in on Basseterre Roads. Dispatches had arrived from Admiral Parker in Port Royal, Jamaica.

Ten

Île de la Gonâve, Saint-Domingue
December 1798

"**G**OOD TO SEE you again, Captain Truxtun. Welcome on board *Redoubtable*. Might I offer you a spot of tea or coffee? Or something stronger, perhaps?"

Thomas Truxtun's hard, sunburned face relaxed into a smile. "I seem to recall, Captain Hardcastle, that the last time I requested coffee on a Royal Navy vessel, I left the after cabin rather tipsy. Dare I try again?"

"By all means, Captain," Hugh Hardcastle said straight-faced.

"Then I shall take it black, no sugar."

"Black, no sugar, it is." He nodded to his steward and then looked toward Richard Cutler. "Lieutenant?"

Richard quickly turned his attention back to Hugh. He had been giving the captain's cabin a quick once-over, wondering how a post captain who had attained such heights of rank and promise in such a splendid service as His Majesty's navy could give it up so easily as Hugh seemed to be doing. "Coffee for me as well, Captain," Richard said, "with sugar—assuming, of course, that it's Cutler sugar."

Hardcastle gave him a rueful look. "I'm told it is. Certainly that is what I ordered the purser to procure. I have my doubts, though. You know pursers. Price is their one and only consideration, and even you must admit that Cutler sugar tends to be rather expensive. And as to what you charge for your rum—well! I am the first to confirm its texture and taste; but good Lord, Lieutenant, how do you get away with demanding such a price?"

Richard grinned. "We don't demand the price, Captain. We offer it. And people pay it willingly. My father has been telling me since I was a child that whatever it is you're selling, make it the best money can buy and price it high, to increase its value in the mind of the buyer and to confirm his good judgment. Do that, and you'll never lack for quality customers. And we never have."

Hardcastle contemplated that. "I look forward to meeting your father, Lieutenant. I daresay I could learn a great deal from him."

"As do I still."

After a pot of rich Jamaican coffee had made the rounds, Thomas Truxtun switched topics to the matter at hand. "What of preparations, Captain? When do you meet with General Toussaint?"

Hugh Hardcastle nodded as if in recognition that the time for polite banter had passed. "We weren't certain exactly when you would arrive here, though we did manage to predict the day. General Toussaint and his entourage arrived on the island this morning. He has with him his personal guard and a general named Dessalines, his most trusted officer. He puts great stock in Dessalines' counsel."

"How many soldiers does he have in his personal guard?"

"Ten."

"*Ten*? Is that all?"

"Yes, Captain, it is." Hardcastle's tone conveyed surprise at Truxtun's question. "His main army is encamped near Port-au-Prince. Transporting a large number of them out here would have been logistically challenging. It would also have raised a red flag for André Rigaud, whose base is on the mainland south of here. Besides, why bring in a larger force? Rigaud may control the southern regions of Saint-Domingue, but our ships have been on patrol around this island for three days and have reported seeing nothing. As we speak, Royal Marines are setting up a perimeter near the cove where Lieutenant Cutler and I will be meeting with General Toussaint later this afternoon. Your Marines are most welcome to assist us. You say you have how many with you?"

"Twenty-four, in addition to our captain of Marines. You met Lieutenant Carter in Port Royal."

"So I did. He seemed a fine officer. As is my own Captain Turner, who commands forty-three. If my math serves, we add your twenty-five to our forty-four and that gives us sixty-nine Marines. Add in Tous-

saint's ten soldiers and we have a grand total of seventy-nine armed
men, not to mention the many sailors and considerable armament we
have on board your ship and mine. So be at your ease, Captain. You
need not be concerned."

"That depends somewhat on Rigaud, does it not?"

Hugh Hardcastle shrugged dismissively. "I don't mean to sound condescending, Captain, but I rather doubt that Rigaud could do much of
anything to anyone on this island even if he had a mind to. I would
take a squad of my Marines, or yours, over a brigade of his picaroons
any day. The same goes for Toussaint's army. We are not discussing
European soldiers here. These men have hardly any military training at
all. Add both sides together and all you have is a horde of ill-clothed,
ill-equipped, ill-led soldiers living on little more than morsels of hope
and sips of promises."

Much like the soldiers of the Continental army, Richard thought,
and they managed to defeat Britain's finest. "But why not parlay with
Toussaint on board *Redoubtable*? You could guarantee security at no
risk to anyone."

"We offered that, Lieutenant, and Toussaint declined our offer. He
prefers to meet us ashore. He is a proud and accomplished man, and I
suspect he prefers to parley within his own seat of power, so to speak,
where he feels most comfortable and where he believes he holds the
upper hand. And that is the key point to remember. Toussaint believes
he does hold the upper hand in our discussions, appearances to the
contrary. In his mind he has more to offer us than we to him. If our
superiors are ultimately to hammer out some sort of agreement with
him, Toussaint must be convinced that he is conceding less than we
are. He trusts us only to a point. In truth, he trusts *no* man outside his
inner circle of confidantes. The only reason he is treating with us at all
is because he believes we can help him achieve his objectives."

Hardcastle's gaze swung to Truxtun after Richard nodded his understanding. "Questions or comments, Captain?"

"Just one, the first one I asked. Exactly when do you and Lieutenant
Cutler meet with Toussaint?"

Hardcastle drew a round, gold-plated watch from his waistcoat
pocket. "It's approaching six bells," he said. "We shall go ashore at
the start of the second dogwatch—in six hours. That will give us three
hours of daylight, more than enough for our purpose."

FROM HIS VANTAGE POINT in the stern sheets of *Constellation*'s gig, Richard Cutler stared ahead to a peninsula jutting out from the western reaches of Île de la Gonâve. Set before a rise of royal purple hills in the far distance was a sunlit white sand beach shaped like a giant arrowhead. The shaft of the arrow extended a good way eastward, toward the interior of the island and beyond, to the mainland of Saint-Domingue and the colonial capital of Port-au-Prince. From what he could observe, the vegetation on this part of the island, the westernmost tip, comprised thick, low-lying brush and scrub, with here and there a scrawny tree thirsting for what meager sustenance its roots could draw from this surprisingly barren land. Nowhere did he find evidence of the multicolored flora, towering coconut palms, or lush green vegetation so prevalent on Barbados, Saint Kitts, and other islands of his acquaintance. This island, in contrast, appeared flogged by the wind and more parched by the sun than enriched by it.

Dead ahead Richard could see the spot where the negotiations with Toussaint L'Ouverture apparently would take place: a grassy stretch perhaps forty or fifty feet up from the waterline. A gray canvas tent had been erected there near a table set between two flaming torches. Twenty feet or so beyond the tent, across a span of hard open ground, began the gnarl of low-lying brush. Within that tangle and confusion the Marines had been ordered to establish a defensive perimeter. How they would do that Richard could not imagine. From his perspective, the undergrowth appeared impenetrable.

He glanced to larboard. Nothing stirred anywhere upon the glassy water, except for the two frigates standing off to westward and, much closer, the jolly boat from *Redoubtable*, its oars dipping and pulling, dipping and pulling, conveying Capt. Hugh Hardcastle and a squad of Marines to the rendezvous ahead. The British Marines, much like his own men, sat still and expressionless on the thwarts, their muskets held upright between their knees. When Richard's eyes met those of his brother-in-law, Hugh touched the forward edge of his gold-rimmed cocked hat. Richard touched his own fore-and-aft hat in reply.

"Toss oars!" the coxswain commanded as the gig approached the beach. Sixteen oars, eight to a side, rose aloft. The gig glided forward under its own momentum until its bow hissed onto the sand next to six other boats that had transported British and American Marines ashore earlier in the day. "Boat oars!" the coxswain ordered. Down came the oars to a position alongside the gunwales. Two bowmen jumped off and held the boat steady as Richard made his way over the thwarts from stern to bow. He stepped ashore and was joined shortly by Hugh Hardcastle.

"Stay here with the boats," Richard ordered Sam Lovett, the sergeant of Marines. Together with his brother-in-law he started up the slight incline of the beach toward a group of men who had emerged from the tent and were now walking down the beach toward them.

Although all of the men were clearly of African descent, their leader's identity was never in doubt. François-Dominique Toussaint L'Ouverture was dressed more like a European emperor than the commander of a rabble army. He wore a sea-blue uniform shirt with a high, stiff collar, the decorative design on its front partially obscured by a white sash running across his chest from his right shoulder to his left hip. A bright gold–tasseled epaulet graced each shoulder, and a second sash of white and red encircled his waist like a belt. His breeches were as white as any British sea officer's, and his knee-high Hessian boots as shiny black as his own skin. From his left hip to his ankles hung a gilt-hafted, ornately designed sword of European provenance.

His personal guard wore a uniform of white breeches, soft leather gaiters, gold breastplates, and plumed shakos. Each soldier carried a gleaming musket a-tilt at his chest. Richard's simple blue dress swallowtail jacket, with its two long vertical rows of brass buttons and a single gold epaulette on the right shoulder, formed a stark contrast to such military finery. The sword attached to a belt at his left hip was American-made and unadorned, save for the silver haft.

Toussaint held up a hand. His entourage stopped ten feet shy of the two naval officers. He stood silent, his eyes taking in first one officer, then the other. Ultimately his eyes settled on Richard, and it was Richard whom he addressed.

"On the one hand," Toussaint said in nearly flawless English, "Great Britain sees fit to send a senior naval commander to parley with me. I know this man. He is respected on these islands. On the other hand, the United States sees fit to send a mere lieutenant as a representative. What message does that send me? Does your government believe I am unworthy of receiving a man of higher rank?"

Taken aback by those questions, Richard had no time to consider his response. He had to rely on instincts. Removing his cocked hat, he advanced one step toward Toussaint and bowed low, placing his left leg forward and his right hand over his heart. In his left hand he held his hat as far out to his side as possible. It was a grand display of deference to

high authority that he had seen performed in the French court, most nota-
bly by the marquis de Lafayette. He straightened himself slowly, his eyes
locked on Toussaint's. "You are mistaken," he said, "if you believe my
government means to insult you by sending me here today. I admit I am
not of the rank or caliber of Captain Hardcastle. Or of you, *mon général*.
But it is not for me to question or explain the reasons why my country has
entrusted me with this most crucial mission. I can only say that the honor
of paying the respects of the United States of America to Your Excellency and discussing the possibility of allying our nations to our mutual
benefit is one I neither deserve nor ever expected to receive."

Still standing at full attention, he gave Toussaint a slight nod, a simple gesture of goodwill between two men. There came a pause as each
took further stock of the other, the height and Anglo-Saxon features
of one standing in sharp contrast to the high cheekbones, snub nose,
narrowed eyes, and longish curly black hair of the other. Toussaint was
a man of less than average height and build who nonetheless exuded
authority and exemplified those hard-to-define qualities that define a
born leader, a man of destiny, without that man having to utter a single
word. The comparison that came instantly to Richard's mind—along
with the knowledge that it would cause his former naval commander to
roll over in his grave—was with John Paul Jones.

"*Eh bien*. Who granted you this so-called honor?"

"My president, *mon général*. Monsieur John Adams."

"You are a friend of *le président?*"

"Not a friend, *mon général*. A personal acquaintance. We live near
each other in the state of Massachusetts."

"I know of Massachusetts. But is it not a commonwealth rather than
a state?" Toussaint allowed himself a trace of a smile.

"That is true, *mon général*," Richard said, impressed by the general's knowledge of a fact of which many citizens of Massachusetts were
ignorant. "My president desires me to tell you, on his behalf, that he
welcomes your correspondence with him. Further, he desires me to tell
you that he holds you and your cause in the highest esteem. Your cause
is America's cause. And he told me to tell you that you remind him of
our own national hero, General George Washington."

With that comparison, Toussaint inclined his head. "*Bien dit*, Lieutenant Cutler," he said. "I can see that you are a man I can trust, despite
your rank. Please, if you and Captain Hardcastle will follow me. We
have much to discuss and our time is short." He turned about and
started walking toward the grassy area.

As Hugh Hardcastle and Richard followed a short way behind, Hugh sidled over to Richard and said, sotto voce, "Well done, old boy. We're off to a good start, thanks to you. Now tell me: from what pile of dung did you dig up that grandiose drivel?"

"I don't know," Richard whispered in reply. "It just seemed the right thing to say. Most of what I said is actually true."

"Well, whatever you have on that shovel of yours, I suggest you continue slinging it."

The crude rectangular table on the grassy stretch had been set up to accommodate six people, with three straight-backed wooden chairs on each side. Toussaint invited the two sea officers to sit on the side facing the gulf. While his personal guard flanked out around the area, he introduced them to Gen. Jean-Jacques Dessalines, a thick-necked, no-nonsense man wearing the grand uniform of his soldiers with a few extra embellishments. Sitting next to him was a third member of Toussaint's party: a young, officious-looking ferret of a man wearing glasses and a thin moustache who had emerged from the tent armed with a quill, inkwell, and sheaf of paper. Five feet away from each end of the table, a torch affixed to an eight-foot-high wooden stake burned brightly within its wicker-shaped metal support, adding light and comfort to what was becoming a pleasantly cool late afternoon.

Hugh Hardcastle spoke first. "Before we begin, Excellency," he said, his eyes flickering from Toussaint to the scribe, who began taking notes, "I am obliged to tell you that Lieutenant Cutler and I are not here in an official capacity. We are not emissaries of our governments. We are here strictly on a fact-finding mission to gather information and report back to our superiors. Whatever decisions may result from our discussions here today will be made by them, not by us. I realize that you are already aware of this, but I have strict orders to be perfectly clear on the matter."

As he spoke, the scribe spoke softly in French to Dessalines, sitting on his right. Apparently this young man was acting not only as scribe but also as interpreter where appropriate. Richard listened intently to what was being interpreted. From what he could gather, the translation was accurate.

"That is my understanding, Captain Hardcastle," Toussaint concurred. "Except for one item you seem to have omitted. I was informed by your agents that although you may not speak for your government, you have the authority to present the terms of what your government is prepared to offer me. I agreed to meet with you and Lieutenant Cutler to hear those terms, and to learn if the United States approves of them."

A man who gets right down to business, Richard thought to himself. And knows how to conduct that business. He found himself admiring Toussaint all the more.

Hardcastle nodded. "My apologies, Excellency. You are correct, of course." He placed his hands on the table and opened them, palms up. "Shall we begin, then? And shall we speak frankly to each other? What my government is prepared to offer you is quite straightforward. As you and General Dessalines are aware, Great Britain holds three military bases on Hispaniola. Your army lacks the means to take these bases from us, should it come to that. Rigaud cannot take them either, so we British are here to stay, should we choose to do so. Having made that point, I am instructed to inform you that Great Britain is now prepared to cede these bases back to you. Including Le Môle, which you doubtless realize is a base His Majesty's government is most reluctant to relinquish."

Toussaint's smile lacked humor. "His Majesty's government is most reluctant to relinquish it, unless, of course, His Majesty's government has concluded that the forces needed to maintain these military bases are best deployed elsewhere, defending islands and waters it deems more critical to its national interests. This is especially true, is it not, if His Majesty's government can convince someone else—a general on Saint-Domingue, perhaps, who commands 60,000 men—to fight its battles for it. You wish to talk frankly, Captain? Then let us talk frankly. You and I are both aware that Great Britain will not commit additional military forces or supplies to Hispaniola or anywhere else in the Indies as long as it is waging war in Europe. The forces and supplies you have here today are, *at most*, what you will have tomorrow and the next day. So you must deploy these forces to your greatest strategic advantage and to your enemy's greatest disadvantage. Take from here, reinforce there, do whatever is necessary to find your enemy's weak points and thrust in hard. It is a basic principle of war, Captain. Surely you read Julius Caesar in one of your excellent public schools in England, which I assume by your polished accent was, for you, either Eton or Harrow."

"Westminster, actually."

"*Vive la différence*. And in your classrooms you surely read the accounts of Alexander of Macedonia, William of Normandy, and Frederick the Great. If there is one lesson we can learn from such military leaders, it is that history repeats itself, especially in times of war. And as I believe a man of your intelligence and upbringing can agree, Saint-Domingue is *not* your enemy's weak point. Am I correct?"

Silence suggested the answer.

"*Ensuite*, I say to you that invading Hispaniola in alliance with the Spanish was *never* in your country's best interests. But what is done is done. To return to the matter at hand, do I understand correctly that your government is now willing to transfer to me intact the bases you hold on Hispaniola?"

Hardcastle's tone in response carried less authority than it had earlier. Even forewarned, Toussaint's erudition had taken him by surprise. "As I said, Excellency, I cannot promise anything specific. I can only state that my government would consider doing that under certain conditions."

"State your conditions."

"There are two. First, that you cease promoting slave rebellion on British-held islands in the West Indies and in the United States." He held up a hand to stem any protest, although none seemed forthcoming. "And, second, that you provide assurances to His Majesty's government that you can, in fact, defeat the forces of André Rigaud, and that when you do, you will not cede back to France the military bases we may now be prepared to cede to you."

Toussaint slowly shook his head. His voice remained calm, yet his expression revealed deep and mounting frustration. "What assurances can I give you," he said softly, "that I have not already given? In numbers, my army is ten times that of Rigaud's. I command the heart and soul of this island, Captain. Its people come in bare feet and rags to fight with me, to fight *for* me. And why is that? Is it perhaps because they trust me, they believe in me, they know I am fighting for them and their freedom? Is that possible of ignorant slaves, you ask? But let us not talk of emotions. Emotions are for women and children and are of minor consequence in such matters. Let us instead talk of war. Let us talk of strategy.

"My forces have Rigaud on the ropes, as you English like to say, despite the weapons and supplies he receives from France. *Encore*, I am fighting Rigaud *and* the French: your enemies, Captain. And yours, Lieutenant. And what do I get in return? What do I receive from Britain and America for fighting your enemies? *Rien*. Nothing. *Zéro*. Not a cannon, not a pistol, not a loaf of bread, not even a thank-you. Lieutenant, you said to me on the beach that my country's cause is your country's cause. Those are eloquent words that stir the heart. But they are meaningless words unless your country is prepared to act on them. Sadly, it is not. How do I know that? Because instead of giving me what I need to win this war, the United States does just the opposite. It maintains a trade embargo on Saint-Domingue. And what does this embargo do? It aids my enemies while it turns my people against you. It makes *you* their enemy. Can you Americans not see this? Are you truly so blind?

"Understand that I am prepared to pay a fair price for whatever arms and provisions you send me. And I will pay you in hard specie or in barter with what we produce, whichever you prefer. But, please almighty God, send me what I need to win this war! Victory is in my grasp—*our* grasp—if you will only do what you know in your heart and mind is in your best interest to do."

Toussaint looked from one officer to the other and did not blink.

"The embargo is not directed at you," Richard intruded into the awkward pause. "It is directed at all French colonies and is meant to starve French military bases into submission." Instantly he regretted the lameness of that statement in contrast to the fluency and logic that preceded it.

"*Peu importe, Lieutenant,*" Toussaint scoffed. "You may report to Monsieur Adams that his embargo is doing precisely that. But to whose advantage? Who is suffering here? It is not your enemies. France does not impose an embargo against Rigaud. No, *monsieur*, those who suffer are those who *fight* your enemies. We both seek to defeat the French, if for our own reasons. And if I lose this war, you may be assured that Saint-Domingue will remain a French colony, and thus your enemy, for many years to come. You may also be assured that my officers and soldiers, all of them, will be executed, and I will be first in line. It will be a bloodbath the likes of which history has never seen. Afterward, there will be few black people left alive on this island.

"Victory can be ours—victory *is* ours—if only you will help us. My army needs weapons. My people need food. I repeat: those who have suffered the most from your mistaken policies are the innocent people of Saint-Domingue. These people do not blame the French or the Spanish or even the English for their misery. They blame the United States. Why? Because the United States is our neighbor, you have fought your own war for independence, and you are in a position to *do* something to help us achieve ours. Thus far, you have chosen to do nothing but sit by and watch."

Richard remained silent, unwilling to answer accusations that he knew to be true. He glanced to his left. Hugh Hardcastle was staring across the table at Dessalines, who returned his stare with arms folded stiffly across his chest.

"What of the French on the island, General?" Richard asked, changing tack. "How many remain?"

"Are you asking how many *white* people remain on Saint-Domingue?" Toussaint asked drily.

Richard nodded. "Yes, I suppose I am."

"The answer is not many. Most of them fled the island a long time ago, leaving Rigaud and the Spanish to do their dirty work. When this war is over, if Rigaud has prevailed, some whites will return to reclaim their estates. Those who do will do so at their peril. Rigaud does not discriminate between your race and mine, Lieutenant. He is prepared to kill blacks and whites alike to get what he wants."

"And that is what, exactly?"

"Self-rule for Saint-Domingue, with himself as colonial ruler and with everything he needs supplied by France. He may tolerate certain whites, the planters and others of wealth, if he believes he can use them for his own purpose. He will not tolerate free blacks under any conditions. If he has his way, he will enslave those blacks he does not execute, just as the British have done." He glanced at Hugh. "I do not have Rigaud's reputation for gratuitous violence. I do not encourage slave rebellion elsewhere, because doing so would cause the deaths of too many of my race. It is not I, Lieutenant, but the French—Victor Hugues and his kind—who have encouraged such rebellions. And I will welcome the whites back to Saint-Domingue, though not as masters; never that. We have confiscated their plantations and we have put former slaves to work on them. We sell what we produce and we earn more money from what we produce than the whites did when the *exclusif*—what you English refer to as mercantilism, Captain Hardcastle—restricted trade solely to France. Do you understand what I am saying?"

Both officers indicated that they did.

"*Eh bien.* This is what I ask you to report to your superiors. If England will withdraw its forces from Hispaniola and cede to me its bases here—and if the United States will end its embargo and send me weapons and supplies to defeat Rigaud—I will open our seaports to trade between our countries. That will benefit you and me and everyone but France, no? And I pledge to do whatever I can to *discourage* slave rebellions elsewhere. What purpose would such rebellions serve? Because of what has happened on Saint-Domingue, whites are now better prepared and will quickly crush any attempt by slaves to resist their masters. Too many Africans would be needlessly slaughtered. When Hispaniola is free and independent, all blacks will be welcome here, wherever they come from." He looked meaningfully at Richard. "And this I pledge to you, Lieutenant: when our ports are open and we are at peace with America, I will grant an *exclusif* of a different kind to foreign companies I want to do business with—companies such as your own Cutler & Sons. Your customers would welcome our coffee. It is the best coffee in the Indies. Some claim it is the best coffee in the world."

Richard remained poker-faced at hearing an offer that whispered bribery while shouting out a financial windfall for his family that would make even Jack Endicott sit up and take note. "You are too kind, Excellency," he said noncommittally. He then asked, to steer negotiations back on the course plotted by Truxtun, "Is the Directory aware that you have requested American aid to achieve your independence?"

"*Qui sait?* We must assume that it is. Rigaud has spies everywhere. Does that concern you?"

"It may concern my government."

"And why is that?"

"There is talk that the Directory now seeks peace with my country. If the United States supports your revolution, that support may not help the cause of peace."

Toussaint looked at Hardcastle. "Does Great Britain support such a peace?"

Hardcastle shrugged. "His Britannic Majesty has no say in the matter, Excellency. England is America's friend in this war, not its ally. We fight a common enemy under separate banners. I can only assure you that England will fight on against France whatever the United States may decide to do."

Toussaint looked back to Richard and opened his mouth to speak, but before he could say anything shouts of warning sounded from the underbrush directly behind the encampment. The shouts were followed by the *pop!* of a musket shot, and then another. A third shot, and a man screamed in agony.

"What in God's name . . . ?" Hardcastle said, half-rising and turning in his chair.

At the sound of the first shot, five of Toussaint's personal guard had formed a human barricade between him and the brush, standing shoulder to shoulder with muskets steady at waist level, aimed toward the threat. From down the beach, where the ship's boats had been pulled onto the sand, a squad of fourteen American Marines came running toward the meeting site.

"Bayonet the bastard!" they heard someone shout from the undergrowth. Richard recognized the voice. It belonged to Lieutenant Carter. A man screamed a curse in French.

Richard ran out on the beach and held up a hand.

"Stand down!" he ordered the Marines. "Sergeant, send four men back to the boats! Make ready to evacuate! Keep the others here and stay low!" He grabbed a musket from a Marine private, a pistol from a corporal. He returned to the grassy area and handed the pistol to Hugh Hardcastle.

They heard another crack of musket fire and a cry from someone hit.

"What do you make of it, Hugh?" Richard shouted. Each had dropped to one knee on the grass, and their four eyes were searching through thick brush and fading sunlight for the source of the shots.

"I can't see a bloody thing in there, Richard. I suggest we get the general off the beach pronto and onto *Redoubtable*. She's closest in."

Just then Lieutenant Carter came running from the brush. Two Marines ran behind him, dragging a fourth man.

"What is it, Lieutenant?" Richard demanded to know when Carter had joined them on the grass and was stooped over, gasping for breath.

"Snipers," Carter managed to report. "Don't know how many. Didn't see them at all until Swanson," referring to a Marine private, "happened to stumble onto one hidden in a pit dug in among the bushes. Then all hell broke loose."

"What of him?" Richard pointed to the man dragged in by the two Marines and now lying face down on the hard ground where he had been summarily dumped. A thin line of red trailed out from his left side.

"He shot at us but missed," Carter answered. "Meyers bayoneted him in the stomach. He's badly wounded. I brought him in so that you could question him." His breathing was easier now.

"What's the status in there, Lieutenant?" Hardcastle demanded.

"Uncertain, Captain," Carter replied. "Captain Turner has them on the run—those we've managed to roust from their nests. There may be others in there. My men are conducting a search."

"Any of ours wounded?" Richard asked.

"Swanson. He took a bullet in the leg. I'm going back in to help bring him out."

Another volley of musket fire sounded, this time from the undergrowth down the beach.

"Right. We'll evacuate Toussaint and his men. And Swanson as soon as you get him out. Captain Hardcastle and I will stand by until all the Marines are off."

"*Un moment, s'il vous plaît, Lieutenant.*"

Toussaint L'Ouverture was approaching them, a pistol in his right hand. Two of his personal guards escorted him, one on each side. The others stood firm in a single line on the edge of the flat, pebbly soil between the grass and the beginnings of the underbrush.

"Pull this man up," he ordered, indicating the rag-trousered mulatto lying on the grass. Toussaint's escorts seized the man and wrenched him to his knees. Blood oozed from the side of the man's mouth and from an ugly gash below the left side of his ribcage. His head, jerked backward when he was yanked up, slowly came level.

Toussaint stepped in front of him. He brought the muzzle of his pistol up against the man's forehead and thumbed back the hammer to half-cock. "*Vous voulez me dire quelque chose?*" he sneered.

The mulatto looked up at Toussaint with jet-black eyes of hatred. "*Je vais vous dire rien!*" he croaked defiantly.

Toussaint thumbed the hammer back to full-cock. "*Ensuite, monsieur, vous êtes un homme mort.*"

The mulatto spat on the ground, then raised his eyes for the final time. "*Je suis un homme mort, quelle que soit.*"

Toussaint squeezed the trigger. The pistol ball exploded through the man's brain and out the back of his head, spraying the two guards holding him with flecks of gore. As the man slumped, dead, to the grass, three shots rang out from the brush. Richard heard the zing of a ball above his head as another ball struck down a soldier standing directly in front of Toussaint. A third ball struck Hugh Hardcastle and spun him around.

The American Marines on the beach riddled the brush with musket fire. Directly ahead, seven of Toussaint's guard also returned fire. A man amid the brush rose into view, took aim, then threw up his arms and fell backward out of sight when a pistol shot hit him.

"Hugh, are you hurt?" Richard cried.

Hardcastle shook his head. "Bastard grazed me, is all." He glanced around. "Seems I was wrong about this place, Richard. I must apologize to Captain Truxtun at the next opportunity. For the moment, however, I suggest we get the hell out of here."

"I'm with you on that, Hugh. Hold steady for a moment." Richard tore off his neck stock, ripped it in two, and wrapped half of it tightly around the wound in Hardcastle's left hand. Richard was relieved to note that the wound was not deep.

"Marines, cease fire!" he commanded after a second volley went off. "Our own men are in there! *Cessez-le-feu!*" he shouted at Touissant's guards. "Sergeant Lovett, the signal to withdraw!"

"Sir!" the ruddy-jowled sergeant of Marines acknowledged. To his squad: "Reload . . . signal to withdraw . . . make ready . . . fire!"

A musket, its muzzle directed straight up, discharged, followed by a second discharge three seconds later, then another and another at three-second intervals until six shots had rung out. That was the pre-arranged signal to those on the island to stop whatever they were doing and hightail it back to the boats.

Richard said to Toussaint: "General, I must insist that you and your men depart immediately for the British frigate."

Toussaint needed no further prompting. He and Dessalines made for the boats down the beach, their scribe following close behind with Toussaint's guards, who helped their wounded comrade.

Richard said to Hardcastle: "Hugh, go with Toussaint. I'll see to everything here."

Hardcastle shook his head. "I appreciate your concern, Richard, but I'll stay here with you. I'll have that pistol back, if you please." He indicated the weapon on the sand that had been dashed from his grip when he was hit. Richard picked it up, checked to see that it was loaded, and gave it to him.

In ones and twos and small groups, British and American Marines emerged from the brush farther down the beach. Red-coated Royal Marines carried the bodies of two comrades and assisted three others who had been wounded. Sporadic gunfire and shouts in French continued to issue from the darkening interior of the island.

"What's the butcher's bill?" Richard asked James Carter once the two were together and Sergeant Lovett had concluded a nose count.

"Swanson is our only casualty, and Isaac will be able to patch him up. I can only estimate enemy casualties. We shot eight, maybe ten. It was a massacre in there. They were clearly a suicide squad. They must have known their chances of getting off this island alive were slim to none once they opened fire."

"I daresay you're right." Richard took in the Marine lieutenant's trousers and shirt torn by thorns and brambles. The exposed skin on his hands and forearms was crisscrossed with scratches of red. "You look a bit the worse for wear yourself, Jim. Get out to *Constellation*. I'll be along shortly."

"I'll do that, Richard. Thank you."

Richard watched him go, then turned back to make a final inspection of the grassy area. Suddenly, another shot rang out from the brush. A Marine private limping toward the boats fell straight forward, a hole torn through the back of his shirt beneath the shoulder blade.

"Everyone down!" Richard cried out. He dropped to his stomach on the sand and brought his musket to bear but could see nothing to aim at within the thick tangle of undergrowth.

Hugh edged his way over to Richard. "It appears that Rigaud's entertainment committee has another act to stage for us," he said with a grimace. "They're cunning bastards, I'll give them that. Cunning and loyal to their cause."

"Jesus Christ Almighty," Richard cried out in frustration. Where are they? *Underground?*"

"That's precisely where they are. Or *were*, and for God only knows how long, biding their time and hiding like rats in a hole." He put a hand on Richard's arm. "Are you all right?"

Richard forced himself calm. He nodded.

"Are your Marines all accounted for?" Hugh asked.

"Yes, all of them."

"So are mine. That leaves only our mulatto friends out there in the bush. He pointed at the two flaming torches perhaps twenty feet away. "Catch my drift?"

Richard nodded. "I'll take the one on the right."

"Agreed. Now before we shove off, might I request a show of support from your Marines? Mine are busy escorting our guests to *Redoubtable*, and I don't fancy those chaps in there having a clear shot at us."

Richard faced around to the Marines lying flat on their bellies a short distance behind him.

"Sergeant Lovett," he said, in a voice softer than normal.

"Sir!"

"Fan out your men." He pointed to the right and then the left. "At my signal, provide covering fire. Captain Hardcastle and I are going in." He indicated the grassy area and the torches.

"Sir!"

When the Marines had formed an inverted V, six on the right side of Lovett at the apex, seven on his left, it was time to go. Richard felt a sickening rush in his intestines and his blood flowing ever faster. "Ready, Hugh?"

"Ready, old boy."

"Right, then. Let's go."

Richard held up his right hand, clenched it into a fist, then chopped it down hard. "Now!" he cried.

"Sir!" At Lovett's command, the Marines rose to one knee, took aim at the underbrush, and opened fire.

"Reload!" Lovett shouted just as Richard and Hugh leaped to their feet and raced up the beach, crouching low and digging their shoes into the sand for traction. They ran up onto the grass and reached the table just as they heard a shot sing out from ahead and the ominous zip of a ball close overhead. Lovett and four Marines stationed at the apex of the V formation stood up and fired a volley at the telltale smoke in the brush.

There was no time to think, only to act. As if they had rehearsed the choreography, each man tore a torch from its bindings, advanced three steps, drew back the metal torch support at waist-high level, and hurled it with all his might before throwing himself down on the hard, pebbly ground. Behind them, off to the sides, they heard a second volley of musketry.

Three shots were fired in reply seconds before the two torches descended in a wide arc and hit the thick, dry brush. Instantly they ignited a conflagration of such intensity that both officers threw up an arm to protect themselves from the fiery heat. They heard a man scream from within the searing white blaze. Another scream, a third, then silence, save for the loud, ominous crackle of parched underbrush burning hot and fast and deadly.

Hugh and Richard slowly rose to their feet and then stepped back a few paces. Together, in silence, each with an arm up before his face, they watched the island burn, mesmerized by the terrible beauty and the unspeakable horror it concealed.

"It's back to our ships," Hugh Hardcastle urged at length. "There's nothing else for us to do except write our reports. And we both know what we're going to write in them, don't we?"

Eleven

USS *Constellation*, 17.11° N, 62.30° W
February 1799

S IX WEEKS had passed since *Con- stellation* had parted ways with *Redoubtable* off Saint-Domingue and returned to station. In his after cabin on board ship in Saint Kitts, Thomas Truxtun had suffered the daily drudgery of organizing convoys and dispatching patrols, along with the myriad other details of naval deployment insisted on by Secretary Stoddert and the Navy Department. Although he performed his desk duties with alacrity, he yearned to be at sea. And that is where he went at the first opportunity, taking *Constellation* southward toward the island of Guadeloupe for a mission of personal reconnaissance. Guadeloupe was not within his designated sector of the West Indies. Nonetheless, as commodore of an American squadron he was given wide latitude to cruise where he deemed it advisable. And he considered it advisable to inspect for himself the French naval base at Basse-Terre.

He found a tidy colonial town with volcanic terrain as a backdrop and a crescent-shaped harbor in the foreground. Dominating the harbor at seaside was a gray stone fortress boasting the tricolor flag of the French Republic and an impressive array of what Truxtun assumed were both 32-pounder and 64-pounder cannon on the embrasures. Anchored within the harbor, from what he could see, was a heavy frigate of the French navy—*La Vengeance*, he assumed, given her impressive size— and a corvette of perhaps twenty guns. Both vessels were anchored within a bevy of smaller double-masted and single-masted vessels. To his surprise—and more, to his concern—Truxtun did not find *Constitution, United States,* or any other American warship from the Prince Rupert Station patrolling the area.

For three days *Constellation* stood off and on the western wing of the butterfly-shaped island, repeatedly sailing close to the range of the fortress' great guns and firing blank charges to windward, challenging the two French warships to come out and fight. Despite their superior firepower, the French ships remained smugly at anchor. Finally, on Monday, February 7, a disgusted Truxtun ordered Nate Waverly to take *Constellation* back to Saint Kitts.

Two days later found *Constellation* five miles northeast of Nevis under all sail to topgallants, despite a low-lying bank of ominous clouds gathering to eastward. A half-hour ago, at noon, the wind had backed and the barometer had begun to fall. Prudent seamanship dictated a reduction of canvas to brace for heavy weather. Captain Truxtun, however, refused to steer the prudent course. Nor would he, he informed his officers, until he entertained no doubt about the identity of the white pyramids of sail visible on the horizon.

When first sighted, the mystery ship was standing to westward on a northerly course. *Constellation* was passing between the islands of Nevis and Redonda on a similar course. Thus the ship, whoever she was, was positioned to the northwest of the American frigate, her topgallants appearing just over the horizon to those on deck. Truxtun immediately ordered Lt. Andrew Sterrett, senior officer of the deck, to crowd on all sail, including studdingsails aloft and a-low, and told Nate Waverly to shape a course in pursuit.

"Storm's comin' up smartly, Captain," Waverly warned, stating the obvious as Sterrett repeated the order to Boatswain Bowles, who repeated it to his mates. A shrill of whistles sent men up the foremast and mainmast yards to extend the studdingsail booms out to windward beyond the reach of the square sails, putting on an extra spread of canvas to catch the wind and add another two or three knots of speed. "Stuns'ls aren't made for the sort of wind that's coming."

"I am aware of that, thank you, Mr. Waverly," Truxtun replied politely. He continued to study the movements of the mystery ship ahead.

With the extra press of canvas, *Constellation* surged ahead. Within the hour the hull of the mystery ship was inching above the horizon. Truxtun glanced at John Rodgers, who held the ship in the lens of a glass.

"What do you make of her, Mr. Rodgers?"

"Can't tell yet, sir. She's ship-rigged and about our length. She's not American. And her beam's too narrow to be Dutch or Swedish."

"Mr. Cutler?"

"I agree, sir." Standing nearer the larboard rail than the others, Richard had to shout over the hum and rattle of the wind in the rigging. "She's either British or French. Maybe Spanish. And you were right, sir. She's no merchantman."

"A ship of war, then?"

"I believe so, sir."

"That is what I recorded in my log, Mr. Cutler, not an hour ago. And that is why we're in pursuit of her. Mr. Sterrett, is the recognition signal ready?"

"Ready, sir. Midshipman Porter and Midshipman Ayres are standing by."

"Very well. I predict, gentlemen, that we'll soon have our answer."

"Shall we beat to quarters, sir?"

"Not yet, Mr. Rodgers. But we would do well to begin preparations."

"I'll see to it, sir."

As Sterrett made his way forward to speak to the boatswain, he had to brace himself against the sharp heel of the ship.

A vessel coming hull-up to those on the deck of another vessel of equal size signifies that the two vessels are approximately three miles apart, that being the distance from any given point to the horizon. *Constellation* was putting on a show of speed sufficient to impress any man's navy and was rapidly closing the distance. Whitewater spewed from her cutwater, bursting over her bows in dazzling rainbows, splattering her yellow-pine planking and foredeck rigging. When Midn. John Dent, his sunburned face flushed with excitement, reported that the chip log he had tossed astern indicated they were making a good sixteen knots, even Nate Waverly could not suppress a smile. For one brief, gleeful moment they were on a joyride, racing on a sleigh heaved forward by a team of galloping, frothing horses as the heart of every man jack on board pumped hard with a bizarre blend of fear, frenzy, and outright exhilaration.

An ear-piercing *CRACK!* aloft that sounded like a cannon shot wiped the smile off Waverly's face. The lower studdingsail boom on the mainmast had broken almost in two and now hung down in an inverted L, swinging back and forth, its torn sail fluttering furiously, impotently, in the mounting wind.

"Leave it!" Truxtun shouted. "Mr. Sterrett, the private signal!"

Andrew Sterrett faced forward and slowly raised and lowered his arms. At the mainmast, David Porter acknowledged and hoisted a red-white-and-blue-striped flag to the topmast. At the foremast, Harry Ayres hauled up a solid blue flag. The combination of those flags on the first two masts was the Royal Navy's private recognition signal for the month of February 1799. Every British and American ship operating in the Caribbean Sea had explicit instructions on how to respond to this signal. Astern, on the mizzen peak, the large American ensign curled and snapped in the freshening breeze. Above, dark clouds drifted over the sun.

Moments merged into minutes, and the minutes dragged on, and still there was no response from the mystery ship.

"Mr. Cutler," Truxtun shouted, "cast loose the starboard guns. Give her a warning shot."

"Aye, Captain."

"Mr. Rodgers, we'll give her one minute to respond. If she fails to do so, we shall beat to quarters."

"Aye, aye, sir."

As Richard made his way to the main hatchway amidships, he made a quick mental calculation. Perhaps a mile of water separated the two ships. The American frigate was proving herself the faster vessel by half. At things stood now, *Constellation*'s guns could be brought to bear within thirty minutes.

Just as he reached the ladder leading below, Richard heard a cry from aloft. He glanced ahead, beneath the taut fore course, its leeches shuddering under the strain of the wind. The mystery ship, now clearly profiled as a frigate, had shifted course to the northwest, bringing the wind on her quarter, presumably her fastest point of sail. That sudden change of course put her on an approximate heading for the Dutch island of Saint Eustatius.

On the gun deck, Richard gave the order. "Loose starboard guns! Open ports! Number one gun, fire a blank charge when ready!"

The gun barked out a warning. Three tons of black iron lurched inboard until checked by breeching ropes.

Men waited, ears primed.

Seconds ticked by. Ten . . . twenty . . . thirty . . . Suddenly a pair of staccato tattoos pierced the air. Gun crews, formed in their divisions, made final preparations for battle. The weather deck above them resounded with the footfalls and shouts of sailors and Marines taking their stations in the rigging, on the fighting tops, and behind the wall of hammocks jammed tight inside bulwark netting.

Richard felt *Constellation* swerve hard off the wind in pursuit just as another round of muddled shouts clamored from above.

"She's hoisting the tricolor, Captain!"

"*L'Insurgente!*" he heard the cry of a sharp-eyed sailor.

Richard cursed under his breath. America had a score to settle with this thirty-four-gun French frigate. American blood was on her decks. God alone knew how many merchant vessels she had seized, how many innocent sailors she had dispatched to the ocean floor. And she had taken *Retaliation* off the coast of Saint Kitts and imprisoned her crew.

"Beg pardon, sir, but why is she running from us? Why show us her heels?" asked Cyrus Moffett. At age twelve he was the youngest and shyest of the eight midshipmen on board. His straight blond hair was abruptly cut off at the nape, and his face was badly scarred by a child-hood bout with chicken pox. Assigned to number two gun, he had come over to where Richard was peering out through gun port number three.

Richard glanced over at the chubby preadolescent whose father was a senator from Rhode Island and a personal friend of Thomas Truxtun. Like the other midshipmen he was dressed in white breeches and a loose-fitting shirt under a plain blue undress coat. Cyrus blinked hard as he returned Richard's look and tried to keep his lower lip from quivering. Despite the cool ocean wind sweeping in through the open ports, beads of sweat had formed high on his brow under the rim of his cocked hat and were trickling down his peach-fuzzed cheeks.

"You'll have to ask her captain, Cyrus," Richard said in a confiden-tial, off-handed tone. Calling a midshipman on duty by his first name went against naval regulations. Nonetheless, it helped ease the lad's anxiety. Richard well remembered his own fear and anxiety as a young midshipman sailing into his first battle. "But I suspect he has orders to avoid a fight."

"Why, sir? If I might ask?"

"His mission is to destroy enemy commerce, not to pick a fight with a man-of-war and put at risk one of the few frigates the French have in these waters."

"I see, sir. I had not thought of that." A hopeful lilt entered his voice when he asked, in hushed tones, "So you think we won't engage?"

Richard shook his head. "To the contrary. We *will* engage if our captain has anything to say about it, and I believe he does. Now, return to station, Mr. Midshipman Moffett. Do your duty. Make your family proud."

"Aye, aye, sir," Moffett said, backing away reluctantly.

More excited shouts from above. "She's taking in her t'gallants!" Then, louder, "She's hauling her wind!"

Richard's eyes swept the gun deck. Gun crews were at their assigned posts, their ports open, implements ready, each gun loaded, extra powder and round shot secured nearby. Everything appeared in order. He touched his tricorne hat to Andrew Sterrett, stationed aft, and stepped up the broad wooden ladder to the weather deck. *Constellation* remained under full sail, despite the threatening clouds approaching fast from the east. Ahead, *L'Insurgente*, her sail plan mirroring that of the American vessel, had come to the wind and was sailing north-northeast directly into the path of the oncoming storm. Apparently, Richard mused, her captain was gambling on the storm providing some means of escape.

Amid a shrill of boatswain's whistles *Constellation* swung to starboard on a course to cut her off, sailing as close to the wind as she could lie.

For the moment, Truxtun controlled the weather gauge, normally an advantageous position that allowed a ship to windward of another ship to dictate battle tactics. But under these circumstances that advantage came at a price. *Constellation* was heeling hard to leeward in pursuit of an enemy on a slightly less than parallel course. Her larboard guns—those that would come to bear on this tack—had their ports clamped shut to prevent seawater from washing in.

Truxtun passed word forward: run out the windward guns.

Richard relayed the order below. Moments later *Constellation* feathered into the wind and the starboard leeches of her great square sails began to slacken and shiver. As soon as the sharp heel came off her, gun crews on the starboard side heaved on ropes and pulleys to haul the massive iron beasts up the slight incline of deck until their muzzles protruded from their ports and their carriages bumped against the hull. When gun captains verified that the guns were secured, *Constellation* fell off the wind and back on course. The added weight extended to windward helped to stabilize the frigate and added another knot or two of speed.

That advantage was lost minutes later when the squall struck the American frigate, forcing her over to leeward. Gear stowed loosely belowdecks came undone, the noise of the crashing and banging audible over the shriek of the wind. Men caught unprepared on deck lost their footing and careened hard against the larboard bulwarks. Up on the weather deck and in the rigging, sailors in the eye of the onslaught grabbed hold of shrouds, spars, ratlines, anything they could hang on to for dear life. Another loud *CRACK!* and the upper studdingsail boom went by the boards.

"Up helm!" John Rodgers yelled through a speaking trumpet. He had his left arm wrapped around the mizzenmast and his left leg braced out. Four helmsmen, fighting to maintain their footing, gripped the spokes of the double wheel and battled the helm over. Slowly, slowly, the frigate turned into the wind. "Let fly all sheets!" Rodgers roared.

As the punishing strain on the top-hamper eased, sailors released sheets from their belaying pins on fife rail and pin rail. Canvas rumbled, then thundered in almighty protest as *Constellation*, the power off her, rounded instinctively head on into the driving squall and came to a standstill. Gale-force winds screamed in the rigging as big droplets of blood-warm rain pounded her decks and cascaded into the sea from her scuppers. The storm blew over quickly, and *Constellation* was back on the chase, her sails once again sheeted home.

Ahead, the howling hammer of wind bashed *L'Insurgente* just as her crew was laid out on the yards in a desperate attempt to reduce canvas. It was too little, too late. The Americans watched in horror as the French frigate's main topmast snapped at the cap, taking the sailors on the main topmast yard down with it. Arms and legs flailing, they tumbled onto the deck or into the sea below. Seconds later, a tangle of spars, rigging, and sails crashed down on top of them. Crews on deck attacked the debris with axes and cutlasses, slashed it to bits, and heaved it overboard.

Escape, always a gamble for *L'Insurgente*, was no longer in the cards. As the storm passed over her and the seas calmed, she stood on a starboard tack and ran out her guns to fight.

Constellation crossed *L'Insurgente*'s wake and ran under her lee. Six bells in the afternoon watch sounded as the American frigate closed to within pistol shot range. Those on deck could see and hear a French officer standing by the larboard taffrail shouting through a speaking trumpet.

"What's he saying, sir?"

Richard vaguely recognized the voice of Frederick Bowles behind him. He was listening intently to the exchange taking place in English and held up a hand for quiet. *Constellation* and *L'Insurgente* were both sailing to northward on more or less parallel courses. The American frigate stood to leeward of the Frenchman, whose once graceful profile had been desecrated by the loss of her main topmast.

"That's the first lieutenant speaking," Richard said, as much to himself as to the boatswain. "He's saying that his captain wants to parley with us."

They waited for Truxtun's response, which was quick in coming. "I have this to say to your captain, *monsieur*," he yelled through a trumpet. "Strike your colors or I shall fire into you!"

Seconds elapsed in translation before the French captain seized the speaking trumpet for himself. "*Reddition sans combat n'est pas une option!*" he shouted back defiantly.

Truxtun's tone in reply was equally defiant. "*Comme vous voulez, monsieur!*" Truxtun rapped out an order to Midn. John Dent, who strode forward at a good clip.

"Mr. Cutler, Captain Truxtun's compliments and you may fire the starboard guns in rotation!"

Richard clambered down the ladder and strode forward. At number one gun he peered through the port, checked the quoin, stepped aside, and nodded to the gun captain: "*Fire!*"

At number two gun: "*Fire!*"

At number three gun: "*Fire!*"

One by one, forward to aft, *Constellation*'s great guns unleashed fourteen rounds of 24-pound shot that streaked toward *L'Insurgente*'s larboard hull at 1,200 feet per second. With each orange-tongued discharge, a red-painted carriage screeched inboard and acrid smoke swept across the deck. Gun crews wormed out, sponged out, rammed home, ran out the guns, and prepared to fire a second round.

The intermittent *boom!* of 6-pounder guns echoed down from the weather deck, and the *pop!* of daisy-cutters came from high up on the fighting tops, all punctuated by the intermittent *crack!* of the Marines' musketry. A savage outpouring of double shot, grape, and lead pummeled *L'Insurgente*'s hull, rigging, decks, and bulwarks. Below, on the gun deck, the first rotation had spent its course and the fourteen guns were repeating the sequence.

L'Insurgente responded with a broadside of her own, most of her guns aimed high, at the rigging. One shot aimed level slammed against *Constellation*'s hull near where Richard and Andrew Sterrett were standing by gun number seven. Instinctively they recoiled from the impact. But the ball bounced off the oaken hull as though it were a rubber ball hitting a wall, inflicting no damage whatsoever. The two officers exchanged a glance, the thought of one read clearly upon the face of the other: *Quercus virens*, the southern live oak at the heart of their ship's frame, had just proved its mettle.

"She's changing course!" someone shouted. The lieutenants peered out through the open port. *L'Insurgente* had indeed changed course— to come directly at them. A horde of French Marines and sailors had gathered on her forecastle and gangways, the polished steel of their pikes, axes, and cutlasses reflecting the afternoon sun.

"They mean to board us!" a young sailor at gun number five cried out, his voice laced with panic. Without another word he raced aft past the two lieutenants, toward the ladder leading below to the presumed safety of the berthing deck. The Marine sentry assigned to the hatches to prevent flight had, for whatever reason, left his post.

"Hold!" Sterrett yelled at the frightened lad. "Return to station, Harvey! Now! I warn you!"

Harvey ignored the warning, kept running. Sterrett drew his pistol, cocked it, took aim, and fired. Harvey fell, screaming, a yard shy of the ladder. He clapped his hands on the upper thigh of his left leg and writhed in agony.

"To your stations!" Richard shouted to the gun crews watching in mute horror.

"Prepare to rake her, starboard guns!" John Dent cried from above. That call to arms brought everyone back to the task at hand.

The change of course had placed the Frenchman in a dangerous position. *Constellation*, seizing advantage of her opponent's vulnerability, ranged ahead of *L'Insurgente* under spanker, topsails, and jib. Truxtun ordered her braces and helm swung over and bore down on an enemy that had apparently realized the mistake and was now struggling desperately to present her broadside.

Constellation tore across *L'Insurgente*'s bow.

"As your guns bear . . . *fire!*" Richard shouted.

One by one as they came to bear on the enemy's bow, the guns sent round shot and canister shot streaking down the length of the Frenchman's crowded weather deck. The shot pulverized the bones and spirit of five, ten, fifteen men, and anything else it touched until it crashed against something hard, a mast or a gun on its truck, upending it with an ugly clash of iron. Case shot and langrage from the smaller elements of *Constellation*'s arsenal added to the bloody carnage until the American frigate had sailed past and could no longer bring her long guns to bear.

Down on the gun deck, Richard's crews could see little of the wreckage their guns had wrought. *Constellation* had moved swiftly past *L'Insurgente*, and her ports provided limited visibility. Only when *Constellation* had rounded up on a parallel course ahead of her enemy did Richard feel it safe to venture topside for a look.

"Larboard guns!" he commanded before he went up, an order that sent crews scurrying across the deck to the guns on the opposite side. Privately, to Sterrett, he said, "Get Harvey below, Andrew. Balfour may be able to patch him up. He's done for either way, but at least let's try to give him his day in court."

"I'll see to it," Sterrett replied, both his expression and his tone suggesting inner conflict. In truth, Richard had been as shocked as the gun crews by what Sterrett had done. Not because of the act itself, or the ethics or legality involved, but because it had been so out of character.

"I'm going topside. The deck is yours."

On the weather deck, Richard scanned *Constellation*'s top-hamper. He could see damage, plenty of it, although at first blush none of it seemed serious. The starboard mainmast shrouds and braces had taken hits, a foremast yard was lost, a chunk of wood had been blown out of the lower topmast, and enemy shot had torn gaping holes in the courses and topsails. *L'Insurgente,* limping along behind them and off to larboard, had suffered a far worse fate. Her mizzen topmast was gone, and without her main topmast she had only her foremast fully serviceable.

Despite the mutilation of the French vessel's top-hamper and what had to be a gruesome litter of bodies and body parts strewn about her decks, the tricolor still fluttered from what was now the cap of her mizzen, and she had run out her starboard guns, less three that had been put out of action.

Constellation, her sails a-luff on the edge of the wind and her great spanker boom jouncing up and down under the lack of strain, waited for *L'Insurgente* to catch up and surrender. Richard glanced aft. Captain Truxtun stood near the helm between John Rodgers and Nate Waverly, the three of them watching the wounded French frigate as though she were simply an interesting spectacle at sea, not the enemy of a few minutes ago that had hurled a half-ton of hot iron in their direction.

When *L'Insurgente*'s splintered bowsprit came parallel to *Constellation*'s stern, Truxtun brought a speaking trumpet to his mouth.

"*Monsieur le capitaine de frégate française,*" he hailed, "do you strike?"

In reply, *L'Insurgente*'s foremost starboard gun flashed fire. The ball missed its mark—whatever that had been—and splashed into the sea a hundred yards beyond *Constellation*'s starboard quarter.

Instantly, white flames shot out from 6-pounder guns on *Constellation*'s weather deck, while below, guns number twelve and fourteen, larboard side, roared out their anger. American Marines, standing or kneeling behind a wall of hammocks, opened fire with muskets. Above, in the tops, Marines brought swivel guns to bear on the Frenchman's deck, peppering it with half-pound iron balls, scrap iron, and langrage, striking men already spent from battle, slicing their flesh into jelly and spatters of skin and bone.

Richard climbed to the weather deck and walked forward, drawn as though mesmerized by this vision of hell fifty yards to larboard. It was now a hopelessly one-sided affair. *Constellation*'s guns were taking a horrific toll, punching at the Frenchman's hull with iron fists, cracking her strakes, smashing through her gun ports, undoing her chain plates and channels, and laying waste to her bulwarks and railing. Each shot that found its mark launched an army of lethal wooden shrapnel into the air. *L'Insurgente* was putting up a brave front, but her cause was hopeless. For every haphazard round she managed to get off, *Constellation* responded with two or three of her own, her aim true with nearly every shot. Months of grueling exercise at the guns had paid off. The battle was over, the victor crowned. At arduous length, *L'Insurgente*'s officers finally accepted the inevitable and ordered their remaining guns silenced and the tricolor hauled down.

Captain Truxtun will be pleased tonight, Richard thought as he made his way back amidships to the ladder leading below. He was considering the ramifications of the victory when suddenly there came a cry of warning from above.

"Mr. Cutler, look out! Above you!"

Richard glanced up to see a broken yard careening off a lower yard, plunging straight down at him. In the few brief, terrifying moments he had to react, he lunged to his left and threw up his hands—too late. The end of the heavy wooden spar grazed his right shoulder and whipped in against the side of his face, sending him sprawling onto the deck, ending thought and claiming the light from his eyes.

"Lieutenant Cutler is coming to, sir. Shall I inform Dr. Balfour?"

"Not yet, John. Let's wait and see what we'll have to tell him first."

Richard heard this brief exchange as if in a dream. Perhaps it *was* only a dream. He prayed it was. His head throbbed. He felt dizzy and nauseous. Even the simple act of moving the fingers on his right hand caused a flame to shoot up his arm to his shoulder, where it combined forces with whatever demons of agony lurked there to send white-hot pain through his neck, head, and body. He opened his eyes, closed them, opened them again. He glanced upward at a confined space he recognized as the sick bay at the forward end of the berthing deck. This, then, was no dream. From the corners of his eyes he saw, standing on each side of the cot, two of the ship's complement: Surgeon's Mate Isaac Henry and a loblolly boy named John Wall. He tried to look more directly at them but found that he could not. Not because of the pain, agonizing as that was. Because he was unable to move his head.

Henry tried to calm Richard's sudden surge of panic. "Do not be alarmed, Lieutenant," he said in his best soothing bedside manner. "You are in what is called a figure-of-eight splint. Dr. Balfour fashioned it himself. See here." He combined thumb and middle finger and gently flicked the finger against Richard's neck below his chin. Richard braced for a jolt of pain. None came, only the light thump of a finger hitting wood. "It prevents you from turning your head, you see, and thus allows the clavicle to heal properly. It's broken, I'm sorry to report. You have other scrapes and bruises, and tendons that require mending. But that clavicle of yours is our main concern."

"It's broken?" Richard rasped. He had no idea what a clavicle was, although he had a good sense of where it was.

"Oh yes, quite broken, I'm afraid. But it will heal as good as new if you remain still for a while. That means no skylarking in the rigging for the next several months." His benign smile comforted his patient. "If it's any consolation, Lieutenant, it could have been far worse. Had that spar struck you a few inches over, or had it not been deflected on its way down, I doubt we would be having this conversation."

Richard winced. "The pain . . ."

"Ah yes, the pain. You'll be feeling *that* for a while yet. It will lessen with time, as the healing progresses. John, be a good fellow and fetch me a vial of laudanum from the chest. Our lieutenant has need of it."

Hours after swallowing the tincture of opium, Richard regained a better degree of consciousness. The dizziness and nausea had eased a little, and he was no longer bone tired. Into his view came the face of David Porter, who rose from a chair at the bedside when Richard opened his eyes.

"Good day, Mr. Porter," Richard managed. He had no notion why the young midshipman was here or why the skin around his eyes appeared so gray and puffy. He looked as though he had either been smacked in a fight or sobbing like a woman. "Assuming it is day."

"It is, sir," Porter replied. "Three bells in the forenoon watch. How are you feeling, sir?"

"I've felt better," Richard said irritably, in no mood for small talk. He waited for Porter to explain himself, which he did after a good deal of hand wringing.

"Sir," he said meekly, "I fear I must apologize."

"Apologize? For what?"

"It was I, sir, who dropped that spar on you."

Richard tried to turn his head, a simple act that caused a frontal assault of searing pain. He clenched his teeth until the pain subsided. "How so?" he rasped.

"Well, sir, as you know, I was stationed in the maintop with the Marines." Porter spoke rapidly, as though eager to explain himself and release a heavy burden of guilt. "Early on during the battle, our mainmast was struck. It began to teeter. Later on it was struck again, and this time it appeared it would topple over. I hailed the deck but no one heard me. So I climbed up to the topmast and cut away the slings." He dropped his eyes. "It seemed the right thing to do."

"It *was* the right thing to do, John," Richard croaked. The lad's remorse had touched him deeply. "You saved the mast. All might have been lost if you hadn't cut away that spar."

"Yes, sir. Thank you, sir. But in saving the mast I injured you. And truly, I would give anything if I hadn't."

"Belay that, John," Richard said over a grimace. "You did your duty. And you needn't worry about me. The surgeon says I'll be up and as good as new in no time. We took *L'Insurgente* as a prize?"

"We did, sir!" Porter exclaimed. "Right after . . . right after you were laid out, she struck her colors."

"Where is she now?"

"Anchored not fifty feet from us, sir. Captain Truxtun has appointed Lieutenant Rodgers her captain, and I am to be one of her midshipmen. We're to remain here in Saint Kitts for another day or two, to jury-rig her for our voyage to Portsmouth. We'll make more substantial repairs there."

"Portsmouth? You're taking *L'Insurgente* to Virginia?"

Porter hesitated. "Yes, sir. And *Constellation* will accompany us. We're going home, sir," he said with an uncontrolled burst of glee.

Home. For David Porter, Virginia *was* home, so his joy was understandable. Virginia, however, was a goodly distance from Massachusetts. Thoughts of home nonetheless flooded his mind—images of his family, of his sons and daughter and brother and father, of Katherine and her loving ways. Then a terrible thought hit him. Could his injury mean the end of his naval career? Would he be summarily shipped off as an invalid to sit on a Hingham beach and ponder for the rest of his years what might have been? To his mind there was no worse fate, and a gnawing fear of that fate persisted in nightmares long after he had fallen back to sleep.

The brilliant light of day was fading into twilight when he awoke to find Thomas Truxtun and George Balfour staring down at him. His captain was dressed casually in buff trousers and a loose white cotton shirt. Richard closed his eyes, willing himself fully awake, feeling ever so much like an animal on display in a cage.

"Well, well, Mr. Cutler," Truxtun announced with a flourish, "I can see for myself that the rumors of your recovery have not been misconstrued. That nasty bruise on your face should keep the women at bay for a spell, and that splint will, for once, force your eyes front and center. But I must say that I am pleased to find your head still intact. We put the method of treatment to a vote, and to a man the ship's company voted for amputation. Fortunately for you, Dr. Balfour here stepped in to save your neck."

Despite his pain and misery, Richard had to crack a smile. He had never seen his captain so exuberant, nor heard him joke in that carefree manner. The glory of victory had something to do with it, no doubt, but so also, he suspected, did the promise of wealth that came along with that victory. Captain Truxtun's three-twentieths share of the prize money would yield him many thousands of dollars—more than a commodore typically earned in a lifetime—whatever value the Admiralty Court might ultimately place on *L'Insurgente*. His own share of prize money, Richard was aware, was no trifling matter. Everyone serving in *Constellation*, whatever his rank, would share in the winnings—along with the U.S. Treasury, of course.

His eyes moved to the studious-looking Balfour, who wore a dark green coat with black velvet lapels and stand-up collar, the badge of office for an American naval surgeon. "Thank you for your care, Doctor," he said.

Balfour inclined his head in reply.

Richard's gaze returned to Truxtun. "What of *Constellation*, sir? She's in need of repairs."

"We're seeing to those." He pointed upward. "Those sounds you hear are hammers and saws on the weather deck. Her rigging's shot up, but her hull shows no damage. None whatsoever," he added pointedly. "And she took many hits. By Jove, that oak *is* worth the misery and suffering its harvest entailed."

"What of casualties?"

"We lost four men. Four dead, that is. The wounded, apart from yourself, have been transferred ashore, along with 173 prisoners, including the French captain, a rather cheeky fellow who actually accused me of causing a war with France. If so, I informed this fellow, Barreaut, then I am glad of it, for I detest doing things by halves." Truxtun smiled.

"What did the French captain do then?"

"Looked at me as though I were something he had found stuck to the bottom of his boot." Truxtun's look turned more serious. "But back to the dead. We lost three in action: Seamen Andrews, Wilson, and Waters. Harvey—well, you know about him."

"Yes, sir. I was there, sir. Lieutenant Sterrett gave Harvey a fair warning. I am willing to testify to that in court, if need be."

"I am sure Mr. Sterrett would appreciate that, Mr. Cutler, though I doubt very much it will be necessary. The facts are what they are, and there are many other witnesses. Now then," he added in that same business-like tone, "here's where we stand. I have appointed Mr. Rodgers captain of *L'Insurgente*. That makes you my first, when you rejoin the ship, though I shall recommend that your promotion take effect immediately. Three days from now, on Thursday, *Constellation* and *L'Insurgente* will weigh anchor for Portsmouth. Mr. Sterrett will serve as my acting first lieutenant during the cruise home. On Wednesday we will see you ashore to the local hospital."

Richard's eyebrows arched upward. "You're sending me ashore, sir? Am I not to be sailing with you to Virginia?"

"No, Mr. Cutler, you are not," Truxtun stated emphatically. "You are hardly in a condition to sail anywhere at the moment."

"But, sir," Richard protested, "I can heal along the way."

"You will heal faster if you remain here, Mr. Cutler. The tropical sun does wonders for the human body. Once you are up and about and the doctors give you permission, you may leave Saint Kitts if you choose and travel to some other island. There are, of course, a number of possibilities, but might I suggest Barbados? I've found it particularly pleasant this time of year."

"Barbados, sir?"

"Yes, Lieutenant. Barbados. It's an island south of here, in the Windwards. Oh, how forgetful of me. You have family there, don't you. Well, what a lovely coincidence that is. I can't imagine a better place for you to recuperate from your wounds. Just keep in mind that *Constellation* will be returning to Saint Kitts in October. When we do, I expect to find you here on the docks looking as hale as Hercules and as tanned as Toussaint. Do I make myself clear?"

"Sir . . ."

"That's an order, Lieutenant."

Truxtun turned to leave but looked back. "Mr. Cutler," he said with feeling, "that was a fine job you did with the guns. A very fine job, indeed. Mr. Stoddert shall hear of it, as will President Adams and the entire Navy Department. Now, please get on with your recovery. This war is not over, and I shall no doubt require your services again in the not too distant future. Good day, my soon-to-be First Lieutenant."

Truxtun saluted and retired aft before Richard could say another word.

Twelve

Barbados
Spring–Summer 1799

R ICHARD CUTLER had no trouble securing passage from Saint Kitts. This Royal Navy outpost east of Antigua (headquarters of the Northern Division of the West Indies Station) and northwest of Barbados (homeport of the Windward Squadron) saw military dispatch vessels come and go on a regular basis. And as it was common knowledge among senior British sea officers in the Lesser Antilles that Richard's brother-in-law was one of their own, Richard was offered a berth on board any Royal Navy dispatch vessel of his choosing. A month after *Constellation* and *L'Insurgente* set off northward for Hampton Roads, he boarded a swift, single-masted packet bound for Bridgetown.

There was little for him to do during the three-day voyage—and little that he *could* do. His right arm remained wedded to his torso in a plaster cast, and he had strict orders from Dr. Balfour to keep the arm firmly bound until a physician on Barbados had examined his shoulder and found it sufficiently healed to remove the plaster. Balfour had assured Richard that while it would take many weeks for the clavicle to heal properly, it *would* heal completely if properly treated. In the meanwhile, he ordered Richard to follow a strict regimen of good food and easy living, and to keep his spirits high.

Balfour had smiled benignly at his patient when giving that order. And who in his right mind, Richard asked himself, would not smile when receiving it? October was seven months away, and he had been given leave by his captain, following a promotion to first lieutenant, to serve out his convalescence among family and friends on one of the most alluring islands in the West Indies. Nevertheless, at the outset of the cruise he had thought constantly about *Constellation*, among other reasons because she carried the letters he had written to Katherine and his father. In them he had summarized the facts of what had happened but included little of his feelings, for he was forced to dictate the letters to Roger Simms, the captain's clerk. Captain Truxtun had promised to forward both letters to Boston as soon as *Constellation* arrived in Virginia. A third letter, to his cousins John and Robin Cutler, had been sent several weeks earlier to Barbados by ordinary mail packet.

As the three-day cruise wore on, the soporific effects of sun, sea, and tropical air coaxed his thoughts in other directions. A memory came often to mind, inspired, perhaps, by the irony it involved. In November 1781, a month after a British grenadier had shot him in the leg during the fighting at Yorktown, Richard had been transported from Virginia to Guadeloupe on a corvette sent ahead by Admiral de Grasse to announce the glorious victory to French naval headquarters. From Basse-Terre he had booked passage on board a Danish lugger bound for Barbados, and there on the docks of Bridgetown he was met by his wife in the company of her brother, Hugh Hardcastle. Richard and Katherine had difficulty reaching one another on the docks, for he struggled with a debilitating limp and she was heavy with child. But it was a reunion he would never forget.

Today, though, as the larboard hull of the packet bumped against that same quay on a splendid sunny morning in early March, Katherine was not there to greet him. Nor were his cousins. Only Caleb was there, dressed casually in an open ruffled shirt and knee-length trousers, his bleached brown hair tied back at the nape of his neck with a piece of string.

"You look the picture of health!" Richard exulted as he squeezed his brother's right hand with his left. Despite their joy at seeing each other, they kept a safe distance apart in deference to Richard's injury. "How long have you been here?"

"Two months," Caleb replied. "I left Hingham the day after Christmas. I've been waiting here at the quays for two days. We knew from your letter when you planned to leave Saint Kitts, so we knew more or less when to expect you here. Our cousins can't wait to see you."

They began walking toward a carriage-and-four with an open front and the Cutler coat of arms on the side doors. Sunburned dockers bustled about them, loading and offloading hogsheads of sugar, molasses, and rum: the wellspring of untold fortunes for the island's English planters, whose produce was meticulously examined by potential buyers and whose accounts were scrutinized by local tax collectors representing the Royal Exchequer in London. Here and there, standing out in sharp contrast to the shirtless, sweaty workers, gentler-born men sporting straw hats adorned with bright-colored linens strolled arm in arm with ladies dressed in the latest European fashions with parasols to shield them from the fierce equatorial sun and the view of the less genteel women who solicited sailors of every stripe and color and state of intoxication. It was a scene well choreographed in Richard's mind, and one he cherished. He had been to Bridgetown many times since his first visit in 1774, and he always looked forward to being back amid the hot, crowded cobblestone streets and dark, shaded alleyways that encompassed the best and worst of the human condition. He was, in a sense, home.

"Well," he ventured to Caleb, "how do you find Barbados?"

Caleb beamed. "It's a paradise, a Garden of Eden compared to Boston. The women here are so beautiful—and so willing! I have no idea why that is, but I've never known anything like it."

Richard returned his smile. "I have a pretty good idea why, and I believe I'm looking at it. So. Making up for lost time, are we?"

"Day and night, I'm hard at it. Though as you'll hear soon enough, Cousin John does not approve of my social life. How long have you been in that sling?"

"A few weeks."

"How much longer will you be in it?"

"A few weeks more."

"Of all the rotten luck. It will certainly hamper your technique."

Richard's smile broadened. Not since childhood had he seen his brother this relaxed and happy.

"Whatever sorry excuse I may once have had for a 'technique' went by the boards years ago, Caleb. And less the pity. I'm content to leave the rutting and sinning to you younger fellows. And when I next see him I shall ask Father Robert to say a prayer for your soul." He had no doubt that the Reverend Mr. Robert Edsen, the Anglican priest of the local parish attended by the Cutler family on Sunday mornings, would pray mightily indeed.

They arrived at the carriage without a lull in their lively conversation. A liveried servant sitting stiffly on the driver's bench held the reins.

"That will not be necessary," Caleb announced grandly. "I have given the matter considerable thought and find that I quite agree with what Reverend Gay used to preach to us in Hingham. God wants us to honor him, does he not? And the miracles of his creation? Well, I figure that's exactly what I'm doing. What better way to honor my Creator than by worshiping that which he created from the rib of Adam?" He opened the door to the carriage, saw his brother inside and tossed in Richard's seabag, then climbed in on the opposite side.

"That's a rationalization if ever I've heard one," Richard quipped.

"That's because," Caleb quipped back, "I have learned at the feet of the master." He thumped twice on the side of the door and the carriage lurched forward.

Their route wound along Front Street, the main thoroughfare of Bridgetown, an appealing avenue lined with cream-white stucco buildings capped with red-tile roofs. On their right, a flotilla of commercial vessels nested next to one another on the quays and at anchor farther out in the harbor. Ahead, high above the terminus of Front Street on the eastern edge of Carlisle Bay, on a hill exposed to the brisk northeasterly trades, stood the majestic facade of Government House, the official residence of the royal governor, set amid clusters of royal palms and lush shrubbery. Beneath it, Fort George held sway over the ships of the Windward Squadron riding at anchor farther below in the harbor. The squadron comprised mostly sloops of war, miniature frigates that relied more on speed and maneuverability to subdue their prey than on the weight or number of their guns. Richard searched in vain for the squadron's flagship, HMS *Redoubtable*. That Hugh Hardcastle was away at sea disappointed him, and not just on a personal level. Since leaving Saint-Domingue in December he had heard precious little about Toussaint L'Ouverture and the War of Knives.

The carriage veered off the cobblestones onto a well-maintained dirt road leading into the interior. Away from the confusion and smells of Front Street, the air sweeping over them carried the delicious scents of tropical flowers. The countryside that now surrounded them was thick with ten-foot stalks of green sugarcane waving in the breeze as far as the eye could see on the gently rising slopes. Here and there a stately plantation house emerged into view, nestled within shade trees and luxuriant undergrowth. Bare-chested men with glossy black skin were processing the newly harvested cane beneath the vanes of tall wooden windmills turning in the breeze. If ships and shipping defined the backbone of a

West Indian economy, the rich sugar harbored within this seemingly endless green sea was its marrow.

"Who's here?" Richard asked as the carriage bumped gently along.

"Everyone's here," Caleb replied. "Cynthia and Joseph returned from England a week after I arrived. The big news is that early last month Julia gave birth to a baby boy. His name is Peter."

"Do say! I had supper with Captain Hardcastle in Jamaica, and he told me Julia was expecting. Mother and son are doing well?"

"Yes, very, though I must say I'm grateful to be lodging with John and Cynthia in their house, rather than with Robin and Julia. It's where you'll be too, in the West Room. I stayed there when I first arrived but got the boot after John received your letter. It's your room, he told me, and you have priority. I worried that for my perceived sins he would banish me to Robin's house. Glory be to God, he didn't. The only guest room Robin has available is a cubicle next to Peter's room. Peter cries all night and keeps everybody awake, especially Anna, his nurse. One look at her in the morning and you know that's a fate you don't want to share."

As Caleb spoke, fond memories welled within Richard. The West Room was where he and Katherine had lived and loved after their arrival in Barbados in 1780, three months after their wedding in England, and he had stayed there during every visit since. Its glass windows opened on three sides to pleasing views of well-cultivated gardens and admitted the heady scents of begonias, hibiscus, ginger lilies, and other tropical flowers. To westward, not far away beyond an expanse of green fields, white sandy beaches and warm turquoise-blue water beckoned.

What of Joseph?" he inquired. "Did the doctors in London find out what's wrong with him?"

"Nothing of consequence, I'm afraid. He's such a nice, gentle boy, Richard. He's intelligent too, though it takes a while to realize just how intelligent. He has a real knack for numbers, but not much interest in other things. I've grown quite fond of him, and he seems to enjoy being with me—if 'enjoy' is ever the right word to use in relation to him. It tears me apart to see him so distant, so removed from everyone and everything around him. I wish to God there was something I could do for him."

"It seems that you are doing something for him, Caleb. You're being a good uncle. I suppose it's all anyone can do, beyond prayer." He grieved for young Joseph Cutler while at the same time giving silent thanks that his own children were so healthy and loving.

"Tell me about the war, Richard. The *Gazette* reports the British side of things, but not so much the American."

"I'll be happy to, Caleb. But first, what news from Hingham? How were Katherine and the children when you left? And how is Father? Letters have been rare down here."

"Everyone was fine when I left. Father has more aches and pains these days, but as he likes to say, growing old is not for the faint-hearted. Katherine and Lizzy are busy planning their trip to England. They're quite excited about it. So are your children. I assume you know all about Captain Hardcastle's wedding, since you said in your letter that you had dinner with him in Kingston."

"Yes. In fact, Hugh and I devised the idea to tie his wedding to Katherine's visit."

"As I suspected. On another subject, when we have time I'll tell you about Father's plans for Cutler & Sons. I've told the gist to John and Robin, though everything remains tentative. Father will want your opinions, of course. . . . Oh, here's something that might surprise you: *Constitution* was in Bridgetown for much of December, in consort with *United States*. Robin told me it was her third extended layover here since August. From what people are saying about these ships, I wish I had been here to see them. But if the past is any indication of the future, *Constitution* will be returning soon."

"*Constitution*? Here in Barbados? How very odd. Do you know why?"

"You're the naval officer, Richard. I was hoping you could tell me. During her last visit, Agee stayed with John and Robin overnight."

"And he gave no reason why he was here?"

"Robin sensed that Agee didn't want to talk about it, and he didn't press him. 'Goodwill visits and coordinating patrols' was all Agee offered as an official explanation."

Something troubling stirred in Richard. He recalled the three days that *Constellation* had stood off and on the French base at Basse-Terre and Captain Truxtun's frustration at not finding any American warships on patrol there. At least now he understood where *Constitution* and *United States* were during that time. But for the life of him he could not understand why these two frigates so vital to the American cause were so far off station in an area of the Caribbean that these days was locked up safe under British control. John Barry of *United States* and Samuel Nicholson of *Constitution* were, respectively, the two top-ranking captains in the U.S. Navy. Surely there was justification for what they had done. But goodwill visits? Coordinating patrols? That made no sense.

"Ah, Richard? Your mind's wandering. You were going to tell me about the war."

"So I was. Sorry."

For the next quarter-hour, as the carriage rumbled along the hard dirt road at a comfortable pace, Richard relayed vignettes from his life at sea, emphasizing the points he assumed would be of most interest to Caleb: the design of *Constellation*, her performance under sail, the composition of her crew, how he injured his shoulder. Ordnance and battle tactics interested Caleb less, which is why Richard suspected early on that their father was right about Caleb. His brother was as tried and true a sailor as any man afloat, but he was more at home in a merchant fleet than a naval squadron.

A FEW MINUTES PAST NOON, the carriage juddered to a stop within a pleasant compound shaded by mahogany and tamarind trees towering over colorful exotic plants. Two substantial one-story houses and a number of smaller outbuildings graced the compound. They were arranged in an oblong circle, with the plantation houses on the north and south arcs and the pebbled drive running through it east to west. Both houses were constructed of coral stone and brick. The windward side of each was built in a semicircle designed to resist hurricane winds.

Northward beyond the circle, in an area less stately yet still pleasing to the eye, were cottages housing the plantation administrators: the agent and his family, the overseer of slaves, and the boatswain, the man who managed the multistep processes of sugar and rum production. Farther on were the slave quarters: simple dwellings of wood and stone that nonetheless bespoke a certain pride, plotted as they were in tidy rows. Each dwelling abutted a cultivated area that yielded a variety of vegetables and fruits to the individual slave families, the members of which, as a rule, were never separated or sold away from one another. A long-standing principle of Cutler slave ownership dictated that Africans and Creoles held in bondage were afforded a degree of self-sufficiency and self-respect. It was a policy neither replicated nor much appreciated by other English planters. Nonetheless, Robin and John were convinced that it was the reason why, year after year, Cutler sugar production outpaced that of its neighbors.

The clop of hooves entering the compound alerted those waiting inside. Julia Cutler was first out the door, smiling broadly as she strode toward the carriage. Once Richard had stepped down, she took him joyfully though carefully into her arms.

"My dear, dear Richard," she exulted, her rosy skin aglow in the noonday sun and her tongue alive with Scottish brogue. She gave him a happy buss on each cheek. "How absolutely wonderful to see you!" She kissed him again, on the lips, laughed a delighted laugh, and then embraced him again as hard as she dared.

Richard hugged her back with his good arm. Julia had been a favorite of his since those sun-drenched days when he and Katherine had stayed with her and Robin on what had then been a second Cutler plantation on the island of Tobago. The family had sold that plantation in March 1782, after the island fell to the French, and had invested the proceeds of the sale in rum production on its larger holding on Barbados. During that visit Julia and Katherine had become the closest of friends, sharing as they did a common birthright, similar dispositions, and a passion for horseback riding.

Cynthia came up to greet him next, though in a more dignified fashion and with less fanfare. She looked thinner than he remembered—perhaps, he thought, from the stress of the long voyage to England and the disappointing results of that voyage.

John and Robin held back until Robin's three older children had added their own mix of greetings. Seth, the oldest at thirteen, had inherited his mother's ruddy complexion, his father's tall and wiry build, and his family's love of the sea. "He'll make a fine ship's master one day," Richard had often remarked, and that same thought occurred to him today as he felt the boy's firm grasp, Seth holding his gaze with an unusual confidence of self that had inspired Richard's observation in the first place. Richard then turned his attention to Seth's sister, Mary, a demure, red-haired lass of eleven who swept a low, graceful curtsy before him, and finally to her brother Benjamin, a lad of six who alone among his siblings possessed the square jaw, bright blue eyes, and yellow hair that defined the seeds of the Cutler family tree.

"Peter's inside, asleep," Julia informed him. "You'll meet him later. Caleb told you about him?"

"He did, Julia, first thing. Congratulations to you and Robin. And to little Peter, for having such a lovely and loving mother."

"And here's Joseph," Cynthia remarked. She beckoned with her right hand for a boy in the shadows to come forward. He did so, reluctantly.

"Come and greet your Uncle Richard from America, Joseph," she urged with forced gaiety.

Richard stepped forward. "Hello, Joseph." He offered his left hand. Joseph took it in his right. His grip was light and his skin was cool to the touch. When he looked up and gave Richard a faint smile, Richard saw written in those hazel eyes and delicate facial features a deep sadness, as though even at his tender age Joseph had grasped that the gulf between his inner world and the real world outside was too vast, too unfathomable, ever to be crossed. Joseph released Richard's hand and dropped his gaze to the ground.

"Well, son," his father said after several awkward moments. "Why don't you and your cousins go on inside and have your dinner. We'll be along shortly."

"Yes, Father," Joseph replied dutifully.

When Joseph and the other children were beyond earshot, John Cutler said, "I'm sorry your arrival here can't be all joy, Richard. We *are* so pleased to have you back with us."

"Good God, John, don't apologize on my account." He gave John a light one-armed embrace and a slap on the back, followed by another for Robin. "There really is nothing that can be done for Joseph?"

"It would seem not," Cynthia said with a heartfelt sigh. "We consulted the best doctors at the Royal College of Physicians, and they offered us no hope. They're as baffled by his condition as the doctors here are. They were kind to him. Everyone is kind to him—Caleb especially. Your brother is a godsend, Richard. Joseph appears happiest when he's with him, if he could ever be said to be happy."

"As are the young ladies of Barbados," John sniffed. In reply, Caleb gave him a cheerful grin. "But I must agree with Cynthia. We are eternally in your debt, Caleb, for the comfort and care you have given our son."

As if by tacit consent, for the remainder of the day and into the next, business and other weighty issues were put aside in deference to personal matters. Julia was especially keen to learn as much as she could about Katherine and the children.

"Will was such a wee babe when you and Katherine sailed home to America, Richard. Yet after all that time, your dear wife still writes me a letter every month or two. Because of her I feel as though I know you and your family as well as your neighbors in Hingham do."

"Probably better than most," Richard commented. It was late afternoon, and he was sitting at a table with a cup of hot tea before him.

About him were the pots and pans, utensils, and bowls and dishes that defined a well-appointed English kitchen. Except that the wood-burning stove was in a separate room connected to the kitchen by a breezeway, to keep the heat of cooking away from the main house. "I wish I could be out on the grounds with Robin and John, to see the new mill we purchased. I mean no offense in saying that, Julia. I do very much enjoy your company."

Julia laughed. "No offense taken, dear Richard. Don't fret. You'll be out of that wretched sling soon enough. In the meanwhile, what harm could there be in walking out to the fields just for a look?"

"A lot, according to the doctors. One slip is all it would take to break the clavicle outright and cripple me for life. I'm ordered to stay put until a doctor here says I can take off the cast."

"Well, you must absolutely heed your doctor's advice. In the meanwhile, Cynthia and I and the children are delighted to have you all to ourselves for at least part of each day."

"I am the beneficiary of that," Richard said.

"And we all have our wishes," she went on as she brought over the kettle for a refill. "Mine? I so wish I could travel to England this summer for Captain Hardcastle's wedding. What joy it would be to see Katherine again. Alas, I cannot travel with a wee babe, and I cannot leave him here with Anna. It simply wouldn't do. I'm urging Robin to go, however. It would do him a world of good. He so wants to see his parents and Lizzy and little Zeke. And guess what? Captain Hardcastle has invited Robin to sail with him to England on *Redoubtable*. His ship is being recalled to Deptford for maintenance during the hurricane season. Quite convenient, isn't it, though I suspect Admiral Parker had a hand in that decision. He's quite fond of Captain Hardcastle."

"So I have observed. I met with them both in Jamaica last summer. That's when Hugh told me about his engagement to Phoebe. Where is Captain Hardcastle now?"

"In English Harbour. He'll be away for a while, though he promised to make every effort to be back in time for the ball."

"What ball?"

"Why, the ball we're hosting in your honor. At Government House. Hugh made the arrangements before he sailed for Antigua. It's to be held on June tenth. You'll be out of that dreadful sling weeks before then."

For Richard, the hours rolled pleasantly into days and the days into weeks. The countryside blossomed in spectacular yellows and reds and whites and pinks as the tropical sun intensified its grip on the Windward Islands in springtime. By the end of March he was allowed to walk into the fields to observe the grinding work of the cut-stone boiling house. The sugarcane juice was channeled into a series of copper kettles and transformed into a sweet syrup, and then either poured into cooling troughs, where sugar crystals hardened around a sticky core of molasses, or transferred directly to the distillery, where the syrup was fermented into rum and aged in charred oaken casks to give it the rich, dark consistency characteristic of Mount Gay rum. March, too, saw a flurry of letters from Hingham now that his family knew where he was and where he would remain for five more months.

Receipt of letters was a highlight of each week. As was her custom, Katherine wrote regularly, numbering her letters in sequence and keeping him informed of the children's progress and the decisions every parent must make on behalf of their children. Often she would seek his advice on some matter—whether a certain teacher at Derby Academy should be dismissed for overzealous use of the cane, perhaps—knowing full well that a decision had to be made before her husband could possibly respond. That didn't matter. What did matter was his sense that he was part of the parenting process. Richard's letters in reply were necessarily brief, but he found as time went on that if he rested his forearm on a table he could scratch out letters that were halfway legible.

As much as the letters from his wife warmed him, those from his father intrigued him. Just as Caleb had described during their numerous discussions on the subject, Thomas Cutler proposed opening a shipping office in Baltimore after peace with France was declared. And that, he believed, would happen soon. Napoleon Bonaparte had consolidated his power in Paris and, according to authorities in the State Department, was keen to end the war with the United States. He had publicly stated that he viewed the rift with America as a distraction—a "family quarrel," he had put it—and he now wanted to focus his military efforts exclusively on Europe. What Bonaparte also wanted, in Thomas Cutler's opinion, was a cooling of relations between the United States and Great Britain that would leave England ever more isolated on the world stage.

Further, it was his father's conviction that Caleb should manage the Baltimore office, assuming that Richard and other family members agreed. And he wrote to say that he had initiated negotiations with John Endicott on opening trade routes to the Orient. First, however, he wanted to better understand what was at stake and what investment would be required. Seizures of American merchant vessels in both the Caribbean and the Mediterranean had fallen off sharply, he explained in one recent letter, and as a result, insurance rates and other costs of doing business had fallen as much as 50 percent. At the same time, worldwide demand for sugar and rum was outstripping the supply, a market dynamic that ipso facto caused prices and revenues to rise for all planters and shippers. Such enhanced profits, Thomas Cutler reasoned, could finance new business initiatives, eliminating the need to borrow funds from a third party or to encumber existing family investments or annual financial distributions to family members.

"What do you think?" Richard asked John and Robin after he had received this letter and allowed his cousins to digest its contents. It was a hot, breezeless day in late April and they were sitting in the center of the compound on two cool, stone-slab benches set beneath the giant trunk of a banyan tree that had been brought over as a sapling from the East Indies.

"Which part of the letter are you referring to?" John asked.

"For starters," Richard said moderately, "my father's recommendation that Caleb manage the Baltimore office."

John shrugged. "He's your brother, Richard. You and your father know him a great deal better than Robin or I do. And neither of us has ever been to America, much less Baltimore. It's your decision, not ours."

"That's not how we do things, John," Richard countered. "This is a family decision. You've both had the opportunity to observe Caleb during these past several months. You've helped him learn the business from the ground up, so to speak. That's why we wanted him to come here in the first place. Is there anything you have observed during that time that gives you pause?"

Richard instantly understood the meaning in John's shrug. "We're not discussing Caleb's social life, John," he said irritably, his patience wearing thin on the subject. "What I need to understand is your business perspectives. I realize you do not approve of Caleb's lifestyle, but I fail to see how that lifestyle disqualifies him from a senior management position."

"It isn't just me," John protested. "Cynthia may not say much about it, but she finds Caleb's running about just as objectionable as I do. Should you ask any other planters, they will tell you the same thing."

"And should I ask those planters whose daughters are pursuing my brother just as ardently, and whose morals are even more suspect by your standards? Ease your sheets a little, John. Caleb was ten years in an Arab prison. By the grace of God he managed to come out of it alive. Isn't that what matters? That he survived and is able to run about, as you put it?"

John stared straight ahead, tapping his fingers on his knee and saying nothing in reply.

"Robin?"

Robin Cutler had listened to the exchange, casually fanning himself with his straw hat as though what transpired was of minor concern to him. Of the two brothers, he had changed the least over the years. Unlike John, whose hair was thinning and whose hairline was receding, Robin retained a full head of russet-colored hair—though now streaked with white—and his sinewy frame and finely chiseled features retained a youthful appearance and vitality. Whereas John delighted in the role and accoutrements of a gentleman English planter, Robin preferred simpler garb and tended to avoid pretensions, despite his marriage into one of the richest families on Barbados. Such differences in style and outlook notwithstanding, John and Robin Cutler complemented each other in ways critical to the prosperity of a family-owned enterprise. Robin Cutler knew how to produce superior products, and John Cutler knew how to sell them.

"As you have heard me say before," Robin said to Richard, "I am quite impressed with Caleb. I have been since the day he arrived. I particularly admire his determination to learn every aspect of the business, whatever it takes and wherever it takes place. One rarely witnesses such enthusiasm for getting one's hands dirty. About the only thing he hasn't done these past four months is cut cane in the fields with the Negroes. And he would have done *that* if John had not threatened to send him to purgatory in Peter's room. What's more, I don't share John's views on Caleb's personal affairs. Neither does Julia. Whom he consorts with and how he does it is his concern, not mine, as long as it does not interfere with the family business and as long as he does it discreetly. Which to this point he has. Do I give him high marks for what he has accomplished here on Barbados? Yes. Do I believe he has the business instincts and acumen to commend him to a senior position in Cutler & Sons? Again, yes, without question."

"Thank you, Robin," Richard said. "We are in agreement, then?"

"You and I are. John?"

John pursed his lips and nodded in resignation.

IN MID-MAY, as the Easter season faded into memory and summer-like heat settled over the island, a physician in Bridgetown removed the plaster cast on Richard's arm for the final time. Pain jabbed at him as he slowly moved his arm this way and that, but the doctor assured him that the discomfort was perfectly normal and would subside once Richard began exercising the muscles that had atrophied during the long weeks of convalescence. And exercise Richard did, right away, with a form he had sorely missed as a semi-invalid. When he returned to the Cutler compound, he walked out not to the cane fields but to the beach, where he stripped to his undershorts and dove into the warm turquoise water. There he lingered for the best part of three hours, swimming an easy side stroke, diving down into the clear depths, relaxing on the sugar-white sand, and then having at it all over again, luxuriating in the clear saltwater and hot tropical sun coursing over him, cleansing him, restoring him. In the late afternoon he returned to the compound, wet and tired, toting six rock lobsters he had plucked off a coral reef and wrapped up in his shirt.

"Supper," he announced happily. He spilled the lobsters, their tails flapping, into a tin basin on the kitchen table. "I'm finally able to start earning my keep around here."

Cynthia gave him a rare beam of a smile. "Oh, how splendid, Richard," she gushed. "How absolutely splendid. Joseph loves lobsters. I must call him this instant." When she returned to the kitchen, she said, "John left today's *Gazette* out for you. There's an article on the front page he thinks you'll find interesting. It's in the parlor."

"Oh? I'll have a look after I rinse off and change clothes."

A few minutes later, still giddy at his newfound freedom and cleanliness, Richard walked into the snug parlor and took a seat in a leather chair bathed in the light of an open window. Beside it was an elegant sandalwood table on which Cynthia had placed a china cup of tea and the latest issue of the *Bridgetown Gazette*. He picked up the paper, snapped it to straighten it, and read a front-page story that John had starred in black ink.

Toussaint L'Ouverture Attacks Rigaud; United States His Ally

Jacmel, Saint-Domingue, 30 April 1799. The civil war that has raged on the island of Hispaniola for a decade has taken a dramatic turn. The army of Negro General Toussaint L'Ouverture, led by his senior officer, Jean-Jacques Dessalines, has laid siege to the

mulatto stronghold on the southern coast of Saint-Domingue. This
assault differs from previous initiatives in that Toussaint's soldiers
appear to be well provisioned and well armed. It is perhaps no
coincidence that as Dessalines attacks Jacmel by land, the United
States warship *General Greene* has blockaded the harbor and is
bombarding the earthworks from the sea. No vessels, including
British merchant vessels, are allowed access to Jacmel in support of
the forces of mulatto leader André Rigaud. Tobias Lear, U.S. consul at Cap François, has refused to comment on what appears to be
a flagrant violation of American neutrality in this affair. Admiral
Sir Hyde Parker in Port Royal, Jamaica, has also refused to com-
ment, although it is widely rumored that he and his superiors in the
Admiralty are gravely concerned over this puzzling turn of events.
Royal Navy frigates have been dispatched to the area, including
HMS *Redoubtable* of the Windward Squadron, recently in English
Harbour, Antigua.

"Son of a bitch," Richard heard himself say. He put the cup down on
its saucer and read through the article again. Overall, it did a commend-
able job of distilling the complexities of the civil war and summarizing
the milestones since the first slave uprisings in 1791. Not surprising to
Richard was its failure to mention the combined British and American
summit with Toussaint L'Ouverture on Île de la Gonâve.

"Son of a *bitch*," he said again, loud enough to be overheard by
Caleb, who had entered the room with young Joseph in tow.

"What is it, Richard? What's the matter?" said Caleb. In a lower
voice: "And pray, watch your language in front of the boy."

Richard glanced up. "It's an article about Saint-Domingue," he
answered vaguely. He had told his family nothing about his experience there, it being decided among those involved to keep the stopper
in the rumor mill for as long as possible. More to the point, he still
had trouble fitting together the pieces of the puzzle. At the time, this
much at least had seemed indisputable: British and American interests
were best served by supporting Toussaint against Rigaud. That is what
Richard had written in his report to Navy Secretary Stoddert, and what
Hugh Hardcastle had assured him he would report to Admiral Parker.
So why were Great Britain and the United States now seemingly at odds
over which side to support? Why would Admiral Parker now succor a
man he had once described as "a mulatto half-breed on a French leash"
who was the sworn enemy of England? And why was Hugh Hardcastle

bound for Jacmel and a possible confrontation with an American brig of war?

"Well, go on. What does the article say?"

Richard was still uncertain how much to reveal, or even if the intelligence he had on the subject had any relevance anymore. "That the civil war there may soon end," he replied. "Caleb, what do you know about Toussaint L'Ouverture?"

"Not much. Only what has been reported in the *Gazette*. The Boston newspapers had little to say about him."

"What's your impression of what's happening on Saint-Domingue?"

"Not much," he repeated. "The way I see it, blacks are fighting blacks on an island populated by blacks. Who cares?"

"Our government, for one. According to this article, the United States has sent weapons and supplies to Toussaint."

Caleb glanced at the headline Richard held out to him. "We're *allied* with him? A former *slave*? Why on earth would we do that?"

"For trading rights. For Toussaint's promise to discourage slave uprisings in America. And who knows, perhaps for a little idealism. Toussaint is trying to do for his country what General Washington did for ours."

Caleb pondered that. "So President Adams has concluded that this fellow Toussaint L'Ouverture can actually win the war. And throw out the French. With whom *we're* at war. Sort of."

Richard grinned. "Cut right to the heart of the matter, don't you, Caleb? You have a bright future in our diplomatic corps." He looked at Joseph, who had been standing off to the side, near the window. Richard couldn't tell whether he had been listening to the brothers' exchange. "So, Joseph. Your mother tells me you like lobsters."

"I do." Joseph spoke so softly the words were barely audible. "Thank you for catching them. That was kind of you. Uncle Richard?"

"Yes, Joseph."

"Will Uncle Caleb have to go to war?"

The two brothers glanced at each other.

"No, Joseph. Uncle Caleb will not have to go to war."

"Then why must he leave us? He won't tell me why."

Richard again glanced at his brother, who shrugged and gave him a helpless look in return. Richard beckoned Joseph over to his side and rested a hand on his shoulder. "Joseph," he said, "Uncle Caleb must return home to Boston because he is needed there. He doesn't want to go, but he must. His family misses him, and his father, your great-uncle Thomas, needs him to help manage our business, just as he has learned to do here on Barbados with your father's help."

"I don't want him to leave. I will miss him. I will miss you too, Uncle Richard." Joseph cuffed his eyes with his sleeve, as close to an outpouring of emotion as Richard or Caleb had ever witnessed from him.

"We'll miss you, too, Joseph. Caleb will especially. He loves you very much. We all do. But we're family, aren't we? And families stick together and support each other no matter what, don't they? Caleb will come back to Barbados. Many times. So will I. And if we're lucky—if we're very, very lucky—you will agree to come to America some day to visit with us and meet your other cousins. Would you like to come to America, Joseph?"

"Yes, I would." Joseph choked on the words. His lower lip trembled and he could say no more. When he looked at Caleb, his eyes welled up, the tears began to flow, and he ran crying from the room.

SEVEN WEEKS LATER, on a rare drizzly afternoon in late June, a post rider brought word to the Cutler plantation that HMS *Redoubtable* had returned to Barbados. The message was written in the distinctive hand of Hugh Hardcastle and contained an invitation to Richard to dine with him two evenings hence in Bridgetown. "I would be pleased to pipe you on board *Redoubtable*," the note concluded, "but I am in serious need of some good shore cooking."

Richard conferred with his cousins and hurried back a reply stating that since duty had prevented Hugh from attending one of the most memorable balls in Bridgetown's memory, and since it was Hugh Hardcastle who had graciously arranged for the gala to be held at Government House, the Cutler family would be honored to have him join them for supper at the Cutler plantation two evenings hence, and to stay the night as their guest. Hugh accepted with pleasure and arrived promptly at six o'clock.

A servant stepped up to take his duffel as Hugh disembarked from a hired carriage. John insisted on paying the driver and then joined the others gathering around the British naval officer bedecked in the spotless white trousers, gold-rimmed blue undress coat, and shiny bullion epaulets of a Royal Navy post captain. His hosts, too, were appropriately attired in the newly adopted fashions of the post-Revolution era. John and Robin wore the unadorned but perfectly tailored full-length dark linen trousers that had been introduced recently in England by

Beau Brummell, along with a fitted tailcoat of similar material and color and an elaborately knotted cravat. In a similar bow to what had become all the rage in Europe, Julia and Cynthia each wore a low-cut dress of rippling silk that fitted closely under the bust and then fell in loose folds to the ankles.

"Welcome," Richard said, clasping Hugh's hand when his turn came. He was dressed for the occasion in a naval uniform that, with more gilt braid, less buff, finer cloth, and an epaulet on the left shoulder to match the one on the right, would have appeared very similar to that of his brother-in-law.

Hugh inclined his head. "Thank you for the invitation, Richard," he said sotto voce, over the clatter of the carriage departing on the pebbled drive. "It's a pleasure to be with you and your family again. You and I have much to discuss. I'm particularly eager to hear about your encounter with *L'Insurgente*."

"That we do. And that we will. After supper."

The Cutlers and their guest moved into John and Cynthia's dining room, a large octagonal space encompassing what in Boston would have been two rooms: the dining room proper, dominated by a large rectangular table of East Indian teak with ten matching chairs—four on each side and one on each end—and a sitting room on the opposite side with cushioned rattan chairs and two round mahogany tables. The floor was of marble and stone, void of mats or rugs—intended, as was the design of the entire house, to retain the cool evening temperatures into the next day and to allow the free flow of air throughout.

Dinner featured freshly caught yellowtail snapper served in a light cream sauce sprinkled with coconut, nutmeg, and ginger. Fresh vegetables and fruits and three of the best bottles of Bordeaux that John Cutler could pull from his inventory completed the menu. Early on in the meal, Hugh Hardcastle scraped back his chair and rose to his feet.

"To our women," he said, holding his glass up. "To those who bring grace and beauty to our lives and without whom we men would be nothing more than mindless barbarians. To my lovely and gracious hosts, Cynthia and Julia Cutler, who have honored me with their kind hospitality this evening; to my sister Katherine, who time and again has had to stoop low to raise her husband up from the depths; and to my intended, Phoebe Clausen, who, in her benevolence, has bestowed upon me life's most precious gifts of love and passion."

"Hear, hear!" the others acclaimed in unison.

Through much of the main course the conversation dwelt on Hugh's upcoming marriage. The wedding date was set for September 24 and would take place in Saint Stephen's Church in Fareham with the Reverend Graham Fenton presiding, the same Anglican minister who had married Richard and Katherine. Hugh and Robin would depart Barbados in a fortnight, bound for England, there to be joined in mid-August by Katherine and Lizzy and the four children.

During a dessert of spotted dog pudding fortified by a hoary port wine, Hugh winked across the table at Caleb Cutler. He had an impish look when he said, in a voice loud enough to capture everyone's attention, "The word in Bridgetown, Caleb, is that at the ball you cut quite a swath among the young ladies of society."

The remark caused John to bristle.

"Pray, take pity," Hugh continued, "on a soon-to-be-married man ignorant of such things and tell me how you manage to rouse these ladies up so. I can see for myself that you are a handsome sort. But surely there's more to it than that. Some sort of love potion, perhaps, sprinkled into a glass?"

Before Caleb could respond, Richard said, "There *is* more to it than good looks, Hugh, but it has nothing to do with love potions."

"Oh? Then what, pray?"

"I can't tell you. Neither can Caleb. It's a family secret."

"Is it, now?" Hugh's tone assumed a tenor of keen disappointment. "And I cannot prevail upon you to divulge this grand secret?"

"No. Sorry."

"Well, then, if you won't tell me, I shall have to inquire of Katherine when I see her later this summer."

"She won't tell you either. My father has often counseled us never to flaunt our advantage and never to reveal the source of our pleasures." That comment inspired general tittering around the table, save from the host at the end. Cynthia brought a hand to her mouth, not in shock, but to suppress a giggle.

"So you are truly going to leave the service, Captain Hardcastle?" she asked once the mirth had faded away, hoping to steer the conversation toward safer waters. She knew that despite her husband's outwardly calm demeanor, a tempest was building within. "We have heard that you might, but of course we have kept that possibility very much to ourselves. *This* secret, if indeed it is one, remains safe with us as well."

"Thank you, Mrs. Cutler. You are most gracious. Yes, I am planning to retire from the service. Not right away, but soon. Unless, of course, I am able to find a steward capable of serving a meal on board ship the likes of which I have enjoyed this evening. That alone might dissuade me."

John joined in the smiles in appreciation of that comment, and Cynthia relaxed.

Richard shared in the gaiety but inside was wrenched by deep regret that he would not be joining his family in Fareham. For so long Hugh's wedding had seemed a distant event. Now, suddenly, it seemed imminent. "I'm sorry I can't be at your wedding, Hugh," he said later that evening when the two of them were seated alone in the parlor. "I should very much like to meet Phoebe."

Hardcastle smiled benignly. "You shall meet her, Richard. Might I remind you that when I leave the service, Phoebe and I are planning to sail to Boston, where we expect the Cutler family to welcome us with open arms and to provide me with suitable employment and a living wage."

"You're in, assuming we can afford your definition of a living wage."

"Which of course you can, once your new best friend Toussaint L'Ouverture grants the *exclusif* he has promised you. Rather ingenious, wasn't it, the way he danced around your president? And the way your president danced around Congress and the whole bloody issue of the embargo? Diplomatic gifts, indeed! The so-called gifts were nothing less than munitions to serve an army and provisions to wage a war. Rather clever of him, I'd say. Your president has made Toussaint a very happy general. A general who, by the bye, continues to labor under the impression that you played a key hand in his good fortune. I daresay his *exclusif* will amount to a rather tidy annual sum for Cutler & Sons."

"Enough to pay your wages?"

"Good heavens no, my dear man! But it should make for a satisfactory down payment."

They chuckled together. From an inside coat pocket Hugh withdrew an elegant silver container on which his initials were inscribed in flowing script. He popped it open, withdrew two six-inch cigars, and tapped the open end of one against the container.

"I hope I didn't offend anyone at dinner tonight, Richard," he said. "I was just having a bit of fun with Caleb. I'm accustomed to dining in far less refined company, but that is no excuse for affronting my hosts. Please apologize for me if you think it necessary."

Richard shook his head. "All's well that ends well, the great bard once wrote, and all ended well this evening. I haven't heard such good cheer in that room for a long time, and we have you to thank for that."

"What about John? I would not wish to upset him. He's not only a friend, he's my host, and an excellent one at that."

"John's fine. Don't worry. Your humor and the wine finally got through to him. He needed that distraction. He tends to take things too seriously. And of course he worries constantly about his son."

"Yes, I'm sure. I was so sorry to learn that the trip to England fell short of expectations. Has there been any change in Joseph since?"

"Actually, I think perhaps there has. Yesterday, Joseph asked Seth and Benjamin to go outside with him to play a game of hoops. Seth agreed, bless him, though he doesn't much care for the game. I realize that may seem somewhat trivial, but you see, Joseph had never before asked anyone to play with him."

"Ah." After a pause, Hugh said, "Excuse me, Richard. Would you care for a smoke?" He held out a cigar. "They're from Hispaniola, in the Cibao River valley. They're really quite exceptional. I must say, the devils on that island know how to make a bloody good smoke."

"Thank you, I would." Richard got up and walked over to John's work desk. He opened a drawer and found flint and steel and a receptacle to use as an ashtray. Striking flint on steel, he offered Hugh a light from the lint, then lit his own cigar.

"That's not all those devils on that island know how to do," Richard said as he resumed his seat. He crossed his right leg over his left and drew in the rich, savory tobacco. Although not historically a smoker, during his convalescence on Barbados he had come to enjoy this occasional luxury.

Hugh slowly blew out a stream of smoke and cocked his head in question, waiting for Richard to go on.

"They also know how to turn friends and family against each other. Seriously, Hugh, what the hell happened to England's support of Toussaint? You and I risked our lives to gain that support. I thought we were in agreement on this."

"We were, and we are."

"Well, then, why were the British trying to get provisions through to Rigaud at Jacmel? And why were *you* ordered there to engage an American warship? I mean no disrespect, but it doesn't add up."

"I quite agree. It doesn't."

"Well, then?"

Hugh took a sip of port and contemplated the ash on his cigar. When he spoke, it was without lifting his eyes from the glowing tip. "We could discuss this for hours, Richard, and someday we will. But here's the nub of it. The commander in chief of the British army in the Greater Antilles—a general named White—took ill and had to return to England. That left in charge a lieutenant colonel named Thomas Maitland—known to many as 'King Tom,' but not in a fond sort of way.

"Maitland, it seems, has no use for colored people, whatever color that happens to be. Black or mulatto, yellow or red, it doesn't matter. He doesn't much care for Americans either. That said, he has a particular aversion for black African Negroes. The blacker the skin, the greater the sin—to his mind at least. And he's by no means alone in that belief. Many whites share it, including many in your country. Few have dared go public with it, however, the way King Tom has.

"As you can imagine, Toussaint L'Ouverture is not high on Tom's list of favorites. A Negro who aims to rule a West Indian island far oversteps his bounds. However he managed it, Maitland convinced Admiral Hyde that Toussaint, who clearly had gained the upper hand over Rigaud after the United States intervened on his behalf, is not to be trusted. His real agenda, Maitland argues, is to incite a slave rebellion on Jamaica, and then to invade the island in alliance with the French and Spanish. His ultimate objective is the capture of our naval base at Port Royal."

"Maitland *believes* that?"

"Oh, I should very much think he does."

"And Admiral Parker? How could any intelligent man be duped by such nonsense? When did he turn about and change his tune so dramatically?"

"When he started listening to a different drummer."

"Meaning?"

"Meaning that while he may have appeared to be in agreement with what we wrote in our reports, his agreement was only on the surface. Deep down, he has long harbored his own doubts about blacks in general and Toussaint in particular, whom he sees as a puppet of republican France. So he had a mind already eager to be twisted by one such as King Tom, who simply provided him with the military justification he needed. The good admiral then decided to get more into the game and play both sides of the wicket, the way everyone else was doing."

"Meaning?"

"Meaning that at the end of the day, Admiral Hyde chose not to end the game. Since the United States was provisioning Toussaint, he would see to it that England provisioned both sides, with a bias toward Rigaud."

"Why Rigaud, for God's sake?"

"To keep the game going, as I indicated. With both sides receiving aid, neither side, in theory, can hold the upper hand. With neither side holding the upper hand, the war can continue for months or even years, with each side killing off the other until, eventually, with enough blacks and mulattoes slaughtered, and with France and Spain distracted in Europe and the United States hamstrung over principles and ethics, we English can march in—or sail in, as it were—and seize control of the entire island. Britain wins and everyone else loses. Quite the simple game plan, once you boil it all down. Mind you, this is not the official version. But it is what I believe to be the truth."

"*Jesus Christ!*"

"Yes, he would be rather appalled by all this, wouldn't he?"

"Hugh, do you mean to tell me that you knew all this when you were ordered to Jacmel? And that to get provisions through to Rigaud you were prepared to engage an American warship blockading the harbor?"

"Never in life, Richard. Yes, I understood the issues, more or less, when I was ordered to sail from Antigua. But never would I have fired upon an American ship; nor was I ordered to. I actually met the captain of *General Greene* near the Bight of Léogâne. His name is Perry. Christopher Raymond Perry. I also met his son, Oliver, who is serving on board as a midshipman."

"I've heard good things about Captain Perry."

"As well you should have. I can tell you without reservation that he is a gentleman and a very fine sea officer."

"But back to Saint-Domingue. What happened to Rigaud after the fall of Jacmel?"

"It's anyone's guess. To my knowledge he has not been captured; nor has his body been found. His officers, those few taken alive, refuse to talk. It matters not a fig. If Rigaud did manage to slip away, he has nowhere to go except France. He's finished on Hispaniola. The game is over. Admiral Hyde made the mistake of underestimating Toussaint and the resolve of his officers and soldiers."

"I see." Richard's voice and facial expression held a faraway quality as he remembered Toussaint's promise of an *exclusif* to Cutler & Sons.

"I congratulate President Adams for picking the winning side," Hugh added, "and you for being a part of it. I doubt that either of you will gain much from it in the long run, however. As much as I respect General Toussaint, I cannot envision a country in this hemisphere governed by black Africans. In any event, perhaps now you understand why I am so eager to retire from the service and settle my affairs elsewhere." He added, "But not before I bestow a gift upon you and *Constellation*."

"A gift?" Richard was at sea.

"Yes, a gift. One I believe that you and Captain Truxtun and your entire ship's complement will quickly come to appreciate. My gift—I should say, the gift of the Royal Navy for services rendered on His Majesty's behalf—is ten carronades, delivered at cost to your Gosport Navy Yard in Virginia. Arrangements have already been finalized between my Navy Board and your Navy Department. My understanding is that they are being installed on board *Constellation* even as we speak. May you have occasion to use them. The French call these guns 'devil guns,' and for good reason. I must say, giving the French a good pasting at sea is one thing I'll miss when I leave the service."

Richard's elation about receiving Hugh's "gift" was superseded several weeks later when, just as he was preparing to book passage north to Saint Kitts, word came to the Cutler compound that USS *Constitution* had sailed into Carlisle Bay under a thirteen-gun salute.

Thirteen

Marie-Galante, French West Indies
September–October 1799

RICHARD CUTLER lost no time getting to Bridgetown. John offered him a horse and carriage, but Richard did without the carriage. Not an equestrian by nature, and made skittish by a fall from a horse in England many years ago, he had learned to ride quite well under Katherine's patient tutelage. Within an hour of receiving word of *Constitution*'s arrival, he had his horse munching feed in a stable on Front Street and the American frigate in sight.

She was anchored in Carlisle Bay on the periphery of the Windward Squadron. His first impression was what he had expected. She looked very much like *Constellation*, only longer—thirty feet longer, he recalled. Her hull was ink black, save for a band of white painted along her gun-port strake. Her beam was comparable to *Constellation*'s in width, but she carried a thousand tons heavier burthen, three dozen sails, and a sail plan exceeding 42,000 square feet. With those great clouds of white canvas now furled tight to their yards and booms, she looked a beauty for the ages as she lay out there beam-on to him. High above, on her three masts, pennants fluttered in the breeze alongside the Stars and Stripes.

A scan of the ships in the squadron and of the pedestrians lining the shore confirmed that many others, sailors and civilians alike, were equally drawn to the graceful lines and stark majesty of the pride of the U.S. Navy.

The immediate question was how to get out to her. The western half of Carlisle Bay housed the ships of the Windward Squadron. Access to those vessels was restricted to ships' boats and to lighters commissioned by the navy yard to transport food and water to the squadron. For the moment, Richard could see no such boat tethered to the quays nearby or coming ashore from the ships. He thus had two choices: he could either wait for one to become available or hire a wherry at the commercial wharves on the eastern half of the harbor. He decided to wait. A wherryman would likely be challenged by a guard boat and ordered to turn back, and the wherryman, his fare already paid, would not likely object.

A half-hour elapsed before Richard noticed a jolly boat being swung out from *Constitution* and lowered into the water. Eight sailors clambered down the frigate's side, followed by the coxswain. He was followed in turn by an individual Richard knew to be an officer, both by his uniform and by the distant squeal of pipes accompanying him off the ship. A sailor in the bow cast off the line, those positioned at the larboard side backed oars, and the jolly boat made for shore, her oars rising and dipping, rising and dipping, moving the boat forward in steady pulses.

Richard moved along the docks toward the point where the coxswain was aiming, an open space along a stone wharf not far away. As it approached, he strained to identify the officer sitting in the stern sheets, but he could not make out the man's features even as the jolly boat bumped gently against the quay a few feet from him.

"Boat oars!" the coxswain cried out.

"Well done, Oates," the officer said admiringly, his voice edged with a Highland burr. Gingerly he stepped onto the quay. To the coxswain he said, "Stand by. I shan't be long, I shouldn't think." To the oarsmen he said, "You men are free to walk about. Just remember my warning. Stay close to the docks and steer clear of the taverns and doxies. I will have no man coming down with the pox." He turned to go but stopped short before the tall blond man blocking his way. "Excuse me, sir, might I be of service?"

"Good morning, Lieutenant," Richard said. "My name is Richard Cutler. I serve as first in USS *Constellation*, currently being refitted at the Gosport Shipyard. I am hoping that—"

"My God, sir!" the officer exclaimed. "*You* are Lieutenant Cutler?"

"I am."

"Well, I'll be snookered," he declared, shaking his head in wonder. "This is a most extraordinary coincidence. *You*, sir, are the very man I was sent ashore to contact. *Constitution*"—he unnecessarily indicated the frigate at anchor—"is at your service. We were ordered to Bridgetown to convey you to Saint Kitts on our return cruise from the Leeward Antilles to the Santo Domingo Station."

"My Lord. Truly?"

"Truly," the officer laughed. He lifted his black fore-and-aft cocked hat. "Allow me to introduce myself. I am Robert Hamilton, *Constitution*'s second."

Richard returned the salute. "I am pleased to make your acquaintance, Lieutenant," he said. "Are you by chance related to Mr. Alexander Hamilton? I believe I have heard him mention your name."

"I am, sir," the handsome, dark-haired officer replied. "I am his cousin. On the Scottish side of the family."

"I see. Well, congratulations on your appointment, Mr. Hamilton. Tell me, is Lieutenant Crabtree on board?"

"He is, sir. He has a slight ailment, else he'd be here in my stead. Nothing serious, I should think, and he seems to be well on a course to recovery. He is most anxious to see you." Hamilton swept an arm toward the jolly boat bobbing up and down along the quay. "Shall we be off to the ship? I see no reason to linger here."

"I'm all for that."

The dirty looks and subdued mutters of the jolly boat's crew as Richard settled into the stern sheets next to Hamilton suggested that they were not as "all for that" as the two officers.

As the boat pulled toward *Constitution*, Richard locked his gaze on the American frigate ahead, taking in the entire ship from her jaunty stern lines to the figurehead at her bow: a scroll, representing the Constitution, guarded on both sides by dragons. He recalled the day when he and his father and brother first approached the fully rigged *Constellation* in Baltimore Harbor. Just as he had back then, he felt a surge of pride that a vessel of such power and glory sailed under the flag of his country.

"Boat ahoy!" a youthful voice cried out from the frigate.

"Aye, aye!" the coxswain shouted up in reply, signifying that he had an officer on board.

With the jolly boat secured at *Constitution*'s larboard fore-chains, Richard, the higher-ranking officer, grabbed hold of the twin hand ropes and stepped onto and up the eleven steps built into the hull. At the entry port he saluted the quarterdeck as a hastily assembled party of ship's boys piped him on board, followed by a second undulating shriek as Lieutenant Hamilton stepped onto the deck.

"This is Lieutenant Cutler, Mr. Sayres," Hamilton said when the shriek was cut short by the boatswain. The young man he addressed appeared to be a midshipman serving as officer of the deck. "We shall go below to visit with the captain. Please pass word to Mr. Hull and Mr. Crabtree to join us."

"Aye, aye, sir."

As the two lieutenants made their way down the broad wooden steps amidships onto the gun deck, Hamilton asked, "How do you find her, Mr. Cutler? Compared to *Constellation*."

"Very much the same," Richard replied, looking about. He stooped slightly when he reached the deck, his eyes sweeping along the array of glistening black 24-pounder guns mounted on blood-red trucks bowsed up one after another against the larboard and starboard bulwarks. He did not need to count them. Every officer in the U.S. Navy knew what armament each of the newly built frigates carried. There would be twenty-six guns to his view on this deck, and four additional guns mounted in the captain's day cabin aft, just as in *Constellation*. "I watched her being built in Boston," he explained, adding, in a softer tone of confidentiality, "Lieutenant, is there anything you can tell me about Captain Nicholson before I meet with him?"

Hamilton gave him a startled look. "Dear me, Mr. Cutler, you *have* been on the beach, haven't you. Captain Nicholson no longer commands this ship. He was relieved several months ago and assigned to shore duty."

"Oh? Who's in command now?"

Hamilton motioned toward a Marine sentry standing at attention before the door leading into the captain's after cabin. "I suggest we see that you are properly introduced."

The stone-faced Marine was dressed in a blue coat with scarlet trim, red cuffs, and a single white cross-belt, and blue trousers. His tall hat was trimmed in yellow and turned up on the left side with a leather cockade attached to it. At his side he gripped a finely polished sea-service musket.

"Lieutenant Cutler to see Captain Talbot," Hamilton informed him.

The Marine sentry snapped a salute, wheeled about, and rapped on the door. He opened it when bidden and announced the visitors. Hearing acknowledgment from inside, he swung the door open and stepped aside.

At the mention of the name "Talbot" an image formed in Richard's mind of a man with whom he had served during the war in Old Mill Prison in Plymouth, England. Despite a ten-year difference in age, they had become close friends during their time in prison. Richard was a former midshipman in *Ranger* and Silas Talbot was a noted privateer captain and major in the Continental army. Such was Talbot's natural charisma that he quickly became the unanimous choice to serve as leader of the American prisoners, all of whom were captured seamen viewed by the British not as prisoners of war but as traitors deserving a traitor's death. Despite that sword of Damocles hanging over him, and a prison keeper who had no love for Americans, Talbot was able to negotiate better terms and conditions for his countrymen before engineering a daring plan that allowed most of the commissioned and warrant officers to escape from Old Mill and return to the war.

When the cabin door swung open, there he was, approaching Richard with a broad smile. Although twenty years had passed since they had last seen each other, Talbot carried his age well. He had gained little weight, his hair was only slightly grayer and flecked in white, and he had the same wide, sturdy cheekbones, the same thin nose with a crook at the end, and the same bright blue-gray eyes that shone either as welcoming beacons of light or as signal fires of danger, depending on whom he was approaching. He was dressed casually in buff breeches, light blue ruffled shirt, and a white linen neck stock. His blue undress coat, identical in design and trappings with the one Captain Truxtun wore, was draped over the back of a chair behind his desk.

"Well, I'll be damned," he exclaimed happily, "if it's not Richard Cutler, here in my cabin. I must say, you lost no time in finding us." He returned Richard's salute, then grasped his shoulders and gave him a jubilant smile.

"Good to see you, Captain. It's been too many years."

"Indeed it has, Lieutenant. How are you? I must say you look fit as a fiddle."

"As do you, sir."

"Yes, well, shipboard fare does tend to keep one trim." He patted his waistline. "Those land snails we lived on at Old Mill were *haute cuisine* compared to what my steward serves me most days."

"I'm sorry to hear that, sir," Richard said, recalling the snails' bitter taste that more than once made him vomit.

"As are my dinner guests." He placed hands on hips. "So. Some years ago the world press announced that you had struck your colors and married that English lass you kept mooning over in prison. Katherine, wasn't it?"

"You have an excellent memory, Captain."

"Actually, I have a wretched memory. It's just hard to forget a name carped out from a baying hound every night for a whole bloody year. One favor that bastard Cowdry"—referring to the prison keeper at Old Mill—"would not grant me, no matter how hard I pressed, was a transfer to the French barracks for one night. One bloody night was all I asked."

Richard grinned. "Katherine and I have three children now, sir. We live in Hingham."

"Yes, thank you. I am quite well versed in your comings and goings, compliments of Mr. Crabtree, who, as you will not be surprised to learn since you had the good sense to employ him, I find to be an excellent sea officer. He has been under the weather, poor fellow, though he's feeling better now. He'll be joining us shortly. It will be like old times, having the three of us together again. I was delighted to receive orders to return to station via Bridgetown and transport you back to Saint Kitts. We intend to weigh anchor just as soon as we're provisioned. And on our cruise northward we might just cause a bit of mischief."

Curious as to Talbot's meaning, Richard was about to ask when there came a rap on the door. Two officers were announced and entered the day cabin. One man Richard knew by reputation. The other he knew by heart.

"I believe you have met Mr. Crabtree," Talbot said good-naturedly. "This other gentleman is Mr. Isaac Hull, my first. Mr. Hull, I introduce you to Mr. Richard Cutler, *Constellation*'s first."

"Welcome on board, Mr. Cutler," Hull said as they shook hands.

Richard knew a little about this lean, attractive, clearly well-bred officer about ten years younger than he. Hull hailed from Connecticut and in recent years had been the master of several merchant vessels. One of these, Richard recalled, had been seized by a French privateer off the coast of Cuba with loss of American lives. What first struck him about Hull physically was the wavy black hair that framed his clean-shaven face, and the long sideburns that inched down to his lower jaw and curved inward toward his chin. His eyes, too, were jet black, and set close together under thick, bushy eyebrows. Richard also recalled that Hull's naval career had been launched with more than a gentle push from his uncle, Continental army hero William Hull, a close friend of Samuel Nicholson.

"Thank you, Mr. Hull. I am delighted to be on board."

Richard's gaze shifted to Agreen Crabtree standing by the closed door next to Hamilton. When their eyes met, Agreen gave him a weak grin.

Talbot observed the exchange. "Well, Mr. Cutler," he said, "now that you have met my commissioned officers, may we invite you to join us for supper this evening here in my cabin? Mr. Davenport, the ship's master, will be joining us. In the event you wish to sleep on board, we shall have a cabin prepared for you. In the meantime, I suggest that you and Mr. Crabtree spend some time at your ease." He stepped back toward his desk, a signal for his officers to take their leave. "Until this evening, gentlemen. And Mr. Cutler, you have my word that the land snails we have in store for us are at least halfway edible."

"Where to, Agee?" Richard asked moments later when they were alone on the gun deck. "How does a brace of fresh air sound?"

"Almost as good as seein' you again, Richard."

Richard slowed his steps to follow Agee up the ladder leading to the weather deck. Topside, sailors in casual, loose-fitting garb and low-crowned black hats worked about them, swinging ropes up and over the lower yardarms to hoist provisions from lighters up onto the deck, then down the wide rectangular hatch onto the gun deck. From there they would be lowered further below to storage under the orlop. Other sailors were lowering away the remaining ship's boats—a long boat, two whaleboats, two cutters, the captain's gig, and a punt—and tying them up astern of the frigate to keep them clear of the on loading. Richard and Agreen returned the sailors' two-fingered salutes and walked forward past the foremast to the forepeak, near the entrance to the head, which at the moment was unoccupied. There, where the massive bowsprit and jib boom extended out from the forecastle seemingly into eternity, they could speak in private.

"My Lord, Agee," Richard marveled as he gazed down the 204-foot length of the flush deck, then upward the same distance to the foremast truck and the mile upon mile of standing and running rigging dedicated to that spar alone. "What an amazing ship she is. I've never seen one like her."

Agreen followed Richard's gaze upward. "Nor had I, Richard."

"How are you?" Richard asked, with concern, when their eyes came level. "What is it you have? Or had. You don't look any worse than you normally do."

Agreen chuckled softly. "Thanks for the compliment. Truth is, I don't know what I have. Neither does the surgeon. Whatever it is, it's takin' its sweet time gettin' the hell out of me. We know what it's *not*, and that's the yellow fever. If I had *that*, I'd be ashore in quarantine quicker than a doxy after a dollar."

"How are Lizzy and Zeke? Have you heard from them?"

"Not since we left Santo Domingo. Since then we've been cruisin' the Spanish Main, chasin' privateers and pirates. And we've had some success doin' it. Took several prizes and sank three of the bastards. If I know Lizzy, there'll be letters for me when we return t' station, though Lord knows when she may have written them. She an' Katherine are bound for England with the children, so neither of us will be hearin' from them for a spell."

"No, we won't." Richard leaned back against the bow. He folded his arms on his chest and studied his friend for several moments. "Agee, I must ask you something."

"I thought you might."

"When Nicholson was captain of this ship, what was he doing here in Barbados all those times? And why was he relieved of duty?"

Agreen gave him a brief nod, as if to acknowledge that he had indeed been expecting those questions. He turned to gaze out to where a Royal Navy sloop of war rode at anchor. Two brown pelicans glided low over the water's surface between the two ships, their broad wings fully outstretched, their eyes searching for schools of baitfish darting about under the floating patches of yellow Sargasso weed. He edged closer to Richard but spoke as if to the sloop.

"The answer t' both your questions is the same," he said. His voice had a distant, secretive quality underscored with acrimony. "And that answer is that Nicholson is a no-account coward."

Richard leaned in even closer. "That's a serious charge, Agee," he half-whispered. "Can you back it up?"

Agreen had to fight to keep his voice low. "Back it up? Jesus, Richard, *you* backed it up just by what you asked. Instead of doin' what we were ordered t' do—chase down the frogs—we cruised for months where the frogs were not. Barbados? It's a lovely island, I'll give you that. And I'm jealous as hell of all the time you've had here t' loll about and chase women. But where are the French? Not here, that's for damn sure. Oh, Nicholson's a fair enough seaman, I suppose. He'd do well as master of a merchant ship. But for the life of me I will never understand why the Navy Department saw fit t' rank him number two on the captain's list. He's no naval commander. He'll do whatever it takes to avoid a fight."

When Richard had no immediate response, Agreen continued.

"Stoddert finally had enough. He fired a broadside, citin' what he called Nicholson's 'litany of failures,' and ordered him t' swallow the anchor. That sure as hell got Nicholson's dander up. He fumed and raged around this deck like an angry peacock. But there was nothin' he could do. Stoddert wanted him out, and out he went. Silas took command, and since then morale on board ship has risen pell-mell from the orlop up t' the weather deck. We've seen our share of action, and Silas aims for us t' see more. At supper t'night he'll tell you about this island off Guadeloupe. It's where we're headin' next. It's a refuge for French privateers, so the British tell us, and Silas figures there might be some ripe fruit in there for us t' pick. Let's hope so. He aims t' restore the honor of this ship, Richard, and by God he'll do it if only Boney will stop talkin' peace and give him half a chance."

As MUCH AS he hated to leave his cousins, Richard ached to get back to sea, especially with the prospect of serving, however briefly, with Agreen Crabtree and Silas Talbot on board the magnificent *Constitution*. In any case, several members of his family had already left Barbados. Hugh and Robin had departed three weeks earlier on board *Redoubtable* and by now should be halfway to England. Caleb, too, was gone. The previous week he had boarded a Cutler merchant brig bound for Charleston to offload hogsheads of sugar and molasses before sailing on to Boston with a cargo of cotton and tobacco that would eventually find its way, together with barrels of Cutler dark rum, to a London dockyard along the Thames.

Caleb's had been a difficult leave-taking, both for Richard and for his cousins. But young Joseph had taken it far better than anyone expected. On Thursday, the day that sea superstition decreed was the luckiest day to weigh anchor, Joseph did for Richard what he had done when saying good-bye to Caleb. On that warm, humid morning he stepped up on his own, without having to be coaxed by his parents, and offered his hand to Richard. His grip was both warm and steady. "Farewell, Uncle," he said, his lower lip trembling only slightly. "Godspeed. Thank you for all you have done for me."

"Thank you for what you have done for *me*, Joseph. I'll see you again soon, either here or in Hingham."

He repeated those same words to Seth, Mary, and Benjamin before taking Peter's tiny hand in his own. He grinned down at the tot, who replied with an expression that could have passed for either scorn or utter boredom.

"Bless you," Cynthia said to Richard. "Bless you and Caleb both." She could say no more. Emotion clogged her throat.

"My love to Katherine and your family, dear Richard," Julia managed during a fleeting embrace. "Although I know you won't be seeing them right away."

Richard nodded at John before boarding a waiting carriage. Then he was gone, his destination His Majesty's dockyard in Bridgetown.

"WE'VE RAISED Marie-Galante, sir," Isaac Hull informed his captain after the officer of the watch had informed the first lieutenant.

"Where away?" Silas Talbot demanded. He had heard the cry from aloft and now scanned a clear horizon.

"Broad on the loo'ard bow, sir."

Spyglasses shifted to an area of water four points to larboard of the course *Constitution* was following. That her officers could see no evidence of the sixty-one-square-mile island that Christopher Columbus had named in honor of his flagship came as no surprise. As the ship's master had informed them that first evening when Richard Cutler had dined on board, the highest peak on the island of Marie-Galante rose a mere 670 feet above sea level. John Davenport, the ship's master, had gone on to explain, much to the officers' amusement, that the island was so flat and round that the French referred to it as *la grande galette*, or "the big pancake."

"Steer northwest by west, a half west," Talbot ordered the quartermaster's mates at the double wheel. "We'll approach by night."

"Northwest by west, a half west, aye, aye, sir," the senior helmsman replied.

Richard Cutler, stationed by the mizzen, set his glass off the frigate's larboard quarter, to where the vessel *Nancy* veered northwestward on a parallel course. She was a substantial sharp-lined, low-freeboard brigantine with square sails on her foremast and a large fore-and-aft sail on her mainmast, but next to *Constitution* she looked like a ship's boat. On her driver gaff fluttered the Stars and Stripes, somewhat deceptively. True, she was an American ship, built and owned, but she was an American vessel known to be trading in contraband with the French. *Constitution* had come upon her unexpectedly the previous day and had given chase. A warning shot fired across her bow persuaded her master to stop running and lie to. Her crew was rowed over to *Constitution* and her master strong-armed aft to Captain Talbot, who, after a word with him, dispatched them all below to the brig. Lieutenant Crabtree had taken command of *Nancy*, along with a skeleton crew of eight sailors and seven Marines. His first orders had been to jettison the vessel's cargo of rice and salted fish and hose down the hold.

"Gentlemen," Talbot had enthused before his officers the evening before, "Providence has smiled on us most kindly. Most kindly," he repeated.

Assembled before him in the after cabin were two of the ship's lieutenants, the ship's master, the captain of her Marine contingent, and eight midshipmen. They stood at attention before his desk, waiting for their captain to explain himself. When he took his time doing so, the burly captain of Marines offered a tentative, "Sir?"

Talbot smiled in mock astonishment. "Why, Mr. Carmick, I am surprised at you. I would have thought a man of your intellect and intuitions would have already guessed my intentions."

"Sorry, sir," Daniel Carmick fumbled. He smoothed his handlebar mustache with a nervous motion and glanced sideways at his fellow officers. They all stared stoically ahead; no one was willing to come to his rescue. "I'm afraid you have me on this one."

"Do I indeed?" Talbot's gaze took in his audience. "You young gentlemen there," he said at length. "A show of hands if you please. How many of you have studied Virgil's *Aeneid*? Come my good lads. Be not shy. I am not your schoolmaster. I shan't require you to recite lines of Latin."

The midshipmen tittered nervously. Three raised a hand halfway.

"Good. We're finally getting somewhere. Now who among you three can summarize for me the story of the Trojan horse?"

The senior officers exchanged quick, muddled glances as seven of the eight midshipmen looked to Roger Jeffrey, at seventeen the senior mid on board ship and the best educated of her junior officers.

"Mr. Jeffrey," Talbot said with a trace of a grin, "it seems the honor of reply has fallen to you."

Jeffrey cleared his throat. "Well, sir," he said in a voice searching for confidence and clarity, "the story takes place during the Trojan War. The Greeks were not able to defeat the Trojans in the field, nor could they take Troy by siege. So they pretended to give up the siege and sail home to Greece. Before they left, they offered the Trojans a huge wooden horse they had built as a tribute to their bravery. But it was not really a gift, sir. It was a ruse. Greek soldiers were hiding inside the horse when the Trojans came out to accept the gift and wheel it through the city gates. That night, as Troy slept, the soldiers hidden inside shimmied down to the ground on ropes. They opened the gates to the Greek army, which in fact had not sailed away, and put every Trojan man, woman, and child to the sword."

"Well done, Mr. Jeffrey. Remind me to put in a good word with your tutor. And so, gentlemen," he exclaimed to the room at large. "What conclusions might we draw from Mr. Jeffrey's excellent summation? What inspiration?"

Men and boys continued to stare rigidly ahead.

"Ah, well," Talbot sighed, "it appears that once again I am forced to explain the pathetically obvious." He was not angry. He was, in fact, having a merry time of it, which only added to his officers' general sense of bemusement. They had experienced their captain's quirky behavior before, but never to this extent.

Talbot rose to his feet and walked over to a larboard gun. "That brigantine," he said, pointing through the open port to where they could see *Nancy* sailing close by in the golden haze of the late afternoon sun, "is our Trojan horse. She will take us into the heart of Troy, with Greeks hidden in her hold. Do you not yet see where I am going with this? . . . Ah, Mr. Hull, I see that the light of day is beginning to dawn on you. On you as well, Mr. Cutler. By God, you are all basking in the glow now. Gather 'round, gentlemen, and listen to my plan."

A LESS RISKY PLAN, Talbot was first to admit, would have had *Constitution* standing off the island of Marie-Galante until they could determine exactly who and what awaited them in the harbor of Grand-Bourg. And that they could have done by sending ashore a covert scouting expedition. But such an initiative would require time, and time was a luxury the Americans did not have. *Constitution* was recognizable even to a lubber as a likely enemy. As for the brigantine, her master had confessed to Silas Talbot that he was on his way to Grand-Bourg and was expected there. Arriving in company with an enemy frigate would raise the reddest of red flags on the island.

According to charts and to British intelligence, access to Grand-Bourg was restricted to a route approximately two cable lengths wide that snaked through a labyrinth of shoals and coral reefs stretching from an area approximately a mile offshore to a cut between two promontories onshore. On the stubbier of the two promontories stood an old stone fort that guarded the narrow entryway to the wide, oval harbor. Although bright yellow buoys marked the route, a night passage was not recommended. Better to wait for daylight when leadsmen stationed on the chain-wales could see the seabed eight fathoms down and the ship's master did not have to rely on buoys that could have shifted position during a hard blow.

At four o'clock the next morning, all hands were on deck. The sea was calm. *Constitution* was rigged for night sailing and was making modest headway in light, fluky winds. Alongside her, *Nancy* kept pace under jib, foremast topsail, and mainmast fore-and-aft sail. Eastward, the first intimations of day had softened the black gloom of night and were giving distinct form to the horizon. Just over that horizon lay the island of Marie-Galante.

At a prearranged signal of flashing lanterns, both vessels hove to.

"I daren't go in any closer, Mr. Hull," Talbot informed his first lieutenant, who was standing at attention by the mizzenmast. "It's time."

Hull saluted. "I understand, sir."

Talbot returned the salute. "Good luck, Mr. Hull. I shall come for you at noon, as prescribed."

"We'll be there, sir."

Hull again saluted before turning to the boatswain. "Lower away the boats, Mr. Nichols. You may begin the transfer. Handsomely, now. And quietly." That last command was issued more by instinct than necessity. Nowhere in sight was there a black shape that would define another vessel under sail.

"Aye, aye, sir," Nichols replied softly.

Twenty-three Marines dressed in ordinary garb went over the side to join the seven Marines already on board *Nancy*. The twenty-five Marines still on board *Constitution* began handing down an arsenal of pistols, muskets, powder, shot, and grenades into the two whaleboats.

Next off, into a longboat, went a hand-picked auxiliary crew of seamen, along with the senior midshipman, a carpenter's mate, a quartermaster's mate, and a boatswain's mate. Last off were two senior lieutenants and the former master of the brigantine, a suddenly contrite, bald-headed man named Phillips.

"Good luck," Lieutenant Hamilton said as Richard gripped the twin hand ropes leading down to the ship's boat bobbing alongside. "I wish I were going with you."

Richard nodded in sympathy. "Understood, Robert, but you're needed here," he said truthfully yet lamely. "I'll see you in a few hours."

On board *Nancy*, Richard took up position beside Agreen at the helm. On deck with them, twelve able-rated sailors dressed in nondescript slop-chest clothing made ready to get under way. The others huddled belowdecks, save for Isaac Hull and Daniel Carmick, who joined the two lieutenants astern. Hull gave Richard a nod, confirming that everything below was secure. Astern, *Constitution* remained hove to, the lanterns on her weather deck gleaming ever less distinctly as her three boats were hoisted back on board and *Nancy* sliced through water stirred to life by a freshening northeasterly breeze. The breeze seemed a good omen. Rarely did the wind in the Indies pick up this early in the morning.

"Relief from the helm, Mr. Crabtree?" Hull asked. "You've been at it all night. Orrick here," referring to the quartermaster's mate, "can take over for now. If this wind holds, we have a good two hours before you need bring her in. A little sleep might do you some good."

"Thank you, sir," Agreen replied. "I'll stay here, if you don't object."

Hull did not object. There was no man that he or anyone else on board the brigantine would rather see at the helm under these circumstances than Agreen Crabtree. "Then you will be pleased to note," Hull said, "that I have requested the galley fire lit and a light breakfast brought up to us." He added in a weak stab at a devil-may-care attitude, "Let's hope the coffee is up to French standards."

Conversation was spotty as *Nancy* sailed eastward. There was little to say beyond what had been said the day before. Each man understood his assignment, and each man standing on deck or crouched below in the hold had now to cope in his own way with the conflicting inner emotions that well up to near bursting when battle is nigh. For most of them, it was not the uncertainty of what lay ahead that they feared, or even the danger. It was the killing. More precisely, how the killing would have to be done. It is one thing to butcher a man two hundred yards away as the result of round shot crashing through an enemy bulwark. It is quite another to kill a man face to face, your sword ripping into his belly, his eyes bulging in unspeakable pain as the steel blade slices through intestines and vital organs, the panic of imminent death silently screaming from a mouth agape, the sudden foul stench as his bowels give way to abject terror. And that assumes that you are the one doing the killing.

"Deck, there!" a lookout cried from high up the forecourse yardarm.

"Deck, aye!"

"It's the fort, sir, dead ahead!"

Hull raised an arm in acknowledgment. He turned to the helm. "Well done, Mr. Crabtree. Spot on target, as usual."

He and Richard strode forward to the bow. Twenty minutes later, through a long glass, they could see the tricolor of revolutionary France fluttering from atop the single turret. Richard glanced aloft. Although the square sails on the brigantine's foremast were furled, she was making good headway on a close haul under the mainmast driver and an array of staysails and jib. Richard estimated the wind at eight knots from the northeast. It would remain so, he surmised, right to the entrance of the harbor.

Gradually the fort assumed a distinct shape. Soon they were close enough in to observe the bright yellow buoys dancing atop the waves. Even at this close distance Richard could see little on the island beyond the fort and the beaches and mangroves fringing its shoreline. Marie-Galante was as flat and treeless as any island of his acquaintance, and he found himself wondering how the island's east coast, be it anything like this, could withstand the onslaught of one of the late-summer Atlantic gales.

"Shall we reduce sail and take her in under reefed driver and jib?" Richard ventured when Hull seemed distracted by what he was observing or thinking.

Hull caught himself. "Yes, Mr. Cutler. See to it, if you will. And my compliments to Captain Carmick and would he please bring Mr. Phillips up here under guard."

Richard touched his civilian-style tricorne hat and departed. Although equal in rank to Isaac Hull, Hull had seniority over Richard by virtue of Silas Talbot having seniority over Thomas Truxtun on the captain's list. More to the point, Silas Talbot had given explicit command of this mission to his first lieutenant.

Moments later a Marine corporal directed Seymour Phillips amidships where the officers had gathered. It was hard not to feel a pang of pity for the man, whatever his alleged misdeeds. He slouched before them, staring down at the deck and shaking his bald head, muttering something incomprehensible. Playacting? If so, Richard concluded, he was one convincing actor.

"Mr. Phillips?" Hull intoned.

Phillips looked up with round, hollow eyes. "Yes, Lieutenant?"

"I want to review with you again the acknowledgment signal for entering Grand-Bourg. I need not remind you that the corporal here has strict orders to keep a close eye on you. That is his sole responsibility until we are back on board *Constitution*. Cross us, and he will blow your brains across this deck."

"You needn't concern yourself, Lieutenant," Phillips groused. "Why would I cross you? You forget that I am an American citizen struggling to feed my crew and family."

"'Smuggling' would seem a more appropriate word for you, Mr. Phillips. You are a traitor to your country, and that, I assure you, I will not forget. Your only hope of survival is to cooperate fully with us. If you do, I may be persuaded to speak for you at your trial. Now then, the recognition signal if you please."

Phillips let out a long, low sigh. "It's as I told you before, Lieutenant. When we approach the fort, you dip the ensign three times. It's critical you do that *before* we reach the fort."

"And if we don't?"

"You know the answer to that."

Hull nodded grimly. "And the guns on the east-facing wall—on the landward side of the fort—they are as you have described them? Higher up than those on the sea-facing walls?"

"They are," Phillips confirmed.

"And to your knowledge there are no other military installations either in Grand-Bourg or elsewhere on the island?"

"Why would there be?" Phillip's frustration was mounting. "Think on it, Lieutenant. Why would the French maintain any sort of force on an island where a fort guards the entrance to its only port? And where armed privateers are normally moored in the harbor? And where a French naval base is but a few miles away?"

Isaac Hull and Richard Cutler glanced at each other, each drawing the same conclusion. What Phillips said reconfirmed the key elements of British intelligence that lay at the heart of their plan.

"Very well, Mr. Phillips. You may remain on deck by the helm. Let those in the fort see you. You may wave to them as we pass by. And you may respond if they hail you. But try to warn them or do anything out of line, and your life shall pay the forfeit."

"Damn you, sir, I am an American!" Phillips vented. "I was selling food to the French, not weapons."

"It's all the same, according to law," Hull reminded him.

Phillips was about to say something—perhaps, Richard speculated, that since no fucking war had ever been declared between America and France, he was free to do whatever he fucking well pleased. In truth, it was a thorny legal point that remained unresolved in American courts and in the opinion of Attorney General Charles Lee. But whatever protest Phillips may have had in mind, he thought better of it and kept his mouth shut.

Her canvas reduced to a minimum, *Nancy* slowed as she entered the well-marked channel leading into the harbor of Grand-Bourg. Less than a mile ahead loomed the fort; beyond it Richard could see masts and white canvas furled on spars. He was leaning casually against the foremast with his arms folded across his chest, as though engaged in a boring routine. He set his hat low on his forehead and tried to count the number of vessels in the harbor, allowing two masts per vessel. It was hard to determine, for the vessels were still distant and were moored close by each other in an area across the harbor where the docks and warehouses were concentrated. His best guess was five vessels of consequence.

As *Nancy* came off the wind to keep within mid channel, Phillips nodded to Hull, who nodded to Roger Jeffrey. *Constitution*'s senior midshipman stood by the larboard signal halyard, dressed, like everyone else, in everyday sailor's garb. Jeffrey acknowledged, seized hold of the signal halyard, and dipped the American ensign one, two, three times. Leadsmen stationed on the chain-wales signaled clear and deep water on the route ahead to where the west-facing wall of the fort was approaching. On its highest tier, black muzzles protruded out from between embrasures. On the lower two tiers, they protruded through square-cut gun ports. As *Nancy* glided along to within fifty feet of the fort's south-facing wall, everyone on the weather deck noted six cannon set on the lowest tier trained point-blank on the brigantine's hull, their round black maws primed to fire conclusively into any vessel attempting a forced entry.

Richard held his breath as he flicked his gaze aft. Agreen nodded back, enmeshed in the same grim memories. They had already been through this drill together—twice. The first time was on board the schooner *Falcon* as she ventured into the harbor of Algiers close by the mammoth guns of an Arab fortification. The second, later that summer of '89 as *Falcon* departed France beneath the fortress at Lorient with refugees Anne-Marie de Launay and her two daughters huddled below in the after cabin.

When they were safely past the fort and lying to, Richard studied the harbor more closely. It was as the British and Phillips had described it. The commercial pulse of what appeared to be a modest Breton town of white stucco buildings with red-tiled roofs was clustered at the opposite end of the broad, oval harbor, where the privateers—or merchantmen, it was hard to determine which—rested side by side, stern in. Their bows faced *Nancy* as she rounded into the wind under a double-reefed driver. Richard glanced up at the fort's east-facing wall. Phillips had told the truth. The cannon up there, on two tiers, were placed too high to bear down on the harbor. Their purpose, apparently, was to protect Grand-Bourg against an assault by land.

Better yet, on the stubby promontory and flat ground between the fort and the town about a quarter-mile away, gray canvas tents and wooden stalls had been erected. Citizens dressed in their Sunday finest were milling around there while listening to merry tunes scratched out by gaudily clad accordion and hurdy-gurdy players. The Americans had known that this festival was under way—it lay at the core of their plan—but its scale was considerably greater than they had anticipated. They could see uniformed military personnel, presumably from the fort, sprinkled in among the civilians. None of them appeared to be armed, but why would they be?

Presently two boats came out toward *Nancy*. A bowman on one of them called out instructions in broken English to douse all remaining sail and heave a towing line out to both boats. He hailed the brigantine's master visible amidships.

"*Bonjour, Monsieur Phillips. Il est bon de vous voir même si vous êtes un américain!*"

His fellow oarsmen started laughing. Phillips waved and smiled back good-naturedly, as though long accustomed to such jocularity. He lifted his tricorne hat over his head and held it there in traditional French fashion.

As they were being towed in toward an unoccupied stone quay where dockers were making ready to warp *Nancy* in sternfirst, the well-laid plan suddenly changed. Richard, at the bow, had been scrutinizing the moored vessels as they neared the docks. It was not the sight of a captured American merchant schooner that made him suddenly flush hot with anger. They had expected to find her there, forewarned by intelligence that a Royal Navy frigate captain had gleaned from a Swedish lugger he had detained after the lugger had sailed from Grand-Bourg. What Richard had not expected to find in Grand-Bourg was the vessel moored two quays down from the schooner, one of uniquely French design that he had seen once before, two years ago in the icy waters of Nantucket Sound.

He strode briskly aft to where Isaac Hull was conferring with Daniel Carmick. "Mr. Hull," he interrupted them, "do you see that armed brig moored over there, the one with the raked bow and angel figurehead?"

Hull scanned the docks. "Yes. What about her?"

"She's an angel of death and I have a score to settle with her."

Hull narrowed his eyes. "Oh? A personal score?"

Richard struggled to control his emotions. "I admit that I have personal reasons for wanting to destroy her."

"Then what I believe you are saying, Mr. Cutler, is that you have a score to settle with her captain. Who may no longer be in command. I mean no disrespect, and I am sorry to disappoint you, but I cannot compromise our mission for a matter of personal revenge, no matter its basis. You of all people should understand that."

"I do understand that, Mr. Hull, and it's why I ask you to reconsider." Richard's voice carried the weight and quality of cold steel. "That privateer, whoever her captain may be, has preyed on American commerce for years. God knows how many of our ships she has seized, how many of our sailors she has taken prisoner or tossed overboard. But never mind that. We need a diversion, do we not? I can give you a far better diversion than the one we have planned." He pointed at the brig. "And I can do it using her own powder."

When Hull hesitated, Carmick spoke up. "He's right about the diversion, sir."

Hull pursed his lips, mentally weighing the pros and cons. His decision made, he nodded at Richard. "Very well, Mr. Cutler," he said. He checked his watch: five minutes past nine. "How many men do you require?"

Thinking quickly, Richard answered, "Four, sir. Mr. Jeffrey and three Marines."

"Agreed. Mr. Carmick, please select the Marines." He checked his watch again as *Nancy* bumped gently alongside a stone quay edged with thick hemp to prevent damage to a wooden hull. Mooring lines secured her in tight. "Keep in mind that we absolutely must keep to the schedule. We *must* be out of here on the ebb tide, even if that means leaving someone behind. Will eleven o'clock serve?"

"Perfectly, sir. I'll go below and make the arrangements."

For the next forty-five minutes Richard sat crouched in a sweaty, crowded hold rife with the lingering stench of salted fish despite the hosing down at sea. Close beside him, Midshipman Jeffrey sat against a Marine sergeant named Kendall, who sat near two Marine privates named Reeve and Jackson. From outside on the quay they heard someone ask in a heavy French accent if Phillips required assistance in unloading his cargo. Phillips shouted back that yes, he would appreciate assistance, but could it please wait until later in the day, mid-afternoon perhaps? They had had a difficult passage from Puerto Rico and he had granted his crew a brief respite at the festival.

"*Bonne idée, capitaine,*" the voice responded. "*À bientôt, ensuite.*"

After that, all was quiet outside, save for the occasional stamp of footsteps on the deck above and the more distant sounds of music and merrymaking. Suddenly, the hatchway above slid open, allowing in a waft of blessed fresh air. Two of the Marines stood up and threw over their shoulders short, white canvas bags such as a sailor or lubber from any country might tote around in port. "Good luck," Richard whispered to them, to which one Marine replied with a salute. Richard immediately admonished him. Out there in the town and on the promontory, he reminded the Marine, they must act like ordinary seamen. Any show of military discipline or deference to rank, until called for, was forbidden. The Marine nodded his understanding and followed his companion up the short ladder leading to the weather deck and down the gangplank onto the quay.

During the next forty-five minutes, pairs of Marines left at five-minute intervals, each dressed as the others, each toting the same sort of canvas bag looped tight at the neck and with only slight noticeable bulges. By 10:15, twenty Marines had left the hold to fan out on the stubby promontory and mingle among the crowd. Belowdecks, within the dank confines of the Trojan horse, six Marines remained in addition to the three assigned to Richard and the corporal. Also remaining below were the ten auxiliary crew members, who had little to do but wait.

They did not have to wait long.

Richard checked his watch: 10:29. He nodded to his small party. Time to go.

ON SHORE, the five Americans walked down the deserted waterfront past a series of long, low, mostly windowless wooden warehouses with hogsheads, barrels, and hemp sacks stacked out front, then turned right and walked past three vessels secured against a quay. First in line, the captured schooner *Rebecca Ann* out of Newburyport lay quietly on her mooring lines, water reflections flickering on the name scripted in black letters on her stern. Second in line was a handsome single-topsail sloop armed with four swivel guns mounted on Y-brackets, two to a side. Next to her, her larboard side snug against a quay ten feet away, was their quarry, *Le Léopard*, the bold gilt lettering on her stern a stark reminder of the riches she had garnered at the expense of American and British merchants. Beyond her, toward the open western arc of the harbor, were smaller quays with brightly painted workboats either tethered to them or pulled up onto the docks.

Richard hand-signaled the three Marines and Jeffrey to stay put and strolled alone up the quay alongside *Le Léopard*. Despite his loathing for her captain, he found it impossible not to admire her gracious lines, the jaunty rake of her two masts, and the length of a jib boom that could support an impressive array of foresails. He counted eight 6-pounders on her weather deck, their black muzzles protruding through ports cut out of the bulwarks.

At the gangway leading from the quay up to the entry port amidships, Richard hailed the vessel in French. In short order a hulking man wearing a red-striped shirt shuffled over and looked down at Richard.

"*Que voulez-vous?*" he demanded. He slurred his words, suggesting that he had pumped on board his own form of celebration earlier that morning.

"*Bonjour, monsieur,*" Richard replied amicably. "*Votre capitaine, est-il à bord?*"

"*Pourquoi voulez-vous savoir?*"

"*J'ai une lettre pour lui.*" As proof, Richard held up a small folded piece of paper.

"*Une lettre?*"

"*Oui. D'une femme en ville. Une femme très belle,*" he emphasized with a suggestive grin. "*Elle m'a demandé de le lui donner.*"

"*Vraiment?*" Clearly the sailor was intrigued by the prospect of a beautiful woman sending a letter to his captain in such a manner. "*Permittez-moi de l'avoir. Je vais le remettre à lui.*"

"*Merci.*" Richard walked up the gangway holding out the paper in his right hand. As he stepped through the entry port, he handed it to the

sailor, who stood there turning over the blank paper in his hands. When
he looked up, baffled, Richard punched him in the solar plexus, dou-
bling him over, then jerked his knee hard into the man's face, straight-
ening him with a faint crunch of bone before striking a blow to his
jaw that sent him reeling backward. The Frenchman crumpled onto the
deck, blood spurting from his nose. Richard seized the man's chin in his
hand and jerked it from side to side. No reaction. He glanced around.
A weather deck that had been deserted save for this one man remained
deserted. No one had sounded an alarm either from the other vessels or
from shore. He beckoned to the others, who sauntered toward him.

"Right," Richard said when they were together on the brig's deck
and he had distributed the pistols from the white canvas bags. He tucked
two of them into the front of his trousers, behind the belt, covering the
butts with the hem of his loose-fitting shirt. "Jeffrey, you come with me.
Kendall, you and your men wait for him by the magazine. You know
what to do when he gets there."

"Count on us, sir," the Marine sergeant whispered. Crouching low,
he turned toward a hatchway leading belowdecks, followed by the two
Marine privates, each brandishing a pistol at half-cock. Please God
they don't encounter anyone lurking down below, Richard prayed. If
they did, they would have to spring a contingency plan of much greater
risk and danger. He was gambling, however, that they would find none
of the crew belowdecks. The festivities were in full swing ashore, and
since the fort guarded the harbor, there hardly seemed a need to keep
hardworking sailors from enjoying themselves. And he had a further
assurance. The last thing Agreen had told Richard before Richard left
Nancy was that he had observed but one man on the brig's deck during
the past hour, and that man now sprawled unconscious in front of him.
Besides, by this hour of the day in the tropics, with the heat and humid-
ity on the rise, belowdecks was hardly a place anyone would choose to
be—unless, of course, he happened to be in the more comfortable ambi-
ence of the captain's cabin.

Richard and Jeffrey waited a moment before creeping down the same
ladder, listening intently for any telltale sound or cry of alarm. None
came. All was quiet forward in the crew's quarters and on the orlop. So
far, so good. At the bottom step they turned and stole aft.

When they reached the captain's cabin, they stopped. Richard
glanced at Jeffrey and then knocked on the door.

"*Entrez*," a bored voice beckoned.

Richard opened the door and stepped inside a snug yet attractive space. Oil paintings of pastoral landscapes graced the walls. The leather chairs, sandalwood desk, and twin teak sideboards appeared to be of high quality. Richly inlaid glass windows gracing the stern and the two quarters confirmed the good taste of whoever had decorated this cabin. Only the heavyset man sitting behind the desk seemed out of place here. He glanced up and took in his two visitors through black, expressionless eyes set amid an unruly shock of red-orange hair, beard, and eyebrows.

"*Bonjour, Monsieur du Bourg,*" Richard said softly, menacingly. He removed his tricorne hat. "*Vous souvenez-vous de moi?*"

At first the privateer captain did not recognize him. Then a slight shift in his eyes indicated that he did. His right hand slid toward a side drawer.

Richard eased a pistol from his waistband and thumbed back the hammer two clicks.

"*Je ne conseillerais pas de le faire, monsieur,*" he hissed. "*Je prendais le grand plaisir de vous tuer.*"

Whether it was what Richard said—that he would take great pleasure in killing him—or how he said it, the privateer captain froze. He raised both hands before him and then gently placed them palms down on the desktop.

Richard stepped forward to the desk. "The key to the magazine," he demanded in French.

The man hesitated, his eyes riveted on the unwavering barrel of the pistol.

"The key," Richard spat out. "I will count to three." He brought the barrel of the pistol six inches from the man's brow and began counting. "*Une . . . deux . . .*"

The captain held up his hands, higher this time. "*Arrêtez-vous, monsieur,*" he shouted. "*Arrêtez-vous, je vous mendie!*" He nodded at the larboard sideboard. "*Il est là, dans le tiroir supérieur.*" He slumped back in his chair.

"Search the top drawer, Mr. Jeffrey," Richard said, his eyes never wavering from the Frenchman. Jeffrey walked over to the sideboard, opened the narrow drawer at eye level, and searched inside with his hand. "There is a key in here, sir."

"It had better be the right one," Richard said, "if this bastard wants to live. Cover him, Mr. Jeffrey."

Jeffrey drew his pistol and held it steady as Richard walked behind the desk. He untied the bandana from around the privateer's neck, rolled it into a gag, inserted it into the man's mouth, and then tied the ends in four knots behind the man's head.

"That should do it," he said. "*Levez-vous!*" he demanded.

The Frenchman stood up. Richard used his own neck stock to bind the man's hands behind him. He checked his watch: 10:48.

"I have him, Mr. Jeffrey. Go below. On the double."

Jeffrey quick-stepped down to the orlop.

"*Maintenant, monsieur,*" Richard said, his voice as tight as the knots on the gag, "*nous attendons. Là-bas.*" He pointed through the cabin doorway and nudged the muzzle of his pistol against the man's back. "*Soyez en tête, s'il vous plaît.*"

The privateer captain led the way, as ordered, to the base of the steps leading up to the weather deck. There they waited, Richard with a pistol in one hand and his watch in the other. Two minutes dragged by. Three. Four. "Hurry, damn it, Kendall," he whispered. Finally he heard footsteps echoing up from below.

Kendall's head popped up through an open hatchway. "Done, sir," he confirmed, then pulled himself up and out. The others followed. "We have five minutes."

"*En haut les pas, vite,*" Richard snarled at the Frenchman, "*à moins que vous ne vouliez mourir ici.*"

The Frenchman clearly had no desire to die there. He stumbled up the steps, followed by Richard, Jeffrey, and the three Marines.

On deck, Richard shoved the privateer captain against the starboard bulwarks. The man's eyes grew big when Kendall handed Richard his knife. With a hard upward thrust Richard cut through the binding on the Frenchman's wrists. Stunned, the man stared at his freed hands just as Reeve and Jackson picked him up by feet and shoulders and heaved him over the side.

"*Au revoir, mon ami,*" Richard shouted down at the splash of water. "*Je suggère que vous nagez très vite.*"

The enraged Frenchman hesitated for a moment, as if considering a return to the ship, then began swimming frantically in the other direction.

"This one's coming to, sir," Jackson said, pointing to the sailor Richard had decked earlier. He was turning his head this way and that, moaning softly.

"Throw him over, too," Richard said. After the second splash he said, "Right! Everybody off! *Now!*"

They had just taken shelter behind stacks of crates and barrels on the docks when the slow-match powder trail ignited by Sergeant Kendall sizzled its way across the floor of the brig's magazine to the main charge of gunpowder and munitions stacked at its far side. A colossal, ear-splitting explosion rocked *Le Léopard* from stem to stern. Yellow and red sparks skyrocketed into the air as her midships arched up off the water. Her two masts teetered, then crashed onto the deck and quay. Fire raced along the downed rigging toward the docks and warehouse, spreading the conflagration. More explosions followed. The brig's deck amidships blew out, causing her tumblehome to cave in on itself and bringing water gushing in through a ragged hole torn through her starboard hull. Then it was over. Within a span of time that seemed impossibly short, *Le Léopard* had been reduced from a proud predator to a listing, battered wreck.

The music and laughter on the promontory faded to silence as the crowd stared in disbelief at the burning hulk, their minds unable to accept such a catastrophe on this lovely, joyous morning. Even the sight of the massive wooden double doors of the fort swinging open and a squad of half-dressed soldiers rushing into their midst did not convince them. What did, finally, start the panic was the line of casually dressed men who had materialized seemingly out of thin air to drop to one knee and point long-barreled pistols at those soldiers.

The French captain defiantly withdrew his sword from its scabbard and held it high, then turned to face his men. Before he could issue the order to fire, a shot discharged from Daniel Carmick's pistol tore into him and dropped him.

The citizens of Grand-Bourg, hitherto riveted in place, started screaming and running from the promontory toward the village and the presumed safety of their homes. A second wave of American Marines, larger than the first, raced against this tide of humanity toward the open doors of the fort. Richard recognized Isaac Hull in the lead.

After Richard's party returned to the brigantine *Nancy*, he watched the proceedings through a spyglass.

"We're in danger of overstayin' our welcome," Agreen warned him. He, too, had been observing the goings-on through a glass. "I say it's time we flew this birdcage."

Richard nodded and walked to the open hatchway. "You crewmen," he called down. "Out you go. *Rebecca Ann* is the schooner on the next quay. Roundly now! Before the fire spreads to her." He eyed Roger Jeffrey. "Your first command, Mr. Jeffrey. Get her out into the harbor and wait for us."

Jeffrey saluted and was off.

To the Marine corporal he said, "Take Mr. Phillips below and bind him. Bring some muskets with you when you come back up. We may have need of them."

"Aye, aye, sir." The Marine pushed Phillips forward, followed him below.

To the sailors assigned to *Nancy* he said, "Make ready to set sail."

Richard raised his glass again, focusing it on the fort. In front of the doors he saw what appeared to be the total capitulation of the French soldiers, guarded by Daniel Carmick and his Marines. Their weapons had been taken from them and tossed into the water, and they were submitting to having their hands tied behind their backs. All seemed secure there. What was happening inside the fort was a story impossible to read. It stood out on the end of the promontory as silent and sullen as the granite stone of its construction. If Hull failed, Richard thought, his stomach churning at the prospect, this had all been for naught. If he didn't spike those guns on the south- and west-facing walls, there could be no escape from Grand-Bourg.

"We're ready to make sail," the boatswain's mate informed him. "And sir, the land breeze is picking up."

"Very well, Morse. We'll have her under way as soon as Mr. Hull and the Marines are back on board."

More seconds ticked by. More minutes.

"Damn, Isaac, hurry," Agreen muttered. He glanced up at the tell-tales fluttering on the mainmast shrouds. Morse was right. The breeze had picked up and was blowing straight out of the harbor. But such a favorable wind would do them no good unless—

"There, Agee. *There!*"

Agreen raised his glass and saw Hull and the Marines charging out of the fort, Hull motioning to Carmick and his men to follow him *now!* No one challenged them, although the French soldiers under guard must have sensed what was coming. They struggled to their feet and ran after the Americans as best they could with their hands tied behind their backs. As the Marines neared the end of the promontory and ran along the arc leading to the town frontage and the burning docks, what had transpired earlier on board *Le Léopard* seemed, in comparison, like child's play with popguns. A tremendous explosion shook the fort with such authority that both land and water trembled. Instantly a volcanic mass of stone shards, iron fragments, and other bits of debris spewed high above the promontory and spread out over the town, docks, and harbor. The mountain of debris seemed to hang in the air for a moment before plunging back down to earth. Richard and Agreen ducked for cover. They doubled up against the brigantine's bulwarks, shielding their heads with their arms as the spew pelted *Nancy* and *Rebecca Ann* and the scarred skeleton of *Le Léopard* in a violent hailstorm.

When it was over, when all was quiet, Richard rose to a knee and trained his glass on the fort—what was left of the fort. Only its east-facing wall remained intact. The rest of it appeared like a giant right triangle of stone rubble propping up that wall, pockmarked here and there with vacant gaps of what had been corridors and gun turrets. Nowhere did he see any stirrings of life.

"Sweet Jesus in heaven, Isaac," Richard said to Hull when, moments later, the first lieutenant and the Marines left the shelter of a stone dockside warehouse and ran up the gangway onto the brigantine. "Where did *you* learn to spike guns?"

"The frogs were a bit sloppy with their munitions." Hull was wheezing, gasping for breath. "And that provided us with a rather splendid alternative."

"Rather splendid indeed," Richard acknowledged.

"All hands! Make sail!" Agreen commanded. Sailors in the bow and stern let fly the lines to the bollards while others raised jib and driver, playing out the sheets to allow the freshening breeze to fill the canvas. *Nancy* slid easily forward from the quay, the wind at her back, her bowsprit pointing toward the demolished fort and the channel leading out.

"You have blood on your shirt," Richard noted with concern.

Hull glanced down. "It's not mine," he said, back in command of himself. "It belongs to the commander of the fort." He withdrew his dirk from its sheath to reveal a blade smeared with red. "When we surprised the garrison, or what was left of it, he put up a fight. That was stupid of him. We had him dead to rights, and the Marines performed brilliantly."

"Casualties?"

"Nary a one. Everyone's accounted for. You?"

"The same."

"That'll make Silas happy." Agreen eased *Nancy* up close to *Rebecca Ann* and waved at Roger Jeffrey at the helm. Jeffrey waved back and ordered his crew to back the jib to coax the schooner out of irons. Once both vessels were in open water and all they could see of Grand-Bourg were clouds of ugly black smoke curling above the town, Agreen said, "Speakin' of our illustrious commodore, gentlemen, have a gander yonder. Unless I miss my guess, thar he blows."

He was pointing to the southwest, where the black hull of an American frigate was rising off the horizon. *Constitution* was sailing toward them, to take them under her wing and shepherd them safely past the French naval base at Guadeloupe, and from there northward to Clarkson's Yard in the harbor of Saint Kitts for a rendezvous with *Constellation*.

Fourteen

In the Atlantic, Northeast of Guadeloupe
February 1800

R ICHARD LEANED BACK in his chair, holding in his hand the letter he had just received up on deck during mail call in the port of Saint Kitts. Slowly, savoring the moment as he always did after receiving a letter from Katherine, he broke the wax seal, spread open the single page, and read:

5 November 1799
South Street
Hingham, Massachusetts
My Darling Husband:

We arrived home late yesterday after what seemed an interminable voyage from Portsmouth. The weather turned foul on our third day out and remained stormy for eight straight days. You would have been proud of your sons. Will and Jamie thrived in the bad weather, and they were of great comfort to Lizzy and me, and to Diana and Zeke. To us, it was terrifying. The seas washed over the ship, and the deck above us leaked, and it was damp and cold. I don't know what Lizzy and I would have done had it not been for their care and attention. They even helped sail the ship when several of the crew took ill. They are born sailors, much like their father, whom we all miss dearly.

Now that we're back in Hingham, such a voyage seems a small price to pay for the joy of seeing my family again. There is much to tell you about Fareham, and we will give you all the details when you return home to us. The wedding was a day we shall always remember. Reverend Fenton, the dear man, was at his best, and everyone attending was caught up in the majesty of it all, including my father, who served as best man along with Jeremy. Hugh and Phoebe make such a handsome couple. They couldn't stop smiling, they were so happy. And can you believe it? Hugh told me what he told you in Jamaica—that they are planning to come to America to live near us in Hingham. My heart is bursting with joy!

I am writing this letter in haste, as I must send word to you that we are home and in good health and spirits. Please God you will be here with us soon. Peace is nigh. You must be aware that President Adams has ordered the frigate United States to Paris with new peace envoys. This time, it appears, they will be received with full diplomatic honors. Monsieur Talleyrand is no longer foreign minister, and Bonaparte has publicly stated that he desires a quick end to this conflict. Your father agrees that the end is near. He asked me to tell you that he will write you himself as soon as he is up and about. He has been a-bed recently, I don't know with what. But be assured that I shall continue to look in on him every day—if Edna will allow me access!

Everyone in my family sends love to you, including my father, who sings your praises every chance he gets. You make him very proud.

You make me so very proud, too, my darling husband. You are forever on my mind, forever in my heart.

Katherine

Richard pressed the paper to his lips and offered a silent prayer of thanksgiving for the safe delivery of his family. An Atlantic crossing in October was not to be taken lightly, especially when sailing against the prevailing westerlies. The thought of the voyage and the dangers it presaged had gnawed at him for weeks. Now worry would feast on him no longer.

His eyes swept over the single page of tight cursive flow. So Bonaparte desired peace now that he had swept the Directory from power and proclaimed himself First Consul of France. Well, why wouldn't he desire peace? The Navy Department had confirmed that thus far in this war a relative handful of American naval and Treasury vessels had captured one French navy frigate and three corvettes, and had captured or sunk more than a hundred French privateers. Not to mention a French fort being blown to kingdom come. Having defeated the world's greatest sea power, Richard mused, the young republic was giving fits to the world's greatest land power.

His mind stuck on the mention of his father's illness, or whatever was keeping him a-bed. That Katherine did not seem overly concerned was reassuring. A red flag stirred nevertheless. Richard had never known his father to linger in bed for any reason. Rarely had he been ill or even acted out of sorts. To those who knew him, Thomas Cutler seemed a paragon of mental and physical heath, the sort of man to whom others turned when *they* were ill or out of sorts.

Richard folded the letter and placed it in the drawer of his small writing desk. His wardroom cabin was warm, but not oppressively so, despite the early evening hour. His cabin was, after all, the most commodious on the ship apart from the captain's suite, and he enjoyed the privacy and relative luxury of the space, especially now that *Constellation* was in port and out of discipline and he could linger there at his leisure, excused from watch duty as a privilege of high rank. Forward, he could hear the muffled laughter of men and women at play on the berthing deck, and up a tier on the gun deck as well. Richard smiled to himself. Captain Truxtun, following an official period of mourning to honor the passing of President George Washington in December, had yielded to the human condition and had allowed wives and sweethearts to come on board ship during the port call. "Wives and sweethearts"—a delightful Royal Navy term that more often than not was a euphemism for local women of easy virtue.

Richard rose to his feet and stretched. Fatigued, his eyes heavy, he glanced at the vest watch lying on his desk: 7:35. Too early to retire. He decided to go up on deck and take the air. Tomorrow morning he would answer Katherine's letter and include it with the others he had written during the cruise.

On deck he met a former midshipman reclaimed from *L'Insurgente* and promoted to third lieutenant by Captain Truxtun during *Constellation*'s layover in Portsmouth. "Good evening, John," Richard greeted him. Both officers were dressed casually in breeches, silver-buckled shoes, and cotton shirts.

"Good evening, sir," Dent replied. "A glorious one, isn't it?"

"Indeed. Reminds me of Boston in late August. A perfect evening to enjoy ashore, I should think."

Dent grinned. "Which is where I'm bound in a few minutes, at the end of the watch. Mr. Sterrett and I are taking supper at a new tavern on Bay Road. We're told it's an excellent place. Would you care to join us, sir? We'd welcome your company."

"Thank you, John, but no. The only place I'm bound tonight is my bunk. I'm done in. Perhaps tomorrow or the next day I'll try this eatery of yours, assuming it passes muster with you."

"You may expect a full report in the morning, sir," Dent announced cheerfully. He took his leave and walked forward amidships in the direction of an open-shirted topman named Wheaton, who was talking quietly to an exotic-looking woman of Carib Indian descent. Her skin was smooth and reddish brown; shiny ebony hair fell straight down to her waist. She was smiling encouragingly at the topman. She might not understand English, but her body language spoke volumes. Wheaton ignored Dent as he walked discreetly past, although the woman's dark olive eyes took in the young lieutenant and then flashed aft, more meaningfully, at Richard.

Richard returned her smile, then leaned against the starboard bulwark and gazed out on a naval base that these days seemed more American than British. The British light frigate *Concorde* lay at anchor amid a clutch of unrated Royal Navy vessels bobbing and straining at their moorings in the light chop. Almost hidden among them were larger vessels of the Leeward Islands Squadron flying the Stars and Stripes: *Baltimore, Pickering, Enterprise,* and *John Adams. Eagle* and the refitted *Insurgent* were out on patrol.

"A pretty sight, eh, Mr. Cutler?"

Richard straightened instinctively. "Sorry, sir. I didn't hear you approach."

"Tut, tut, man. Relax. Do not naval regulations regarding a ship out of discipline include her first lieutenant?"

"I believe they do, sir," Richard said.

"Well, then, be at your ease."

Thomas Truxtun joined Richard at the railing, his gaze on the five short-barreled, wide-bore carronades lined up before him along the starboard bulwarks between midships and taffrail. Five others of equal bore and design were positioned across on the larboard side. Each was mounted on an immovable wooden bed equipped with a slide that absorbed the gun's recoil when fired. The outer end of the bed was secured to the deck by a heavy bolt. On the inner end were two wheels designed to swivel like casters and provide greater ease in swinging the gun from side to side. Just as lethal as traditional long guns, these 24-pounder carronades were considerably lighter and smaller, and thus suitable for installation on the weather deck. And only three men were required to service each gun. Their single drawback was that they were effective only at short range.

"We owe Captain Hardcastle a great debt for securing these guns for us," Truxtun said, adding, with a touch of pride, "*Constellation* is the first ship in the U.S. Navy to carry them. Though I doubt she will be for long. Once Captain Talbot gets wind of this, he'll demand the same for *Constitution*. And if history is any judge, Stoddert will find a way to give him what he wants."

Richard understood the bitterness in his voice. During *Constellation*'s refitting in Portsmouth, Truxtun had traveled north to New Jersey to visit his family. There, out of the blue, a letter from Benjamin Stoddert had informed him that the Navy Department had officially awarded Silas Talbot seniority over him. It was an issue that had been hotly contested for more than two years, and its resolution had infuriated Truxtun, who felt compelled to resign his commission. What had happened next was somewhat vague. Truxtun refused to talk about it, and each officer harbored personal opinions that in the aggregate only served to muddle the facts. What *was* clear was that both John Adams and George Washington had intervened in the drama, the former president by inviting Truxtun to Mount Vernon to appeal to Truxtun's patriotism and sense of duty, and the current president by venturing to Perth Amboy to present his most accomplished sea officer with the gold medal awarded him by Congress and to convince him not to quit the service. Truxtun had agreed to withdraw his resignation on the condition that he never be placed in a position where he would have to report to Talbot. Stoddert readily agreed and Truxtun reported back for duty in *Constellation,* finally setting sail for Saint Kitts six weeks behind schedule.

"Think we'll have occasion to use these guns, sir?" Richard asked to steer their conversation away from dangerous waters. The open feud between Talbot and Truxtun had been a trial for him, for he held both naval commanders in the highest personal and professional esteem.

"This war shouldn't last much longer. Our envoys have been in Paris for a number of weeks. Perhaps terms of a treaty have already been worked out."

"Perhaps. But until we're at peace, we remain at war. When peace does come—and I agree that it will come shortly, there is no need to drag out his affair—it's home for us again, this time on a more permanent basis. You will be leaving the service then, Mr. Cutler?"

"That's my intention, sir. And I shall do so with great regret. I will miss the Navy more than I thought possible."

Truxtun nodded sympathetically. "I understand," he said. "The Navy has a way of growing on you, doesn't it? It's why I decided to return to service rather than retire, as logic and justice dictated I should. And since you feel the same as I do, why not do the same and stay in the service? The Navy needs officers of your caliber."

Richard shook his head slowly. "I have considered that, sir, assuming there's a place for me in a peacetime Navy. And I would do it under different circumstances. But I find it hard to be separated from my family for such long periods. I have a young daughter who needs her father at home. My wife tells me that our younger son, Jamie, is anxious to follow in my footsteps and join the Navy. So he may be leaving home soon. And I cannot disappoint my father. He has high hopes for me in Cutler & Sons."

"I cannot speak for your father, Mr. Cutler, but I can speak for Secretary Stoddert. Should you decide to remain in the Navy, you need not be separated from your family. I have it on good authority that Stoddert is about to introduce the Royal Navy practice of allowing certain qualified officers to remain in the service on half pay during peacetime. You'd be on furlough—on the beach, so to speak, and a Hingham beach at that—but you would remain a commissioned officer who would return to duty if and when another war threatens. I'd be delighted to recommend your name for that list, if you'd like me to."

"I *would* like you to, sir," Richard replied without hesitation, "and I would be honored if you would." He could not resist a smile.

Truxtun smiled as well. "Consider it done."

"Thank you, sir." After a pause, Richard returned to the subject of the carronades. "I suppose, then, that the prospect of peace means we shall not have occasion to see these 'devil guns' in action."

"To the contrary, Mr. Cutler, I believe we will. And soon."

"Soon, sir?"

Truxtun nodded. "Quite soon. The Royal Navy may not have many ships left in the Indies, but they still have a vast network of spies. And British spies on Guadeloupe report that a French frigate has put in to Basse-Terre to take on passengers and provisions. They report she's planning to depart for France within a fortnight. When sighted, she was sailing in the company of a 28-gun corvette. I was informed of this not thirty minutes ago in a note sent over from *Concorde* by Captain Sweeney."

"If she's a frigate, sir, she must be *La Vengeance*."

La Vengeance was a frigate of 54 guns, the largest and by all accounts the last French naval vessel of consequence in the French West Indies. For three weeks *Constellation* had scoured the waters and recesses of the Lesser Antilles in search of this ship as an angler might stalk a monster fish rumored to inhabit a lake. They hadn't found her, but the cruise had provided ample opportunities to drill the men hard at the new 18-pounder guns that had replaced the 24-pounder long guns on the gun deck to better stabilize the frigate and make her less top-heavy.

"The British have confirmed that indeed she is *La Vengeance*. And if her captain intends to flee the Indies, I intend to stop him. Please advise Boatswain Bowles that we sail tomorrow with the tide at six bells in the afternoon watch. And advise him to see these ladies off—graciously, mind you, but *off*—and to recall everyone on shore leave. As of midnight tonight, Mr. Cutler, *Constellation* is a ship *in* discipline."

AT DAWN ON FEBRUARY 1, on the third day at sea, *Constellation* sighted a ship sailing far out in the Atlantic. At that distance even the most keen-eyed lookout could distinguish only that she was ship-rigged.

Richard was standing by the taffrail, squinting astern through a long glass. "Run up the English colors," he ordered James Jarvis, the junior officer of the watch. "And please inform Captain Truxtun that his presence is requested on deck. Walk, if you please, Mr. Jarvis," he called after him when the young midshipman scampered off in a young mid's eagerness to obey a command.

"Aye, aye, sir. Sorry, sir."

Richard next addressed the boatswain and master's mates at the helm: "Prepare to wear ship."

As the signal midshipman retrieved the British ensign from the flag locker and made ready to hoist away, James Jarvis went below to report to the captain. In short order, Truxtun appeared on deck in full undress uniform, save for his cocked hat.

"Good morning, Mr. Cutler," he greeted his first lieutenant. "Mr. Jarvis informs me that we have sighted a ship."

"Good morning, Captain. Yes, sir, we have. She's to the southeast, following a northerly course. On the chance she's English, I have ordered the British ensign raised. We are standing by to wear ship. I am assuming you want to give chase."

"What is our present position and course?"

"Antigua is ahead to larboard, sir. Barbuda is to starboard. Our course is northwest by north."

"Very well, Mr. Cutler. If she is British she'll respond quickly enough. You may wear around and calculate a course of interception."

"Aye, aye, sir." Richard stepped forward and brought a speaking trumpet to his lips. "All hands! Stations for wearing ship! Man clewgarnets and buntlines! Spanker mainsail brails! Weather main, lee crossjack braces! Handsomely there, you men!" Instantly his orders were piped through the ship.

The helmsmen at the big double wheel coaxed *Constellation* off the wind until it came from dead astern. Sailors stationed aft and amidships brailed up her spanker and mainsail to allow the other sails on the main and mizzen to be all in the wind. With afteryards braced up sharp for the new tack and foreyards squared, headsheets were shifted over and foresails braced around to catch the wind and help turn the ship's stern through it, just as the mainsail was reset and the spanker hauled out. Within minutes, *Constellation* was turned about on a reciprocal course and sailing full and by, with her foreyards braced up and her weather bowlines hauled taut.

Approximately fifteen miles separated the two ships. Although *Constellation* was now on a course of interception, the other ship was following an oblique course relative to the American, which meant that several hours would pass before the other ship could be positively identified. *If* she maintained her present course for all that time.

Which she did not.

"Deck, there!" the lookout in the foremast cried down some time later.

"Deck, aye!" Harry Ayres, stationed at the base of the foremast, acknowledged. "What is it, Laird?"

"She's coming about, sir! She means to show us her heels!"

Ayres quick-stepped aft.

"Thank you, Mr. Ayres," Thomas Truxtun said when the midshipman had made his report. Immediately he issued the order for *Constellation* to come off the wind in pursuit. "You may return to station." He rubbed his chin. "What do you make of it, Mr. Cutler?"

Richard replied slowly, thoughtfully, as if seeking to convince himself as well as his captain. "She can't know our identity, sir, any better than we can know hers. By now she should have spotted the British recognition signal. If so, we may conclude she's not British. If she were, she would not turn and run once she realized we were giving chase. She would either maintain her course or turn to come straight at us. Were she a neutral ship, Dutch or Swedish, perhaps, *why* would she run? In any event, we know that this vessel is ship-rigged and of considerable size, a ship of war by anyone's bet. The Dutch and Swedes don't have vessels of such size in the Indies. And Spanish frigates are long gone from these waters. That leaves only one conclusion."

"Mr. Sterrett?"

"I agree with Mr. Cutler, sir," the second lieutenant replied. "She showed her colors the instant she came about."

"We must assume, then, that she's French. And if she's French, she's *La Vengeance*. By God, gentlemen, I think we've found our quarry!"

"Yes, sir," Richard said, the thrill of the chase upon him. "Her captain must have decided that since he can't outrun us, his best bet is to try to make it back to Guadeloupe. Perhaps he has important passengers on board who have no stomach for a fight."

"That could very well be the case, Mr. Cutler. Now hear this: I want every inch of canvas clapped on, including stunsails. Have the yards slung with chains and the ship cleared for action."

"Aye, aye, sir."

With the extra press of sails, *Constellation* surged ahead on a larboard tack heading south-southeast. The other ship pursued a course to the south-southwest, back toward the southern reaches of the Lesser Antilles. Guadeloupe lay perhaps twenty miles over the horizon. If reaching the safety of that island were her strategy, the tactical question, for those on board both ships, was whether or not the mathematics of pursuit would allow the pursuer to cut off the pursued.

As the chase continued through the morning and into the early afternoon, the distance between the two ships narrowed. Just as the hull of the other ship was rising up to the south, the wind shifted and turned fluky. The massive sails of the American frigate luffed, filled, and luffed again, as though living beings gasping for air. Helmsmen struggled to keep *Constellation* on course in what was quickly becoming a game of catch-as-catch-can with the wind.

Truxtun remained undeterred. "We'll work this to our advantage," he stated optimistically to his officers. "We're the lighter of the two vessels and we have a copper bottom. I doubt that ship does—most French ships do not—so in this light wind the growth on her bottom should slow her down. It may take longer to catch her, but catch her we will. It's just a matter of time."

Time they had, and plenty of it during the long hours of sluggish pursuit, to weigh the consequences of actually running down their quarry. Every officer on board *Constellation* was keenly aware that *La Vengeance* was a heavily armed ship; 18-pounders on her gun deck, 12-pounders on her weather deck: fifty-four guns total. By comparison, *Constellation* carried twenty-eight 18-pounders on her gun deck and ten 24-pounder carronades on her weather deck. Richard had done the math, as had even the lowest-ranking petty officer. A full broadside from *La Vengeance* carried 582 pounds of hot metal; a broadside from *Constellation* only 372 pounds. In other words, the French had a 50 percent advantage in weight of broadside. And if *La Vengeance* did manage to come within sight of the naval base at Basse-Terre, the French corvette, were she still there, would surely sail out to add her twenty-eight guns to the balance.

In early evening, as the breeze freshened and the distance between the two ships continued to narrow, Truxtun ordered the British ensign hauled down, the American ensign hauled up, and battle lanterns lit. "And you may run out the guns, Mr. Cutler," he said. "Both sides."

"Shall we reduce sail, sir?"

"Not until it's absolutely necessary. Have the men stand by to brail up the courses."

Richard relayed the order to Midn. David Porter, acting as aide-de-camp, who relayed it below to Lieutenant Sterrett and the gun captains.

Night was settling over a black sea framed by a bright starlit sky and a half-moon lying low to the west. On board *Constellation* there was no need to beat to quarters. Men had been at battle stations for nearly twelve hours, had eaten an early supper next to the guns, and had taken rest in rotation on the gun deck. Three hundred yards ahead, *La Vengeance*—her name encrypted in gilt lettering beneath the tinted glass of her heavily decorated stern gallery—sailed on toward Guadeloupe as though oblivious to the American frigate creeping up on her from astern.

At nine o'clock, as the quartermaster of the watch sounded two bells and *Constellation* approached to within hailing distance, Truxtun strode forward to the forecastle and brought a speaking trumpet to his mouth. "Ahoy, *La Vengeance*!" he shouted out. "This is USS *Constellation*. I order you to haul down your colors and surrender to the United States of America!"

Every man on the American frigate stood by at attention, ears primed for a response that was not forthcoming. Save for creaks in her block and tackle and the whisper of wind ghosting through her top-hamper, silence reigned on *Constellation*.

"Ahoy, *La Vengeance*!" Truxtun tried a second time. "Surrender or I shall fire into you!"

When his demands were once again met with silence, Truxtun walked aft to the helm. "Let the log reflect that I gave her fair warning," he said blithely. "Have the courses brailed up, Mr. Cutler. Mr. Waverly, bring her up a point."

Before Truxtun finished speaking, two tongues of orange lashed out from the stern ports of the French frigate. Balls of hot iron howled through the air, screaming ever louder as they approached until the air above was rent by the rip of canvas not far from the maintop where James Carter had stationed his Marines. Their trajectories expended, the two balls plunged into the dark ocean astern.

"Bring her up another point," Truxtun said calmly to Waverly. "Starboard guns may fire when ready."

Midshipman Porter relayed the order to the gun deck. Sterrett acknowledged and passed word to Lieutenant Dent stationed aft. *Constellation* edged up closer to *La Vengeance*, her bowsprit now drawing even with the Frenchman's larboard quarter, her aft guns handspiked as far forward as possible.

"*Fire!*" Sterrett's order was repeated down the line. Fourteen guns erupted at five-second intervals. Most were aimed level at the hull of the French ship, visible a hundred yards distant beyond the close-quarter flashes of yellow, white, and orange. Round shot and double shot smashed into the Frenchman's bulwarks, splintering them. Spears of jagged wood rocketed through the air and across her deck, impaling flesh and tearing into vital organs. From above, in *Constellation*'s fighting tops, Marines at the swivel guns rained canisters of grape onto the

Frenchman's deck. The barrage was reinforced by a rain of musketry fired from the tops and from behind walls of hammocks stuffed into netting along the weather railing.

Not every long gun was aimed level. Some were aimed high. One shot scored a direct hit on the enemy main-topmast, which shattered and toppled over like a twig in a child's hand, taking with it a jumble of topsail, royal, and mizzen staysails.

La Vengeance answered. True to her name, she came up on a starboard tack and launched a broadside of her own, concentrating fire on her enemy's top-hamper. *Constellation*'s lower mainmast took a glancing blow that nonetheless punched out a sizable chunk of wood, exposing an ugly gash of white Virginia pine. On her lower mainmast shrouds, a breast backstay parted beneath its outrigger. Nearby, a sailor climbing to the crosstrees cried out. For what must have been a terrifying wisp of time, he gaped down at his left leg blown clean off before letting go the shrouds and ratlines and tumbling below to the deck. Blood spurted from the red jelly mass of the stump like some gruesome water pump before a quick-thinking waister rushed out to seize the deformed body and drag it against the larboard bulwarks.

"Fire as they bear!" Truxtun shouted out. "Mr. Waverly, maintain a parallel course! Range up on her quarter!"

For another hour, and an hour after that, the two great frigates battled it out, strength of broadside against strength of broadside, lighting up and roiling the short span of Atlantic separating them. It was as though two great armies had come together on the field to pound each other unmercifully until one side had taken all it could take and was forced to stand down. The French boasted superiority of guns, the Americans superiority of drill. For every broadside *La Vengeance* managed to get off, *Constellation* answered with two, evening the odds, then with three, giving her the edge, over time, in shipboard structures and skeletal frames and gun mounts ravaged, dismantled, or blown apart.

La Vengeance was suffering terrible damage to her planking, *Constellation* to her rigging. The American ship's mainmast had taken multiple hits. Shrouds and stays on all three masts had been shot away. Dead Marines and sailors littered her weather deck. Others, badly wounded, moaned and struggled to pull themselves up, their pitiful cries for succor ignored because no man could be spared to carry them below to the surgeon. Not three feet from where Richard stood as stoically as an inhuman blend of terror and discipline allowed, a Marine private, felled from the mizzen top, splattered supine onto the deck. His hollow eyes rolled over to Richard, his mouth opening and closing in silent supplication, his body shivering and shaking as though from freezing cold, until the lifeblood drained out of him and he lay still, his glazed eyes, even in death, locked on the first lieutenant.

"They mean to board us, Captain!" Richard warned, forcing himself free of the Marine's dead gaze when *La Vengeance* suddenly shifted course and came at them bow on. In the ghastly glow of sporadic cannon fire they could see French Marines and sailors assembling on the foredeck brandishing a lethal assortment of muskets, pistols, boarding pikes, tomahawks, cutlasses, and belaying pins. It was *L'Insurgente* all over again.

"Bring her off, Mr. Waverly," Truxtun commanded. "Down helm!"

"It's no good, sir!" the ship's master yelled back, a rare hint of panic in his voice. "She won't answer! She's too shot up!"

"Mr. Cutler! The carronades!"

"Aye, aye, sir!"

"Mr. Porter, pass word to Mr. Sterrett to load with double shot and hold fire until he hears the carronades. Then, by God, tell him to give them everything he has, aimed at her foredeck!"

"Aye, aye, Captain!"

The two ships closed to within seventy yards, sixty, fifty yards—every yard bringing the snub-nosed devil guns within a more deadly range. Loaded with 24-pound shot in two of them, langrage and grape and case shot in three, they were swung on their casters to bear directly on the Frenchman's bow.

"Steady, men," Richard encouraged the five three-man gun crews.

Forty-five yards.

"You see your target. Wait for my command."

Forty yards.

On board *La Vengeance*, the men in the bow held up weapons and shouted heated words of defiance. A bow-chaser barked, then another. The Americans ducked low, but the round shot merely bounced off *Constellation*'s hull and dropped into the ocean.

Thirty-five yards.

"Steady . . . steady . . ."

The long guns on both ships fell silent. French Marines held the Americans in the foretops at bay with a steady stream of musketry. *La Vengeance* loomed, a giant black silhouette against a slightly lighter backdrop of gloom, gliding closer and closer, until the distance separating the two ships was a mere twenty-five yards. On board *Constellation*, sailors on the starboard side armed with pistols and pikes clutched long wooden poles to fend off and prevent the enemy from grappling hold, pulling the American frigate in close, and unleashing her legions of hell.

"Steady . . . steady . . . *Now, men! Now! Fire!*"

Five carronades roared as one, seconds before a measured broadside of long guns erupted on the deck below, all guns trained on the enemy's bow. Masses of hard, hot metal pummeled the French frigate, caving in strakes, shoving her bow off the wind and broadside to *Constellation* as the rage of carronades tore through enemy ranks like so many bowling balls on a green, cutting, slicing, and carving in a macabre feast of death, destruction, and mayhem.

"Reload!" Richard shouted on the weather deck.

"Reload!" Sterrett shouted on the gun deck.

The broadside was repeated. *La Vengeance*, dangerously cut up and caught unaware by the carronade onslaught, fought to come off the wind and turn away from the devastation. On her foredeck, French sailors and Marines threw up their hands, staggered backward, cried out in agony. American Marines in the tops added to the onslaught, lobbing grenades onto *La Vengeance*'s deck and bringing swivel guns and musket fire back into action. It was sheer butchery. No Frenchman was left standing. Some, perhaps crawling aft, were pinned in tight against the smashed-in bulwarks, escaping the bodies and body parts strewn in expanding pools of blood forward. After a third broadside exploded from *Constellation*, the great ocean fell silent, as though the two combatants, each stunned to the core, had paused to take stock of the carnage and chaos each had wrought against the other.

As *La Vengeance* slewed off the wind, nothing but her bowsprit, lower foremast, and mizzenmast remained standing. Nonetheless, the sails on those damaged spars remained functional. As she drifted apart and away, she began listing to larboard, suggesting that at least one shot from *Constellation* had hulled her at the waterline.

"*Damnation!*" Truxtun swore under his breath. He watched in agonizing frustration as the lights in his enemy's gun ports faded into specks in the distance. *Constellation*'s body was too bruised and battered to give chase. "We had the bastards!"

"*Have* them, is how I see it, Captain," Waverly countered. "If that floating hulk isn't done for, then I'm a farmer from Tennessee."

"Watch out the mainmast!" Boatswain Bowles suddenly cried out, pointing upward.

With an almighty rip and a resounding *crack!* the mainmast, which had teetered ominously during the engagement, its supporting shrouds and stays sprung by enemy fire and its base battered by multiple whacks of round shot, snapped in two just above the deck and toppled sideways. Crashing against the larboard bulwarks, it lay motionless for a split second like a giant oar shipped inboard, balanced on its yards, before it rolled over and splashed into the Atlantic, still tethered to the ship by two lengths of rope. Four topmen went with it, along with James Jarvis, midshipman. One topman, still alive, slung an arm listlessly over a yard and was dragged behind in the water. Two others floated beyond him, belly down. Jarvis was nowhere to be seen, presumably trapped somewhere under the heavy shroud of canvas.

Richard glanced at Truxtun, who gave him a brief nod in reply.

"Mr. Bowles!" Richard shouted forward. "Retrieve those men and ax those ropes! Get the wounded below to the surgeon! Fix stoppers to the two masts and rig temporary shrouds and stays!"

"Aye, aye, sir," Bowles called back. A shrill of whistles from his two boatswain's mates awoke the crew from their postbattle stupor and drew their attention away from the horrific sight of their shipmates lying about them, many of them dead, dying, or grotesquely maimed.

As the gruesome work got under way, Nate Waverly stood with hands on hips, surveying the damage to *Constellation*'s rigging. Halyards, lifts, braces, sheets. Lines of every purpose and description lay in unruly coils and long serpentine formations all over the deck. Aloft, from what could be seen of holes and tears in the faint light, not a single sail had escaped damage. "We'll have a hell of time beating north with this rig," he commented matter-of-factly, his creased face gray with fatigue and concern.

Forward, despite mind-numbing exhaustion, sailors worked feverishly to comply with the first lieutenant's commands, motivated, perhaps, by the simple blessing of being alive and *able* to work. No one, from captain to captain's clerk, paused to think of the horrors about to unfold on the surgeon's table down on the orlop. Or of the sharks beginning to circle and thrash about in the waters close by, drawn to the surface by the smell of blood dripping from the scuppers. Soon enough, these demons of the deep would be rewarded with a banquet of sawed-off limbs heaved overboard by a surgeon's mate.

"I quite agree, Mr. Waverly," Truxtun said, his voice containing a neutral, faraway quality that was unusual for him. "Which is why we are not returning to Saint Kitts. "

"Where to, then, sir?"

"Port Royal. We can make repairs there."

Constellation WAS CRIPPLED. Her body and soul remained intact, but her mobility was threatened by the loss of her mainmast and the damage to her rigging. Her rudder, while serviceable, had also taken a hit. The odds were long, but should an enemy warship happen upon her, she would be hard-pressed to present her broadside.

Jamaica lay approximately 700 miles to the west, and Saint Kitts only 150 miles northward. But Nate Waverly was right: sailing upwind under these conditions would prove challenging if not impossible. Heading westward meant that *Constellation* would have the wind at her back, a point of sail that would put the least strain on a makeshift jury-rig and allow stability for carpenters and sail-makers to make minor repairs and adjustments along the way. Better still, since the trades blew predictably from the northeast, it was unlikely that *Constellation* would have to alter course until she reached Port Royal.

First order of business: clear away the debris on the weather deck and make *Constellation* as shipshape as possible. Second order of business: burial at sea for the fifteen American dead. Captain Truxtun in full dress uniform presided over the somber proceedings alongside his commissioned and warrant officers and the ship's complement of Marines, less those six lying alongside their nine shipmates amidships, each entombed in a pure white shroud of flaxen sailcloth. After Truxtun had read the service and committed the bodies to the deep, Richard dismissed the mustered divisions. As a reward for a job well done—and as an act of mercy—he divided the crew into four watches of two hours each rather than the customary two watches of four hours each, a watch bill first introduced to the Continental navy by Capt. John Paul Jones. Such a regimen allowed the men, in rotation, to sleep for eight hours straight, a rare luxury at sea but one desperately needed by men living on the edge.

The week's voyage to Jamaica proved uneventful but ultimately disappointing. The morning after *Constellation* dropped anchor off naval headquarters at Port Royal, Admiral Sir Hyde Parker was piped on board with full military honors. He was keen to learn more about the battle with *La Vengeance*—the first details of which had begun to wend their way through the ubiquitous web of British intelligence—and unhappy to inform Captain Truxtun that, alas, he was unable to supply a new mainmast for *Constellation.*

"I must apologize on His Majesty's behalf," he said to Truxtun and his first lieutenant in the after cabin, "but we have no spars to spare. The war in Europe, you understand. You can see for yourself that I command a somewhat smaller squadron than I did during your last visit. Of course, ever since your navy entered these waters, our navy has had less need of our own ships, which is why My Lords of the Admiralty have recalled so many of them to home waters." He smiled as a steward bowed before him, offering a glass of claret from a tray. "You have been most helpful to our cause, and for that His Majesty is most grateful. I am pleased to report that attacks on our merchantmen are down considerably from a year ago. Most sectors report no hostile activity of any sort in months. As a result, your merchant captains, and ours, are free to sail wherever the winds of profit take them." He raised his glass. "Cheers, Commodore. Cheers, Lieutenant. Here's to ridding the seas of vermin." He took a healthy sip, as did Captain Truxtun. Richard left his glass on the table.

"What of Toussaint L'Ouverture?" Richard asked after Hyde had set his glass down with a contented sigh. He well recalled his conversation with Hugh Hardcastle in Barbados and was curious to know the extent to which the term "vermin" applied in the admiral's mind.

"I am pleased to report that General Toussaint has succeeded in his campaign," Parker replied, as though Richard's question fitted comfortably within the scope of the conversation and his own ethical view of the world. "He doesn't rule the entire island—by agreement, the Spanish have retaken control of the central and eastern portions—but he does control all of Saint-Domingue—or Haiti, as he intends to call the colony once Napoleon grants independence. You should be proud, Lieutenant. As Haiti's first president, Toussaint will preside over a government based on your American model." He smiled broadly. "A rather impressive achievement for a former slave, what? Makes one rather proud to have had a hand in the making."

"Yes, sir," Richard said, inwardly thinking, a slippery fellow, this Admiral Parker. A man of rank and polish and apparent sincerity who manifests no guilt for the duplicitous role he played in the affair—or remorse for the thousands of lives that role had claimed—and who now takes credit for the outcome! In truth, Toussaint had prevailed not because of men like Hyde Parker, but in spite of them. But Richard decided not to press the point. Doing so, he realized, would serve no purpose.

Truxtun, perhaps reading Richard's thoughts, changed tack. "Admiral," he asked, "is it true you have no notion of where *La Vengeance* might be at the moment? Or her disposition?"

"Just so. We know where she is not: Basse-Terre. What we suspect, assuming she remains afloat, is that she is somewhere off to the south where the prevailing currents would take her. We shall soon have this puzzle solved, and when we do, we will notify your Navy Department posthaste." He glanced over at Richard. "By the bye, Lieutenant, you will be interested to learn that Captain Hardcastle has put in for duty at Spithead, and his request has been granted. More's the pity. He was my finest officer and I shall miss him. I hope he finds the action he is seeking."

"Yes, sir," Richard said straight-faced, knowing full well why Hugh Hardcastle had put in for duty at Spithead.

"Well then, Admiral," Truxtun ventured, "I think our business here is finished. I offer my thanks once again for allowing us to transfer our wounded to your hospital ashore. In a few days we shall be sailing for Virginia. I understand there are American merchant vessels in Kingston who wish to depart with us."

"Quite so, Captain. In the meantime, let our dock master know what provisions we can supply for your cruise home and what repairs our dockyard might make to *Constellation* before you leave. I am putting a dispatch vessel at your disposal, should you wish to send word ahead of your intentions."

"Thank you, Admiral. That is most generous of you."

"My honor, my dear sir. My honor."

A week later, under a more substantial jury-rig, *Constellation* weighed anchor and accompanied a convoy of seven American merchantmen northward through the Windward Passage. Helped along by fair winds and the swift-flowing Gulf Stream, she reached Hampton Roads in respectable time. Awaiting her at the Gosport Navy Yard on a cool, blustery, brilliantly sunny afternoon in late March was a welcome whose like no one on board could have anticipated.

Hardly were they within the confines of the large natural harbor when seventeen warships—a fair representation of the forty-eight warships that now constituted the U.S. Navy—erupted in a series of sixteen-gun salutes. Officers and Marines on deck and sailors arrayed in the top-hamper on ratlines and footropes stood in silent tribute to *Con-*

stellation as she coasted to her mooring. Ashore, fife-and-drum bands struck up lively tunes as civilians who had assembled en masse at the docks waved hats and added their huzzahs to the din of rockets exploding high overhead.

The next few hours on board ship were frenetic. Dignitaries of various political and military stripes either came on board or sent word that they would be coming. Excited chatter abounded about the battle with *La Vengeance*, to such a degree that fact became difficult to distinguish from fiction, heroics from bravado. This much, at least, was known: *La Vengeance* had made it to the Dutch island of Curaçao, where her captain—a Frenchman named Pitot who reported to his superiors that he had been attacked by a ship of the line—had driven her onto a sandbar to keep her from sinking. On board, among other passengers, were thirty-six American prisoners-of-war who were subsequently released for helping to save the lives of a large number of distraught French dignitaries. *La Vengeance*, however, could not be saved. She would never sail again.

Accounts of the battle—relayed to the American press courtesy of British intelligence, reports sent ahead by Captain Truxtun, and several of the thirty-six American prisoners on board *La Vengeance* who had recently arrived back in the United States—electrified the young nation. Accolades poured in via congratulatory speeches, letters, and written communications dispatched from the halls of Congress.

Not all of the communications were of that sort, however. On the day Richard arrived in Hampton Roads he received a letter by military post that was addressed simply to "Lt. Richard Cutler, USS *Constellation*" and written by the hand of the one he held closest to his heart. He stared down at the cursive flow, wondering how on earth she could have known his whereabouts and troubled by what that knowledge might portend.

As quickly as decorum allowed, he withdrew to the privacy of his cabin. He sat down on the chair by his desk, unfolded the letter, and read.

27 February 1800
South Street
Hingham, Massachusetts
My Dearest:

I do not know where you are or where you are bound. I am thus sending a copy of this letter to every British and American naval base of which I am aware, in the hope and prayer that somehow by God's grace you will receive it and act upon it, if duty and circumstances permit.

Your father has taken a turn for the worse. We understand it is his heart. There is no immediate danger, I think, and Caleb is here, which gives him great comfort. But he is calling for you, and I must confess, I am concerned that he is being so adamant. It's as though he may sense something that Dr. Prescott cannot.

Come if you can, my darling. If you cannot, we will all understand, your father first and foremost. But come if you can.

Katherine

Fifteen

Hingham, Massachusetts
April 1800

ASSUMING FAIR WINDS when returning to home port from the east or south, Richard Cutler normally charted a course between the Graves and Green, the two islands located farthest out among the thirty-odd islands fringing Boston Harbor. Once past those islands he would tack around to a southeasterly course toward Boston's commercial wharves, careful to keep the shoals of Deer Island and the Winthrop Peninsula well off to starboard. He would hold that course until he came abreast of the lighthouse on the northern tip of Long Island, at which point he would order his crew either to make final preparations for docking at Long Wharf, often his initial destination, or to steer around the southern end of Long Island eastward toward Hingham Bay. From there it was an easy lope through the sheltered waters of the bay to the docks at Crow Point, always his final destination.

Today he asked the captain of USRC *Massachusetts*, the Treasury cutter on which he was a passenger, to steer sharply to westward as they approached Great Brewster Island. From there they could cut through Hull Gut, a fifty-yard gap of water separating Peddocks Island from the mainland at Pemberton Point. That course would lead them directly into Hull Bay and on into the eastern reaches of Hingham Bay and save many hours of sailing time.

That request gave pause to Robert Thomas, the cutter's broad-shouldered captain in command by the tiller. Thomas hailed from nearby Scituate, and thus had personal acquaintance with the vicious cross-seas spawned by an ebb tide spilling out from Hull Bay into the Atlantic through the gap that locals referred to as "Hell's Gut." They might save time on that course, he conceded. But if the timing were off, or if the currents and rip tides swirling within the gap were up more than usual, he could be putting his vessel at risk. And if something did go awry, how would it look if this recently refurbished vessel of the Revenue Cutter Service were damaged on her first cruise?

Whether it was the look on Richard's face or his insistence that they were approaching slack tide at low tide, meaning that the fierce flow surging in reverse would more likely assist than impede them, he was persuaded. Into Hull Gut they dove, plunging into a confused array of roiled waters under jib and foresail, foremast course and furled top-sail, and a large quadrilateral driver, all canvas drawing full and their leeches fluttering madly in the cold of a stiff northwesterly wind that seemed to gather strength as they pounded through the narrow passage. The few people walking on the pebbly beach at the tip of Pemberton Point stopped to admire this graceful image of sail power laid hard over to larboard, her taut weather rigging shuddering in the wind as icy spray doused her shrouds and deck. Finally, the white trail left in her wake had faded back to indigo blue and she was safely beyond Bumkin Island.

"Thank you, Captain," Richard said at the gangway amidships after the cutter lay secure against a quay at Crow Point. Her crew of eight, stationed forward and aft and out on the dock, were preparing to cast off and get under way again. "I am very much in your debt."

"To the contrary, Lieutenant," Thomas said. "I am the one in debt here. It may have been your good fortune that I had orders to Boston at this time, but I have had the distinct honor and pleasure of a war hero's company these past few days. Congratulations again on your victories. You and *Constellation* have done us all proud. Alas, I fear I shall never experience that sort of glory. Unless, of course, I am fortunate enough to happen upon a tax shirker or, better yet, a Cutler cargo that is not properly documented."

Richard grinned although his voice remained serious. "You under-estimate yourself and your service, Robert. Revenue cutters have dis-tinguished themselves throughout this conflict. I am told that *Pickering* captured ten privateers before she was taken into the Navy. And I understand that Captain Preble has added to her glory since."

"Aye, quite. What I mean is, I shall not encounter such opportunities while in command of a cutter based in Boston and with the war nearing its end."

Richard picked up his seabag and tucked it under his left arm. "You are certain I cannot offer you accommodations here in Hingham? A meal perhaps? Lodging for the night? My family would be honored."

"Thank you, no. My orders are explicit. I must report to Customs House at my earliest convenience. Besides, my friend, you have quite enough on your plate as it is." He offered Richard his hand. "I wish you Godspeed, Richard. And I wish your father a swift and full recovery."

"Thank you, Robert. I greatly appreciate that. Godspeed as well to you and yours."

Richard strode down the gangway. On the dock he turned left, waved good-bye to the cutter a final time, and walked briskly along the quay and out onto a route he had followed countless times since his earliest days of boyhood wander and wonder. On every road, past every sight, the memories of a lifetime weighed heavily upon him. Memories of his brother Will, who had died much too young and who continued even in death to hold sway over Richard's mind. Of his mother, Elizabeth, the family matriarch, who had devoted her life to him and his siblings. And especially of his father, who had summoned him home, but who, Richard desperately needed to believe, had somehow managed to defy death's dark tentacles. He convinced himself that he would find his father either writing at his desk or, more likely on such a promising spring afternoon, puttering about in his garden, planting the seeds that come July would yield a harvest of fresh fruits and vegetables to grace family suppers over which he would preside, as he always had done.

As he turned onto North Street and then South Street, citizens of Hingham recognized him despite his knee-length navy-blue coat and the tricorne hat set low on his forehead. He doffed his hat to those who greeted him but avoided conversation with everyone except for a slightly stooped, gray-haired widow who been a family friend for decades and who approached him purposefully as he made his way along South Street. "God bless your father, Richard Cutler," she said gently, earnestly when she was at his side. She gave him a quick but heartfelt embrace. "God bless him. Everyone in Hingham is praying for him."

"Thank you, Mrs. Bigelow," Richard said. "Thank you very much. I am certain that our prayers will be answered." He squeezed her arm and moved on, his spirits buoyed by her kind and revealing words. His father clearly was still alive. But with what prognosis?

He went first to his own home on South Street, two hundred yards past its intersection with Main Street, on which his father lived. As much as he yearned to turn left and go straight to his father, he needed to see Katherine first, to understand his father's condition.

As he approached his two-story gray clapboard house, he spotted his daughter in the sun on its lee side. She had a pair of saddles set up on a long sawhorse and was busily cleaning their leather attachments. She had her back to him and did not hear him approach.

Richard set his seabag gently on the ground. For several moments he stood quietly, reveling in the simple pleasure of a parent observing his offspring at work or play. Almost two years had passed since he had seen her, and it came as a shock to him that she was no longer a little girl. In his absence Diana had blossomed into a comely young lady. At twelve years of age, her lithe body and long chestnut curls captured the very essence of her mother, whom Richard had met in England when she was just three years older than her daughter was today. As he watched Diana oil and scrub the leather straps leading down from saddle to stirrups, emotions welled up in him anew.

As if with a supernatural sense of someone watching her, she turned around and saw her father. The sight sent soap and brush tumbling to the ground. Diana made to come toward him then remembered herself, straightened, and bent her right knee in respect for her elder. "Oh, Father, you're home!" she gasped. "Mother will be so pleased! And Pappy has been so wanting to see you!"

"I am home," Richard exclaimed, his spirits lifting further at Diana's words. "And to welcome me home, Daughter, you're going to have to do a lot better than that sorry excuse for a curtsey."

He dropped to a knee and spread out his arms. She smiled at that and came running, melting into his embrace and throwing her arms around his neck the way she used to do when she *was* a little girl.

"Oh, Father, you're home," she cried again. "Finally! We've been waiting and waiting for so long. Pappy . . ." She stopped short and pulled away from her father, her delicate features a sudden testament to misery and woe. She blinked her eyes hard, her lower lip trembled. Then she collapsed back into his arms, burying her face against his neck and shoulder and weeping openly. "He's dying, Father. Pappy's dying. Even Mother admits it."

Richard clasped her to him, his spirits plunging from on high down into a black abyss. He felt his inner defenses crumbling but fought back the urge to succumb to despair, determined to remain strong for his daughter. "It's all right, Diana," he managed. "It's all right." He rubbed her back and stroked her soft curls. "It's all right, Poppet." When her sorrow had run its course and her sobs had softened to intermittent sniffles, he held her apart from him, dabbing at the dampness on her eyes and cheeks with a handkerchief drawn from his coat.

"Are you all right now?" he asked gently.

She nodded.

"Is your mother home?"

"No. She's at Pappy's. With Aunt Anne and Aunt Lavinia."

"I see. Where are Will and Jamie?"

"Down at Harrison's boatyard. They're building a boat."

"Good for them. I look forward to seeing it." He stood up and rested a hand on her shoulder. "I'm going right over to visit with Pappy. Do you want to come with me?"

"Yes, but wouldn't you like me to tell Aunt Lizzy that you're here? She will so want to see you. Edna is at her house and she can look after Zeke. I wish I could tell Uncle Caleb, but he's in Boston. Something important came up and he had to leave."

"Well, I'll see him tonight, I trust. Yes, please do tell Aunt Lizzy I'm home. We can walk over to Pappy's together and you can go on to her house from there."

At the entrance to his childhood home, Richard waved to his daughter as she continued on toward Pleasant Street. He opened the front door and walked into the parlor, listening for some telltale sound as he removed his hat and coat. He heard only one: a *clink* coming from the kitchen. When he cracked open the door to the kitchen, he saw Katherine stooped over before the hearth, stirring what was likely some sort of stew in a black iron cauldron set above a low-burning fire.

She started when she heard the door creak fully open. When she saw Richard standing in the doorway, she placed the ladle gently inside the pot, wiped her hands on her apron, and rose to her feet. Their eyes remained locked on each other until they met halfway across the room by the long dining table. He took her in his arms and held her, as she held him, silently, for a span of time broken only when a mantel clock in the parlor struck four times.

"How's Father?" he whispered.

"He's sleeping now. He sleeps much of the day. Anne and Lavinia are upstairs with him. They've been here a week."

"Is there any change? Any hope at all?"

She bit her lip as she slowly shook her head no. "I'm sorry, Richard. The end cannot be too far off. Doctor Prescott is doing everything he can, but there isn't much more he can do. He agrees with me that your father is hanging onto the hope and prayer that he will see you again. Perhaps it's that hope that is keeping him alive. I daresay there's something he wants to tell you. It will mean everything to him that you're here."

Richard closed his eyes to the reality, the finality of it all. "Should I let him sleep?" he asked softly. "Or should I wake him?"

"Wake him, by all means," she said. "There's no rhyme or reason for when he sleeps, and sleep is not what he needs at the moment. But first I must ask: can you stay with us? Or must you return to your ship?"

"I can stay, Katherine. Captain Truxtun granted me indefinite leave after I showed him your letter. *Constellation* is in for major repairs, and by all accounts this war will be over before she's ready to put to sea again."

"Oh, thank God," she breathed, almost choking on the words. She brought her hands to his cheeks and her lips to his, not with passion or longing, but with a quarter-century of love and respect coupled with a profound relief that he was home in time to see his father, and that they, she and her husband, the two of them, were once again together as one.

"Go, Richard," she urged. "Go to your father."

Glossary

aback   In a position to catch the wind on the forward surface. A sail is aback when it is pressed against the mast by a headwind.

abaft   Toward the stern of a ship. Used relatively, as in "abaft the beam" of a vessel.

able seaman   A general term for a sailor with considerable experience in performing the basic tasks of sailing a ship.

after cabin   The cabin in the stern of the ship used by the captain, commodore, or admiral.

aide-de-camp   An officer acting as a confidential assistant to a senior officer.

alee or *leeward*   On or toward the sheltered side of a ship; away from the wind.

amidships   In or toward the middle of a vessel.

athwart   Across from side to side, transversely.

back   To turn a sail or a yard so that the wind blows directly on the front of a sail, thus slowing the ship's forward motion.

back and fill   To go backward and forward.

backstay   A long rope that supports a mast and counters forward pull.

ballast   Any heavy material placed in a ship's hold to improve her stability, such as pig iron, gravel, stones, or lead.

Barbary States   Morocco, Algiers, Tunis, and Tripoli. All except Morocco were under the nominal rule of the Ottoman sultan in Constantinople.

bark or *barque*   A three-masted vessel with the foremast and mainmast square-rigged, and the mizzenmast fore-and-aft rigged.

bar-shot   Shot consisting of two half cannonballs joined by an iron bar, used to damage the masts and rigging of enemy vessels.

before the mast   Term to describe common sailors who were berthed in the forecastle, the part of the ship forward of the foremast.

before the wind   Sailing with the wind directly astern.

belay   To secure a running rope used to work the sails. Also, to disregard, as in "Belay that last order."

belaying pin   A fixed pin used on board ship to secure a rope fastened around it.

bend   To make fast. To bend on a sail means to make it fast to a yard or stay.

binnacle   A box that houses the compass, found on the deck of a ship near the helm.

boatswain   A petty officer in charge of a ship's equipment and crew, roughly the equivalent in rank to a sergeant in the army.

bollard   A short post on a ship or quay for securing a rope.

bower   The name of a ship's two largest anchors. The best-bower is carried on the starboard bow; the small-bower is carried on the larboard bow.

bowsprit   A spar running out from the bow of a ship, to which the forestays are fastened.

brace   A rope attached to the end of a yard, used to swing or trim the sail. To "brace up" means to bring the yards closer to fore-and-aft by hauling on the lee braces.

brail up   To haul up the foot or lower corners of a sail by means of the brails, small ropes fastened to the edges of sails to truss them up before furling.

brig   A two-masted square-rigged vessel having an additional fore-and-aft sail on the gaff and a boom on her mainmast.

Bristol-fashion   Shipshape.

broach-to   To veer or inadvertently to cause the ship to veer to windward, bringing her broadside to meet the wind and sea, a potentially dangerous situation, often the result of a ship being driven too hard.

buntline   A line for restraining the loose center of a sail when it is furled.

by the wind   As close as possible to the direction from which the wind is blowing.

cable   A strong, thick rope to which the ship's anchor is fastened. Also a unit of measure equaling approximately one-tenth of a sea mile, or two hundred yards.

cable-tier   A place in a hold where cables are stored.

camboose   A term of Dutch origin adopted by the early U.S. Navy to describe the wood-burning stove used in food preparation on a warship. Also, the general area of food preparation, now referred to as the galley.

canister shot or *case shot*   Many small iron balls packed in a cylindrical tin case that is fired from a cannon.

capstan   A broad, revolving cylinder with a vertical axis used for winding a rope or cable.

caravel-built   Describing a vessel whose outer planks are flush and smooth, as opposed to a clinker-built vessel, whose outer planks overlap.

cartridge   A case made of paper, flannel, or metal that contains the charge of powder for a firearm.

catharpings   Small ropes that brace the shrouds of the lower masts.

cathead or *cat*   A horizontal beam at each side of a ship's bow used for raising and carrying an anchor.

chains or *chain-wale* or *channel*   A structure projecting horizontally from a ship's sides abreast of the masts that is used to widen the basis for the shrouds.

clap on   To add on, as in more sail or more hands on a line.

clewgarnet   Tackle used to clew up the courses or lower square sails when they are being furled.

close-hauled   Sailing with sails hauled in as tight as possible, which allows the vessel to lie as close to the wind as possible.

commodore   A captain appointed as commander in chief of a squadron of ships or a station.

companion   An opening in a ship's deck leading below to a cabin via a companionway.

cordage   Cords or ropes, especially those in the rigging of a ship.

corvette or *corsair*   A warship with a flush deck and a single tier of guns.

course   The sail that hangs on the lowest yard of a square-rigged vessel.

crosstrees   A pair of horizontal struts attached to a ship's mast to spread the rigging, especially at the head of a topmast.

cutwater   The forward edge of the stem or prow that divides the water before it reaches the bow.

daisy-cutter   Another name for a swivel gun.

deadlight   A protective cover fitted over a porthole or window on a ship.

dead reckoning   The process of calculating position at sea by estimating the direction and distance traveled.

dogwatch   Either of two short watches on a ship (1600–1800 hours and 1800–2000 hours).

East Indiaman   A large and heavily armed merchant ship built by the various East India companies. Considered the ultimate sea vessels of their day in comfort and ornamentation.

ensign   The flag carried by a ship to indicate her nationality.

fathom   Six feet in depth or length.

fife rail   A rail around the mainmast of a ship that holds belaying pins.

flag lieutenant   An officer acting as an aide-de-camp to an admiral.

footrope   A rope beneath a yard for sailors to stand on while reefing or furling.

forecastle   The forward part of a ship below the deck, traditionally where the crew was quartered.

furl   To roll up and bind a sail neatly to its yard or boom.

gangway   On deep-waisted ships, a narrow platform from the quarter-deck to the forecastle. Also, a movable bridge linking a ship to the shore.

gig   A light, narrow ship's boat normally used by the commander.

grape or *grapeshot*   Small cast-iron balls, bound together by a canvas bag, that scatter like shotgun pellets when fired.

grapnel or *grappling hook*   A device with iron claws that is attached to a rope and used for dragging or grasping, such as holding two ships together.

grating   The open woodwork cover for the hatchway.

half-seas over   Drunk.

halyard   A rope or tackle used to raise or lower a sail.

hawser   A large rope used in warping and mooring.

heave to   To halt a ship by setting the sails to counteract each other, a tactic often employed to ride out a storm.

hull-down   Referring to another ship being so far away that only her masts and sails are visible above the horizon.

impress   To force to serve in the navy.

jack   The small flag flown from the jack-staff on the bowsprit of a vessel, such as the British Union Jack and Dutch Jack.

jolly boat   A clinker-built ship's boat, smaller than a cutter, used for small work.

keelhaul   To punish by dragging someone through the water from one side of the boat to the other, under the keel.

langrage   Case shot with jagged pieces of iron, useful in damaging rigging and sails and killing men on deck.

larboard   The left side of a ship, now called the port side.

lateen sail   A triangular sail set on a long yard at a forty-five-degree angle to the mast.

laudanum   An alcoholic solution of opium.

lee   The side of a ship, land mass, or rock that is sheltered from the wind.

leech   The free edges of a sail, such as the vertical edges of a square sail and the aft edge of a fore-and-aft sail.

lighter   A boat or barge used to ferry cargo to and from ships at anchor.

loblolly boy   An assistant who helps a ship's surgeon and his mates.

manger   A small triangular area in the bow of a warship in which animals are kept.

muster-book   The official log of a ship's company.

ordnance   Mounted guns, mortars, munitions, and the like.

orlop   The lowest deck on a sailing ship having at least three decks.

parole   Word of honor, especially the pledge made by a prisoner of war, agreeing not to try to escape or, if released, to abide by certain conditions.

petty officer   A naval officer with rank corresponding to that of a non-commissioned officer in the Army.

pig   An oblong mass of metal, usually of iron, often used as ballast in a ship.

poop   A short, raised aftermost deck found only on very large sailing ships. Also, a vessel is said to be "pooped" when a heavy sea breaks over her stern, as in a gale.

post captain   A rank in the Royal Navy indicating the receipt of a commission as officer in command of a post ship; that is, a rated ship having no less than twenty guns.

privateer   A privately owned armed ship with a government commission authorizing it to act as a warship.

prize   An enemy vessel and its cargo captured at sea by a warship or a privateer.

purser   An officer responsible for keeping the ship's accounts and issuing food and clothing.

quadrant   An instrument that measures the angle of heavenly bodies for use in navigation.

quarterdeck   That part of a ship's upper deck near the stern traditionally reserved for the ship's officers.

quay   A dock or landing place, usually built of stone.

queue   A plait of hair; a pigtail.

quoin   A wooden wedge with a handle at the thick end used to adjust the elevation of a gun.

ratlines   Small lines fastened horizontally to the shrouds of a vessels for climbing up and down the rigging.

reef   A horizontal portion of a sail that can be rolled or folded up to reduce the amount of canvas exposed to the wind; the act of so rolling a sail.

rig   The arrangement of a vessel's masts and sails. The two main categories are square-rigged and fore-and-aft rigged.

rode   A rope securing an anchor.

round shot   Balls of cast iron fired from smooth-bore cannon.

royal   A small sail hoisted above the topgallant that is used in light and favorable winds.

scupper   An opening in a ship's side that allows water to run from the deck into the sea.

sheet   A rope used to extend the sail or to alter its direction. To *sheet home* is to haul in a sheet until the foot of the sail is as straight and as taut as possible.

ship-rigged   Carrying square sails on all three masts.

shipwright   A person employed in the construction of ships.

shrouds   A set of ropes forming part of the standing rigging and supporting the mast and topmast.

slops Ready-made clothing from the ship's stores, or slop-chests.

slow-match A very slow burning fuse used to ignite the charge in a large gun.

stay Part of the standing rigging, a rope that supports a mast.

staysail A triangular fore-and-aft sail hoisted upon a stay.

stem The curved upright bow timber of a vessel.

stern sheets The rear of an open boat and the seats there.

studdingsail or *stunsail* An extra sail set outside the square sails during a fair wind.

swivel-gun A small cannon mounted on a swivel so that it can be fired in any direction.

tack A sailing vessel's course relative to the direction of the wind and the position of her sails. On a "starboard tack," the wind is coming across the starboard side. Also, the corner to which a rope is fastened to secure the sail.

taffrail The rail at the upper end of a ship's stern.

tampion A wooden stopper for the muzzle of a gun.

tholepin or *thole* One of a pair of pegs set in a gunwale of a boat to hold an oar in place.

three sheets to the wind Very drunk.

top A platform constructed at the head of each of the lower masts of a ship to extend the topmast shrouds. Also used as a lookout and fighting platform.

topgallant The third mast, sail, or yard above the deck.

top-hamper A ship's masts, sails, and rigging.

topsail The second sail above the deck, set above the course or mainsail.

touchhole A vent in the breech of a firearm through which the charge is ignited.

tumblehome The inward inclination of a ship's upper sides that causes the upper deck to be narrower than the lower decks.

waist The middle part of a ship's upper deck between the quarterdeck and the forecastle.

wardroom The messroom on board ship for the commissioned officers and senior warrant officers.

watch A fixed period of duty on a ship. Watches are traditionally four hours long except for the two dogwatches, which are two hours long.

wherry A rowboat used to carry passengers.

windward   Facing the wind or on the side facing the wind. Contrast *leeward*.

xebec   A three-masted Arab corsair equipped with lateen sails. Larger xebecs had a square sail on the foremast.

yard   A cylindrical spar slung across a ship's mast from which a sail hangs.
yardarm   The outer extremity of a yard.

About the Author

WILLIAM C. HAMMOND is a literary agent and business consultant who lives with his three sons in Minneapolis, Minnesota. A lifelong student of history and a longtime devotee of nautical fiction, he sails whenever possible on Lake Superior and off the coast of New England.